DRAGONS OF ASRED

HR MOORE

Published by Harriet Moore
Copyright © 2023 HR Moore

All rights reserved.

No portion of this book may be reproduced in any form without written permission from the publisher or author.

Titles by HR Moore:

The Relic Trilogy:
Queen of Empire
Temple of Sand
Court of Crystal

In the Gleaming Light

The Ancient Souls Series:
Nation of the Sun
Nation of the Sword
Nation of the Stars

Shadow and Ash:
Kingdoms of Shadow and Ash
Dragons of Asred

Stories set in the Shadow and Ash world:
The Water Rider and the High Born Fae
House of Storms and Secrets

http://www.hrmoore.com

MAP

For an online version, go to:
www.hrmoore.com/knownworld

Chapter One

Fyia couldn't move. The dragon had pinned her arms to her sides, and was huffing hot, sulfuric breaths at her face. Any hotter, and she was sure her skin would blister.

She seemed to be in a cavern, although Fyia couldn't make out much of her surroundings, only the impression of heat, other beasts circling, and a reddish-orange glow that lit the space. She struggled to make sense of it all.

'Fyia,' said a rich, male voice from somewhere above her.

Cal. She looked up, and the dragon did the same, squeezing her harder in the circle of its tail. But it was no good. Her voice refused to heed her, and the dragon narrowed its eyes in victory.

The dragon's smug expression sent a heavy ball of searing anger into Fyia's gut. She saw red, and the emotion grew, multiplying at a furious rate.

The dragon went still, every trace of haughty satisfaction wiped from its features. Fyia grasped that which was growing inside her and pushed it outwards, towards the mighty beast.

'Fyia, are you okay?' said Cal, with an edge of panic. 'You're hot, and …'

The dragon dropped Fyia.

She should have hit the ground, or fallen into the magma pit below, but instead, the heat abated, and Cal's cool, soothing hand was on her forehead.

'Thank the Gods,' said Cal, pulling Fyia into his arms. Relief washed over his features, his muscles relaxing under the press of her fingers, and she inhaled him greedily, expelling the hot, acrid air of the cavern, replacing it with his wild scent of gorse and snow.

'What happened this time?' said Cal, who was pale and drawn. Fyia had been pulled into dragon dreams on each of the four nights they'd been flying north, and the sleepless nights had drained them both.

'The same, give or take,' said Fyia, not wanting to re-live it. 'Although, at the end, the dragon seemed almost … scared.'

'Of what?' said Cal. He hooked a finger under her chin and looked down at her with his deep, green eyes.

She held his gaze, drinking him in, then said cockily, 'Of me. I think I did something magical.'

Cal half smiled and kissed her gently. 'You're making it up,' he teased. 'Your magic is pitiful.'

She smiled into his mouth, then pinched between his ribs. He squirmed, and she took advantage of his distraction, rolling away and making for the window.

He came after her, wrapping his arms around her waist, his chin resting on her shoulder as they both took in the view through the airship's porthole.

'It's …' said Cal.

'Barren,' said Fyia. Her eyes searched for anything of note, but ice was the landscape's only feature.

'Stark,' said Cal, 'but it has a certain beauty.'

The sun illuminated a sea of ice crystals below. 'I suppose it does. But it will be more beautiful when we melt it.'

'You don't know what's underneath,' said Cal, nipping her ear.

'Anything is better than … wait, what's that?'

'What's …'

The flash of red came again, and they raced for the door as one. They grabbed their cloaks and stuffed their feet into fur-lined boots, then flew up the stairs.

'Movement on the port side!' Fyia shouted at the top of her lungs, flinging herself through the door and out into the frigid northern air.

Fyia's wolves whined at the excitement, rubbing against her legs as she plucked a telescope from a crew member's hand. Not for the first time, she missed Edu. If he'd been here, she and Cal wouldn't have been the first to spot movement in the snow. But Starfall needed him more than she.

'There,' said Fyia. 'It looks like … like a fight!'

'Gods,' said Cal, looking through his own telescope. 'We should help them.'

'Which side?' said Fyia. A strange elation filled her. They'd seen no sign of another soul since they'd left the coast, and now this? It felt absurd to happen across a fight here. 'Are they tribes?'

'The ones in red are from the Kraken Empire,' said Cal. 'They're dressed like the men who attacked us in the north.'

'Change course!' Fyia shouted. The memory of their attacker's hands on her made her want to wretch; she wouldn't stand by and let the dead Emperor's soldiers do the same to anyone else.

'It could be a trap!' said Opie, their pilot.

'Or it could be our one and only chance to discover what the Emperor wanted up here,' said Fyia. 'Change course.'

Opie hesitated for a beat, then ran across the airship, calling orders. The ship came around, and Fyia pressed the telescope to her eye once more, following the fight as best she could.

The soldiers of the Kraken Empire wore heavy woolen coats and tasseled hats. They used ropes with weights at the end, which they whirled at their enemy. It seemed the Kraken soldiers were under attack, for they were only half visible, poking up through a hole in the ground, their legs mostly hidden, while warriors clad in wolf skins advanced on their position.

The Kraken soldiers stood in a small, circular formation, and were trying to climb out onto the snow, to put themselves on a level with their attackers, but their attackers outnumbered them two—or maybe three—to one.

What was this place? A military outpost? A safehouse? A trading station?

'It could be a mine,' said Cal, standing close by her side.

He was right. They'd heard reports that the former Emperor had set up mining operations, and the local tribes were not happy.

'Look,' said Fyia. She pointed to a disturbance in the snow fifty paces from the fight, where a sea of soldiers poured out onto the snow from another hole. They were dressed all in white, but their tasseled hats gave them away.

'*Warrior*,' Cal breathed.

'Bows!' shouted Fyia. She ran to snatch a bow from the stash of weapons along the outside of the airship's central cabin.

Cal grabbed a bow of his own, and most of the crew surged to join them.

'Stop!' screamed Opie, the panic in his voice enough to halt Fyia in her tracks, despite the adrenaline flooding her blood.

'Stop!' Fyia echoed, and all movement ceased, the deck turning still and expectant.

'If everyone runs to the bow, our nose will go down,' he said, testily, 'and we will likely all die.'

He was right. Both Essa and Opie had warned of the importance of weight distribution, although in the heat of the excitement, the thought had fled Fyia's mind.

'Ten with me,' said Fyia. 'Everyone else line the sides, and be ready to shoot, or throw projectiles.' They'd stored piles of rocks in baskets at intervals along the railings for that exact purpose, and Fyia was glad they'd done so now, even though the extra weight had slowed them down.

She and Cal stood side by side as they unleashed hell on the Kraken soldiers' ambush. Fyia nocked her bow, waiting a tick for the others to ready themselves before saying, 'Fire at will.' She let fly, then nocked a second.

Fyia loosed and drew in a steady rhythm, each of her arrows finding their target. While she was not a warrior—proudly so, for that was not where her skills lay—she had always had a knack for archery. When a bow balanced in her hand, she acted almost without conscious thought, her arrows seeming to find their own way to the target.

By the time the airship hovered above the fight, it was over. The Kraken soldiers lay dead, their blood seeping out in crimson stains across the snow, and those wrapped in wolf hides had disappeared below the ground.

'Fyia …' said Cal, taking her hand, 'that was … I knew you killed King Antice with a bow, but … that was …'

'Magic,' said Fyia, with a coy shrug. 'Or at least, I think so.'

'It was incredible,' he said, squeezing her fingers. Fyia had loosed three times as many arrows as the others, and every arrow had hit true.

'Now we must hope those we helped are friendly,' she said, squeezing back. 'Opie, set us down!'

Opie nodded curtly, obviously unhappy, but not voicing his concerns, then set about doing as she asked.

By the time they'd landed—a little way from the hole—disembarked, and picked their way through the dead bodies, a group of five men and women awaited them.

'Greetings,' said Fyia. 'Do you speak the tongue of the Five Kingdoms?'

'A little,' said a large, bearded man. Under his wolf fur, his torso was bare and corded with heavy muscle. It made Fyia cold just to look at him, and she pulled her own fur cloak closer around her.

'I hail from the Five Kingdoms, and my friend is from the Black Hoods,' said Fyia.

Cal, who stood beside her, inclined his head. 'Greetings,' he said.

'You have flying machine of Kraken,' said the man, narrowing his eyes suspiciously.

'I stole it from the Emperor, who you might not know is dead,' said Fyia.

'Liar,' said a similarly muscled woman, from behind the man.

'I killed him with my own hands,' said Cal, holding his hands out wide.

'The Kraken Empire is now ruled by an Empress,' said Fyia.

The group went silent. 'We not believe you,' said the woman.

'You don't have to believe us,' said Cal, 'but confirmation will reach you soon enough from other mouths.'

They stood in silence again, the man's eyes roaming over Fyia's wolves. He dwelled on them for a long time, then looked back at Fyia. 'You Queen.'

Fyia took in the group behind the large man. 'You King?' she said, deciding all were deferential to him, aside from the woman who'd spoken. 'Or chief? Or …'

'Me Senshi,' he said. 'Warrior.'

'And I daughter of Dōtai,' said the woman, stepping forward. 'Daughter of our leader. Why are you here?'

'We were flying past,' said Fyia. 'We saw the fight and came to help. We are no friends of the former Emperor, and those were his soldiers, were they not?'

'Ya,' said the woman. 'Now you leave?'

Fyia's pulse leapt. 'We had hoped to see inside,' she said. 'To discover what they were doing here.'

'Why?' said the man, the Senshi.

Fyia shrugged. 'Curiosity.'

The woman's brow creased in suspicion, so Fyia continued. 'We seek the dragons. We are heading to the northern temples for that purpose.'

'Ahhhh,' said the woman, nodding. She clapped her hands once. 'You may come.'

Fyia and Cal followed as the woman and the Senshi descended into the hole. Fyia's wolves joined them, but her guards remained outside, with the other members of the tribe.

They passed down through layer upon layer of thick ice, until finally the walls changed to a light rock containing bits of stone that sparkled where the light hit. 'You mine the crystals?' asked Fyia.

The woman grimaced. 'No. They everywhere. Worthless. We mine for that.' She pointed along a corridor supported by columns of ice, where pickaxes lay strewn alongside half-filled carts.

Fyia stepped carefully over the dead bodies of the Kraken soldiers, moving closer so she could examine the gleaming metal seam that ran in a thick and swirling strand along the wall.

'What is it?' she breathed. She reached out to touch the metal, which turned pink and blue, green and brass as the light of their torches played across the surface. It was reminiscent of the four metal balls Fyia and Cal had collected, although not exactly the same.

'It special,' said the woman. 'Needed for dragon. Emperor may not take.'

'Why do the dragons need this?' said Cal. He removed his glove and traced a swirl with his finger.

'Because they do,' said the woman. 'Our tribe protects mine. That our job in Order of Dragon.'

Fyia's eyes flicked up to the woman. They were from the Order of the Dragon? She hadn't thought to find members of their ranks so far from their temple. But then, there was much she didn't know.

'You have a temple here?' said Cal.

'No,' said the woman. 'We visit Temple of Dragon when dragon return. When north thaw. When journey not treacherous.'

'Are there many mines in these lands?' said Fyia, finally pulling her hand back from the seam.

'Ya,' said the woman. 'Now, we go.'

They emerged back through the hole to find teams of dogs waiting on the snow, sleds tethered behind them. Fyia's wolves stilled beside her, their heads going low, but the members of the Dragon Order wasted no time before loading themselves and urging the dogs forward.

'We wish you luck on your quest,' said the woman, as she sped past.

'Until we meet again,' Fyia called after her, 'on the steps of the Dragon Temple!'

They watched until the devouts disappeared behind a hill of ice, and then Fyia pulled out the tiny piece of metal she'd pocketed from the mine. Cal's face split into a broad grin as he pulled out his own, slightly larger piece.

'I'm planning to give mine to Essa for analysis,' said Fyia. 'What's your excuse?'

'Don't you worry, I have plans for it,' said Cal, flashing her a mischievous smile.

Chapter Two

SEVERAL SPINS OF THE HAND after they re-boarded the airship, a lookout spotted a series of spires reaching up into the sky, skewering the horizon.

'There!' he shouted, and Fyia and Cal jammed their own telescopes against their eyes.

'Yes!' said Fyia. 'Opie! You see the temple?'

'I do, Your Majesty,' Opie said, with an edge of sarcasm.

'Just making sure,' Fyia shot back, arching an eyebrow as she smiled. Nothing could temper the excitement bubbling in her chest, for this was it. The dragon eggs had to be here. There was nowhere else they could be.

Cal slipped an arm around her waist as they sailed closer. 'You really think they'll be there?' he asked, dropping a kiss against her temple.

'Yes,' said Fyia. 'You?'

'I scarcely dare to hope.'

Opie set the airship down several leagues from the temple, the only place they could find flat enough to accommodate the hulking airship, and Fyia preferred a trek across the snow to aimlessly searching for a place to land. She itched to get going, her legs dying to run.

She even searched for nearby eagles, hoping to summon one of the giant birds to carry her to the temple, but there were none to be found. So instead, she strode out near the front of their group, pressing the men and women in her guard to hurry.

'We must be careful,' said the most senior of the guards. 'The ice is treacherous …'

'I know, I know,' said Fyia. 'Be careful, but go quickly.' Fyia knew she was being unfair, and if Edu—the head of her personal guard—had been here, he would have chastised her for pressing them. Their safety was important, but she was like a child upon the eve of the Winter Solstice, unable to contain her excitement.

Her wolves raced ahead, and that only heightened Fyia's impatience.

'There are two temples here, are there not?' said Cal, clearly trying to distract her.

'You know very well there are,' she said, throwing him a dark look.

'Which do you think will contain the dragons?'

'How should I know?' she said, although her mind latched onto the question.

They trudged in silence for several moments before Fyia said, 'The Temple of the Mother would seem the obvious place to hatch the eggs.'

Cal did his best to hide his smile, which was to say he did a terrible job. Fyia refrained from swatting him.

'Although, what are dragons if not children of the Warrior?' she continued.

'I suppose we shall find out soon enough,' said Cal, nodding at the guards ahead, who had stopped dead.

Fyia and Cal moved up beside them, to where a path disappeared down into the snow, under an overhang of ice, but the temple's spires were still a hundred paces further across the snow. Steam swirled in the air above the path, and Fyia and Cal looked to one another, elation bubbling between them.

They rushed forward together, Fyia's guards not quick enough to stop them, calling after them and scrambling to try and keep up. Her wolves had already disappeared under the overhang, into the gloom, and Fyia felt nothing to concern her through the Cruaxee bond, so the risk seemed small.

But as Fyia and Cal moved further along the path, a terrible creaking filled the air. They spun as one back the way they'd come, but the floor beneath their feet began to shift. The path disappeared, plummeting down, down, down, and taking Fyia and Cal down with it.

Sensis surveyed the land below her. *Her* land, or at least, the land of Lady Sensis Deimos of Altergate. The title fit like a too-small pair of shoes, which was to say, it pinched, and Sensis much preferred the one she'd truly earned—High Commander of the Armies of the Five Kingdoms.

Lady Starfall—Fyia's aunt, whom Fyia had left in charge after departing for the north—had granted Sensis an airship to take her to her new estate in the Kingdom of Moon. The estate Fyia had given Sensis after executing its former owner, Lord Eratus Venir. Starfall had decreed that one could not let estates run themselves—although as far as Sensis could tell, that was exactly the approach Starfall took with her own lands—and had sent her on her way.

Sensis sighed deeply, because Starfall was right. These people were not used to Sensis as their liege. There was much work to do here, weeding out those still loyal to their former master, working through the accounts, checking inventories, ensuring the continuation of trade relationships with the other High Houses of the Five Kingdoms.

The other *High Houses*, because Sensis now ran a High House of her own. And with that title came extensive responsibilities. How could she both lead the armies of the Five Kingdoms and fulfil her new duties? She could take a husband to see to her domestic affairs, but the thought made her shudder.

They floated over fields and orchards, fruit pickers out in force, lugging baskets filled with apples and pears and plums. The pickers cast wary glances upwards, for although most across the Kingdoms would by now have heard of the great flying ships, few had seen them in the flesh.

The airship landed on the lawn in front of a vast stone house. A circular drive ran around the perimeter of the sprawling lawn, lined with the rare alterwood trees that gave the estate its name—Altergate.

The airship's crew had barely rolled the rope ladder over the side before an angry-looking man came charging down the wide stone steps connecting the drive to the mansion's imposing front door.

'Here we go,' Sensis said under her breath, then took a deep, sustaining lung full of air and launched herself over the side, shunning the ladder.

'Sensis,' said Lord Sollow Antice, inclining his head the barest fraction as he pulled himself up before her.

No title. 'Antice,' said Sensis, not bothering to incline her head at all. Her use of his given name made him visibly flinch, and it was all Sensis could do not to laugh.

'I would prefer you call me Lord Antice,' he said curtly.

'Then you should call me Lady Deimos ... or Lady Altergate, if you prefer, as I believe is tradition for the lady of this particular estate.'

'Unless you wed my uncle, there is no Lady Altergate.'

Sensis softened. She'd assumed word would have already reached Antice's ears, given his fingers were in many pies across the world, but ... 'I regret to inform you your uncle is dead.' Antice's forehead scrunched, and his lips pressed firmly together. 'He was working with the Kraken Emperor and conspiring against our Queen. She took his life as punishment, and passed his titles and estates to me.'

Antice went white. Sensis thought she detected sorrow in his honey-colored eyes, but the rest of his features were set like clay fired in the hottest of ovens. 'No,' he finally said. 'This will not stand.'

'You question the wisdom of your Queen?' said Sensis, a note of warning in her tone. He was most likely in shock, but even so, Sensis would not excuse dissent, especially from one who associated—or maybe even led—the rebels fighting Fyia's rule.

Antice looked for a moment like he might spit in her face, and say his Queen could burn in the Seven Hells, but he held his tongue. He spun away and made for the house, and Sensis strode after him. If he hadn't already known about his uncle, he wouldn't yet have hidden the ledgers, and Sensis wasn't about to give him that chance.

Veau watched from the entrance as Isa and Axus huddled over the strange model on the floor. It was a series of circular stones connected by lines in a pattern he couldn't make sense of, some stones with a small pebble on top, a few without.

As he watched, a pebble slipped sideways off another, disappearing in a puff of smoke as it hit the floor.

'Another has fallen,' said Axus, the strain clear in his tone. 'Should we …'

'No. We should not,' said Isa.

'But …'

'Stop,' said Isa, her head snapping up to look at Veau where he hovered by the entrance.

'Sorry,' said Veau, the word out of his mouth without conscious thought. Surely with her all-powerful magic, the leader of the Fae'ch would have known he was there?

'Come,' said Isa, turning her attention back to the stones.

Veau approached, but stopped a few paces away, not wishing to crowd them. He furiously scanned the structure, searching for any hint as to what it could possibly represent. Again, he came up blank. Not the stars, nor the rivers, nor the temples. The aqueducts, perhaps? Something to do with the hot springs that littered the kingdoms? But there didn't seem to be enough lines to represent all of those …

'It is. Time,' said Isa, in her usual halting, waiflike way. 'You must. Repay your debt.'

Veau's insides contracted. His debt? What debt? Axus must have seen the panicked confusion on his face, for he said, 'You did not think your carefree existence under the Fae'ch Mountain was free … did you?'

'I …' Veau's mind went blank, refusing to supply words.

'Regardless,' said Isa. 'Reports say. Your sister has. Gone north.'

'Back to the Black Hoods?' said Veau. Nervous tension pulsed through him. He couldn't lose his home here; it was the only place that had accepted him and his magic. If he returned to the Five Kingdoms, some would call for him to lead, to usurp his sister, while others would call for him to be locked away, on account of his dangerous magic. Veau had no stomach for any of it.

'To the. Temples of the. Warrior. Mother,' said Isa.

That made sense. Fyia had visited the other major temples already in her search for dragons.

'Why?' said Isa, her eyes intensely expectant.

'Why what?'

'Why would she. Go there?'

'To search for the dragons, I should think.'

Isa made a hissing noise and swiped her hand through the air. 'She thinks. She will find the dragons. There?'

Veau shrugged, not understanding. Surely that was the obvious place for Fyia to look. 'Where else would she go?' he said. 'She searched the other temples and found nothing. She searched here, and the egg was missing …'

Isa hissed again, and Veau fell silent. 'Go,' she ordered. 'But we are not. Done.'

Starfall brought the meeting to order by rapping on the table with a gold candlestick.

'I do wish you would have some respect for the ancient artifacts of our lands,' said Lady Lyr, the Warden of the Starlight Kingdom.

'There are a great many things I wish you would do or not do, Lady Lyr,' said Starfall. 'Indeed, there are a great many things I wish for in general, but I have come to accept, recently, it is not my lot to get the things I wish for.' For ever since Fyia had gone gallivanting north with her betrothed, Starfall's life had become an endless string of problems, even more so than before. She was beginning to tire of all this, wondering how much longer it would be until she could return to the Temple of the Night Goddess, and her carefree, hedonistic existence.

Starfall didn't miss the Spider's scowl. The spy master was no fun. Never had been. 'I call this meeting to order,' said Starfall, taking in the diminished group, with Fyia absent, Lord Venir dead, and Sensis at her estates, which was presumably the reason Lord Antice's seat was also empty. Only Lady Lyr, Lady Nara, Lord Fredrik, Essa, and the Spider looked back at her.

'The first order of business,' said Starfall, 'is to find a suitable Warden for the Sky Kingdom, to replace the recently deceased Lord Venir. I need not remind you, Venir was also Master of Coffers, thus we must fill that position also.'

Endless conversation ensued, where each of them put forward candidates. Only Essa sat sullen and silent, apparently unconcerned about who would next dole out the research money she relied upon.

Eventually, Starfall brought the discussion to an end. They had a short list, some of whom could fill both vacant roles, as Lord Venir had done, and some of whom could fill only one or the other.

'We shall research the short list, so we may present our preferred options to the Queen upon her return,' said Starfall.

'Which will take place during a meeting of this council?' said Lady Lyr, distrustfully.

'Naturally,' said Starfall.

Lyr gave a sharp nod, and Starfall chose not to rise to the bait, for if she did, they would be here all day. 'Next, we must discuss the changes required to the various laws of each of the Five Kingdoms, so when our Queen marries the King of the Black Hoods, she will not relinquish control of her position, power, or assets to him.'

Lady Nara sighed. 'Why she rails so against the laws that have served us …'

Starfall silenced her with a look, and Nara's cheeks turned pink.

'Lady Nara's point should not be ignored,' said Lord Fredrik, ruffling his feathers. 'These changes will not be well received by most, and we are still recovering from the last rebel attacks. Is it necessary to give them more reason to rebel against our carefully constructed and effective order?'

'Effective for whom?' said Starfall. 'For you? For others like you? It is not effective for me. It does not serve the women of our kingdoms.'

Lady Nara coughed self-importantly. 'You do not speak for all women.'

Starfall laughed harshly. 'And you believe you do? Most women do not have the luxury of large estates, unlimited funds, and the ability to fill their time as they wish. That your father allows you a life of such freedom is your blessing,' said Starfall. 'Most are not so fortunate.'

'Then let us compile guidance for the men of our lands …'

'Stop,' said Starfall. 'Even if I agreed with you—which I do not—this council serves the Queen. Our opinions matter not in the face of a direct order. Our duty is to determine *how* to make such a change, not *if* the change should be made. Thus, what would it take?'

Silence descended, and Starfall let it stretch for many moments.

'We are not experts in the law,' said Lady Lyr.

'Then we will find and summon experts from every kingdom,' said Starfall, 'and seek their guidance. Spider, I assume this is a task we can entrust to you?'

The Spider inclined her head. 'Of course.'

'Next,' said Starfall, 'an update on repairs to the capital after the rebel bombs. Lord Fredrik, Lady Nara, the floor is …'

'Seriously?' said Essa, exploding to her feet in an uncharacteristic display.

Starfall arched an eyebrow. 'There is something you wish to say?'

'We sit here and discuss marriage and council seats, when there is only one topic that truly matters: the clocks.'

'Yes,' said Starfall, 'we will get to …'

'Nothing else matters!' said Essa, slamming her hand on the table. 'The clock in the Temple of the Sea Serpent has fallen.'

'It has been like that for many years,' said Lady Nara. 'Nothing bad has happened, so why the dizzying rush?'

'We have been lucky, but the future will not be the same,' said Essa.

'You have evidence?' said Lady Lyr.

'Plenty, which I have explained to this council several times before.'

'A single clock falling from its perch, and magma below the Queen's new palace,' said Lyr. 'What else is there?'

'The steam is increasing from the hole where the clock once sat in the Temple of the Sea Serpent,' said Essa.

'According to a bunch of priestesses who are probably high on Cuttle Stars at least half the time,' said Lyr.

'That is not fair,' said Nara.

Starfall looked at the clock above them, sending a silent plea to the Gods to spare her this agony, which meant she saw the moment the wooden strut came free from the ceiling, hurtling down to where they sat. She had no time to move her big, heavy seat, but let out a cry just before the strut landed on the council table.

'Goddess,' said Essa, jumping to her feet. 'See! The infrastructure that keeps us safe is crumbling!'

'The infrastructure that keeps us safe,' Lyr mimicked, her tone scathing. 'We should tear the things down.'

'Oh?' said Starfall. 'I thought it was your view we should treat relics from our past with respect?'

Lyr screwed up her face.

'You are all ignorant,' said Essa. 'Can you not see what is slapping you in the face? Queen Fyia would take this seriously, and I will act, even if you refuse. Please, Starfall, summon the Guild of Engineers to repair the clock here. I will travel to the Temple of Sea Serpents to close the hole there ... or at least try, and I will have my students comb the archives for anything that might give us the slightest bit of help.'

Starfall studied Essa's impassioned form for several beats. Essa was not the type to make a fuss about nothing. 'I will do as you ask,' said Starfall, 'and I will send envoys to our allies, advising them to check their own clocks.'

Essa closed her eyes and took a loud breath. 'Thank you.'

Chapter Three

FYIA FLUNG OUT HER HANDS and hurled a stream of magic at the floor, almost without conscious thought. Whatever magic she'd managed slowed her sufficiently that she landed with only the smallest of thuds. Cal was not so lucky, if the crunch to Fyia's right was any indication.

'Cal?' she said, struggling upright. He'd landed on a stack of wooden crates, whereas Fyia had landed on a pile of plants with thick, cotton-like heads the size of dinner plates.

'I'm okay … I think,' he said, easing himself up. 'I guess the crates broke my fall a little.'

It was better than landing on the hard rock, she supposed. Fyia helped him to sit, then crouched in front of him. 'Where does it hurt?' she asked, running her hand through his short, dark hair. It had grown a surprising amount in the short time since he'd shaven it.

'I'm fine,' he said. 'Although I'm beginning to agree with those who council patience …'

Fyia huffed out a laugh. 'Edu's been trying to teach me that for years.'

'Help me up.'

She did, and Cal gingerly tested his limbs as they cast their eyes around the surprisingly well-lit space. 'Where's the light coming from?' said Fyia. The stark light of the sun illuminated their surroundings, but she could see only a few holes where it shone directly into the cavern.

'I … wait … is that a crystal in the wall? And another there …'

'They're reflecting light from outside?'

Cal shrugged.

'My Queen!' called a shrill voice from above. 'Are you alive?'

Fyia's wolves whined through the hole.

'Yes,' Fyia called back.

'Is King Cal alive?'

'Alive and kicking,' said Cal.

'Can you see a way out?' said the guard.

'Hang on,' said Fyia. 'We need to look around.'

'I'll send guards back to the airship for a rope, just in case.'

'Very good,' said Fyia, the words habitual.

Cal was already exploring the strange subterranean garden they'd fallen into. It felt curated, highly so, with raised metal planters filled with foliage.

'Why couldn't I have landed in one of those?' said Cal. He pointed to where five round, deep-looking pools lined the edge of a circular mosaic.

Tall trees with long, pointed leaves at their crowns reached up around the edges of the cavern, and Fyia realized the air was hot. 'They would probably have burned you alive.'

'Hmm,' said Cal, holding his hand over the top of one. 'You're right.'

The perfectly circular pools were reminiscent of the metal balls they'd discovered in place of the dragon eggs. 'What if the eggs are down there?'

'Or maybe the metal balls are the dragon eggs,' said Cal, repeating the thought they'd shared many times already.

'The pools could be the way to hatch them …'

'Or maybe we were too late, and the eggs hatched years ago. Maybe someone found them before us.'

Fyia frowned. 'Why would you think that?'

'Your dreams,' he said. 'They seem so real.'

'Yes, but if dragons still existed in the world, they couldn't hide. They would need to hunt, and roam, and …'

'I know,' said Cal.

'Do you think we can get to the temples from here?' said Fyia, scouting the perimeter, looking for an exit.

'I can't see a way out,' said Cal.

'We should summon your Cruaxee. Your bear's senses will …'

'Or we could enjoy a few moments alone before the guards return with a rope,' said Cal, moving to Fyia's side.

Fyia smiled and tilted her head back. 'That's not the worst idea,' she said, and then Cal's lips were on hers, hot and firm and soft.

But moments later, Fyia sensed movement above them. She pulled away and turned just in time to see a winged figure drop through the hole in the ceiling. He fell gracefully, preventing himself from slamming into the floor with a single, powerful flap of his sandy-colored wings.

Fyia went rigid. 'Hello,' she said, meeting the fae's piercing blue eyes.

The fae tilted his head to one side.

'Do you live here?' said Fyia, looking around for anything she could use as a weapon. He didn't seem hostile, but then, he didn't seem friendly either.

The fae cocked an eyebrow. 'No.'

'Just visiting?' said Fyia, wishing he would give her something more to work with.

'Fyia!' shouted a voice from above. A voice she would know anywhere. A voice she was equal parts delighted and shocked to hear. 'Let Leo fly you up!'

'Edu!' Fyia shouted back. She picked her way around the waterways to where Leo awaited below the hole. 'You have wonderful timing.'

'It's nice to see you too, *Your Majesty*,' said Edu.

Uh oh; he was definitely pissed.

Leo lifted Fyia into his arms, and with only a handful of flaps, flew Fyia up through the opening.

As soon as they were through, Leo deposited Fyia, then dropped back down to get Cal.

'Edu …' said Fyia, but her eyes snagged on the young woman in his grasp. Edu had pulled her hands behind her back, holding her securely before him.

'Who's your friend?' said Fyia. The woman was no warrior. Fyia could tell that from the way she held herself, the way she planted her feet.

'I am Alba,' said the woman, a defiant spark in her eyes.

Fyia immediately warmed to the woman.

'They were following you,' said Edu.

'And a good job too,' said Alba, as Leo set Cal down next to Fyia.

'The guards would have had us out in no time,' said Fyia, with a dismissive wave of her hand. 'You're Fae'ch? From the mountain?'

Leo and Alba exchanged a glance, clearly reluctant to reveal anything at all. 'I'm assuming Isa sent you to spy on us?' said Fyia. 'To track our progress and report back?'

'She wants to see if you're a good partner for the Fae'ch,' said Alba.

Leo scowled, throwing a fearsome look at the short, curly-haired woman. 'We do not know that to be the case,' he said.

'No,' Alba conceded, 'but she seemed to imply …' Leo shook his head, and she snapped her mouth shut. 'Sorry.'

Fyia laughed. 'You two are together, right?'

Alba's eyes met Fyia's for only a fraction of a tick before flitting away, but it was enough to convey so many messages. Alba would say no more, but she wanted to, which meant Fyia would find out in time.

A maid placed a generous plate of food in front of Sensis, then headed to the other end of the ludicrously long table to lay a plate before Lord Antice.

Sensis ignored him as she spread rich, thick, yellow butter, and coarse, herb-filled pate over her sourdough bread, popped a slice of pickled onion on top, and bit down. She refrained from letting free the hum of appreciation building in her throat; a perfect combination, if ever she'd tasted one.

Sensis washed her mouthful down with a swig of the alcoholic cider they fermented on the estate, then returned her attention to the ledger open beside her. She'd spent every moment since touching down pouring through the books, which painted a fascinating picture of Lord Venir's ruthless cunning. It was clear the man had had a remarkable head for business, but also that he cared not whom he extorted along the way.

'It is rude to read at the dinner table,' said Antice, who seemed genuinely shocked, his knife and fork frozen above his plate.

Sensis sent him a disdainful glare. The High Houses insisted on rules for everything: eating, walking, dressing, who could address whom first at a party. She had little tolerance for the pointless practices that served only one real purpose, as far as she could tell, which was to single out those not born of a High House.

'It is my dinner table,' said Sensis, 'so I may do as I please. And it was rude of you to address your host in that disrespectful manner.'

Antice reared back, but Sensis returned her eyes to the ledger, not giving him the satisfaction of engaging further.

'How long do you intend to remain here?' said Antice, throwing down his cutlery and leaning against the back of his seat.

Sensis ignored him.

'It is considered polite to answer when asked a direct question.'

He really wasn't coping well with his loss of power. Sensis picked up her goblet and took a long sip, swilling it around her mouth as she assessed him.

'How long do you intend to remain a *guest* in my house?' said Sensis.

'It is not your house,' Antice hissed. 'It has been in my family for generations, and I intend to appeal the Queen's decision upon her return.'

'You wish to have a dagger pierce your heart?' said Sensis. 'Like your uncle?'

'Is that how the *Queen* deals with those who contradict her?'

'Not generally,' said Sensis, 'but it seems a good way to deal with treason.'

'I have not …'

'But your uncle did.' And most probably Antice, also. Sensis let the unsaid words hang in the air.

Antice pursed his lips.

'You believe treason should go unpunished?' said Sensis.

He shook his head as though he couldn't quite believe her audacity. 'How long are you planning to stay, Sensis?'

Something about her name on his lips made her shiver. It had been that way since they were children. 'Is there a reason you want to be rid of me, Antice?' said Sensis, cocking an eyebrow.

'My name is Lord Antice.'

'And mine is Lady Deimos.'

Antice banged his fist on the table and threw back his chair.

Sensis smirked. 'I think that little outburst broke a number of your own rules.'

He strode for the door.

'Lost your appetite?' said Sensis. It was childish, but it was also fun.

He slammed the door behind him.

Moments later, a guard poked his head around the door. Sensis nodded, and he went scurrying away, off to watch Antice like a hawk.

The following morning, Sensis rose early. She pulled a housemaid from her work building a fire in the great hearth in the entrance hall. 'I'm in need of a guide to show me around my house,' said Sensis.

Right now, Antice had the upper hand. He knew the territory, and most likely owned the hearts of the people. But Sensis would level the playing field, starting today.

'My lady,' said the maid, 'I have duties … I …' But then she seemed to remember that Sensis was now in charge, and bobbed her head.

'Don't worry, I will explain your absence to the housekeeper.'

The maid was apprehensive, skittish, and kept flitting her eyes towards the stairs. Sensis wondered why. Because Antice might come down for breakfast and see her helping the enemy?

'What's your name?' said Sensis.

'Raya, my lady,' said the maid, dipping into a quick curtsey.

'Well, Raya, where do you suggest we start?'

'I … uh …' She seemed surprised to be asked her opinion.

Sensis waited, giving her space to think.

'Well … I, um … guess we could start at the top and work down?'

Sensis nodded. 'Very good.' She held out her hand, palm up, and gestured towards the stairs. 'Lead the way.'

Raya led Sensis up three flights of stairs, then opened a plain wooden door, which revealed a further flight of much steeper, narrower steps. 'The servants sleep up here,' said Raya, holding up her dress as she skipped up the stairs.

They emerged in a long, dimly lit corridor with doors set into the wall at regular intervals on either side, each identical to the next. The only light came from the few open doors, and Sensis poked her head inside each one.

Most rooms were tidy, with neatly made beds and few possessions. One or two looked as though they'd been hastily vacated, but the beds were still made, the sheets just a little askew. Lord Venir had kept a strict house, apparently, but that was no surprise.

'How many staff live in the house?' asked Sensis.

'Around twenty, I think,' said Raya, counting on her fingers.

'They all sleep up here?'

'All but the Housekeeper.'

'Then some of these rooms are empty?'

'Yes, my lady.'

'Good. I will have my guards occupy those that are spare.'

Raya paled. 'Oh,' she said. 'Um …'

'They won't hurt you, if that's what you're worried about,' said Sensis. 'I don't tolerate those kinds of men.'

Raya still looked nervous, but she plastered a fake smile on her face and headed for the stairs. Sensis wondered about her reaction, adding it to the growing list of things to dig into.

They toured the rest of the house, which took most of the morning. The upper two floors contained endless bedrooms, most of which sat empty, including the one that had belonged to Lord Venir. Sensis had taken one of the lesser—although still impressive—suites, having no desire to sleep in a bed that had, until recently, been occupied by a man like Venir.

Raya had refused to enter Venir's room, terrified by the very thought, so Sensis went in alone, and gave it a cursory search for anything interesting, or better yet, incriminating. She found nothing of note, but she would send guards to conduct a more thorough search. In fact, she would get them to search every room, including Antice's.

The first floor held grand reception rooms, while the kitchen, pantry, and utility rooms were housed in the basement. Unlike the residences of the former kings and queens of the Five Kingdoms, this house had been built for show, not for strength. No turrets nor arrow slits, no moat nor portcullis. It was designed to impress the guests that whisked up the drive, not repel them. The place sprawled, and had many doors and large windows through which an attack would be simple. It spoke of a carefree existence, of arrogance and power.

By the time the tour was done, the sun was high in the sky, and Raya hurried off to finish her duties. Sensis descended the worn stone stairs that led to the kitchen, and felt immediately more at home as she sat at the long wooden table.

'Anything I can get you, my lady?' said Cook, putting down his knife. He had a round face, and a slight podge around the middle, which boded well.

'Lunch, please,' said Sensis. 'Whatever you have that's quick.'

Cook nodded and filled a bowl with stew from the pot bubbling above the fire.

'Shall I get someone to bring it upstairs?'

'Here is fine, thank you,' said Sensis, accepting the bowl gratefully, the scents of rosemary and bay filling her nose.

Cook nodded again, then went back to chopping onions.

'You don't have a cook stove?' said Sensis, surprised.

'Don't like them,' said Cook. 'Don't trust them. With a fire, you know where you are. Heard too many stories of burnt food and variable temperatures. I won't have my reputation tarnished by no stove.'

Sensis smiled into her stew. 'This is delicious,' she said, before taking another mouthful.

'Thank you,' said Cook, in a way that said he knew. 'Seen the house now, have you?'

'Most of it; there's a lot to see.'

'Will you be staying long?'

He seemed to be asking out of curiosity, but it was likely anything she said would get back to Antice. 'Maybe.'

'Any foods you like especially? Or don't like?'

'I'm a soldier,' said Sensis. 'I'm not fussy. Although I am partial to strawberries dipped in chocolate.'

Cook laughed. 'That's easy enough.' Chocolate was rare, but apparently sourcing luxury items wasn't a problem for Venir's cook.

They went about their business in silence for a few moments, then Cook said, 'Expect you'll be touring the estate grounds next?'

'Yes,' said Sensis. 'Who should I select as my guide?'

Cook fixed her with a surprised expression that matched the one Raya had given her earlier. 'Well,' he said, 'the Gillie's the obvious choice, but if I were you, I'd ask the Under-Gillie. Twice the Gillie's experience, and far more sense.'

Sensis nodded. 'I'll do that. Thank you.'

Sensis used the kitchen door to leave the house, and poked around in the woodshed, coal, and cold stores for a bit. She found nothing of interest, and after that, it didn't take long to find the Gillie's office, not far from the kitchen. She rapped her knuckles on the glass-paned door.

'Yes?' said a young, blond man, who didn't look up from his ledger.

'I'm looking for the Under-Gillie.'

'Under the alterwoods,' said the man, still absorbed in his numbers.

Sensis closed the door and strode around the side of the mansion, through a beautiful, sweet-scented rose garden, until she reached the steps at the front of the house. She signaled to a guard, told him to commandeer the Gillie's ledgers, then strode towards the alterwood trees that lined the drive.

It took a while to locate the Under-Gillie, for although Sensis knew about tracking, the Under-Gillie, apparently, knew more. She eventually spotted him, cocooned in the roots of a colossal old tree, its bark dark and hard, its leaves deep green saucers.

'Cook recommended I ask you to show me around,' said Sensis.

The man faced away, wrapped in a mud-colored cloak. 'That's because he has a sense of humor,' said a voice she recognized.

'Antice?'

'Lord Antice,' he replied. 'Or Under-Gillie, if you must.'

'Your skills of concealment are impressive.'

'You sound surprised,' he said, making no move to get up.

'That's because I am.'

'There are many things about me I am sure you will find surprising.'

'You say that as though you plan for us to spend enough time together for me to discover those things. After your retreat last night, I thought you might have left.'

'I apologize, my ... lady.'

'How kind, my lord.' Sensis didn't hide her triumphant smile, which he ignored. 'Do you plan to show me around the estate, or should I rouse the Gillie?'

Antice got to his feet in a fluid movement. 'This way,' he said, with a look Sensis couldn't decipher. Then he strode off down the drive.

Chapter Four

CAL HELD UP HIS TORCH as they entered the Temple of the Mother. The sun was only just past its height, but it didn't penetrate the space, so it was hard to see the intricacies of the interior. It was unlike any normal temple; no grand hall, nor impressive statues.

They'd continued along the collapsed path, Edu making them move with painstaking care, until it had eventually deposited them in a rectangular space edged by columns, enclosed above, with only five small circular holes in the ceiling. In the center sat a rectangular box made of stone. It looked like a casket, and Fyia shivered. Was this a tomb?

Edu stepped in front of her, a warning on his face, and Fyia waved her hand in submission. After her antics of earlier in the day, she held no high ground from which to wage a war.

Edu carefully explored the space, testing each tile before he stepped, insisting on silence, so he would hear any clicks or scrapes or footsteps other than his own.

It was tedious, and Fyia longed to make a dash for the mysterious box. Instead, she rested back against the wall and studied the Fae'ch spies sent by Isa.

They were a funny pair. Leo, a male of few words, and Alba, a woman of many. He was smitten with her, of that there was no doubt, and considering they'd been sent to spy, Leo spent a great deal of time staring at Alba, especially when he thought no one was watching.

Alba seemed similarly taken with the sullen fae, but they were almost nervous around one another, suggesting their relationship was a new one.

'Were you two a couple before Isa sent you to spy on me?' said Fyia, her tone light.

Alba whirled, biting her lip to try and suppress her broad smile.

'Yes,' said Leo. He took Alba's hand and tugged her focus back to Edu's exploration.

'Does she approve of the match?' Fyia pressed, a smile pulling at her own lips.

Leo scowled at Alba, who shrugged off his touch with a scowl of her own. 'I don't know,' she said. 'I don't think she's against it … but, you know what she's like; it's hard to tell.'

'I don't, actually,' said Fyia. 'Not really. I only met her once, and she expelled me from the mountain with barely a word.'

'Did you steal it?' said Alba, her eyes wide. 'The dragon egg?'

Fyia laughed. 'No. There was no dragon egg.'

'You think that's where the metal ball you took from the Emperor came from?' said Alba.

Fyia's insides lurched in surprise. 'You concealed yourselves well that day, then.'

Alba turned sheepish, and Leo shook his head at her. He was trying to be stern, but he mostly just looked indulgent.

'It's a mystery how the Emperor acquired the ball,' said Fyia, 'but we think it had something to do with the witch he had with him.'

'You didn't happen to recognize her?' said Cal. 'Or see where she went?'

'No,' said Alba. 'So much happened so quickly, and she was gone in a flash.'

'Do you know who she is?' said Fyia.

Alba shook her head. 'Do you, Leo?'

Leo took a deep breath, obviously uncomfortable, but he shook his head also.

'Isa might know,' said Alba. 'We can ask her.'

'You think she'll help?' said Fyia, hope unfurling in her chest. 'Because that's not the impression she gave me.'

'I think something has changed,' said Alba. 'She told us it might be time ... although time for what, I don't know. I think maybe she meant it's time to work with you?'

'We don't know that,' said Leo, through gritted teeth.

'We don't know that,' Alba agreed. 'But what else could she have meant?'

'A great many things, I would suppose,' said Leo.

Edu reached the middle, and Fyia's chest leapt. She raced to Edu's side, the others hot on her heels as she scanned the stone box for clues.

'Do not even think about opening it,' said Edu, his tone brooking no argument.

Fyia ignored him as she ran her hands over the smooth stone, searching for hidden inscriptions.

'Here,' said Cal, who stood at its foot. 'There's a dragon. A five-headed dragon.'

Fyia moved to his side and traced her fingers over the outline. 'And underneath,' she said, 'is that a crown?' She ran a finger around the circular band that contained no points or adornments.

'The Dragon King wore a band of plain gold, did he not?' said Cal.

'You don't think ...' said Fyia, meeting Cal's eyes.

'It could be,' he said.

'Don't even think about opening it,' Edu repeated. 'If the Dragon King's remains are inside, it's most likely booby-trapped.'

Fyia waved her hand. 'Fine,' she said. 'I'll leave it to you to find a safe way in. We'll explore the rest of the temple.'

'Fyia ...' said Edu, but she was already moving.

'It's a temple ... the Temple of the Mother, who is nurturing and kind. Her temple should be a refuge, not a gauntlet.'

'My mother was neither nurturing nor kind,' Edu shot back, 'and neither was yours.'

'Nor mine,' said Alba. 'She abandoned me. And not Leo's either ...'

'Alba,' said Leo, his tone sharp, and Alba's lips clamped shut.

Interesting.

Fyia headed deeper into the temple, and gooseflesh spread across her skin as she travelled further into the dark, foreboding space. There were no windows, so even if the temple hadn't been half-buried by snow, there wouldn't have been any light, which seemed strange to Fyia, for a temple dedicated to the Mother.

Edu pushed past Fyia and strode ahead. 'Stay at least ten paces behind me,' he said, his voice full of frustration.

The unease settling in Fyia's gut meant she didn't argue. She considered whether they should turn around and find another way in, but then Leo spread his wings and flew ahead. Apparently he was the silent, impatient type.

'It slopes upwards,' Leo called back, then a few moments later, 'and ends in a circular chamber with a statue of the Mother in the middle.'

Fyia dutifully paced behind Edu, resisting the impulse to rush, and they eventually emerged in the dingy space. They held up their torches to illuminate the only interesting feature in the room, a statue of a woman nursing a baby that stretched almost to the curved stone roof, at least thirty paces above.

On the other side of the sphere-like room, steps descended to double doors made of wood.

'Maybe we came in the back door?' said Cal, eyeing the much more impressive entrance.

'The Mother looks a lot like a warrior, don't you think?' said Fyia, walking a circle around the statue, studying the carving from every angle. 'She has a sword at her hip, and her clothes look like armor.'

'You think it's the Warrior?' said Alba, running her hand over the stone.

'Maybe it's both,' said Leo, surprising them all with his contribution.

'One God with two sides,' said Fyia, liking the idea.

'And one temple with two sides to match?' said Cal.

'Strange for the remains of the Dragon King to be in the Temple of the Mother,' said Edu.

'But not the Temple of the Warrior,' Fyia countered.

Edu tilted his head in acquiescence, and Fyia made for the double doors, flinging them open before Edu could stop her.

'I thought we'd agreed to be more patient,' Cal whispered in her ear as he entwined their fingers.

'Old habits die hard?'

He chuckled.

After a few paces along another corridor, they emerged into a colossal hall, wide and tall, the walls sparkling white, and, 'Gods,' gasped Fyia, as her eyes took in the sea of dragon scales hanging in the air below the vaulted ceiling.

'Wow,' said Cal.

'What's holding them up there?' said Edu, moving this way and that, squinting at the scales.

Leo hopped into the air and ran his hand above a scale.

'Magic?' said Alba.

Leo nodded.

'Decorations, or a trap?' said Fyia, tentatively stepping towards them.

'Don't,' said Edu, but Alba was already halfway to the middle of the space, and there was no way Fyia was going to let all the discoveries be hers.

Edu shrugged, and Fyia and Cal stepped under the scales. Fyia gasped, as did the others, for the scales above their heads began to move, to spin. They made slow, stately turns, nothing alarming or hostile, just … beautiful, mesmerizing, and Fyia couldn't pull her eyes away. She took another step forward, then another, until she stood in the very center of the chamber, below the largest of the scales.

Cal went with her, and they shared a look of mutual wonder. But then she gasped again, because behind Cal's ear was a faint golden glow. His fire-touch …

'Fyia,' said Cal.

She turned her eyes upwards, following his gaze, and found the tips of the floating scales emitting the same glow. The light climbed slowly higher with every revolution, until the scales were fully lit, the air a spinning mass of gently glowing gold.

Antice led Sensis down the grand, wide, alterwood-lined drive, the air between them tense, charged, waiting for an angry spark to set light a blaze. In the surrounding wood, the leaves were shades of orange, yellow, and burgundy, but not the alterwoods, which remained a brilliant, deep shade of green.

It had always been a mystery how they could sustain themselves through the long, arduous winters with their waxy, circular leaves. All anyone could come up with was that it must be magic, a fact the old kings had suppressed, like they'd done with anything they didn't understand or control.

'You can almost feel it,' said Sensis. She held her arms out to either side as they trudged past yet another pair of impressive trees.

'Feel what?'

'The magic,' she said, raising a provocative eyebrow.

He held her gaze for a beat, then looked away, his expression unreadable.

'Does that hurt?' she pressed. 'The mention of things you don't understand?'

'You think you have me all figured out?' His flirtatious tone brought Sensis up short, the surprise stealing her brain function.

Antice laughed, the sound provoking but not hostile.

'I don't presume to know you at all,' she eventually replied. 'As you do not know me.'

'Oh, come now. How can you say such things when we practically grew up together?'

Now it was Sensis who laughed. 'You were a prince. My parents served your father. I was never your equal ... well, aside from the one time you agreed to spar with me. But then, we weren't equals that day either.'

'I should thank you for handing me my pride that day,' he said. 'Before then, I'd dreamed of being a warrior. You taught me my calling was elsewhere.'

'I could have told you politics was more your speed without first putting you on your arse.'

'Such an ugly word,' he said. 'Politics. I prefer leadership.'

'You stir up bad sentiment, then incite mob behavior and terrorist action. Politics is a nice word for your work.'

'You think that's what I do?'

'I know that's what you do.'

'You know nothing,' he said, stopping suddenly.

Sensis halted too, the enormous wrought-iron gates only twenty paces away. Stone dragons sat atop the pillars, others carved into the stone of the gatehouses on either side.

'Do you believe in them?' she said, nodding to the statues.

A smile pulled at Antice's lips. 'Of course.'

'Then why work against the Queen?'

Antice turned away. 'This is the northernmost gate. Feel free to use it.'

When Sensis made it clear she wouldn't be using the gate, Antice took her to the stables, where they mounted a beautiful pair of bay geldings. Antice showed Sensis all the gates on the estate—large, small, and even a few hidden in the bushes—each accompanied by the hint that she should see herself out.

Eventually, exits exhausted, he also showed her the fields, estate cottages, and orchards where the estate workers gathered the last of the cider apples.

They cantered back to the stables and left their horses with the grooms, then headed back to the house, past the outbuildings where the apples were stored.

'Do you remember the year …' said Sensis.

'When we made cider?' Antice finished, meeting her eyes with a mischievous grin.

A flush of warmth bloomed inside her, and she turned her head away. 'Don't,' she said. Her parents had come to the estate regularly to trade when Sensis was young, and occasionally they'd brought her with them.

'Don't remind you of the time I had my first kiss against the back of that barn?' he said.

'Oh? With whom?'

'Don't pretend you don't remember,' said Antice, his voice low.

'You can't mean …'

'You were the only girl I knew.'

They'd been fourteen years old, gangly, and awkward. Sensis had cared only for swords and combat, her parents convinced it was a phase she would leave behind, desperate for her to don dresses and attend parties. To snag a powerful husband.

Antice had indulged her love of combat that first year. They'd shared tips and talked for hours about military strategy, arguing over the best engagements of all time. The hatred and harsh words and distance had come later, after he'd surrounded himself with lordlings from influential houses he'd met at his exclusive, boys-only school.

But that first year, he'd waited until no one was watching, the sun having set, alcohol flowing, so everyone forgot all about them, and tugged her under a table, then out of a hatch in the barn's wall. He'd barely hesitated before pushing her back against the stone and pressing his lips to hers, and she'd let him, the sensation like nothing she'd ever felt before.

It wasn't her first kiss. A boy she sparred with had cornered her once after training. She'd gone along with it, keen to see what all the fuss was about, but she hadn't let him do it again. Maybe because it hadn't felt like it did with Antice. It had been sloppy and hard and rushed, but the kiss with Antice was eager, but also gentle. He had explored her lips and mouth and tongue with something akin to reverence, and she'd done the same to him, consumed by him, lost in his thrall ... until the banging of a door had made them jump guiltily apart, and they'd run as though they feared for their lives.

By the time Sensis snapped out of her reverie, they were almost back at the house, the sun low in the sky.

A guard hurried down the shallow front steps to meet them. 'General,' he said, 'Lady Starfall has sent word. The Queen's Small Council has requested the assistance of the Guild of Engineers. The clock in Selise is structurally unstable and needs urgent work. Lady Starfall has also requested that any leader responsible for a dragon clock check its integrity with urgency.'

'Thank you,' said Sensis, following Antice up the stairs to the house.

'Curious,' said Antice, 'that the Small Council should care about the clocks.'

'If you had been there, as you are supposed to be, you could have shared your curiosity with them,' said Sensis. 'Did the Queen not threaten to strip you of your lands and titles if you did not attend council meetings?'

'I obtained a leave of absence from Lady Starfall,' said Antice. 'The Queen's changes have not been easy on the Kingdom of Moon, and there is much to settle.'

Sensis scoffed. 'You have done little to make it easy on the people of Moon, and the university and guilds should have admitted women all along. It's not such a hardship to allow us an education, or to admit us to the army ... sometimes we're even an asset, as I, Essa, and many others have proven.'

'Admirably,' Antice agreed.

'Then you'll send the engineers?'

'I do not control the guilds,' said Antice. 'They govern themselves, as they have always done.'

'I was not born yesterday, Lord Antice ...'

'But I will encourage the Guild to aid our Queen,' he said, mockery edging his words.

'What an upstanding Warden of the Moon Kingdom you are,' said Sensis, matching his tone.

Antice strode off into the house, and the guard gave her a questioning look, but Sensis waved him away. Tonight, Sensis would follow Antice herself.

Starfall prayed to all the Gods to give her strength as she entered a lesser chamber in the council building, on account of the main chamber being structurally unstable. The Guild of Engineers had sent a team to fix the problem, so at least Essa would be happy.

Starfall faced down the lawmen staring back at her as she strode to her place at the head of the table. They were all men, and dressed in the ridiculous robes and wigs they insisted on wearing to *uphold the traditions of their great profession*. There wasn't much evidence of greatness among the paunchy, greying men, although a couple of their underlings stirred her interest, from what little she could see of them, pressed back against the walls as they were.

The Small Council filed in behind Starfall, taking their seats as she called the meeting to order.

'We all know why we are here,' said Starfall. 'The Queen wishes to change the laws of her kingdoms. That the changes will be made is not for discussion, and this meeting will address practicalities and considerations, nothing more. For clarity, the changes in question are to allow women to maintain their independent status and property when they marry, and to grant women equal rights to men in all things.

'I propose we hear in turn from the experts of each kingdom, and save discussion until the end. Are there questions before we begin?'

'Lady Starfall,' said a wig. He was old and haggard, and didn't bother getting to his feet. 'I really must object. The proposed changes are too radical, and too contentious to be forced through in this rushed manner. We must take small, steady steps.'

Almost all the wigs around the table nodded in vehement agreement, and most of those lining the walls, too.

'It will cause further riots,' said another. 'Instability of a sort we have never seen before.'

'We must seek commonalities to bring the kingdoms together, not press sores that will pull us apart.'

Lady Lyr, Warden of the Kingdom of Starlight, and one of Starfall's least favorite people, nodded along too. 'They're right,' she said. 'As I have been saying all along, this is lunacy.'

Lady Nara stood, and the wigs reluctantly gave her their attention. The Warden of the Kingdom of Sea Serpents was young, beautiful, and threatening to these old men. They would rather see her married, housebound, and impregnated than sitting at a table of power.

'Maybe there's a middle ground,' she said, not quite forcefully enough, given her audience. They sniggered, and a couple even exchanged lewd glances. 'The Queen will not change her mind on this matter, but maybe we could change the laws as they apply only to royalty and nobles, at least to begin with, and then roll out the changes more broadly over time.'

'Lady Nara,' said a rotund man who looked to be in his fifties. His face had a ruddy hue, and his fingers—which he was now waving in animated fashion—were short, chubby things. 'Leave this business to the men. That the Queen has selected women to advise her is only natural, I suppose— strength in numbers, and all that—but I implore you, leave this to us; we know what is best.'

Nara sank back to her seat, but Starfall would not let his words stand. 'It is a shame,' she said, leaning casually against the arm of her chair, 'although not surprising, that your inflexible, male brains have not grasped the facts. Seeing as you seem to require the treatment of toddlers, I shall explain once more, and this time, I will go slowly. Perhaps you will do us *women* the courtesy of keeping up.

'We will be changing the laws to reflect the Queen's wishes. And not only those relating to marriage, but also those that discriminate against the magic folk. If this is out-with your abilities, I will happily accept your resignations on behalf of the Queen.'

'Lady Starfall …' the old wig began, but Starfall cut him off.

'You do not wish to be considered for the role of Warden of the Sky Kingdom?' she said. 'For that is your home kingdom, is it not?'

The man's mouth fell open, and he said no more.

'This will not stand!' said the chubby wig.

'I agree,' said Starfall, turning her eyes to him, 'the position of Master of the Coffers would not suit you. Do not make the mistake of assuming that because the Queen is not here, you can patronize her, for you will not like the consequences when she returns with her dragons.'

Some of them paled, some scowled, a few at the sides hid smiles, but they all held their tongues.

'Now,' said Starfall, 'let us resume. Whichever of you is from the Starlight Kingdom, we will start there, and please, try to stick to the agenda.'

The meeting lasted endless hours, but they eventually agreed a way forward. The law men would draw up the changes, and they would reconvene when it was done. Starfall wanted nothing more than to find the nearest public house when it was over, but she held Nara back as the others filed out.

'Yes, my lady?' said Nara, her sails hanging limp, devoid of wind.

'Lady Nara,' said Starfall, with a stern sigh, 'these men would happily breed you like a prize sow. That your father allows you to enjoy considerable wealth and freedom is your very great fortune, but make no mistake, a husband may not afford you the same privilege. It would be wise for you to remember that.'

Nara nodded, then stalked away, her shoulders slumped. Starfall sat back in her seat. 'Spider,' she said, when they were finally alone.

'I will watch the old men,' said the Spider, 'and the young ones, too. For they are hungry, ambitious, and let us hope malleable.'

'Just how I like them,' said Starfall, with a salacious flash of her eyes.

Veau listened with rapt interest as Storm, an old Fae'ch from the deep, explained why she'd summoned the water riders to her. Veau was not a water rider—a member of the Fae'ch with magical skills attuned to riding the great beasts of the lake—but whatever this was, it was significant, and he wanted to know more.

Veau had never met a Fae'ch from the bowels of the mountain, but something grave had drawn this woman to the surface. And she'd practically pounced on Veau earlier that day, telling him to meet her here, because she wanted to know more about Fyia.

Of course Veau had come, the intrigue too great to ignore. He'd asked around about the woman, and if rumors could be believed, there was a deep rift between Storm and Isa, for they both loved the same fae male. The male, Gabriel, had shunned their leader and chosen Storm instead, but under the mountain, Isa was all-powerful, and could order them to do anything she pleased. Had Isa ordered Storm here today? Was it some strange punishment?

'It is no exaggeration to say we face an existential threat,' said the short, curvy blond.

Veau's pulse spiked, and a tense hush fell over the crowd.

'I called for water riders because I have a mission for you. One that will appease the Children of the Lake, and bring us back into balance with those ancient and powerful beings. Our mission is to rouse a slumbering beast from the deep, with scales so rare they're prized almost as highly as the scales of a dragon.'

Why did the Children of the Lake need to be appeased? They'd dwelled under the mountain since long before the Fae'ch had sought refuge here, and Veau had never heard mention of issues with them.

The assembled crowd shuffled uneasily, and Storm scowled. 'Where are the real water riders?' she said, rounding on Axus. 'The ones with the magic of the water? The ones who would bite my hand off for an offer such as this?'

Axus looked blankly back, and the others seemed confused, just like Veau. The water riders were a group that congregated often at this end of the lake, and rode great, serpent-like beasts that lived in the water. It was not for the faint of heart, and many had lost their lives to the canny creatures.

'No …' said Storm, disbelief thick in her tone. 'There aren't any?'

Veau frowned, trying to keep up.

Axus shrugged. 'What good are water riders?'

'What good are water riders?' Storm repeated. 'They'd come in useful right about now, don't you think?'

So those who gathered to ride the water creatures were not actually water riders after all?

'This isn't a run-of-the-mill occurrence …' said Axus, off kilter in a way Veau had never seen before.

'There was one,' said Regio—Axus' son, and one of the cockiest Fae'ch Veau had ever met. 'At least, I think that's what she was.'

A few of the others began nodding.

'Alba,' said a fairy.

'Yes,' said Regio. 'It would explain a lot if her magic was literally made for water riding.'

'And where is Alba?' said Storm.

'Not here,' said Axus, 'and we have no way to bring her back.'

Storm growled. 'We must appease the Children. They were here first, and we are here at their mercy, safe only so long as we give them what they need.'

'Magic,' said Veau, part of him surprised he'd spoken up.

Storm nodded. 'Magic. Not too much, and not too little. Just enough. We must find a source to provide that, and I suppose this sorry group will have to be enough.'

'What will happen if we fail?' asked Regio.

Storm's eyebrows lifted, and she appraised them anew. 'If I were you, weak as you are, I'd pray I never found out.'

A shiver of unease travelled down Veau's spine. Life under the mountain was anything but perfect, and there were those on the outside he missed, but this was the first place he'd lived without the constant fear of his magic hurting those he loved. For it to be snatched away so soon ...

Storm split them into groups, and Veau stepped away, perching on the rocks and observing for the rest of the session. Storm drilled them for hours, everyone demoralized and sullen when it was finally over.

Veau was the only one to hang back, the others racing for the exit. 'You wanted to speak with me?' he said.

Storm waited until they were alone, then gave Veau her full attention. 'Why did your sister come to the mountain?'

Veau hesitated, deciding what to say, but the truth was public knowledge. 'She sought the dragon egg guarded by the Fae'ch.'

'Did she indeed ...' Storm watched him for several long ticks. 'I want to learn about your sister. Fear not, it's nothing bad. I'm ... intrigued by her. I believe she intends to welcome the magical back to her lands, and I want to know if it's a call I should answer.'

Veau's jaw dropped open.

'It can't be so much of a surprise,' said Storm, laughing at his reaction. 'Life under the mountain is hardly ideal.'

'Especially for you,' said Veau, then immediately regretted it.

'Especially for anyone,' she parried. 'So, tell me, is your sister a queen worthy of the name?'

'Yes,' said Veau, without hesitation. 'My sister is … I don't know. She's infuriating most of the time, and stubborn, and once she gets an idea in her head, there's no reasoning with her.'

'Like conquering five kingdoms?' Storm said, with a chuckle.

'Like bringing back the dragons.'

Storm stilled, taking him in. 'You think it a foolish quest?'

Veau shook his head. 'No. I think if anyone can do it, it will be her, but …'

He trailed off as footsteps approached, and a tall, dark-skinned fae with black wings appeared through a tunnel. Few were brazen enough to show off their wings, for Isa had deemed it impolite while under the mountain, something this fae seemed to care little about.

Storm looked warmly at the male, then said, 'Gabriel, this is Veau, Queen Fyia's brother. Also fire-touched, in case you hadn't noticed the river of scales across his face.'

Veau frowned.

'Don't mind her,' said Gabriel, his voice deep and slow. 'She's insensitive.'

'It's rude to call people names,' said Storm.

He wrapped an arm around her. 'Pot, kettle ... It is nice to meet you, Veau, brother of Queen Fyia.'

Veau gave a half smile just as Isa appeared in front of Gabriel, materializing in a whirl of smoke. Isa laid a hand on his chest, and Storm looked as though she might implode. Veau suddenly wished to be anywhere else.

'Where have you been?' said Isa, her voice distant.

'I've been busy,' said Gabriel, his tone clipped, the easy smile of moments before long gone.

'Doing what?'

'Asking around in the deep for food we can use for the Children.'

'The Children are nervous,' said Storm. 'They ...'

'You will placate them,' said Isa, not even looking at Storm.

'As you wish, leader,' said Storm, with a mock bow. 'But where is the one they call Alba?'

Isa clenched her jaw, then sneered as a cloud of smoke wrapped around her. She all but disappeared, only her head remaining, her deadly eyes fixed on Veau for a tick before she turned to Gabriel. Her hand reappeared from the smoke, and she used it to cup Gabriel's face, running a thumb across his cheekbone. 'Come to me tonight, my love. Oh, and I see you've found your son.'

Isa vanished, and it took several long moments for Veau to process her words. At first, he thought she must have meant someone else, but then Storm and Gabriel turned identical looks of shock on him, and his eyebrows pinched together as the implications hit him one by one.

A deathly hush descended, accompanied by a sucking sensation in the pit of Veau's stomach. And then Storm disappeared, leaving only Veau and Gabriel—Isa's beloved, a powerful fae, and his ...

father—standing alone, staring at one another in the gloomy light of the cavern.

'I thought the King of Starlight was my father,' said Veau.

'Apparently not,' said Gabriel. 'I did not know …'

'Then it's a surprise for us both.'

Gabriel nodded. 'I'm sorry.'

'For what?' said Veau. 'Impregnating my mother?'

'I … well …'

Silence settled as Veau tried to claw back his racing thoughts. 'Did you love her?'

'No,' said Gabriel, with no hesitation. 'I'm sure your mother is a wonderful woman, but I barely knew her.'

Veau snorted. 'My mother is anything but wonderful … but, if you didn't know her … why?'

'Isa,' said Gabriel.

'Oh.' Gods, no. So many thoughts warred for space in his mind, but he couldn't grasp a single one.

'Isa was angry her efforts to get with child were not bearing fruit, and then your mother came to the mountain. I believe she intended to find a magical sire for her own child, and Isa wanted to punish me, so …'

'So she forced you?' said Veau, feeling sick.

'Yes,' said Gabriel, 'she forced me, but that has no bearing on how I think about you … or how you should think about yourself. You can hardly be judged because of the actions of Isa and your mother … and me.'

'I'm sorry,' said Veau. 'For both our sakes.'

Silence covered them like a blanket as their new roles settled on their shoulders.

'Lucky you didn't inherit my wings,' said Gabriel. 'Unless you're hiding them with magic …'

'No,' said Veau, shaking his head. 'I have only weak, erratic magic. That, and the scales across my face.'

'Well, you didn't get those from me, although your ears have a very slight point. We can attribute those to your fae blood.'

'It finally makes sense why Isa agreed to let me live under the mountain,' said Veau. 'For you. Because she loves you.'

Gabriel scoffed. 'That woman doesn't know how to love. She brought you here to torment me, or use you as a hostage.'

'Rumor says Isa is head over heels in love with you …'

'What she feels isn't love, despite what she may believe,' said Gabriel. 'She cares only for power. She's desperate to keep her place as leader of our kind, but fears the long-lives in the deep might get rebellious ideas … or up and leave. Now your sister's welcoming us back to her lands, Isa walks a precarious line.'

'You would leave?' said Veau. 'I never really believed any of the Fae'ch would take up Fyia's offer.'

'Why not? You think we enjoy living under this damned mountain?'

Veau thought for a moment. 'Honestly, yes,' he said. 'That's how it looks from the outside, but maybe that's because Isa allows no one in.'

'Come,' said Gabriel, kindly, 'let us go to Storm; she wishes to know more about your sister.'

'Half-sister,' said Veau. 'Unless …'

'No,' said Gabriel. 'It happened only once.'

Veau huffed out a laugh. 'People in the Five Kingdoms made such a fuss when I gave my throne to Fyia, and it turns out she was the rightful heir all along.'

'You are still the son of the Queen of Starlight,' said Gabriel. 'Magic- and fire-touched. That's not nothing.'

'I hardly think my paltry magic warrants the title.'

'It is strong for a human, is it not?'

Veau shrugged. 'It's hard to say. Until Fyia took over, anyone with even a hint of magic hid their talent for fear of persecution, or death.'

'We will test it,' said Gabriel. 'But first, we will speak with Storm.'

Veau's mind was reeling with all that had happened, and Isa seemed rankled, so much so, Veau was scared to enter her quarters when she summoned him, several days after she'd revealed he was Gabriel's son.

'Get in. Here,' said Isa, as Veau hovered at the door to her large, lavish cave.

'Is that …' Veau pointed at the ceiling, where it seemed as if real sunlight poked through a series of cracks. When had he last seen the light of the sun?

'Yes,' snapped Isa.

Her complete attention suddenly landed on Veau, and he froze at the sight of her wild eyes.

'Storm sought you out, did she not?'

Isa likely already knew the truth, so there was little point in trying to lie. 'She did.'

'She wants to know about your sister?'

'Yes.'

'Why?'

'I'm not sure, exactly,' he said. It was a half-lie, given Storm had told Veau in no uncertain terms she was thinking of going to Fyia's side. 'She asked what Fyia wants.'

'To which you said?'

'Dragons.' Isa seemed volatile … likely to lash out, and Veau feared for his safety for the first time since coming to live with the Fae'ch

'And you are training with Storm and the water riders?'

'I'm an interested observer. I have no affinity for water riding, but I want to help if I can. If the Children of the Lake were to …'

'You will spy on Storm and Gabriel,' she said, cutting him off. 'Whatever they do, I must know. I cannot be everywhere at once, so you will lend me your ears and eyes.'

'Of course,' he replied, because that was the right answer, but unease filled him. This woman had forced Gabriel to have sex with his mother. She was a monster, delusional, whereas Storm and Gabriel had been nothing but warm. Gabriel whim about magic, and treated him like he was worth something.

Veau had little choice but to obey the Fae'ch leader—he'd sworn an oath to do so, as had every Fae'ch under the mountain—but his heart would not be in it, for his loyalties lay firmly elsewhere.

Chapter Five

SCORPIA LOOKED OUT ACROSS the mirror-still bay, the water so clear and pure she could see crabs scuttling across the sand twenty paces below. She'd heard whispers on the wind of all that had happened in the north; falling clocks, the Emperor toppled from his perch, the engagement of Queen Fyia and King Cal.

There had never been a shortage of gossip from the Five Kingdoms, nor the Kraken Empire, in all her long life, but also, never had it been quite like this, so much all at once. Her old bones creaked with glee, for the gossip heralded the coming of something greater and more terrible. She'd caught it, like the faintest whiff of a foreign scent on the air, barely there, yet unmistakable all the same.

'Your Majesty,' said her equerry, stepping through the billowing fabric of her veranda.

'Yes?' she said, reluctantly turning her head.

'An envoy has arrived from the Five Kingdoms. Lord Fredrik Feake.'

She inhaled deeply and sat a little straighter on her throne, then waved her hand, her many bracelets jangling.

A slight, brown-skinned man with a demeanor of humble self-importance strode to the spot before her. 'Your Majesty,' he said, bowing low.

'Welcome, Lord Feake,' said Scorpia, motioning for him to sit in the chair her equerry had placed by her side.

'Most kind,' he replied. He angled himself to face her as he sat, his features stoic. 'I hope Your Majesty will forgive my abrupt style this day, but I come with grave news.'

Scorpia bit back the smile fighting to take hold of her lips. The young were always so earnest in the face of a crisis. Why it took so long for them to realize a deep frown or serious pinch of one's eyebrows made no difference in such scenarios, she had never fathomed. Her own wit prevailed at even the direst of moments, a fact of which she was inordinately proud. That, and her ability to keep her head when everything was going to shit around her.

'Please,' she said, with a wave of her hand, 'let there be no ceremony on my account.'

'Thank you, Your Majesty. I appreciate it.'

Scorpia almost rolled her eyes, but if she had, Feake would no doubt note the gesture, and his solemnity would only increase.

'The Lady Starfall requested I travel to the Scorpion Lands to inform you the dragon clocks in the Five Kingdoms are crumbling. Essa Thebe, the Queen's engineer, seeks to rectify the damage, for she believes the clocks to be significant. She requested we inform our allies, and advise them to carry out any and all repairs that might be necessary.'

'Is that so,' said Scorpia.

'You do not believe the clocks to be important?'

Scorpia scoffed. 'I am relieved to hear the Five Kingdoms are finally taking the threat seriously. The Scorpion Lands have always done so, and our clock is in pristine condition.'

'You ... really think there's a threat?' said Lord Feake, suddenly uncertain.

Scorpia's mouth fell open. 'Urgh ...' She struggled to find words to adequately express her derision, so in the end, she simply said, 'You may leave.'

Feake scampered out of her sight, and Scorpia turned her attention back to the water. There it was again, that scent of promise.

'Prepare my ship,' she said to her equerry, who hovered just out of view. 'Something is coming. I will travel north on the morning tide.'

Essa hated the Kingdom of Sea Serpents with a passion. She didn't love her home kingdom—Moon—any better, but that was because the people there were backward and full of prejudice. Here they were more progressive, no doubt because the Priestesses of the Sea Serpent—and their magic—were feared and revered in equal measure. But there was something about the kingdom's relationship with the sea that felt dangerous to Essa, as though her life was always in peril, nowhere safe.

She trudged across the great undulation in the land that stood between her and the temple, past houses and shops that seemed newer than most of the surrounding settlements. She wondered at that, but the burning sensation in her legs chased away the thought as she climbed the steep steps to the plaza in front of the temple's entrance.

Unease settled on her shoulders as she caught her breath at the top, but she shook it off, then headed inside. She made for the dark, foreboding tunnel that led to the place where the temple's dragon clock had once stood. Before it had fallen, and smashed to pieces on the rocks below.

Priestesses scurried this way and that, more animated than Essa had ever seen them. Was it because they were once again able to practice their watery magic, or had something else sent them into a spin?

She hurried to the tunnel, careful not to snag her clothes on the sharp fangs guarding the entrance, then felt her way along the uneven ground.

When she finally emerged onto the ledge above the sea, she found the High Priestess sitting on her knees, her arms spread wide, head bowed, robes blowing in the wind. The hole where the dragon clock had once sat spouted boiling steam into the air, foreboding, and scented with sulfur.

'Priestess?' said Essa, her prickle of unease now a bolt of electricity shooting up her spine.

The woman looked up slowly, an unreadable expression on her face, her mismatched eyes seeming to look straight through Essa's flesh and bone.

'Priestess?' Essa repeated. 'Are you … okay?'

'You are too late,' said the woman, her voice vacant yet unwavering.

'Too late for what?'

'To save us.'

'You … what …? You mean to fix the clock?'

'When the clocks doth strike thirteen, the dragons shall return. But if the clocks do fall before, then fire will reign supreme,' said the priestess, turning her gaze to the sea. She smiled a whimsical smile as she watched the rolling waves.

'It's not too late,' said Essa. 'The clocks have not struck thirteen.' *Whatever the Seven Hells that meant.* 'Fyia has not yet found the dragons.'

'The clocks have fallen.'

'And we can fix them,' said Essa, although her voice betrayed her uncertainty.

'Wishful thinking,' said the priestess. 'The Fae'ch will never help us, and the creatures have already returned.'

'Creatures?' said Essa. Her heart raced wildly as she willed her mind to decipher the true meaning of the priestess's words. 'What creatures?'

The priestess's eyes were still locked on the sea, following one particularly large wave. The priestess rose to her feet in one lithe movement, her arms held out to her sides, what looked like a fish bone resting in each upturned palm.

'Priestess!' said Essa, as the woman moved dangerously close to the edge, where one misstep would mean a sheer drop onto the jagged rocks below. But that wasn't what most worried Essa, who backed up towards the tunnel, ready to dart inside. The bulge in the water was close now, close enough to see it wasn't a wave at all. It was a …

An enormous tentacle broke the surface, and Essa gasped, shying back into the tunnel. The priestess didn't flinch. She began to chant, swaying slightly, still holding out her hands.

The tentacle was joined by a second, and a giant head followed the fearsome limbs. The giant head of a … it was, truly … a kraken. The kraken's head was that of a serpent, its body coated in shiny scales, fangs protruding from its pointed mouth, but below the water, snake became squid, and eight deadly tentacles splayed out around the monster.

The kraken plucked the bones from the priestess's hands and deposited them in its mouth. It let them sit on its forked tongue a moment before swallowing them down, then watched as the priestess dropped to her knees, her arms on the ground in front of her, prostrating herself before the monster. But the kraken took no mercy. It plucked her from the ground and threw her like a rag doll into the air.

'The map!' the priestess screamed, before the kraken caught her in its mouth, skewering her on a fang.

It took Essa a moment to realize the priestess was shouting to her. A map? What map? Essa cast frantically around as the kraken tossed the priestess up again, then caught her and swallowed her whole.

Gods. *Gods.* Essa couldn't think, her terror almost consuming her as the kraken's beady eyes fixed on her. If she didn't move, she would be next. She would die, and take with her the knowledge of what she'd witnessed. But as she retreated, the wind whipped a piece of paper off the ground, and Essa moved without thinking. She darted forward, caught it before it disappeared into the steam, then, as a tentacle hurtled towards her, she fled.

Fyia wasn't sure how long they all stood there, taking in the spectacle, the scales showing no sign of ceasing their display. But before she'd even begun to grow bored with watching, a set of clipped footsteps grabbed their attention, and an extremely short man with dark hair, dressed head to foot in furs, stepped through the open set of doors on the far side of the hall.

'You made it, finally,' said the man, his voice surprisingly deep, considering his stature. There was something familiar about his features, but Fyia couldn't place him.

'Hello,' said Fyia.

Fyia's wolves growled, and Cal pulled Fyia closer to his side.

'I'm Fyia Orlightus.'

'Yes, yes ... come,' said the man, then he spun on his heel and clipped back the way he had come.

'But, who are you?' Cal asked, as Fyia's wolves growled louder.

'All in good time,' the man said, without looking back.

They had little choice but to follow, Alba and Leo already moving, and Fyia hadn't come this far to hover in the entrance hall, but she couldn't ignore the unease firing through her bond with her Cruaxee.

They stepped through the ornate golden doors, and Fyia looked back over her shoulder. The scales were dimming, and Fyia tugged on Cal's hand to make him look too.

'Your ears lit up,' Fyia said quietly, 'but it's gone now.'

'You think the scales put on that show because of our fire-touch?' said Cal.

Fyia shrugged. 'Or maybe they do that for everyone.' She threw him a satirical smile. 'Maybe we're not as special as we like to think we are.'

Cal dragged the nail of his thumb across her palm, and a jolt of lightning shot through her. They held each other's gaze for a tick, two, and then he tugged her after the others.

The small man led them down a wide, open corridor lined with gleaming pillars, the same carving of five interlinked circles in the spaces between every one.

'What is that?' asked Alba, walking so close to the man as to be almost on top of him.

The man kept walking, providing no answer.

'And you have the eyes of an elemental,' Alba continued, unperturbed. 'You are Fae'ch?'

The man spun at that. 'I am no such thing,' he hissed, with a look terrifying enough to make even Alba shrink back.

'What do you mean, *the eyes of an elemental?*' said Fyia, a little too eagerly. When magic had been banned in the Five Kingdoms, they'd ripped every trace from schools, libraries, and public life. It had been illegal to even mention magic, so Fyia was hungry for every morsel she could snap up.

The man gave a small shake of his head, then began walking once more.

'Those with elemental magic have mismatched eyes,' said Alba, falling in beside Fyia.

'Not all of them,' said Leo, in a censoring tone.

'Telling them this won't hurt,' she snapped, then turned back to Fyia. 'I mean, I'm no expert, but those with the magic of earth, air, fire, water, and *other* have mismatched eyes. Or at least, some of them do.'

'You know not of what you speak,' said the man, as he took a turn in the corridor.

Alba scowled. 'Well, that's what we were taught. I don't know the ins and outs of it; they weren't forthcoming with magical information under the mountain, but it's something to do with elemental magic.'

'Does everyone with magic fall into some group or other?' asked Fyia. She supposed that could make sense.

'Of course,' said Alba, 'although it's not clear cut. Maybe for some … like me, but …'

Leo grabbed her hand. 'Alba,' he said, his tone fierce.

'Oh, fine, whatever. But … we don't have to be secretive anymore.'

'He's wise to be cautious,' said Edu.

'Edu is caution personified,' said Fyia, throwing Edu a provoking glance.

'Which is good, considering your approach is the very opposite,' he snapped.

'Oh come now, I'm not *so* bad.'

Edu looked ready to outline precisely how bad she was, but the man led them under a sweeping archway into a light-filled atrium, and their voices instantly died.

The circular room contained five circular pools, just like the chamber they'd fallen into earlier. But here, four sat around the outside, and one in the middle. From the middle of the central pool protruded a column of shimmering rose-gold, which splayed into a complex web of metal limbs. It had the air of one of Essa's scientific contraptions, or maybe an artistic sculpture, and looked as though it might spin and whirl in some convoluted pattern, if one could find the right lever to make it start.

The sound of trickling water filled the air, the outer ring of pools all connected by water moving in a constant cycle from one to the next. The physics was not obvious, and Fyia supposed magic was at play, although she didn't care how it worked, she cared only to find out what this place was, and what the metal contraption was for.

Inscribed in front of each pool, a symbol had been scratched into the gleaming stone.

'Symbols of the Gods,' said Alba, circling the outside pools. 'The Whore, the Sea Serpent …'

'The Dragon,' said Cal, looking at the symbol by his feet.

'The Warrior and Mother are together,' said Fyia, standing over the combined inscription.

'For the Warrior and Mother are one and the same,' said the man, who watched them closely. 'Two sides of the same coin.'

'Explains the strange temple,' said Alba.

'Explains a lot about my mother,' said Edu.

'And mine,' Leo muttered, almost too quietly to hear.

'What is this place?' asked Cal. He reached out to touch the metal structure, but the man halted him with a sharp tut.

'I wouldn't do that if I were you,' he said.

Cal pulled back his hand. 'Why not?'

'That is the only way to bring back the dragons. Damage it, and kill the dreams of your betrothed.'

Fyia's blood rushed in her ears, her mouth went dry, and her feet moved of their own accord towards the structure. 'You know how to hatch the dragons?' she said, hope squeezing her chest tight, making her voice small.

'That is why you are here, is it not?' said the man.

Fyia nodded, her eyes roaming over the metal, searching for any small clue how to use it.

'And I believe you have the missing pieces …'

Fyia's eyes snapped up to his. 'The metal balls?'

'The eggs.'

'The … what?' said Fyia.

The man snorted. 'Dragons don't lay eggs, but the balls are a seed of sorts, hence the name.'

Fyia reeled. 'They don't lay eggs?'

'Dragons give birth to live young, or are made from the very fabric of magic.'

'Then, we have to make the dragons?' said Fyia. 'Using these?' She held up one of the strange metal balls she and Cal had found.

'We have only four,' said Cal. 'Is that enough?'

'The legends all say we need eggs,' said Fyia, unable to let go of the notion. 'Five of them.'

'Yes, well, legends are dangerous things,' said the man. 'One step removed from fabrication. And one ball was never removed from the mechanism. To remove it would have meant full destruction.'

'And we must place the others inside too?' said Fyia, eying the metal structure once more. 'That will make new dragons?'

Now Fyia was faced with the reality of finding them, a freezing, boiling terror filled her bones. She'd never thought much past the image of her atop one of the fearsome beasts, had never considered the practicalities.

The man looked away. 'Perhaps we should take things one step at a time,' he said. 'We should not act in haste.'

Fyia nodded. He was right. Although Fyia tended towards alacrity in all things, this was not something to rush. The stakes were too high, and they would only get one shot.

'Come. I will tell you the things you do not know.'

Sensis crouched in the shadows beside an alterwood tree, still and watchful as she waited for Antice to show himself. He had stolen out of the house every night since she'd arrived, and given her guards the slip every time; a well-trained Under-Gillie indeed.

Tonight, though, she wouldn't let him get away … if he showed.

She'd been hiding for hours with no sign of him, and he usually headed out shortly after dinner. Maybe he had a mistress, or went hunting, or simply enjoyed being outdoors. Or maybe he was up to something. Knowing Antice, Sensis would put coin on it being the latter. So she waited, and waited, and waited.

It wasn't long before dawn when she finally heard the whisper of a crunching leaf on the lawn. Antice was good, but he didn't have the eyes of an owl, and in the moonless, cloud-filled sky, a slip-up was almost inevitable. But she waited, because if she were Antice, she would lay decoys to throw pursuers off her scent. And as magic ran through the bloodlines of all their ancestors, she supposed his having the eyes of an owl couldn't be entirely ruled out.

Sure enough, the sound of a snapping twig cut across her thoughts, then a spin of the hand later, a thud—probably a stone hitting the ground further down the drive. Sensis waited still, for she could sense him more than see him, moving between the trees, heading her way.

She stayed in the alterwood's shadow, letting him come to her, as any slight movement might betray her position. She'd had a hunch he might come here. This was where she'd found him hiding before, after the Gillie had said he would be among the trees. Which raised the question, why? Why would a busy man, who presumably cared little about the day to day running of this estate, spend so much time here?

As it turned out, the answer came swiftly, for on the other side of the tree behind which Sensis crouched, Antice muttered something she couldn't hear, and then a slight whoosh of air buffeted her face.

Sensis launched to her feet and made a blind grab for the vague outline of Antice as he disappeared through a hole in the ground. He gasped and tried to yank free, and Sensis didn't resist. She let him pull her down into the hole, so they landed in a heap together on the damp earth at the bottom of a set of rudimentary steps.

A gentle glow of pure white light suddenly filled the air, the hole above now closed, and Sensis found herself sprawled across Antice, his body her cushion. Their faces were close, and his eyes were furious.

'Get off me,' he hissed, shoving at her.

'But I was just getting comfy,' she said, wriggling a little, as though burrowing into a couch cushion.

'Sensis, I'm warning you ...'

'You mean Lady Deimos, Antice?'

'*Sensis.*' He flipped them, and Sensis quite enjoyed his shocked expression at finding himself on top of her, the length of his body pressed along hers, his lips so close they could accidentally brush against her own. 'Why did you do that?'

'Do what, exactly?' said Sensis, her tone mocking.

He got to his feet. 'Why didn't you resist me when I turned us over?'

'Because that's what you wanted me to do.'

'You gave me the upper hand.'

'And,' said Sensis, rolling to her feet, 'you did nothing with it.'

'You'd rather I stabbed you?'

Sensis smirked. 'I'd like to see you try. What are these lights? They're magical?' she asked, her tone full of equal parts incredulity and wonder.

Antice looked away. 'They have been here a very long time, since before magic was outlawed.'

It made no difference, and they both knew it, but Sensis let it drop, more interested to see where the tunnel led.

'No,' said Antice, making a grab for her hand as she started walking.

She easily sidestepped him, then walked backwards a few paces along the tunnel. 'We both know you can't best me in a fight,' she said. 'So what's it to be? Come with me, or stand here sulking?'

'This place isn't for you.'

'Oh?' she said. 'And why is that?'

'You're not of the right ....'

Sensis sneered. 'For the love of all the Gods ... you're still peddling that crap? Your blood is better than mine?'

'No, Sensis, that's not ...' he trailed off. 'Well, don't say I didn't warn you.' He held out a hand, inviting her to lead on.

'I wasn't born yesterday, my dear Sollow.' His eyes bulged at her use of his first name. 'You're going in front.'

Starfall eyed the Spider across the table, and wondered how it could possibly be that she, the prudish, sensible Spider, was Starfall's only ally in the shit-show that was Fyia's Small Council. If one could call it Fyia's, for they didn't respect their Queen, nor did their Queen sully her own hands by leading them ... too busy chasing myths. Never before had Starfall missed the comforts of the Temple of the Night Goddess quite as she did now; there, she'd still be happily abed.

Starfall sucked in a weary breath. 'I call this meeting to order,' she said. 'What crises must we avert this day?'

The faces around the table—many short of the number that should be present—looked awkwardly at each other.

'The engineers think they've shored up the clock in the council chamber,' piped up Lady Nara, her tone hopeful.

'Essa will be pleased,' said Starfall. 'Although her news to us is grave.'

'Oh?' said Lord Fredrik, Warden of the Kingdom of Plenty, who had recently returned from the Scorpion Lands. He had reported a successful mission, and was still smug about it, despite the great ease of his task.

Starfall almost couldn't bring herself to share Essa's words—part of her didn't want to believe them—but Essa was not one prone to dramatics. 'The High Priestess is dead,' said Starfall.

Lady Nara gasped. As Warden of the Kingdom of Sea Serpents, the news was most pertinent to her.

'She was killed by a kraken,' Starfall continued. 'Essa observed the event with her own eyes, although she was the only witness. She believes the High Priestess offered herself as a sacrifice, possibly to atone for our failure to preserve the clocks.'

'A stretch,' said the Spider. Starfall once more marveled that the Spider, of all those present, had thoughts most similar to her own.

Starfall inclined her head. 'Regardless, the High Priestess is dead, the clock is still damaged, a kraken has returned to our land, and it is Essa's view that the Fae'ch hold the key to our salvation. She is on her way to the Fae'ch Mountain presently.'

'Then I suppose there isn't much we can do but wait,' said Lady Lyr, Warden of Starfall's own home kingdom, the Kingdom of Starlight. 'And while we wait, we should deal with the unrest in the streets of Selise.'

'A few skirmishes by those with nothing better to do with their time,' said Starfall, with more confidence than she felt.

They were still rebuilding the capital after the rebel attacks of less than a turn of the moon ago. The death and destruction had made them all edgy, and the leaders of the rebellion were still at large. Further attacks were perfectly possible, although they'd deployed troops to deter any who might try.

Starfall would feel better if Sensis were here, but she'd sent word to say she was extending her stay on her estate. Thankfully, it seemed Sensis being in Moon was also keeping Lord Antice out of the Small Council's hair, but Starfall could only let his absence slide for so long ...

'Unrest has been reported across the Kingdoms,' Lyr pressed. 'The people are yet to accept Fyia's rash ways.'

'People don't like change at the best of times,' said Starfall, 'and Fyia has given her subjects many adjustments to grumble over.'

'Changing laws,' said Lyr, 'letting the *magical* back into our lands, forcing the market owners to ...'

'Enough,' said Starfall, exasperated. How many times must they have the same conversations? 'This is not a cake shop. We are not here to gossip and grouch. We are here to see that the will of our Queen is done. Should you take issue with ...'

The doors to the temporary council chamber swung open, and a harried-looking guard bowed low.

'Come,' said Starfall.

He straightened, then strode towards her, a scroll in his hand.

'Sorry to interrupt, my lady, but the envoy said it was of the utmost importance. He was ... animated.'

Starfall broke the seal—that of the former King of the Kingdom of Sky—and quickly read the missive. Then re-read it to ensure she wasn't hallucinating.

'What is it?' said Nara, leaning forward, concern scratching deep lines in her forehead.

Starfall passed the parchment to the Spider, then sat back in her seat. 'It would seem this day is determined to try us,' said Starfall, 'for Lord Billington, of the Kingdom of Sky, reports that Hell's Canal—through which his kingdom does much trade—is boiling, and the fish, upon which they rely, have thrown themselves onto the land.'

Sensis followed Antice along the dank earthen corridor for only a short way before they hit a crossroads. A stone pillar sat in the middle—a signpost, Sensis realized, arrows scratched into the stone, along with writing she couldn't make out.

'There's a whole network of tunnels?' said Sensis, but Antice ignored her question, instead turning right and continuing without check.

'Antice ...'

He didn't stop.

'*Lord* Antice.'

His steps faltered for a moment, but then he resumed, saying, 'There is much you and your Queen do not know about this kingdom.'

Sensis was crafting a suitably tart response when the corridor opened out into a room of sorts. Small shafts of light from the rising sun filtered in from above—presumably spy holes—and in the center of the space sat a desk, crafted from the roots of the trees. Ancient-looking books and piles of parchment perched atop the uneven surface, and Sensis rushed towards them, hope swelling in her chest that she might finally learn something interesting.

'Don't,' said Antice, and Sensis paused, her hand a hair's breadth away.

'Why?' she asked, turning slowly to face him.

'They do not belong to you.'

'This tunnel, unless I am very much mistaken, is under my estate. Thus, the tunnel, and everything inside, is mine.'

Antice strode forward, stopping so close in front of her, she could see the specks of amber in his eyes, even in the dim light. Sensis was tall, but Antice was taller, and as he looked down at her, her heart pulsed harder. Then he slid his hand over hers, entwined their fingers, and pulled her away from the desk.

'This place is special,' he said in a low voice, still holding her fingers.

His eyes dipped to her lips, and Sensis had to work very hard to focus, refusing to let him distract her, as he was so desperately trying to do.

'*Special* indeed, if you're attempting to seduce me into submission.'

He sucked in a shocked breath. 'Sensis, I ...'

'Yes, Antice?' she said, holding up their joined hands in question.

'I'm not ...'

She shook off his hand and stepped around him to the other side of the desk. 'Now,' she said, picking up the nearest scroll, 'what exactly are you trying to hide?'

Sensis cast her eyes over the ornate script. A family tree—the Antice family tree—made up of an endless string of kings all the way back to the time of the

Dragon King himself. Although, they were not direct descendants, if the parchment could be believed.

She cast aside the family tree, and those detailing other royal houses. 'You seek to undermine Fyia's claim to the throne?' said Sensis. She looked up to find Antice watching her closely, a resigned expression on his face.

'No,' he said, and to her surprise, Sensis believed him.

Under the scrolls was a book, which she pulled towards her, finding it open on a chapter entitled, *The Role of the Dragon in Maintaining Balance*.

Her eyes darted back to Antice, who gave nothing away.

She flipped a few pages until she reached the next chapter, *The Role of the Fire-Touched in Controlling Dragons*.

She closed the book and read the title: *The Aqueducts, Magma Streams, and Dragon Clocks of the Ancient and Most Glorious Kingdom of Asred*.

'What the fuck is this?' she said, picking up the tome and brandishing it like a weapon.

'It's a book,' said Antice.

'This is treason,' said Sensis, moving menacingly towards him. 'Punishable by death.' As she said the words, something unpleasant clenched in her guts. 'You have withheld vital information from your Queen.'

Antice shook his head. 'It matters not,' he said, holding his ground and meeting her gaze, his broad shoulders set square, 'for the Queen does not have dragons.'

'It is not only about dragons,' said Sensis, flipping through the pages. 'It's about *Maintenance of the System*, and *Consequences of the Clocks Falling*,' she said, reading off the headings, 'and *Replenishment of Minerals*, and … *Warrior's Balls* … *The Hierarchy of the Fire-Touched*?' Sensis' eyes snapped up. 'You're searching for a way to replace her.'

Antice snatched the book from her hands. 'Keep your voice down,' he hissed, his eyes darting to the space behind them.

What? 'Why?' she said. 'The spy holes? You're worried someone will hear?'

'No,' said Antice. 'We must go. *You* must go.' He threw the book back onto the desk and grabbed her hand. 'Now, Sensis.'

Sensis pulled back, easily freeing herself from his grasp, and Antice put his hands on the roots and closed his eyes. Silence fell over them for a handful of ticks, and then he sucked in a deep, regretful breath. 'It is already too late.'

'Too late for what?' said Sensis, feeling the invisible, nefarious hands of something she didn't understand closing around her.

Antice pulled himself up to his full height. 'What are you doing?' he exclaimed. 'How did you get down here?'

'Antice …'

'*Lord* Antice to you,' he replied.

Sensis clamped her mouth shut. There could be only one reason for him to act this way. She picked up the book and slipped it into her cloak, then turned back to face him.

'What is this place?' she said.

'That is none of your concern.'

'Where do the tunnels lead?'

'Many places,' said a woman, who stepped out of the darkness, flanked by two burly men. She had stars tattooed below her right eye, and Sensis recalled the description of the rebel leader given to her by the caretaker of the council chamber in Selise. Was this woman one of those responsible for the attack on their capital?

'How did she get down here?' said the short, dark-haired woman, eying Antice suspiciously.

'I would like to know the same thing,' said Antice.

'And I would like to know what you're doing on my estate without my leave,' said Sensis.

'Restrain her,' said the woman, 'and bring her with us. She may be useful.'

Fyia picked at the roasted snow rabbit before her. She didn't want food; she wanted answers, but the strange man with mis-matched eyes was reluctant to share. 'Eat first,' he said. 'There is time yet, and nothing good was ever achieved on an empty stomach.'

How could anyone think of food at a time like this?

They ate in what appeared to be the kitchens, the table wooden and functional, the coals in the hearth's pit glowing an enticing shade of red. A red that reminded Fyia of her dragon dreams.

Fyia let her fork clatter to the table as the phantom scratch of a talon travelled up her spine. The memory of those fearsome creatures, the peril, the feel of their being so very close—close enough to touch—took hold of her mind, and she leaned into the feeling, chasing it.

Cal grabbed her hand under the table, tugging her back, and she found everyone's eyes upon her. Had someone asked a question?

'Well?' said the man.

'What is your name?' she asked, deflecting.

The man gave her a blank look. 'I have many names,' he said evasively. 'But for now, you may call me Cinis.'

'Cinis,' Fyia repeated, testing the word in her mouth. It tasted like ash, something not quite right about it. 'What is your role here?'

'I am the keeper of the temple,' he said, 'tasked with maintaining this place for as long as it might take.'

'To return the dragons?' said Alba, leaning across the table.

Cinis gave a non-committal shrug.

'But how do we do that?' said Cal, still holding Fyia's hand. 'The dragons are gone, and you say dragon eggs are a fiction, so how do we make new dragons?'

Cinis sat back in his seat and steepled his fingers. 'The balls are the keys, the metal structure the lock. Together, they hold the magic of fire at bay. The magic needed to make dragons. When we set free the magic, the fire-touched may once more use their scales to create new dragons, as they have done since the beginning, and then ... then we will return our broken world to its rightful state, wings beating across the sky at dawn, nights filled with the roars of those great beasts. We have been waiting for one such as you, Queen Fyia.'

Fyia bristled. 'I am not the only one with the fire-touch,' she said, squeezing Cal's fingers.

'No,' Cinis conceded, 'but you are the only one who has done anything with it.'

Fyia didn't like his tone, but he was right, she supposed.

'How do we do it?' said Fyia.

'I will show you.'

'You expect us to take your words at face value?' said Cal. 'Trust that you are not lying to us?'

Cinis chuckled. 'You have come all this way. Shown no respect for tradition. Broken the magical bindings to retrieve the keys with nary a thought for risk, and now you've reached the final hurdle, you shy away? Have I misjudged you, Queen Fyia?'

'Goading me won't work,' she said, a half-smile on her lips. 'And your deflection makes me wonder if you do have something to hide ...'

'We all have our secrets, do we not?' said Cinis, getting to his feet. 'But in this, I speak only truth. The dragons occupy the space between. Between our world and the next ... pure magic personified. They regulate the magic in our world, ensuring it ebbs and flows to just the right degree. Without them, magic pools in all the wrong places, and so the north has frozen, the land has lost its fertility, and our kingdoms have crumbled to a shadow of their former selves.

'Our ancestors built a system so great, so ambitious, so wonderful ... and what have we done with their legacy? Squandered it, and fought among ourselves.'

Fyia wasn't sure she followed. 'Our ancestors built the system?' she said tentatively. 'The magic didn't just, exist?'

Cinis threw a frustrated hand across the air. 'They *harnessed* the magic, used it to its full potential, invented ingenious solutions to the problems they faced. Our ancestors were chased from their homeland across the Blue Mountains, and found nothing here but a barren sea of ice. From that wasteland, they crafted the world we know. They reclaimed the land beneath, bit by bit, harnessing the fire, thawing what was frozen, building channels of magma to keep it so, regulating the system with supreme engineering feats.'

'The clocks?' said Fyia, finally catching on.

'The clocks, the aqueducts, and the rivers of magma that flow beneath. All built by our ancestors. Together with the dragons and the fire-touched, the system keeps our world in balance. We must return the magic, so we can restore the system before it fails entirely, for the end has already begun.'

Rivers of magma crisscrossed her lands? The thought was terrifying, although Fyia supposed it at least explained all the hot springs. 'So Essa was right,' said Fyia. 'The clocks are important.'

'And if you bring back the fire magic, you will have the power to fix them,' said Cinis, holding up his hands as though never a more perfect solution had been set forth.

'And if we don't?' said Fyia.

'You must know the saying,' said Cinis. 'One of the few truths to have passed down from the old times to the new.'

'When the clocks doth strike thirteen, the dragons will return. But if the clocks do fall before, then fire will reign supreme,' said Cal.

'But what does it mean?' said Fyia. 'When will the clocks strike thirteen?'

Cinis turned his back, clearing dishes from the table. 'When the magic requires it.'

'And when will that be?' said Fyia.

Cinis shrugged.

Was he being evasive, or did he truly not know? It mattered little, for if they didn't fix the clocks, *fire would reign supreme*. Whatever that meant. Something to do with the magma, presumably. 'So by unleashing the fire-magic,' said Fyia, 'we'll be able to fix the clocks?'

Cinis spun slowly to face her. 'It is the variety of magic required,' he said.

'And once we've fixed the clocks, then we can create more dragons?' said Fyia. 'To help us keep the system in balance?'

'It will certainly be possible.'

'But how do we fix them? How does returning the magic help us?' said Cal, now squeezing Fyia's hand a little harder than was comfortable.

'There are books in the library here that explain it all.'

Fyia imagined how excited Essa would be to delve into those books.

'Then we should read them first,' said Cal. 'Before we do anything …'

'The magic will take time to return,' said Cinis. 'You can read while you wait.'

'You said the dragons keep the magic from pooling in the wrong places,' said Fyia. 'How? Simply by flying around?' An image flashed before Fyia's eyes of a soaring dragon, pulling behind it a cloud of magic, droplets of power falling like rain in its wake.

Cinis laughed. 'Sometimes.'

'The aqueducts?' said Alba. 'It has something to do with the water?'

'Close,' said Cinis.

'The magma,' said Leo. 'Dragons are made of fire.'

Cinis turned an impressed gaze on Leo. 'Exactly.'

'They swim through the magma?' said Cal. 'Why?'

'How do they get in?' said Fyia. She'd always known the dragons were the key to thawing the north, but she'd never given much thought to *how* the dragons would achieve it, and had certainly never imagined the clocks would have a part to play.

'When the clocks doth strike thirteen, of course,' said Cinis, with a coy smile. 'They open, and the dragons fly inside, assuming the clocks are intact, and that the dragons are well-trained.'

Something hot that felt faintly like terror writhed in Fyia's stomach. The dragons were only part of the answer. The fire-touched—she and Cal and Veau—

would have to train the dragons. Merely creating them wasn't enough.

'Will you teach us?' said Fyia. 'How to fix the clocks and control the dragons? How to bring our system back into balance?'

'I will do what I can,' he said. 'Now come, for the sun is setting. It is an auspicious time to return the fire magic to our world.'

Chapter Six

Sensis tried to take in every detail of her surroundings as her captors shoved her along the subterranean corridors. She lost any sense of direction, and they walked for several turns of the clock, so they were a long way from her estate by the time they popped out of the ground through another alterwood tree.

Her captors bundled her into a waiting carriage, then squashed her onto a bench between Antice and one of the burly men. The woman with the star tattoo took the bench opposite, and the last man sat beside her. The woman didn't take her eyes off Sensis for a single tick. She was sensible, because, although heavily outnumbered, Sensis was still a formidable threat.

'We're heading for Medris?' Sensis guessed. They headed east, and not much else lay that way, aside from Moon's capital, perched in the mountains.

'We are,' said the woman.

It was a risk, taking Sensis to Medris. Sensis commanded the city's military academy, which meant these people were either confident in their abilities to keep her hidden, or they were stupid.

'Report,' said Antice, his tone clipped. He opened the curtain covering the window far enough that Sensis could see through, the sun high in the sky.

The woman eyed the curtain warily; *not stupid, then*.

'You want me to …' said the woman, whose eyes flicked to Sensis.

'Report,' Antice repeated, and although she obviously questioned his judgment, she didn't argue.

'There is unrest in the city because the Lord of Laws announced changes to the marriage rules as decreed by the Queen. Women are to own their own property, retaining ownership even when they marry.'

Antice nodded. 'That is not a surprise.'

'No,' the woman agreed, 'but the people are not happy.'

'Curious that you should not wish to own that which you have worked for,' said Sensis.

The woman gave her a withering look. 'You know nothing of what I want,' she replied. 'I doubt you are capable …'

'Letitia,' said Antice, stopping her dead. The name did not suit the lethal-looking woman, and smacked of high birth. *Interesting*. In her baggy pants and heavy overcoat, she looked anything but noble.

'There have been worrying reports from the Scorpion Lands,' Letitia continued. 'Specifically, from the Valley of Death. Hell's Canal is boiling.'

Sensis blinked in surprise, and Antice's head snapped away from the window, first to the woman across the carriage, then to Sensis. 'Did you know?'

Sensis prickled with annoyance. 'No.'

'If it's true,' said Antice, 'it will mean disruption to our trade routes.'

'Really?' said Sensis, with a disbelieving laugh. 'You hear a canal is boiling, and your first thought is about how it will hit your pocket?'

'Our people need to eat,' he parried.

'There are alternative routes,' said Sensis.

'There have also been reports that the giant krakens have returned,' said Letitia. 'The High Priestess of the Sea Serpent was plucked right from her temple. Our trade routes are at risk.'

'Then it is lucky we have ships that fly in the air,' said Sensis, hiding her shock at this new revelation. 'The important question is *why* these things are happening.'

Letitia sneered. 'Is it not obvious? It is because the *Queen* is stirring up magic. Bad things follow wherever the magical lead.'

'*Letta*,' said Antice, although his voice was gentler than before, her soft nickname at odds with the woman's frosty exterior. 'We do not *know* that to be the cause.'

Letta made a choked sound. 'No?' she managed. 'What other explanation is there?'

'It is not that simple.'

'Or maybe it's not that complicated.'

They stared at each other for several long moments, stuck in a stalemate.

'Sorry to interrupt your tiff,' said Sensis, 'but why are we headed for Medris?'

'The Guild of Magic has knowledge they would like to share,' said Antice.

Letta made another disbelieving noise. 'Anything else you'd like to tell the High Commander of the Armies of the Five Kingdoms?' she snarled.

'Not presently,' said Antice, pulling the curtain shut. It wouldn't be long until they arrived in the city, and traffic on the roads would increase the closer they came; they were already halfway to the top of the mountain.

The sun was hovering just above the horizon by the time their carriage rounded the final corner of the climb. The ground flattened as they passed through the fearsome steel gates to the city, entering the first level—the level of Roaches—that housed the markets and brothels and fighting pits.

The city was a remarkable construction, a series of terraces carved from the mountain, the purpose of each level unique. The higher one travelled, the more affluent the streets became, with the prestigious university perched at the very top, presiding over them all.

The university had been the seat of Antice's royal forebears, the control of knowledge integral to the wealth and personality of their kingdom.

The military academy, over which Sensis had authority, was the only structure that spanned multiple levels, stretching all the way from the level of Roaches to just below the university at the top. Military recruits entered at the bottom—regardless of their wealth or background—and climbed the terraces as they progressed through their training. The highest honor for a military leader of the Kingdom of Moon—or indeed, for any of Moon's people—was to be invited to the university, to dine at the Dean's table, and for their opinions to be valued.

The carriage travelled the switchback road from Roaches to Boards, where the theatres and dance halls had their homes. Then past the upmarket shops and eating houses of Silver, below which the well-to-do rarely ventured, not pausing until they'd travelled to the far side of Obsidian—the level below the university, and the domain of the guilds.

The streets here were almost as densely packed as they were in Roaches—space at a premium throughout the city—but the colleges of the guilds had been lovingly crafted from stone and glass, carvings of all manner of mythical creatures adorning the walls of the winding passages, enclosed arch bridges, and ancient doorways.

The buildings intertwined, connecting in the strangest ways, having been swapped and bartered between the guilds over time. Each guild's buildings reflected its personality, the lecture halls, laboratories, dormitories, studios, and even gardens carefully constructed to present a precise image to the world.

The Guild of Magic was no exception, but unlike the others, they hid themselves away, displaying only the barest hint of that which was contained within. And beside their simple, stone-arched gateway, tucked against the back wall of the Obsidian terrace, was where the carriage finally stopped.

A shiver travelled down Sensis' spine as the carriage door swung open. For all the time she'd spent in this city as a child, or leading the military academy more recently, she'd never so much as glimpsed what lay behind those walls.

Antice smiled knowingly, then followed the other men out of the carriage. He helped Letta down, and then Sensis. Both women accepted his assistance, something about her predicament making Sensis take comfort from his touch. So much so, she didn't immediately release his hand.

'Why are you making no attempt to hide me?' she said, her voice low, so only he could hear.

'No need,' he replied, then turned towards the open gate. The Guild's door, set into the stone of the terrace wall, opened as they approached, and a short woman with copious rustling skirts swept towards them.

The woman's dark hair was pulled back in an elegant, respectable up-do, crystal earrings swinging from her lobes, and her features ... well, they matched Letta's too perfectly for her to be anything other than a close relation.

'Mother,' said Letta, with a small incline of her head.

'You've brought a guest,' the older woman replied.

'Lady Otterly,' said Antice, smoothly stepping forward and kissing the woman on each cheek. 'Have you been introduced to Lady Deimos? Perhaps during her time at the military academy?'

'I have not had the pleasure, Lord Antice,' said Lady Otterly, her polite words laced with disapproval.

'Lady Otterly,' said Sensis, inclining her head the barest fraction.

'Lady Altergate,' Lady Otterly replied, the first to use Sensis' new title.

Antice visibly bristled, and Sensis tamped down her misplaced feeling of triumph, for this woman was no ally of hers.

'Let us continue inside,' said Antice, holding out his arm and ushering the others ahead.

Sensis hung back.

'If you're planning to stage an escape, I wouldn't bother,' said Antice. 'This whole area is protected by magic. Those outside the boundary can't even see you, and if you make a run for it, the wards won't let you through.'

'I thought magic was considered abhorrent,' Sensis countered.

'Ah, but one must seek to understand that which one considers abhorrent, so as to more effectively stamp it out.' He finished his words with a crispness that implied he wished to convey more than she could decipher, but she had no time to dwell.

The entrance was like stepping into a box of pure, white marble, the floor, walls, and ceiling all gleaming in an unnatural light that had no obvious source.

Lady Otterly strode ahead, taking the middle of three corridors, which headed in a straight line deeper into the building. Deeper into the mountain. The hairs on Sensis' forearms prickled with unease.

'Wait in there,' Lady Otterly said to Sensis, pushing on a section of wall. A large chunk of marble swung inward, revealing what appeared to be a common room beyond. An untidy one.

Sensis hesitated.

'I'll keep her ... company,' said Antice, sounding mildly irritated at the inconvenience.

Sensis shot him a suspicious look, but complied. She stepped into the dimly lit room with wood-paneled walls, green leather wingback chairs, and a bar on a raised platform in the back corner. The remnants of a party—a wild one—lay scattered about. Tankards and bottles and silver cutlery were strewn everywhere, along with silver candle arbors that lay on their sides, and wet patches on the floor.

Antice stepped up behind her as the door swung shut, his smell of apple blossom and malting grains suddenly strong. He stopped so close to her back they were practically touching.

'What are you doing?' she asked, in a quiet voice.

'They're listening,' he whispered into her ear, his breath on her skin the most intimate contact she'd had in ... well, longer than she cared to admit. 'And I wish to share with you that this place, although in possession of a party trick or two, has no magic of note.

'It is a glorified drinking club for the firstborn sons of the highest echelons of Moon society. A couple of them boast weak magic, and they brew expensive potions to ward off pregnancies and relieve colds. Their mothers trade the concoctions over tea and cake, while whispering in hushed, excited voices.'

His words were a sensual caress, and Sensis willed her mind to concentrate on their meaning, and ignore whatever game he played. But the warmth of his breath on her neck, and the barest brush of his lips against the shell of her ear, made it all but impossible.

'They enjoy generous stipends,' Antice continued, 'and a comfortable life playing ill-advised drinking games, while enjoying the kudos and mystique of being a member of this guild. They hit balls with silver trays, and aim the corks of the finest sparkling wine at targets pinned to the roof, all in the name of entertainment. But really, they are an embarrassment, and my ancestors worked hard to keep them locked away.'

'Careful, Antice, that smacks of resentment,' Sensis teased.

Antice caught her dismissive hand as it waved through the air, and her breath hitched in her throat.

'They may be magically useless, but politically, they are anything but,' he murmured. 'Lady Otterly carries considerable sway. Her ancestors were tasked with controlling the use of magic, the first King of Moon bestowing wealth, access, and other privileges on her family, and the Otterlys have quietly increased their empire over time. Lady Otterly and her daughter should not be underestimated.'

Sensis nodded, causing Antice's nose to slide along her ear. She tried to focus, to think of questions that would prepare her for whatever Lady Otterly had in store, but her brain blocked out everything but the feel of his skin against hers, and the warmth of his fingers in her hand.

Neither broke the connection, and Sensis was tempted to lean into him, to press her back to his chest with the hope he would envelop her in his arms. But the threat of rejection was too great—not to mention the threat of discovery. She wouldn't give him the same power she had when they were children, nor give him the satisfaction of knowing she wanted to touch him. It was a game to him, and it always would be. So she pushed away, just as the door swung open.

Antice refused to relinquish her hand when she tried to tug it free, and Sensis froze in place. He slid his thumb across her skin, once each way, then released her and spun to face Lady Otterly in a confident, well-practiced movement.

'Well?' he said, his tone that of a prince used to being obeyed.

'They are ready, Lord Antice,' said Lady Otterly, who had come alone. She waited for them to follow before taking off along the gleaming corridor.

Antice trailed Sensis. Showing Antice her back made her uncomfortable, but the way Lady Otterly held herself made Sensis believe Antice's warning. The woman was dangerous, and Sensis would not underestimate her. In a way, it made Sensis happy, finding this force of a woman who'd carved out a place of power for herself within the patriarchy of the Moon Kingdom.

Her joy was short-lived, however. They climbed a spiral stone staircase, and what waited at the top—inside the university itself—made Sensis' blood boil.

Otterly led them into a great, round chamber, vines creeping up the walls, and others falling down from shelves that sat at seemingly random intervals.

In the middle, stood a strange table made of many materials. One end dragon glass, the middle dragon steel, then alterwood, obsidian, and some material

Sensis had never been able to identify that looked like stone shot through with metal.

A throne of intricate gold sat against the far wall, below an enormous, lavishly decorated dragon clock that presided over the room. The sun's final rays shone through the domed glass ceiling and gleamed off the metal.

But Sensis had seen all this before, and barely cast a glance over the impressive room. Instead, she homed in on the cozy scene at the far end of the tall, chair-less table, where the recently appointed female Dean chatted merrily with Letta and a handful of men donned in the red robes of the Guild of Magic.

The Dean had been appointed at Essa's recommendation, and to see her so firmly in the establishment's bosom, so soon into her tenure, made Sensis want to rage. Had this been the woman's intention all along? To convince Essa of her suitability, and then turncoat the instant Fyia's advisors turned their backs?

'Oh, General, don't look at me with such derision in your eyes,' said the Dean, meeting Sensis' gaze.

'You've been quick to ingratiate yourself with the locals,' said Sensis. 'I don't recall that forming a part of your job description.'

'Yes, well,' said the short-haired, brown-skinned woman, 'we all do what we must.'

Sensis sneered. 'Is that how you justify selling out your Queen?'

The Dean went very still, and the air seemed to flee the room. 'It is how I justify protecting the female students of this noble institution. They were being insulted, attacked, and harassed. Should I have stood aside and let that continue?'

No good would come from pointing out that the very people the Dean had allied herself with were those who had made those students' lives a misery. The Dean had capitulated at the first sign of stress, and had presumably received personal favors as part of the bargain, but the Dean's weak spine was not Sensis' primary concern.

'Why is the General here?' said a doddery old white man in an ancient-looking red cloak. 'The matter we wish to discuss is sensitive.'

'I brought her,' said Letta. 'She found her way into the alterwood subways, and she may prove useful.'

'You want the Queen to know …' said the old man.

Letta cut him off. 'Report, my lord, or I will do it for you.'

The table allowed for standing only, as the king who'd built the university—hundreds of years prior—had deemed anyone unable to stand for the duration of his meetings unfit for his service. Had the Guild of Magic upheld the same logic, this old lord would have been dismissed. He almost toppled to the floor, clutching the table for support.

Two of the younger men in red cloaks rushed forward, carrying a chair between them, and the old man slumped onto its cushioned pad. He waved another man forward, this one somewhere in his third or fourth decade, and the tall, broad man stepped up to the glass section of the table. He flattened a large scroll across it, pulling weights from his pockets to hold the document in place.

'When the new Queen ascended to the throne of Moon, some time ago,' said the man, not waiting for leave from his older colleague to begin, 'the Controller—Lady Otterly—ordered a search for anything pertaining to the Queen's mission to return the dragons.'

'A foolish endeavor,' said the old man from his chair.

'Regardless,' the man continued, his tone matter-of-fact, borderline bored, 'the search of the Guild's archives has thrown up some interesting findings, the most notable of which is this map.'

The others crowded around to see the details, and Sensis elbowed the younger guild members out of her way, taking a prominent place at the table.

'The map shows the aqueducts, clocks, and magma streams that flow not only through Queen Fyia's five kingdoms, but through the whole known world,' he said, sweeping a hand above the document.

The existence of magma streams under the known world didn't seem to shock anyone else, so Sensis kept her own surprise at bay.

'And overall control of the system—a careful balance of magic and precise mechanics—sits here.' He pointed to a spot on the Great Glacier, far in the north, and the blood drained from Sensis' face.

'Should the Queen wish to return the dragons,' interrupted the old man, waving his hand to catch their attention, 'she can do so from there.'

'What have dragons got to do with the aqueducts?' said Sensis.

'Much,' said the old man. 'But if the Queen restarts the system when clocks are missing …'

'She can't restart the system,' said Letta. 'She doesn't have the key.'

'What key?' asked Sensis, her heart pounding in her ears.

Letta remained silent under Sensis' expectant gaze, and Sensis realized that was because she didn't know.

'We can safely assume the knowledge has been lost to time,' said the old man. 'So even if the Queen has the key—whatever it is—and even if she possesses magic, as she claims to, she couldn't possibly know how to use both together …'

Lady Otterly tisked. 'Conjecture,' she said, but as the word came to an end, a deeper, richer, metallic noise boomed out across the chamber.

Their heads swiveled as one towards the clock, and the noise came again, this time louder.

'What the fuck is that?' said Letta, looking to the old man for an explanation.

The man's face turned sheet white. He spluttered ineffectually, then wheezed, 'Get me up,' to the two younger guild members. They rushed to help him, but instead of heading towards the clock to investigate, he instructed the men to assist him in a cowardly retreat, making for the double doors out of the chamber.

The others didn't hesitate, racing after him. They shouted questions, but the guild members didn't answer.

Sensis grabbed the map before following, the clock now making an ominous creaking noise behind them. It sounded very much like something inside wanted to get out, and whatever it was, it was big, and fearsome, and Sensis had no desire to face it.

'The first step,' said Cinis, pacing the edge of the room, 'is to place the balls into the mechanism.'

Cal had insisted on a trip to the library before they agreed to use the metal balls … eggs … whatever they were, and Fyia had acknowledged it was the sensible path. Cinis had put book after book in front of them, each detailing how, without magic—and dragons—the system would diminish. How, should the system be shut off for any length of time, the land would freeze, and how a good flow of magic was required for all manner of things, including creating dragons.

When Cinis had shown them twenty books or more, even Edu had found it hard to question restarting the mechanism, although his features were still arranged in a firm scowl. The final book had explained how the mechanism was key to all, that without it, nothing else could function.

'But … where do they go?' said Fyia, unable to find a place designed to hold the balls, try as she might.

Cinis laughed. 'They go in between, of course. As the dragons draw on the magic between worlds, the balls slot into the spaces between the metal.'

It was almost obvious, now she knew what to look for, the gap popping out at her.

'Simply slide the balls into the mechanism,' Cinis continued, but Fyia's pulse was so loud in her ears she could barely hear him. She'd dreamed of returning the dragons since she was a girl, and this was the first step. Her heart leapt to her mouth, because she knew, deep in her bones, it would be no smooth endeavor, but her hand reached forward anyway. Nothing worth doing was ever straightforward, and she had not come this far to turn back now.

'Wait,' said Cal, halting her. 'This is all so …' he searched for the right word, 'hasty. We should think it through.'

'We already have!' said Fyia. 'What else is there to think through? We are either here to return the dragons, or we are not.'

'Yes, but …' he lowered his mouth to her ear, and whispered, 'there is much we do not know. Cinis could have motives of his own.'

'Even so,' said Fyia, her own voice barely more than a murmur, 'what choice do we have? How do you plan to learn more, when Cinis is the only soul here?

And you saw the books; the mechanism must function for the magic to flow ... they were crystal clear on that fact. What else can we do? Where else can we turn?'

'What about the Fae'ch? They sent Leo and Alba ...'

'To spy on us!' she said, with a shake of her head. 'Isa is not to be trusted.'

'And Cinis is? Based on our knowing him for less than three hour turns?'

Fyia looked away, to where Edu, Alba, Leo, and Cinis stood watching them. Edu would certainly council restraint, as would Leo, Fyia suspected, and her wolves were still uneasy. But eagerness was painted plain as day across Alba's features, and Cinis wore an expression that seemed almost reproachful.

'Placing the balls into the mechanism will not return the dragons,' said Cinis, 'but it will unlock the magic required, and I cannot teach you what you need to know until the magic has returned.'

Cinis could be lying, it was true, but what else could the mechanism be for? It was activated by the balls they'd found where the dragon eggs should have been, and Cinis wasn't forcing them. He'd answered their questions and shown them books from the library.

'This is the temple of the warrior,' said Cal. 'What if we unlock a weapon?'

'The Warrior *and* the Mother,' countered Fyia. 'And magic is a weapon, as it is also a route to prosperity.' With magic, they could make dragons, which would thaw the north, and the needless rebellions in her own lands would cease in the face of those beasts. 'Think of what this could mean for your people,' she added.

Cal scowled. 'Don't do that. I care deeply about my people, but something about this feels off. *Cinis* feels off.'

Fyia couldn't argue with him there, but it was bound to feel strange, and uncomfortable, and she hadn't achieved so much by shying away from things that gave her gooseflesh.

She took a breath. Returning the magic benefitted everyone. 'We'll take it one step at a time. We'll use the balls to return the magic, then restore the clocks, and only then create new dragons.'

Cal was right to be cautious, but what choice did they have? And for Fyia, that was the heart of it. 'We do this, or we do not,' said Fyia. 'Those are our only choices. There is uncertainty, but we take a risk, or return to our lands empty handed. There is nowhere else to look for answers.'

And Fyia would rather face the consequences of something she'd done, rather than those from something she had failed to do. It was scary, but if by returning the magic they could create new dragons, then the risk was worth it. So she reached out to the structure and rolled the ball in her fingers between two strands of metal.

The ball seemed to defy gravity a moment, hovering before it began its ponderous route downwards, twisting and turning through the sculptured metal until it dipped below the water and out of sight.

Taut, expectant silence stretched thin across the room, everyone seeming to hold their breath, waiting for the unknown. When nothing happened, Fyia lifted another ball into the same space, then another.

Still nothing, and now only one ball remained. Cal held it in his hand and met Fyia's gaze. 'We're really doing this?' he said, the half-smile of someone about to do something reckless pulling at his lips.

Fyia's face split into an excited, throw-caution-to-the-wind grin, and something enormous flapped its wings in her chest, the expansive movement threatening to crack her open from the inside. 'Looks that way,' she said.

Cal's eyes blazed with excitement as he pressed the final ball into the mechanism. 'No going back now,' he said, as the ball plopped into the water. Fyia's stomach clenched as she hoped against hope they'd done the right thing.

Fyia slipped her hand into Cal's, holding on tight as she scarcely dared to breathe. She could barely believe the dream she'd chased for so long was coming true. She'd killed five kings, then found the metal balls, but she would mark this as the true beginning. This moment would change the course of their world's future in a way nothing else could. Soon they would have the means to create dragons, and with dragons, they could make her changes stick, thaw the north, and not only that, but finally her people would respect her.

A handful of racing heartbeats passed, and Fyia began to worry nothing would happen, that it had been dormant too long, or the mechanism had been damaged. But then a quiet whirring noise reverberated around them, and the water in the pools rippled, and then, from the heart of each of the empty pools, rose a tall metal structure. The structures were reminiscent of the one they'd slid the balls into, but smaller, with fewer pieces, and each contained a ball, now lit from within, casting golden light with hints of pink, blue, and metallic green.

The structure beside Fyia began to gently spin, and when she looked down, she found a metal ball sat in the center of this one too, a gentle glow radiating from it.

But the structures were far from the most remarkable part, because Fyia could now feel magic coursing under her feet and through the air. She felt powerful—more so than ever—like she could reach out and hold the magic, and bend it to her will.

'You feel it,' said Cinis. 'I can see that you do. And this is a fraction of what is out there, stored in the world, ripe for the taking.'

Fyia's face split into a smile, until his words sank in. 'Ripe for the taking?' she repeated. 'I don't want to *take* anything.'

'Aside from the dragons?'

'I …'

'You don't want to command them?'

'Well, I …'

Someone gasped from the entryway, and Fyia's eyes went wide when she saw the face of the man there. It was … Cinis, only much taller and with eyes that looked shockingly familiar.

'What have you done?' said the man, rushing forward, suddenly next to Fyia. He tried to prize the ball from the mechanism, but it wouldn't budge, and his hands grabbed Fyia's arms, accusing eyes boring into hers.

Cal stepped forward, as did Edu, their weapons already in their palms, her wolves snarling.

'Unhand her,' Cal said slowly.

'Cinis told us this would bring back the magic,' said Fyia, panic beginning to flutter in her stomach. 'He said we needed to, so we could fix the dragon clocks, then make new dragons. He said …'

'I am Cinis,' said the tall man.' He followed Fyia's gaze to the other side of the room, to where the short man had morphed into a woman, her features altering until it wasn't Cinis who stood before them, but the mad magical woman who had stood at the right hand of the Kraken Emperor. The woman who'd disappeared after the Emperor's death.

'Asesh,' said the man, his voice a snarl as he lunged for her. But she was too quick, there one tick and gone the next.

Cinis—the real one—dashed from the room, faster than should have been possible, but he returned moments later.

'She has gone,' he said.

'Who is she?' said Cal. 'And why was she impersonating you?'

Cinis made his way from one structure to the next, trying to dislodge the balls, but to no avail. 'She was the Dragon Kings' consort. Not just to one of them, but to every one for many generations. Since before even they called themselves the Dragon Kings. She whispered in their ears about power and greatness, and single-handedly brought down an empire that had been in balance for eons. That witch has caused more harm than any other, and you played right into her hands.'

Fyia's stomach bottomed out. 'What exactly did we do?'

'You restarted a system of magic and mechanics that has been dormant since the time of the last Dragon King—magma ducts, aqueducts, and dragon clocks. A system that is crumbling, and does not have wardens stationed at every point of weakness, as it once did.'

'Leo and Alba have gone,' said Edu, striding into the room. When had Edu left? Fyia hadn't even noticed. 'I'd wager they're heading for the Fae'ch mountains, to report to Isa.'

'She'll know before they get there,' said Cinis. 'Or, at least, she will feel the effects, even if she is unable to connect the dots.'

Fyia's mind raced. 'How so?'

Cinis whirled and strode from the room, and Fyia could do nothing but gape.

Chapter Seven

Essa breathed deeply as she awaited Isa, the legendary leader of the Fae'ch. Essa was neither a diplomat, nor did she have the sales skills of the merchants. She was an engineer—blunt and logical—not cut out for this line of work. But there was no one else, and time was not on their side.

Essa had no magic of her own, but even she could tell something was shifting. She'd seen the mighty kraken with her own eyes, and the few beings she'd passed on her way into the mountain had seemed on edge, so different to when she'd first been here, only a score of days before.

'Did Veau not make it clear the last time?' said Isa. The fae woman had suddenly materialized in front of Essa, who sat on the floor of a dingy cave, before a pile of stones. 'He does not want to see you. He came to live with us because you could not offer him what he needed.'

'I'm not here to see Veau,' said Essa. She knew Veau's reasons better than anyone, and would not give Isa the satisfaction of failing her little test. 'I am here because the clocks are falling, yet the magic is building. You turned away the envoy Lady Starfall sent to tell you this.'

'He could tell us nothing we did not already know,' said Isa. 'If that is. All …' Isa's speech became halting, and she began to fade from view.

'That is not all,' said Essa. 'The High Priestess of the Sea Serpent gave me a map before a kraken plucked her from her temple.' Essa pulled out the parchment, and Isa cocked an eyebrow. 'I understand now how the system fits together. About the ducts, and how the clocks are doors for the dragons, and I know the cogs lining the approach to this mountain are taps to shut off the flow of magma.'

Isa smirked. 'They are not taps to shut it off.'

'Then what are they for?' said Essa, not sure whether to believe her.

Isa's eyes roamed over the stones on the floor before returning to Essa. 'They control the flow, but that matters not.'

'How so?' said Essa, a thrill of panic rising in her chest.

'The system is crumbling; no one could hope to use it now.'

'But what if the clocks strike thirteen?' said Essa, not understanding how Isa could be so blasé about the threat of destruction.

Isa laughed. 'You refer to the nursery rhyme they sang to children in the time of the Dragon Kings?'

Essa stayed silent. It was a saying everyone knew; a warning passed from generation to generation.

'Leave,' said Isa, and the next moment, Essa was outside the closed portcullis at the mountain's entrance, looking at the cogs she'd so dearly hoped might be their salvation.

'Is it possible?' said Isa, tramping down the edge of horror that flared in her chest. Their latest intelligence suggested Queen Fyia and King Cal had gone to the Great Glacier. It was possible they'd discovered the truth about the eggs, although Isa couldn't imagine serious, imperious Cinis ever explaining how the lock worked. But the Queen had defied everyone's expectations, and Storm continued to insist something was amiss with the magic.

'Well?' she snapped at the long-life. She'd found him in the deep and ordered him to meet with her. He couldn't refuse, for like most under the mountain, he'd sworn an oath of obedience to her, but she'd sweetened the deal with the promise of a crate of Cuttle Stars in return for his help.

'It is certainly possible for one to restart the system,' he said. 'My forebears created a simple enough mechanism. It would probably need some repairs—it has been dormant a long time—but so long as it is still in working order, there is no reason why one could not ...'

'What about the taps?' she demanded, cutting him off. His long-winded answers infuriated her; she required only a yes or no.

'What about them?' he asked, his tone ponderous.

'Several clocks have fallen. Can we use the taps to shut off the magma flows, should the system restart?'

The tall, thin fae was old, even for their kind, his hair mostly grey, the lines around his eyes beginning to deepen. His brow creased. 'Why would anyone restart the system if clocks have fallen? It would be far more sensible to fix the clocks ...'

'Yes, of course,' said Isa, her blood sizzling at his statement of the obvious, 'but that does not answer my question.'

The man paused as he considered the problem. The silence stretched, and Isa's attention wandered. She let her subconscious guide her, first across the lake, where Storm was training the water riders, then to the guilds, where her people traded as usual, then to the deep, in search of the one who made her heart flutter. She'd found herself observing him more and more of late, wanting his every waking moment for herself.

She scowled when she found him, for he was training Veau—his son, and Queen Fyia's brother. Isa hadn't intended to reveal Veau's identity so soon. She'd planned to stretch it over years, to make Gabriel wait until he begged to know, until he was willing to give her anything, to *give up* anything for the knowledge.

No matter, for Veau was under the mountain, and Gabriel would never leave his son. Not to mention, it was prudent to have one with the fire-touch under her control, given all that was happening in the world.

'It is possible to use the taps to prevent magma from flowing through a given loop in the system,' said the engineer, finally having collected his thoughts, 'but only for a short while. They were designed primarily for flow regulation …'

'But it could work?'

He sighed. 'We used them in that way for maintenance, shutting off the magma for a short time, but the mechanisms would eventually give way under the pressure, and then we would have no way to control the flow at all; it would be worse in the long run. But why do you ask these questions? Who would restart the system if it is broken?'

An impulsive, reckless Queen, Isa's mind whispered. But surely even Fyia would listen to reason, and Cinis would provide reason in spades. For all his faults, Cinis cared little for power, and Isa could not believe he would help Fyia restart the system in its current state. But the Children of the Lake were restless, Storm felt something ominous in the air, and all of it together meant unease sat like a squatter in Isa's gut.

Veau responded to Isa's summons with a fake smile, forcing a spring into his step, because since he'd learned Isa's true nature, he could muster not the barest thread of respect for his leader.

His true father, Gabriel, was reserved when speaking of Isa, but Storm was not. The stories Storm told of Isa's manipulations and deceit had shocked Veau, and his heart broke for Storm and Gabriel.

Isa would not accept that Gabriel loved another, convinced her magic had chosen Gabriel as her lifelong mate. And for Gabriel and Storm, having Isa as the third wheel in their relationship was nothing short of hell.

'My leader?' said Veau, looking around the cave with the stone structure on the floor.

Axus stepped out from behind a pillar, and then Isa materialized out of the air. Veau wasn't sure he would ever get used to that.

'Tell me about Gabriel and Storm,' said Isa, no hint of her usual faraway tone.

'Storm continues to train the water riders,' said Veau, his eyes flicking to Axus, 'although it is not going well. We are not natural ….'

'And Gabriel?' said Isa.

Veau thought for a tick. There was no use denying what he suspected Isa already knew. 'Gabriel is training me to use my magic.'

'Why?'

'Because it's erratic, and I would rather not be a danger to others, or myself.'

'I am sure my love has more important duties to attend.'

'I cannot speak to that,' said Veau. 'I am not privy to all the details of Gabriel's life.'

Isa sneered. 'Don't get smart with me.'

Fear spiked through Veau's veins. 'I meant no offense. I would never …'

Isa silenced him with a wave of her hand. 'Tell me what they are plotting.'

'Plotting?' said Veau. Were Gabriel and Storm plotting against Isa? If so, they'd never told Veau.

'To leave. Tell me their plans.'

Oh. 'I do not know for certain,' said Veau. 'Only what I told you before. Storm asked me about my sister … about whether she was a good leader.'

'Storm still wants to leave? It wasn't a bluff?'

'I believe she wants to go,' said Veau, 'although she's committed to calming the Children of the Lake. I don't think she would go if she believed them to be a threat to the Fae'ch.'

'The Children will *always* be a threat,' Isa fired back, then disappeared for a moment before returning. 'Your sister …'

'Yes?' said Veau, holding his breath. What had she done now?

'Would she do *anything* to bring back the dragons? Even if it meant hundreds—or thousands—would die?'

'I … no,' said Veau. 'She wants to return the dragons, of course, but … has something happened?'

'Axus?' said Isa. 'Has something happened?'

Axus bowed his head. 'There has been no word from Leo and Alba. We believe them to be on the Great Glacier, with Queen Fyia. It is remote. However, several clocks are badly damaged. Should your sister return the dragons at this moment, many will die.'

Veau's mouth went dry. 'Does Fyia know?'

'We could send word,' said Axus. 'Regio could take a message to his brother.'

'You seek to remove your son from the dangers under the mountain?' said Isa, rounding on Axus.

The dangers under the mountain? Veau knew about the Children of the Lake, but ... were there more?

'The Queen is a long way from doing anything of note,' said Isa, '... of bringing back the dragons. She doesn't know how. Staying out of human affairs has served us well during our time under this mountain, and it will serve us well now.'

Sensis burst out onto the plaza in front of the university, where an enormous statue of Antice's father stood. Curious academics heading home for the evening turned their heads to watch as the Dean and all those who'd been in the throne room hurried past. The academics threw questioning looks at one another and then hurried away.

Others poked their heads through the windows of various academic buildings. Presumably, they could hear the ominous banging from the clock radiating through the old stones.

Sensis ignored everything but the need to get free and report to her Queen. She would send a rider to Starfall too, and find out where Essa was; she'd want to see the map.

Sensis had only to make it to the military academy. Once there, no one could stop her, for the full might of the force stationed in Medris would be behind her. But halfway down the nearest set of steps to the Obsidian level of the city, a hand grabbed hold of her arm.

Sensis whirled, finding Antice behind her, his lips set in a determined line. 'How did you do that?' said Sensis. She hadn't heard him coming …

'We have to get out of here.'

'We … what? You kidnapped me. I'm getting out of here, but I couldn't give a rat's uncle what you do.'

'We should go together to the Queen,' he said, urging her to keep moving down the stairs.

Sensis planted her feet, and Antice exhaled loudly, looking at the terrace wall as though words to convince her might magically appear.

'I … there are … reasons,' he said.

'Such as,' said Sensis, acutely aware the longer they stood, the more chance of someone preventing her escape. She should just dump him on his arse and run. She'd be inside the academy walls before he so much as made it to his feet, but something went tight in her chest, resisting the idea. 'Well?' she pressed.

'Can't you just trust me? That I want to help?'

Sensis couldn't help the bark of laughter that escaped her lips. 'I stopped trusting you when we were kids. And you're a rebel leader.' At the look on his face, she added, 'Don't pretend otherwise.'

'I … it's … complicated.'

'I have to go,' she said, turning her back, even if she didn't want to.

'Sensis, I …'

She raced down the steep steps.

'Stop,' he called, and something in his tone made Sensis pause.

'It's easier if I show you.'

She turned to find him unbuckling his breeches. 'Antice, what in the Seven Hells …?' But before she could get the words out, he yanked them open, and Sensis gasped.

Cal pulled Fyia close to his side as they followed the new Cinis away from the metal structures, which were now gently spinning. Cinis led them deeper into the temple, through a series of perfectly straight corridors, until they turned into a haphazardly arranged room entirely out of keeping with the rest of their surroundings.

'It may look like mess,' said Cinis, waving an arm to indicate the stacks of books, maps attached to the walls at strange angles, and whirring metallic models, 'but everything is where it should be. Touch nothing.'

Cinis busied himself clearing a space for them to sit around a low table, and Cal moved his lips close to Fyia's ear. 'That man has your eyes,' he whispered.

Fyia looked up at him, and Cal was struck again by the similarity of the blue shot with topaz.

'He certainly seems familiar,' she said.

'And his hair,' Cal continued.

'I know,' said Fyia, tersely. 'He has a streak of white, just like I do.'

It was almost hidden in the man's short hair, and camouflaged amid the grey speckles of age, but there all the same.

'What's your point?' said Fyia, a challenge in her eyes.

'Could you be related? Do your parents have siblings?'

'Not as far as I know … aside from Starfall.'

'Sit,' said Cinis, moving the final stack of books from the low, cushioned seating around the table. 'We might as well be comfortable if we're to discuss matters that are the opposite.'

Edu had reluctantly taken Fyia's wolves back to the airships, to tell the crew to ready for departure, so only Cal and Fyia remained. Cal pulled his seat close to Fyia's, then sank onto the warn, cushioned pad.

'What does that mean?' said Fyia, balling her hands into fists.

'Yes, you're right, we might as well cut to the chase.' Cinis leaned back and steepled his fingers, just as Asesh had done when impersonating him. 'You have restarted a system that has lain dormant for hundreds of years. Not much will happen for a few spins of the hand, for it will take time for things to ramp up, but the level of the magma is, at this very moment, rising, for the caps that were containing it have opened.'

'Asesh said we were releasing magic back into the world?' said Fyia, who had gone white as a sheet.

'After a fashion, but not really,' said Cinis. 'The magic will swell, as much is stored in the magma that was trapped deep underground. And magic has collected in pockets around our world … that will spread through the system as it chugs back to life … even more so when the dragons do their part.'

'But there are no dragons,' said Cal.

'Asesh told us we needed to release the fire magic to make them,' said Fyia.

Cinis snorted. 'Did she indeed. Well, she lied. She knows as well as I that dragons still exist in our world.'

Fyia went still, and Cal thought back to her dragon dreams—how real they had seemed. 'Where?' she whispered.

'Where they belong,' said Cinis. 'In Hell.'

'Hell's Mouth?' said Fyia. 'But I've been there. I threw the crowns of the old kings into the flames.'

'Poetic as that may be, the dragons are a long way from the surface. Although, I received word only yesterday that the canal in the Valley of Death is boiling, so maybe they're not as far from the surface as they once were.'

'How can that be?' said Fyia, recoiling.

Cinis huffed. 'It's truly amazing how little you know. I suppose I should start at the beginning …'

'It would be refreshing,' said Cal. The north hadn't kept magic under wraps in the same way as Fyia's five kingdoms. On the contrary, they'd embraced and celebrated it, but he was still woefully out of his depth. How could it be that no one knew dragons still lived in the world?

Cinis stood and paced to a map on the wall. 'The land west of the Blue Mountains and East of the Kraken Empire was once uninhabitable. Nothing but a sea of ice in the north, and terrible heat below the Valley of Death, getting hotter and hotter, until the land itself boiled at the bottom of the world.

'Our ancestors fled here, over the Blue Mountains, thousands of years ago, chased out of their homelands by their enemies. They possessed magic, Cruaxees, and the touch of fire, but their gifts did little, aside from keep them alive, and scrounging for survival is hardly any life at all.

'So they imagined beasts of fire made flesh, cut from the very fabric of the magic, yet tethered to a solid form using one of the fire-touched's own golden scales.'

Fyia gasped. 'How?'

'They cut the scales from their flesh, then worked the dragons around them, spinning magic into solid form. A sacrifice must be made to tether a dragon to this world.'

Cal imagined losing one of his own scales, and the urge to vomit filled him. Fyia only had one … what would happen if she lost it?

'And those with the fire-touch led their people?' said Fyia. 'Using the dragons?'

'Yes,' said Cinis. 'The dragons were a weapon with no compare. But there were also those without the touch of fire, who, knowing they could never compete, sought their own source of power. They were magic-touched and had Cruaxees, and they searched for an upper hand, experimenting in any way they could devise.

'They infused small creatures with magic, and found rare minerals with magical properties they used as poisons or potions, and then, in the caves of the Kraken Empire, they discovered creatures that were almost human, but with wings like birds and bats.

'The creatures were peaceful, and unable to defend themselves, able to communicate in only the most rudimentary way. And yet they were alluring, and had a kind of magic that was unique … pure … powerful … compulsive.'

'They bred with them?' Fyia guessed.

Cinis nodded. 'And made the fae.'

Cal sucked in a breath. The fae had been made? If anything, he'd assumed the fae had existed before the humans.

'They made all manner of creatures, some more successfully than others, and sent extinct many native species in the process.'

'Is Asesh fae?' said Fyia.

Cinis nodded heavily. 'She was one of the earliest of their successful creations, and was always bitter that her kind, and her creators, were considered less worthy, despite their considerable power and abilities. They built not only new races, but magnificent structures, and many ingenious things.

'So Asesh came here, to what was the heart of the world back then, determined to teach them a lesson. She seduced the head of one of the fire-touched families. He was young and impulsive and obsessed with Asesh. He showered her with gifts, then took her to wife, but children did not follow.

'Asesh was distraught, mostly because, through a child, she could have led the most prominent of families, and by extension, wielded power over all those touched by fire. She instructed her husband to take a second wife—one from another of the fire-touched lines—and they had a son. Asesh seduced him when her husband was an old man, for Asesh did not age in the way of humans. She looked the same when her husband was seventy as she had when they'd first met, and back in those days, she was very beautiful.'

'Did she have a child with the son?' said Fyia.

'No,' said Cinis, 'but he and his descendants were the route to Asesh's revenge. Through them, she made the fire-touched fractious and competitive. She convinced them to in-breed to the point where they were all closely related, and the most prominent family, who had the largest dragons, began dubbing themselves the *Dragon Kings and Queens*, leading to even more unrest.

'The inbreeding meant most children of the fire-touched didn't survive, or went mad, and their magic became weak, until they couldn't even control the dragons, let alone make new ones. And Asesh's work was finally done.'

'So they locked the dragons away?' said Fyia, who gripped Cal's hand so hard it was almost painful.

'Many of the dragons fled before it came to that, and have never been seen again, but the loyal remained, eager to serve their masters, or perhaps just addicted to the rewards the system offered.'

'What rewards?' asked Cal.

'The balls that come from the dragon clocks,' said Cinis. 'They are made of a mineral the dragons adore, but cannot extract themselves. The Dragon Order mines the mineral, not far from here, in fact.'

Fyia looked at Cal. 'And the Kraken Emperor wanted those mines, because Asesh told him about them?'

'Probably,' said Cinis. 'The extraction takes place here, in this temple, using another set of pools. I was collecting the latest haul from the miners' cache when you arrived. There was an attack, and they wanted to offload what they had, in case the Emperor's soldiers returned.'

'Do you think Asesh planned the whole thing? To get you out of the temple when we arrived?' said Fyia.

'It seems likely,' he said. 'By the time I felt your presence here, I was too far away to prevent your mistake.'

They lapsed into silence for a moment, Cal wondering what disasters could have been avoided if they'd met the real Cinis first.

'And they shut away the remaining dragons?' said Cal.

Cinis nodded. 'Lured into Hell; the only place that could contain them. And without the dragons, the dragon clocks and magma ducts couldn't function. The Order of the Dragon shut down the system and hid the eggs, prophesying that when a worthy ruler rose, they would restore the system, and the dragons would return.'

Cinis took a seat, and Cal mulled over his words.

'What happened to Asesh?' said Fyia.

'She was half mad herself by then, although she'd finally achieved the destruction of those who had looked down upon her race. But she miscalculated. Once the system of magma ducts was shut down, nothing remained to unite the kingdoms. The last Dragon King, by then also considered mad, was assassinated, and the few remaining fire-touched went their separate ways, barely a shred of magic between them.

'The Great Kingdom of Asred fell, the north slowly froze, and eventually new kings emerged in the middle kingdoms. But with little magical power of their own, those kings outlawed magic, leading to further persecution of Asesh's people.

'But you have released the dragons along with the magma,' said Cinis, getting to his feet once more, 'so we must prepare.'

'The dragons?' said Fyia.

'We released the dragons?' said Cal, his mind racing. Could it be true?

Fyia turned her head slowly to look at Cal, and so much passed between them in that moment. Shared excitement at the promise of Cinis' words, but also confusion and fear and the yawning chasm of everything they didn't know ... not to mention the new responsibilities they'd pulled down onto their shoulders.

But they had done it. They'd bloody done it.

'The magma is rising,' said Cinis, with a shrug. 'The system is gearing up. The magic is restless. Soon the levels will be such that the dragons can leave Hell's Mouth through the magma ducts. They'll hammer on the clocks, demanding to be let out, and of course, it's only a matter of time ... assuming they don't find a hole first ...'

'Only a matter of time before what?' said Fyia.

Cinis' expression turned grave. 'Until the clocks toll the time of the birds.'

'Until … what?' said Fyia. Cal's stomach plummeted anew. He'd momentarily forgotten that the system was broken, and that magma would soon flow through its creaking bones, presumably to spew out through its open wounds.

'The clocks automatically strike 13 when the magic needs to be moved. Too much magic has built up in pockets. It must be shared around the world, and once the magma ducts are sufficiently full, the clocks will chime, putting the dragons to work.'

'Can we remove the balls?' said Fyia, her tone frantic. 'Shut it down again before the magma gets high enough?'

'You can if you know how,' said Cinis, 'but that is not knowledge I possess.'

Shit.

Cal held tight to Fyia's hand, even when she tried to pull away. They had done this together; it was not for her to carry the burden alone. But Cal sent a silent prayer to all the Gods that the clock in Anvarn would hold, that his people would not suffer because of their actions.

Fyia slumped in her seat. 'I should have waited,' she said, her voice small.

'*We* should have waited,' Cal corrected.

'You told me to be cautious,' said Fyia. 'You told me to wait.'

'But I didn't truly try to stop you, and I rolled the final ball into the lock.'

Cinis made a frustrated noise in the back of his throat. 'It matters not,' he said, dismissively. 'You should have exercised caution, yes, but we all make mistakes. The question is what you will do about it. Whimper over your shortcomings like self-indulgent children? Or will you do all in your power to forge forward and make the best of the situation you have created?'

Fyia got to her feet and stalked slowly towards the tall man, the similarities between them impossible to ignore.

'No one can accuse me of whimpering like a child,' Fyia hissed, 'nor of cowering from a fight, no matter how improbable my success. Do not chastise me for a single moment of regret. There have been others touched by fire, yet none who stepped up to do what was required. I stepped up, and now I will stare down every dragon we released into the world, and bring them to my side.'

'Good,' said Cinis, a curious expression on his face that looked almost like … pride, 'because I would expect no less from any child of mine.'

Chapter Eight

Outside the walls of the Council Building, a mob had gathered, their chants and jeers filling the air around Starfall and the Spider.

'Apparently,' said the Spider, dryly, 'the people of Selise like the Queen's new marriage rules even less than the people of Medris.'

'And according to Sensis, they liked it not at all,' said Starfall, resting her back against the doors to the outside world. She was no coward, but no part of her wanted to face the restless crowd.

'We must deal with the leaders of the Moon Kingdom.'

'One problem at a time,' said Starfall, mentally adding that to her endless list. 'I wish Sensis had brought her message in person; I'd feel safer with her here.'

The Spider raised her eyebrows in agreement. 'It is curious that she and Antice should be heading north together …'

'That's one word for it,' said Starfall. 'There's keeping your enemies close …'

'And then there's getting into bed with them?'

Starfall barked out a laugh. 'Did you just make a lewd joke, my old girl?'

'I believe there are those who consider me incapable of such things,' said the Spider, cocking an accusing eyebrow.

'I believe you *capable* of a great many things, but I do love a surprise.'

'Oh, good,' said the Spider. 'I'm sure the mob will be delighted to provide several ... should you muster the courage to face them.'

'Urgh,' Starfall growled, steeling herself. She nodded to the guards, but before they could open the doors, racing footsteps sounded from the stairs.

'An eagle!' shouted the approaching guard. 'From the Queen!'

Starfall inhaled deeply, dreading what Fyia might have decreed now. She snatched the parchment from the guard and quickly unrolled it, then scanned the brief words.

'Open the doors!' Starfall shouted. 'And get everyone away from the clocks!'

Starfall handed the parchment to the Spider, who stood still for several moments, then snapped to action, heading back into the building. 'I will alert my web.'

Starfall barely heard her, for as the doors creaked slowly open, the roar of the crowd became deafening. The booing and jeering ratcheted up to a new level now they had someone at whom to aim their vitriol, but Starfall didn't hesitate, stepping through and holding up her hands, trying to quiet them.

If anything, their roars grew louder and more frenzied, the front row of protesters shoving against the soldiers forming a human shield at the bottom of the steps. Starfall held her arms high, but the crowd had grown since the Small Council had determined this the best course of action. Then, it had been too small to be a threat to the soldiers stationed outside. Now, as Starfall cast her eyes over the sea of humanity, every sensible part of her screamed at her to run. To protect the council building and let the mob brawl ... fight themselves out.

But Fyia's note had been clear. The clocks were not safe. They were in imminent danger. They had to get everyone away. But what could Starfall do? How could she calm them?

The shoving grew worse, and Starfall shied back as someone threw a flaming glass bottle over the heads of the soldiers protecting the steps. It smashed far from where Starfall stood, but several soldiers fell.

They hurried to fill the hole, but the protesters acted first, and from Starfall's vantage, it was obvious the protesters would break through the line. Starfall had no choice but to pull back, to regroup, to find some other way to get their attention.

The protesters surged forward, and two soldiers in the front row went down. The protesters didn't hesitate, surging again, forcing their way through the weakness in the line.

Starfall whirled and ran, screaming at the guards to close the doors. Her heart hammered in her chest, but she told herself she would make it. This was not her day to die ... she just had to keep moving.

But just as she was crossing the threshold, the doors already half closed, a great, deep, bone-shaking boom sounded from high above. Then another, and another, and then everything suddenly went still.

Starfall spun back to see the protesters faltering, those who had been sprinting for the top—for her—now rooted to the spot, their eyes turned upwards to the dragon clock.

'The hands!' a woman shouted, raising her arm and pointing at the clockface.

Starfall moved back through the doors, far enough that she, too, could see the clock. A hand was indeed spinning, but not one of those that usually spun. An additional hand had appeared, and was now turning a ponderous circle around the clockface, past the mysterious symbols inside the numbers that none of them understood.

They all watched as it pointed straight down, then headed back up the other side, and Starfall knew deep in her gut where it would stop. At the top. Where a dragon's head sat between the numbers twelve and one.

Starfall couldn't tear her eyes away as another boom sounded, this one followed by an ominous cracking. She should probably run. Head for the secret tunnels inside the council building and send word to Fyia, but she couldn't force her feet to move.

The hand was almost at the top now, and Starfall cast an eye across the crowd. They were collectively holding their breath, watching and waiting with grim fascination, because whatever would happen when the clock hand reached the top would probably not be good.

The engineers had shored up the clock as best they could, but would the repairs hold? Or would the whole building come crashing down atop where Starfall stood?

It was too late to wonder, for the hand finally reached the head of the dragon, and stopped dead. A low bell pealed, and the crowd gasped.

The bell rang again, and Starfall realized the booming had ceased. For some strange reason, that made her more fearful than anything else, like whatever made the noise knew it was getting what it wanted.

The bell tolled again and again, until it had tolled twelve times, and tense anticipation buzzed like lightning across the plaza.

There could be only one reason for this. Fyia—whatever she'd done in the north—surely the cause. And then the clock tolled one final time, and the crowd gasped as the clock face spun open from the center, until only a black space remained.

And then the crowd cried out in shock and fear and adoration, for from that black space sprang a beast of legend; a mighty, winged terror with pointed fangs and great, green scales that turned golden in the sunlight.

'A dragon!' screamed a voice from the crowd, snapping many out of their reverie. Some fled, banging against those that still stared skyward in wonder, and then chaos broke forth.

Starfall couldn't tear her eyes away, following the beast's slow wing beats as it lifted itself heavily into the air.

Fyia had done it. That which no one had thought for a moment she could do. Starfall had never truly believed this day would come. That they would see the dragons soaring above the Five Kingdoms as they had in the times of old.

An icy finger of dread chased down her spine. Dragons could bring them prosperity, it was true, and that they were magnificent, no one could question, but they were also a terrible, terrifying weapon. Almost impossible to kill, if legend could be believed. Ferocious, wild, and with appetites that were hard to satisfy.

The dragon turned its sights back on the clock. The face had closed, the extra hand was gone, and the dragon seemed to look for something, scanning the wall beneath the clock. But as the dragon waited, it flapped its wings in a way that seemed ... agitated.

Shit.

'Get away!' Starfall screamed. 'Everyone leave!'

But it was no good. The crowd was now cheering and chanting and making noises of pure wonder. None of them saw the threat until it was too late. Until the dragon plunged towards the earth and closed its mouth around three bodies in one swift movement.

'Run!' screamed Starfall, but they were already scattering in every direction. The dragon landed, squashing another handful of the terrified crowd, and Starfall cursed, desperately searching for a way to distract the beast.

But then the clock made a familiar metallic sound, like metal cogs turning against each other. Starfall could barely hear it over the screams, but the dragon heard it, its head snapping up, its pointed ears suddenly erect and pointed forward.

A metal ball released from the usual place near the top of the clock, tipping into the copper tracks that zig-zagged across the front of the building. The dragon dropped its feast, leaving body parts strewn forgotten on the ground as it launched into the air and made a beeline for the ball.

It snatched the ball from the runners, then took to the air, beating its wings fast as though fleeing a foe. Starfall tracked the beast until it disappeared into a cloud bank, then staggered back into the council building, saying in a quiet, thin, timid voice that sounded nothing like her own, 'Close the doors.'

Elowyn inched along the tunnel towards the platform where the colossal kraken sat, as though on a throne. Three Priestesses of the Sea Serpent had made the journey since the monster had eaten the High Priestess, but none had lived to tell the tale.

Elowyn questioned her own sanity as she crept closer. She was almost at the end of the tunnel, and could see a giant, suckered tentacle flicking back and forth. She considered turning back, because to continue was to give the kraken a chance to eat her too, but she wanted to be High Priestess more than she'd ever wanted anything, and to do so, she must sit on the kraken platform for a turn of the sun. A simple task in recent times, for the krakens had all but disappeared. Until now …

Elowyn wondered briefly if the stories were true. If the High Priestesses of old had really commanded the krakens, or more accurately, the water inside them. She possessed water magic, even though she'd hidden it all her life, only experimenting when she was sure she was alone. Practicing magic had been forbidden, and if she'd been discovered, she would have been cast from the kraken platform onto the teeth-like rocks below.

She knew in theory she could command the water, as she had been doing every spare moment since Queen Fyia had legalized magic, but that did little to quiet the nagging voice at the back of her mind telling her she was about to die.

'I am not about to die,' she whispered, as she inched forward. 'My magic was made for this.' Her magic had swelled in the last turns of the sun, as though something in the atmosphere had changed … something in the water. She felt more powerful than ever before, making her believe maybe she could command the kraken off the platform, back into the sea.

But just as she was summoning the courage to take the final steps, a hissing noise filled the air, and then the kraken screamed. The tentacle disappeared, and Elowyn rushed forward to see what had happened.

The kraken had abandoned the platform, the hissing, roiling noise coming from the hole where the dragon clock had once sat, louder with every passing tick, while thick, black smoke billowed into the air.

The heat became unbearable, so Elowyn shied back from the hole, her heart hammering, her brain yelling at her to run. But sick fascination held her in place, some reckless part of her needing to see what would happen next, and wondering if this was part of the test. But then a glowing orange light rose through the smoke, and terror gave her feet wings.

'You are a hypocrite,' said Sensis. She slammed her hands on her desk, on the map she'd stolen from the Guild of Magic as they'd run for their lives.

'Are we finally going to do this, then?' said Antice, leaning back against the flimsy wooden wall of the airship and watching her closely.

Essa had made modifications to the original airship design when she'd created Fyia's fleet, one of which was to make them lighter, reducing the amount of wood. So if they argued, it wouldn't just be those in the next-door cabins who would hear, but the whole damn crew.

Sensis wasn't sure she cared. This fight had been brewing since Fyia had given her Venir's estate … Gods, it had been brewing since Antice had shunned her when they were little more than children. Since he'd given her hope that someone as influential as a prince would accept her as she was—regardless of what society deemed appropriate—then ripped it away.

She forced aside the thought. Yes, they were finally going to do this. Sensis slammed her hands down once more. 'You should have told your Queen,' she said, glaring at him, the full force of her infuriation on display.

'Which bit?' he said with his usual cocky nonchalance. He folded his arms and shifted onto one leg, shuffling a bit to get comfortable, but Sensis would not react to his deliberate antagonism.

Instead, she stood straight and pulled back her shoulders. 'We can start with your involvement with the rebels, then move to your aiding the Guild of Magic in withholding information from your Queen, and then, I don't know, maybe circle back to the row of scales hidden in your groin?'

Sensis' errant mind wondered if he had ever had sex. A secret like that was too valuable to ever risk …

'You missed the bit where I was a dick to you when we were kids,' he said.

'You're like that to almost everyone, so it was no more or less than I expected.' Although her heart gave a traitorous thud as he pushed off the wall and moved towards her.

'I regretted it instantly,' he said, his voice uncharacteristically soft. 'I wanted to impress the lordlings I was with, and I …'

'I don't care, Antice,' she said, but suddenly she couldn't meet his eyes. 'And we have more important matters to discuss.'

'I never truly supported the rebels,' he said, still moving towards her. 'I had to maintain appearances, and certainly couldn't stand in their way, but I never did more than I had to. Venir, my uncle, was a strong supporter of the rebel cause—despite also sitting on the

Queen's Small Council—and I couldn't afford his suspicion.'

'So instead, you stood by while the rebels bombed the capital? While Letta led the charge?'

Antice faltered, but didn't ask how she knew Letta was involved. 'I withheld nothing of true value from the Queen,' he said, 'and my fire-touch ... well, that is a private matter. I am under no obligation to share my personal brand of magic with the world.'

'Is that what *this* is about?' said Sensis. She pulled the book she'd taken from the chamber under the alterwoods from her cloak.

Antice eyed the tome for a moment, then tipped his head to one side. 'Yes, and no.'

'You're trying to trace the fire-touch back through your bloodline? So you can stake a claim as the dominant line?' The book contained an entire section on the hierarchy of the fire-touched, which Fyia would need to understand if she wished to perch at the top of that growing tree.

'No,' he said. 'I care little for the hierarchy, and more about who may sit within it.'

'You think there are more with the touch?'

'Veau, Fyia, and I all have it,' said Antice. 'Veau couldn't very well hide his, and Fyia chose to make hers public—or her parents did—but nobody knows about mine. My parents hid the touch, and swore those who attended me to secrecy. They had leverage over every single servant. But if I have gone through life without the world knowing, then how many others have done the same? Until Fyia came to power, magic was forbidden, and the old kings didn't take kindly to anyone with the touch.'

'They always were pathetically insecure.'

Antice shrugged. 'Turns out they had a lot to be insecure about.'

'Did you find others?'

Antice shook his head. 'That book only recently came into my possession. I heard a whisper through the alterwoods, and …'

'You … what?' said Sensis. 'A whisper?'

'The alterwoods are the only trees native to our land, and their roots form a network infused with old magic. They pass whispers. Hard to hear—impossible for many—but I have spent my life sitting among the trees, straining to hear, and I can make out some of what they say.

'An alterwood grows inside the Guild of Magic, and the roots told me of a book the Guild had found alongside that map, so I snuck in and stole it.'

'You're magic- and fire-touched,' Sensis said bitterly. 'Do you have a Cruaxee too?'

Antice shook his head. 'More people have magic than the old kings liked to admit. My father, the King of Moon, included.'

'Not me,' said Sensis, hating how sour her voice sounded in her ears.

Antice laughed gently, and Sensis froze as he rounded the desk between them.

'You think you are without magic?' he said, taking her hand.

Sensis knew she should snatch her hand back and chastise him for touching her this way, but her touch-starved skin luxuriated in the feel of his warm, callused fingers.

'Antice,' she said, the hint of a warning lacing her tone.

Tears threatened to prick Sensis' eyes at her confusion … the danger. She hadn't felt this way in years, but her body wanted to turn itself inside out at the memories her mind was dredging to the surface. The horror of them went some way to breaking the thrall of Antice's touch, and her brain spiraled. Was he manipulating her? Trying to turn Sensis against Fyia because he wanted the crown? Or maybe he'd felt vulnerable under the rule of the old kings, just like she had. Maybe he shared their vision for a different kind of world …

'How could you fight as you do without magic?' he said. 'You are a wonder.' He lifted his free hand to her cheek, caressing her skin with his thumb. 'Magic manifests differently in us all, but everyone has some spark within them … something that makes them shine. Whether that is magic of the water, or fire, or of the warrior, or the trees …'

'Bullshit,' she snapped, finally yanking herself away, immediately feeling the loss of him. 'You expect me to believe you care about anyone but yourself and your high-born friends? You forget I know who you are.'

'Yes,' he said quietly, 'you know both sides of me. You know the arrogant, insecure boy who shunned you in front of his friends, but also the boy content to pick apples in the orchard, so far under your spell, he threw aside the rules laid down for him, and kissed you.'

Sensis turned away, her cheeks flaming. 'Did you find more?' she said, trying to focus on what really mattered—her duty to her Queen. 'With the touch of fire?'

Antice remained silent for several ticks, and Sensis forced herself to suck in a long, centering breath as she waited. Antice had spent his life listening to the whispers of trees, but she had spent hers learning to master her emotions. To stay calm under pressure. To predict the movements of her enemies, always two steps ahead.

'I already told you I have not.'

Had he really?

'I have suspicions, but little more,' he said, stepping up behind her.

Her back was vulnerable, so Sensis turned and gave a sharp nod, Antice now so close she had to look up to meet his eyes. She found it suddenly hard to breathe, her chest constricting as he lifted his hand to her neck.

Sensis froze, neither pulling away nor rocking forward, as most of her wished to do. But then his lips lowered and pressed against hers, and arcs of lightning shot through her, slaying her restraint quite thoroughly.

He slipped his hands into her hair, the sensation of his nails scraping against her scalp sending a shiver down her spine, but as she pressed into his touch, he pulled back, holding her head in his hands as he looked down, a question in his eyes.

He waited for her to make the next move, forcing her to acknowledge she wanted this too, that she was in it, an active, willing participant, never able to brush her involvement aside as an impulse, or say she'd been caught up in the moment.

Her gaze dipped from his hooded eyes to his tempting lips, and she swayed towards him. He gently dug his nails into her scalp, and Sensis gasped, then tipped her head back, going up on her tiptoes so she could reach his lips. He held her off, forcing her eyes back to his, and then he kissed her.

It started slowly, each of them making small, exploratory movements, pressing, and nipping, and pulling, and then Sensis probed into his mouth, massaging and flicking his tongue with hers. Antice groaned his approval and slid a hand to her backside, holding her to him.

The kiss deepened, until there was nothing but the two of them, the press of their bodies, the euphoria of each other's touch. Their mouths found a primal rhythm, their hands roaming, hips pulsing, and then

Antice slid his hand inside her leather pants, cupping her backside, massaging, pulling her against the bulge in his breeches. Sensis broke away, clutching his neck with one hand as she rested her head against him.

'We should stop,' she said, breathing hard.

'Should we?' he said, kissing her hair as he slipped his hand out of her leathers and wrapped his arm across her back.

Sensis inhaled him as she steadied her pulse, clutching him close, any shred of dignity long gone. 'I do not wish to get with child,' she said. It had been months since she'd seen a witch. The magic might still be intact, but it would be foolish to risk it.

'We could do other things,' said Antice, kissing and stroking her until she was soft in his hands.

'We have much to do,' she said, but her eyes were closed, lapping up his attention. 'Our duty to our Queen …'

'Yes, yes,' he said, then stepped suddenly away. Sensis wanted to chase him, but she kept herself rooted to the spot. 'Duty before everything.'

His words were bitter, because, of course, Antice knew all about duty. His parents had drilled him practically since the day of his birth on his obligations as future sovereign. But what choice did they have? Duty did come before everything.

Sensis tore her eyes from him, pushed her long hair back over her shoulder, then bent over the map, which detailed how the magma ducts and aqueducts and dragon clocks worked together. Sensis wished they'd paid Essa's warnings more heed, because if Fyia used the balls before fixing the clocks, many would die.

The Guild of Magic assumed Fyia couldn't restart the system, because she lacked the key. They were wrong. The map showed five circles over the Temple of the Warrior, and Sensis knew exactly what those circles were, even if the Guild did not.

Her bruised lips tingled, distracting her, pulling her back to the kiss, to Antice. She tried to shake the feel of him against her, but it was an impossible task, and she feared she would never get him out of her head.

'The navigator still awaits our decision,' she said, balling her fists. 'To the Fae'ch Mountains? Or should we seek Fyia, wherever she is?' The Fae'ch were closer, but the likelihood of them cooperating was miniscule. The old kings had persecuted and exiled them, and their memories were long.

'Sensis,' said Antice, his voice urgent enough to make Sensis look up. He was staring through the window, and when she followed his gaze, she gasped at what she saw. She blinked rapidly. Had someone fed her poison? Was this a dream? That would explain a great many things …

'Do you think it will attack?' said Antice, his eyes still glued to the great winged beast in the sky, its purple scales glinting gold whenever they caught the light.

'I hope not,' said Sensis, now beside him. She didn't have space for fear amid the wonder flooding her body. Fyia had done it. The dragons were real. The legends were true.

'Dragons are almost impossible to kill,' said Antice.

'And this airship can't outmaneuver a flock of birds, let alone a dragon …'

The beast slowed its movements, falling in beside the airship, wing beats leisurely, so it stayed by their side.

'What's it doing?' said Sensis, tearing her gaze away to glance at Antice. But Antice was lost in the dragon, fixated on the beast. 'Antice?'

'I … think something is happening to me,' he said. 'I think … my scales … they feel …' Antice clawed at his belt, then yanked down his breeches, giving Sensis an eyeful for the second time in as many days. But this time, nothing could distract her from the row of little golden marks in the crease that ran south from his right hip, because a soft golden light radiated from them.

'Oh my Gods,' said Sensis. 'What … what does it mean? Did the dragon seek you out?'

'I …' Antice looked through the window, and the dragon turned its head to look back, and as their eyes met, a bolt of cold, hard fear finally permeated her awe.

Chapter Nine

Isa may have kicked Essa out of the mountain, but that didn't mean she had to leave empty-handed. She'd spent the time since studying the taps and pipes built into the rock channel on the approach to the mountain's entrance, then traced the pipes all the way to where they punched into the mountain itself.

If Essa could understand more about how this great system of magma ducts and mechanical clocks had been constructed, then maybe she could repair it herself. Or, better still, maybe she could replace it with a new one that didn't pose such a risk to life.

Fyia would certainly never give up on thawing the north—especially now she was marrying the King of the Black Hoods—and the magma ducts were the key to that. The problem was, the Fae'ch controlled a crucial piece of the infrastructure, and Essa still didn't fully understand how it all worked. And she was running out of time ... she could feel it in her bones.

Essa was ready to call it quits for the day, to head back to the uncomfortable bed in her makeshift camp. Her airship was waiting in the woods at the bottom of the mountain, and the thought of her plush bed, and a glass window that kept the weather at bay, was almost enough to turn her feet down the mountain. But she had a job to do, and would not leave until she'd followed every pipe she could find. Surely one of them would tell her something of use ...

She tramped back to the hollow in the rock that held her sleeping mat, and crouched under the small awning she'd strung over her head. She sighed as she pulled dried meat and an apple from a canvas bag, but after no more than a single bite, the sounds of screaming echoed through the air.

Essa went still, listening for the noise she hoped she'd imagined. Or maybe the Fae'ch had finally become bored with Essa sniffing around, and were playing a trick to try and drive her away, as was their nature.

But as she listened, the sound came again, then again, louder, and Essa jumped to her feet, her food forgotten. She crept forward, climbing the short distance towards the mountain's entrance, finding a rock to hide behind where she could see down the length of the approach, all the way to the open portcullis.

A few Fae'ch emerged from the dark space, their faces ashen, distraught, then more behind them, until a steady stream of bodies exited the mountain. They shrieked and cried and clutched one another, some waiting around the entrance, pointing back into the mountain, others rushing towards where Essa stood, fleeing whatever threat lay inside.

Essa knew she should follow them. She should run down the mountain and escape into the sky, but her feet were blocks of lead holding her in place, her eyes frantically searching the crowd, scanning each new face for any sign of Veau.

More and more poured out, and then suddenly, the flow ceased, and a tense silence settled. Essa wished she knew what that meant. Was everyone else trapped? Had there been a cave-in? But the Fae'ch had magic, and Isa could move through time and space. Surely they had a way to deal with such things.

Or maybe their clock had fallen also. Fyia had told Essa about the dragon clock that presided over their great hall. Could it be that the clocks had struck thirteen already? That at this very moment, magma spewed out into the mountain, melting all that stood in its way? Melting Veau?

But then another group emerged, the crush now so dense Essa couldn't see who it was. They parted enough that she glimpsed a woman shouting at the crowd to get back, moving them along the chasm, shooing them away. Most obeyed, still clutching each other, or sobbing, or walking like animated dolls, shock having sucked them dry.

Beside the entrance, Isa lay on the ground, looking up at the woman who'd told the others to get away. Isa was screaming, telling the woman to go back inside, to placate the Children of the Lake.

Two men stepped up to the woman's side, and then Essa finally caught a glimpse of Veau, his scales reflecting the dying light of day. Essa inhaled sharply, tramping down the well of emotion threatening to overwhelm her, trying not to draw attention to herself. She studied Veau as he watched the altercation between the two women, scanning him for any sign he was hurt.

And then a man raised his voice, dragging Essa's attention away from Veau's light-haired form. The man—a big, dark-skinned fae with bird-like wings—looked lovingly down at the woman fighting with Isa, and she smiled warmly back at him. 'We will go to the Queen of the Five Kingdoms,' he said, his voice carrying to where Essa stood, 'for there is a disturbance in the air, and Queen Fyia will need those with magic to help her. She believes in a better, fairer future, and I applaud her.'

Essa could barely believe her ears. Isa was no longer in charge. The Fae'ch were leaving the mountain. They wanted to help Fyia. It was more than any of them had ever hoped for, and Veau was with them ...

'You are welcome to join us,' said the woman. 'To make a new life for yourselves in the light.'

And then the crowd of Fae'ch headed towards Essa, and her feet moved without command, scrambling to the ground in front of them.

'Veau!' she shouted, rushing towards him, her usual cool reserve forgotten.

'Essa?' said Veau. The fae man turned questioning eyes upon him.

Veau rushed to greet Essa and pulled her into a tight embrace, lifting her off her feet as he laughed into her ear.

'What are you doing here?' he said, setting her down then easing back, so he could see into her eyes.

Essa squared her shoulders, winching some fraction of her composure back into place, then said, 'Funny, I was going to ask you the same thing.'

The woman, who Essa learned was called Storm, her fae companion, Gabriel, and Veau, joined Essa on her airship, although she refused to take off until they told her what in the Seven Hells had happened.

'The Children of the Lake left the lake,' said Veau, who seemed on edge, still visibly shaken.

'Hot, sweet tea,' Essa called to one of her crew, then settled herself at the long table in the ship's plain mess. 'Please,' she said, inviting the others to join her. She was glad to hide behind the familiar formality, doing her best not to look too hard at Veau.

'Who are the Children of the Lake?' said Essa. 'And why did they leave the lake?'

Veau and Gabriel turned their eyes to Storm—a short woman with a blond bob. Storm had an aura of power that draped around her shoulders like a blanket, and it made Essa wary ... made her think she should give the magnetic blond a wide berth.

'They left,' said Storm, 'either because, if they had stayed in the water, they were at risk of death, or because there was something outside the water they desired.'

'Which do you think it is?'

Storm shrugged. 'Impossible to say.'

'What happened to Isa? Why were you arguing?'

'You didn't hear?' said Veau, glancing at Storm with a wary expression.

Essa shook her head. She'd never seen Veau quite like this, and she wondered if something was wrong. Was he still scared of his magic? Was he afraid of Gabriel and Storm?

'Isa was a tyrant,' said Veau, 'but every Fae'ch swore an oath to follow her, for as long as they lived under the mountain. They couldn't leave, for fear of persecution at the hands of the kings, and once Isa had our oaths, we had no choice but to obey.'

'Until Fyia legalized magic,' said Essa.

'Exactly,' said Storm, her lips pulling up at the corners. 'But Isa—my half-sister—inflicted much damage in her time as our overlord.'

'Oh,' said Essa, feeling her cheeks heat.

A pregnant silence filled the air, and Essa hated to think what exactly Isa had done to them. 'But there is little she can do now we are outside. Her magic is weaker than ours, and we will never trust her again.'

'And many of her followers are dead,' said Veau. 'Axus is dead.' He choked on the words, and Essa wondered what exactly Veau had witnessed.

'We want to return to our lives as they were before the dragons disappeared,' said Gabriel, 'when we lived peacefully alongside humans.'

It was more than Essa had ever dreamed possible.

'They want to help Fyia,' said Veau. 'Do you have news of her?'

Essa shook her head. 'Last I heard, she was travelling north, to the Great Glacier.'

'To the Temple of the Warrior-Mother?' said Storm.

'I think so,' said Essa, not dwelling on the combined name, unfamiliar as it was, 'but I'm worried she's going to restart the magma ducts before we fix the clocks.' The map from the High Priestess had shown how the magma would rise, and if that happened while there were still holes …

'What do you mean?' said Storm, with new intensity.

'Unless someone on the Great Glacier has told her, Fyia doesn't know about the magma ducts that travel across our world. Honestly, there is much I still do not know—perhaps you can educate me—but what I do know is that the clocks are crucial, and several have fallen.'

'They've … what?' said Storm, sitting up even straighter in her seat. 'How likely is it Fyia has found all the eggs? That she's used them?'

'That she's hatched them?' said Essa. There was something about Storm's words that gave Essa the tingling sense she was missing something.

'To stretch the metaphor,' said Storm, although her expression said she too realized something wasn't quite in line.

'The metaphor?' said Essa.

'The eggs are not real eggs,' said Storm. 'That was their nickname, because they were small and round, and when all five were used together, they gave life to the magma ducts. But dragons do not hatch from eggs. They give birth to live young.'

'And the dragons remaining in the world were trapped in Hell,' said Gabriel. 'But they will escape when the system restarts.'

'Gods,' said Essa, leaning back in her seat, fisting her hands in her hair as the implications of Storm's words sank in. 'Then I would say it's very likely she's used them—assuming she has them all, and assuming she can work out how—because Fyia has no idea what they are.'

'If she's already done it,' Gabriel said to Storm, 'could that be what the Children of the Lake were running from?'

'Or running to,' said Storm. 'Dragons are almost impossible to kill, but the Children have done so before. They would give much to gorge themselves on the magic of a dragon, and have been waiting a long time for the chance.'

'Will they leave the mountain?' said Veau.

'Maybe,' said Storm, 'although the dragons could just as easily kill the Children, especially the older, cannier ones. The Children will be wary. They are more likely to huddle by the mountain's clock ...'

'Waiting for a dragon to come to them,' said Gabriel.

Essa's blood ran cold. 'We have to get to Fyia ... have to warn her.'

'Indeed, we must,' said Storm, 'but it is likely already too late.'

Veau knocked on the door to Essa's cabin. He was nervous in the way of a teenaged boy asking a girl to a banquet, and he chastised himself as he waited for an answer.

'Come in!' she called.

Veau steeled himself, then turned the handle and pushed his way inside. Essa hunched over her desk, looking between a notepad with untidy writing scrawled across its surface, and a map she'd strapped to the desk's top.

He stood watching her for a few moments, not wanting to interrupt her absorption, content to reacquaint himself with the set of her brow, the purse of her lips, and the way she flicked her pencil as she pondered a problem. It might take a full turn for her to remember him, and he was happy to wait, few things in this world as impressive as Essa's mind in full flow.

After only a few short spins of the hand, she threw down her pencil and pushed away from the desk, a frustrated noise rumbling in the back of her throat.

'Want to talk about it?' said Veau.

'No.'

Veau chuckled, then finally tore his eyes from her long enough to take in her cabin. It was small, the bed pressed up against a large window built into the side of the airship, not much else in the room aside from her desk and a single armchair.

Essa sat on the bed, and Veau joined her, leaving a conservative distance between them.

'You look well,' said Essa. 'Life with the Fae'ch has been kind to you.'

'You look well also,' said Veau, fighting the temptation to take her hand.

'I don't feel well,' she said, slumping a little. 'I feel as though the world is about to implode, and there's nothing I can do about it.'

'If it does, it's not your fault.'

Essa huffed a laugh. 'I know. It's all on your sister, but knowing that doesn't make me feel any better. It won't make the families of those who die feel any better, either.'

Veau bowed his head, looking at his hands. 'But if she's truly returned the dragons …'

'… which Storm seems to believe is likely.'

Veau met Essa's eyes, and understanding passed between them. If Fyia had returned the dragons, then they were in uncharted territory, in a new era of their existence, with a new set of rules to define and obey.

'What's the deal with Storm and Gabriel?' said Essa, scooting back on the bed and folding her legs beneath her. 'You seem to know them well?'

Something that felt a lot like guilt pulled at Veau's gut, and shame. Would it be unwise to tell the world Gabriel was his father? Would that have ramifications for Fyia? Not that anything would matter if she truly had dragons …

But Essa wasn't the world, and he could trust her, so he tamped down the discomfort that threatened to render him mute, and forced his brain to form words. 'I learned a lot inside the mountain,' he said, although he couldn't meet her eyes. 'Gabriel taught me to control my magic, and Storm taught me about rocks with magical properties, and the Children of the Lake, and

Fae'ch politics. And Isa taught me that the former King of Starlight is not my father ... Gabriel is.'

Essa didn't react to the news. She barely blinked. 'Is he Fyia's father too?' Her engineer's brain cared only for details, and Veau's mouth split into an involuntary smile.

'No. I don't know for sure who is, but my mother was ambitious, so we can't rule out the possibility she found another magical being.'

'How?' said Essa. 'How did your mother even meet Gabriel?'

'She went to the mountain, seeking a magical sire.'

Essa tutted with distaste.

Veau shrugged. 'Isa used it as a way to punish Gabriel. She forced him to ...' Veau couldn't bring himself to say the words, but Essa understood well enough.

'Isa wanted to have a child with Gabriel,' Veau continued, 'but it never happened. She blamed Gabriel. But then he fathered me, and Isa had a son with Axus ...'

'Maybe Isa and Gabriel just weren't compatible.'

'But Isa claims her magic identified Gabriel as her soulmate.'

Essa cocked a questioning eyebrow. 'Is that really a thing?'

'So Isa's ancestors have always claimed.'

Silence settled for several beats, both of them gazing through the window, letting the story settle.

'But Gabriel taught you to control your magic?' said Essa, still looking through the window.

Veau inhaled sharply, then considered his answer, taking extreme care over the selection of his words, because if he couldn't convince Essa he had his magic under control, all hope was lost. 'Gabriel identified what was wrong. Why things were so erratic. I was trying to control too much, and the magic doesn't like it. I had to learn to be a conduit, to direct the flow rather than trying to block it, or the magic builds up, and eventually breaks free.'

'You're sure it's safe?' said Essa, finally meeting his gaze with her sharp, grey eyes. 'That you won't hurt anyone?'

'It hasn't been long,' said Veau, 'only a few days. I suppose I could relapse, but it feels different now, like something missing has slotted into place. So long as I don't let the magic accumulate, as I did before, I don't see how it could be a danger.'

Essa nodded slowly, years of history and heartache ebbing and flowing between them.

'You want us to get back together?' said Essa, blunt as always, and Veau loved her for it. He never worried she would temper herself around him, or lie to him. She would tell him the things he didn't want to hear, then do whatever she could to help. She was selfless, and committed, and driven by logic to such an extent that she had packed him off to the Fae'ch to seek help without a second thought.

She'd told him it was the only way. The Fae'ch the only ones who could help him. She'd told him the people of Starlight didn't deserve a king whose magic might accidentally lash out at his subjects. Just as they didn't want a queen who had stood by and let that happen. So instead, she'd turned her back on any hope of ever occupying that position, and sent him on his way.

'The threat of my magic has gone,' said Veau, 'and that was all that stood between us. I still love you … will only ever …'

'You know if Fyia has truly returned the dragons, you could claim one as your own?'

Veau tensed, the conversation taking a turn he would rather avoid. 'Maybe, although that's not what I want.'

'You would squander your power?'

'I would live happily with you for the rest of our days, serving our Queen and living contented lives.'

'Your sister will need your fire-touch.'

'You don't know that. And what about what I need?' said Veau, bunching his hands in the linens.

'Nothing matters but the Crown,' said Essa. 'Isn't that what your parents used to say?'

'You know that's bullshit ...' said Veau, his heart beating hard in his ears. He searched for a way to reel the conversation back in, then asked the question he feared. 'What do you want, Essa?'

She snorted. 'I want a lab at the end of the world where no one disturbs me. I want to invent things, and work with brilliant people, and uncover the many secrets of our world.

'I won't lie to you, Veau, you know that is not my way. I love you as much now as I ever have, but neither of us knows what the future may hold. We should not be hasty; not after all we have been through already.'

He froze, watching her for tick after tick, then batted aside the sinking feeling in his chest. He moved to sit against the headboard and placed a pillow across his lap, then patted it with an open palm. 'We can take it slow,' he said, patting the pillow again when she looked at him with wary eyes. 'We can just be friends to start.'

'Do friends stroke each other's hair?' she said, her eyes flicking to his hand. But after a beat, she shifted her weight and shuffled closer, then curled up beside him, resting her head on the pillow.

'I'm sure Edu strokes Fyia's hair all the time,' said Veau, digging his fingers into her blond locks and gently tugging.

Essa giggled, the sound so uncharacteristic that Veau laughed too, digging his hands in anew, something easing in his chest at the contact.

Essa sighed, shifting so her nose pressed against his torso. 'I suppose we can try,' she said, her eyes fluttering closed, 'but things are complicated, especially if the dragons really have returned, and … I don't want to lose you again.'

Cinis made Cal and Fyia wait at the edge of the chamber they'd fallen into only that morning, entering through a secret tunnel they'd failed to find. It seemed a lifetime ago they'd landed in a heap, then been rescued by Leo, but less than twelve spins of the hand had passed.

'Stand there and don't move,' said Cinis. 'If you get in the way, you may ruin the whole batch, or worse, die.'

Cal wrapped an arm around Fyia's shoulders, and she leaned into him as fatigue finally settled over her. Less than twelve spins, and yet the whole world had changed. They'd learned they knew nothing, and her believing Asesh could already have resulted in many disasters. Were the dragons even at this moment eating people alive? Were the fallen clocks spewing magma into the world?

'It's not your fault,' said Cal, pulling her, so she stood in front of him, then pinning her back to his chest.

She tipped her head against him and took a deep, regretful breath. 'Who else's fault could it be?'

'The kings who outlawed magic and let the clocks go to ruin,' said Cal, no hint of uncertainty in his tone. 'Asesh. The Fae'ch; they knew you planned to return the dragons, and yet offered no warning …'

'Quiet,' said Cinis. 'What is done is done, and I need to concentrate.'

'Yes, *Father*,' said Fyia, in a sarcastic tone, because after Cinis had dropped his bombshell, and confirmed that yes, he meant Fyia was his daughter, he had refused to say more.

Cinis scowled. 'I told you, I will explain all later. Right at this moment, all that matters is making Dragonsprite, which means I must focus; the process is not easy.'

Fyia inwardly rolled her eyes. She'd insisted on sending eagles to Starfall, the Fae'ch, the Temple of the Sea Serpent, and the Black Hoods, but there had been little time for anything else. Worry gnawed at Fyia's insides, and standing around watching was not one of her strengths, angst coursing through her bones.

But then Cinis pulled a concealed lever here, and twisted a dial that looked like it was part of the flower beds there, and suddenly, metalwork rose through the five circular pools of water.

Fyia gasped, and Cal gripped her harder.

'I take it you are responsible for the hole in the ceiling?' said Cinis, not looking away from the twisted metal sculptures as they ascended. They were all different colors—gold, silver, bronze, copper, and a dull grey. Some had dish-like parts, some had bits that looked like funnels, and others contained only twists of metal.

'Yes,' said Fyia. 'The path gave way.'

Cinis nodded, but didn't look up. The sculptures came to a halt, all at different heights, and Cinis began retrieving bits of half-pipe from around the place, hidden here and there among the trees and plants.

Fyia looked up at Cal, who met her gaze with equal astonishment. Their wonder only grew as Cinis attached the half-pipes to four of the metal structures in a convoluted pattern.

'What in the Seven Hells?' said Fyia.

'Shush,' snapped Cinis, as he pulled a lump of something copper and blue from his pocket. Fyia recognized it as the metal the Order of the Dragon mined from below the ice, and she couldn't tear her eyes away as Cinis placed one piece after another between the twists of the dull, grey sculpture—the only one not connected to the others.

Just like the metal balls had earlier, the pieces travelled through the sculpture's twists until they disappeared below the surface of the water. But then nothing happened.

Fyia frowned, but Cinis didn't move. He waited, watching the structure in the next pool over, his shoulders relaxed, features expectant.

And then a gurgling noise sounded, and the dish that sat like a strange flower at the top of the bronze structure filled with a shining silver liquid. It ran out of the dish, down the pipe Cinis had attached, flowing into a funnel in the silver sculpture in the next pool. The liquid traveled through the closed twists and turns at speed, as not two ticks later, it was in the next half-pipe, now the color of copper.

It was more viscous than before, moving slowly. Cinis watched it carefully as it progressed down the steep pipe to the copper structure, where it mixed in another dish with a purple substance that flowed in through a hole in the dish's side.

The mixture swirled for several long moments, then pulled together to form a silver ball, which rolled down the final half-pipe onto a waiting plate. A whooshing noise like the fall of a guillotine filled the air, something within the golden structure hammering down so fast it was difficult to see, and the ball cracked into four. It reformed itself into four perfectly round, golden spheres, then rolled slowly out of the mechanism, into Cinis' waiting hands.

'Let us be off,' said Cinis, carefully pocketing the balls, then quickly dismantling the structure.

'You're not going to tell us what that was?' said Fyia, watching the metalwork sink back into the water.

'The balls used in the dragon clocks?' said Cal. 'Or, at least, they're the same golden color.'

'Yes,' said Cinis. 'Now the dragons have returned, the clocks will only release balls when they strike thirteen, and they only do that when the area around the clock needs more magic. The dragons desire the balls, so when a clock strikes, they either fly, or swim through the magma, competing to get the ball first. Magic clings to them, and they pull it along in their wake, distributing it around the world.'

'What if two dragons show up at once?' said Fyia.

'They will fight. It is a brutal business, but these balls are the best way to control the dragons. We must take all we can. Come … carry these,' he said, pulling open a hidden compartment filled with sacks.

'Take great care not to puncture them,' he said, placing the newest balls into a sack shot with cobalt-colored strings. He carefully sealed the top. 'If the dragons smell the balls when we are on your airship, we will all die. I have infused these sacks with magic to disguise their contents, but one little nick is all it would take.'

Fyia and Cal gingerly hefted a sack in each hand, as did Cinis, saying, 'We shall have to hope this is enough for now. This temple is the only place we can make Dragonsprite.'

Fyia was silent as they trudged to the airships. She scanned the sky, half expecting to see dragons circling in the air, but there were none to be seen. Which was for the best, given there was still so much she didn't know. She didn't know how to control a dragon, or use her magic, or if her actions had already led to the deaths of great swathes of her people, swallowed by the rising magma.

'We will go to the Temple of the Dragon,' said Cinis, in a tone that did not invite argument. Fyia cocked an eyebrow. 'The Circus there was designed for training dragons.'

Fyia wondered if they could trust this man any more than they should have trusted Asesh. She couldn't dispute his features bore a striking resemblance to her own, but even if he were her father, as he claimed to be, that didn't mean his motives were pure. Maybe he was in league with Asesh, or had some long-game of his own.

'I won't lie,' said Cal, 'I will be glad to see my people.'

Fyia nodded. She was happy to go to the land of the Black Hoods, but not only for Cal. She had no desire to face her own subjects until she knew more; until she both understood and had a solution to the problems she'd caused. And she wanted to learn about her magic, and how to control the dragons, away from the scared, judgmental eyes of her courtiers and councils.

Fyia inhaled deeply. It had been a long road, and her people would surely hate her more than ever, but a feeling low in her gut made Fyia fear the worst was yet to come.

Fyia's wolves sat on her feet and rubbed themselves against her as she took her seat at the head of the table next to Cal. She petted them, their presence reassuring, something inside her settling back into place at their familiar presence.

Cinis had overseen the storage of the sacks of Dragonsprite, then joined them in the large dining room, all of them glad of the wine and meat pies awaiting them.

Edu refused to sit, instead hovering behind Cinis, casting suspicious looks at the back of his head. Fyia didn't have the energy to roll her eyes, suddenly bone-weary and looking forward to her soft, warm bed. But there was much to address first.

'Why the Temple of the Dragon?' said Edu, before Fyia could form words of her own. She had relayed to him all Cinis had told them, but apparently he had questions of his own.

'Because it is the best place to train the dragons,' said Cinis, turning awkwardly in his seat to look at Edu.

'Why?' Edu pressed.

'Because the Black Hoods were no fools. They didn't try to hide it when their magic weakened, when their hold on the dragons became fragile, and they searched for solutions. They built a training ring, and stashed Dragonsprite, and hoarded dragon scales.

'And they created a home where the dragons could live peacefully, and breed, deepening the connections between the dragons and their fire-touched, intensifying the bonds that held them together.'

'You really think we can control the dragons?' said Fyia, accepting a glass of ruby red wine from a guard.

'I think your best chance is at the Dragon Temple,' said Cinis. 'But you must also learn to master your magic. It is of reasonable strength, and will compete with your fire-touch if you do not.'

A prickle of excitement ran from the top of her spine to the ends of her toes, because she had always wanted to learn about her magic. But for perhaps the first time in her life, she wouldn't start the task this very moment. She took a fortifying sip of wine, then said, 'I will look forward to discussing it further in the morning. It has been a long day, and I am going to bed.'

Fyia was already half asleep by the time Cal joined her in bed, both washed and glad to be rid of their dirty clothes. She rolled into him as he joined her under the covers, breathing in his scent of fresh gorse and wind-swept, snow-covered hills.

She lay her head in the crook of his shoulder, and he wrapped an arm around her, playing with the bare skin of her back.

'I can't believe we were here, in this bed, only this morning,' said Fyia, awareness stirring in her core as his fingers caressed her.

'So much has happened,' he agreed. 'Cinis, Asesh, the Dragonsprite. And you returned the dragons …'

'*We* did,' she said, lifting her head to look him in the eye. 'You can't blame me for all of it.'

Cal rolled her onto her back, his hand tracing up her side, skirting her naked breasts. Desire stirred low in her belly, leaching into her blood as his eyes raked over her, his thumb strumming a nipple.

Fyia pushed up on her elbows and studied him in return. 'I'm tired,' she said, arching her back.

'Me too,' he replied, leaning forward to kiss her stomach. 'We should sleep.'

Fyia's insides clenched. 'We have dragons to train.' Her voice became strained as he kissed higher.

'We need our strength.' He flicked her nipple with his tongue.

Fyia gasped and fell back on the bed, sliding a hand to his neck to pull him down with her. He yanked the sheets aside and settled atop her, moving his mouth to the other side. The cool air hit her wet nipple, and Fyia writhed impatiently beneath him, wrapping her legs around his waist and clenching her thighs.

He rocked forward, slowly brushing her core, and Fyia let out a frustrated moan. 'Don't tease me.'

He pinned her arms above her head, then kissed her neck as he slid inside her. She exhaled, rightness saturating her very being.

His lips slowly devoured her neck, sucking and licking, and Fyia luxuriated in the sensations, content to let him take the lead.

He kissed his way up her neck, along her ear, then skirted her hairline until his lips brushed her forehead, and a tingle of sensation cascaded back across her scalp. He released her arms, traced a single finger down her nose, and pressed it against her sensitive lips.

He watched her as he rocked his hips, then kissed her until she didn't know which way was up, pleasure spreading, web-like, across her body.

Fyia leaned back into the soft mattress and let herself sink under Cal's weight, languidly absorbing everything he gave. He moved slowly, and the slower he went, the tighter Fyia wound, her body amplifying every ounce of delicious friction.

'Don't stop,' she heard herself say, and Cal buried his head in her neck, his hips maintaining their perfect rhythm.

But then he did stop, and Fyia's muscles clenched around him, so close to release. 'Cal,' she whispered, clutching him, trying to move against him. He made tiny pulsing motions with his hips, hitting her just where she needed him, again and again. 'Gods ... yes ... Cal ...'

Convulsions wracked through her with such force, she was surprised her body held together, then Cal's fingers found her nipple, and she cried out as the waves intensified. Fyia was only vaguely aware of Cal groaning and stiffening above her, then their bodies pressed together as they both panted hard, Fyia still sensitive, clenching her legs around him to keep him inside her.

She fisted her hands in his hair, and he lifted his head, studying her, then kissing her deeply. A glow emanated from behind his ears, and Fyia's mouth split into a broad smile. 'It's happening again,' she said, tracing his hairline.

Cal pulled back and rolled her so he could see the single glowing scale at the base of Fyia's spine. He kissed her hip. 'Why?' he murmured against her skin.

Fyia shook her head. 'We could ask Cinis, but ...'

'Telling your newly acquired father that your scale glows after ...'

'Okay, thank you,' said Fyia, pulling him back down on top of her. She still didn't know how to feel about Cinis. How it changed everything ... and nothing at all. Her parents were still wicked, selfish people who cared little for anyone but themselves. She wondered how they were adjusting to life under the new Empress, whether they were already attempting to weasel their way into her good graces. If Adigos was counseling her wisely ...

'We're going to find the dragons, you know,' said Cal, pulling her back from her thoughts.

Fyia cocked an eyebrow. 'We're going to do more than that, my love. We're going to train them, and then we're going to reign over our untied, peaceful, prosperous kingdoms forevermore.'

'What if we're challenged?' he said, resting his head on her chest. 'Veau is also touched by fire, and there could be others.'

'Oh, don't stomp all over my freshly minted fantasy,' she said, tugging his hair. He nuzzled her with his stubble, and she wrapped her arms around him. 'We can worry about the practicalities tomorrow, but just for tonight, I'm content to dream.'

Chapter Ten

DAYS LATER, FYIA AWOKE TO shards of the rising sun cutting through the cabin. That, and Cal's fingers playing with the skin below her breast.

She hummed with contentment, embracing the feeling she knew would disappear the moment they left the bubble of their cabin, blocking all thoughts from her mind aside from Cal, the sun, and the warm, soft cocoon of their bed.

Part of her dreaded reaching the Dragon Temple, and she was glad of their circuitous route, Opie—their pilot—flat out refusing to take the airships overland, given the air currents they would meet. So they'd flown southeast, to the sea, and would soon head north, now on the other side of the canyon that concerned Opie. And Fyia and Cal had had precious time together.

Fyia's mind conjured an image of a dragon—her dragon—gleaming silver and gold in the rising sun, beating its wings with powerful strokes that kept it in line with the airship. Cal was kissing his way across her stomach, along her hip bone, and Fyia almost lost the dragon in her haze of pleasure, but then the scale on her back became warm, and shock focused her mind.

'Cal,' she said, twisting so he could see her back.

'It's glowing again,' he said, sliding a finger across her fire-touch. 'And it's hot.'

Her dragon forced its way back into her mind, and Fyia threw back the covers, rushing naked to the window.

'What is it?' said Cal, pulling on his breeches as he followed her.

'My dragon,' she said, searching through the glass, trying to catch a glimpse of a wingtip.

'*Your* dragon?'

'I just had another dragon dream, but this time, it was underneath the airship.'

'Warrior's tits,' said Cal, snatching up Fyia's clothes and helping her dress. 'We have to warn the crew.'

'It doesn't want to harm us. It feels … excited, happy … playful.'

'Playful,' said Cal, his voice dripping with disbelief.

'Wouldn't you want to play if you'd been locked up for hundreds of years?'

'I … well, *I* might, but I'm not sure you would.'

Fyia swiped him on the arm, then pulled on her boots before rushing to the door.

They raced up the stairs, then to the railing, tipping themselves as far over as they could. Fyia's wolves bounded to her side, and Fyia pulled back a little, scared they might accidentally tip her over.

'What are you doing?' said Edu, his tone laced with suspicion and concern.

'Looking for something,' said Fyia, practically shaking with excitement.

'Looking for …'

But before she could decide what to say, an enormous beast, its silver scales gleaming gold where the sun struck, swooped out from under the airship. 'For that!' Fyia shouted, clapping her hands and whooping with excitement. 'My dragon!'

'*Your* dragon?' said Edu.

'He found me,' said Fyia. 'I don't know how, but here he is, almost close enough to touch.'

'The dragon that tried to kill you in the dreams?' said Edu, casting a concerned look at Cal.

'That wasn't him,' said Fyia. 'That one had red scales, and the tips of his ears were wispier. My dragon would never hurt me.'

'Fyia,' said Cal, alarm edging his tone, 'we should be cautious. We know little about the dragons.'

'Do you think he would catch me if I leapt onto his back?'

Cal grabbed her hand, squeezing hard. 'I know you're excited—we all are—but you're not acting like yourself. You seem … drunk.'

'Do I?' said Fyia, Cal's words bringing her up short. She did feel a little strange, but that was surely just euphoria, the excitement at having finally found what was hers. The relief. The ability to prove once and for all that she wasn't crazy, or lost in legend, or whatever it was everyone said about her, to make themselves feel better.

'A dragon has chosen you,' said Cinis, from behind them.

Fyia tore her eyes away to look at him. 'How do we communicate?'

Cinis thought for a moment, as though working hard to dredge up a distant memory from the depths of his mind. 'I never had a dragon, obviously, but if I correctly recall, some could silently command their dragons, while others used words or movements. There is no standard method; you must work it out between you.'

Fyia tentatively reached out with her mind, as she would with her Cruaxee, and her dragon twisted its head sharply towards her.

'Fyia …' said Edu, her name a warning. They were leagues in the air, and if her dragon attacked, they would all die. But she couldn't wait, and her dragon wouldn't hurt them.

She reached out again, but only brushed lightly against the impression of her dragon's mind, halting when she felt the barest hint of his consciousness. *It's okay*, she said silently, reassuring and coaxing. *I'm just happy to meet you, that we can finally be together.*

Her dragon pressed back against her mind with such ferocious joy that Fyia staggered back a pace. Edu and Cal grabbed her arms, their disquiet barely registering as a child-like laugh broke from her lips.

Exactly, she said to her dragon. *That's how I feel too.*

'Airship ahead!' shouted a member of the crew, and Fyia reluctantly turned away as the deck became a frenzy of moving bodies.

'It's Essa!' called Edu, pulling the telescope from his eye. 'Opie! It's Essa! Can we come alongside?'

Opie appeared beside them. 'It can be done,' he said, 'although it is not without risk. A single finickity air current could smash us together. Or …' he cast a sideways glance at the dragon, 'a single beat of that thing's wings.'

'I'll tell him to keep his distance,' said Fyia. Airships would be new for the dragons, but she was sure she could convey the message.

'Dragon!' screamed someone in the bow. 'Another one!'

Fyia's stomach plummeted, and she felt once more for her dragon. He didn't seem concerned, even though he must have registered the other beast.

'It's friendly!' Fyia shouted back. 'Everyone, stay calm. No hostility!' And then a second airship emerged from the clouds behind the second dragon, and Fyia gripped the handrail so hard her knuckles hurt.

'That airship is flying the High Commander's flag!' shouted Edu.

'Sensis,' breathed Fyia, a different kind of excitement swelling in her chest. The promise of her friend's capable, level presence was buoying. She turned to Opie. 'Raft us up, my dear pilot.'

'My Queen,' said Opie, with an incline of his head. But although he accepted her order, tension filled his shoulders as it never had before.

Fyia wondered for a tick if she should give the order to land instead, but they were skirting the coast of the Kraken Sea. She could see nowhere obvious to set down four airships, and Fyia was ever impatient.

It seemed to take hundreds of spins before they were close enough to even shout to each other, and then another thousand or so for them to come alongside. The two dragons circled one another, wary but not hostile, the new dragon about the same size as Fyia's, only a little smaller than the airships.

Fyia kept a careful eye on the dragons, sending soothing thoughts to hers as the ships inched closer and closer together. They seemed content enough to circle, riding the currents, and Fyia wondered how long it would take for them to tire. Would they ever tire?

Essa's crew flung ropes to Fyia's, Rouel—a member of Fyia's own personal guard—among them. He threw an irresistible grin first at Fyia, then at Edu.

'Rouel!' said Fyia. 'It's good to see you.'

'And you, Your Majesty,' he said, with a bow. 'When you left without me, I jumped aboard Essa's ship, seeking adventure.'

'Did you find it?'

'Do you not see the dragons?' he replied with a laugh. 'They said you couldn't do it, but I always knew you could.'

Fyia beamed as she turned in search of Essa, a myriad of emotions warring for space in her chest. But before she found her old friend, her eyes settled on another, one with a streak of shining gold across his face.

'Brother!' she cried, rushing to the side, where the crew were hastily constructing buoys from anything they could find.

Veau grinned. 'My Queen,' he said, bowing, then reaching out to take her hand across the narrow space.

'What are you doing here?' Fyia's eyes flicked to where Essa hovered nearby, watching their reunion. 'What about your magic?'

A big, dark-skinned fae dropped out of the rigging above Veau's head, scooped Veau into his arms, as though he weighed nothing at all, then flew him over the gap between the ships.

'This is Gabriel,' said Veau.

'And I am Storm,' said a short, blonde woman from behind Fyia. How had she got there? She had no wings …

They both bowed to Fyia, who nodded her head in acknowledgement.

'This may sound strange,' said Veau, 'but Gabriel is my father. He taught me to control my magic.'

Fyia pulled Veau into an embrace, tears threatening to flood free. After many ticks, she finally pulled back, but refused to release him, holding his arm as she said, 'This is Cal, and that's Cinis.' She pointed to where Cinis stood by the railing, tracking the dragons as they soared. 'Turns out he's my father, so it doesn't sound strange at all.'

Veau's mouth fell open. 'It seems there is much about our parents we do not know.'

'And much they kept from us,' she replied, as Veau and Cal grasped forearms in greeting.

'I hear you're betrothed to my sister,' said Veau.

Cal nodded. 'It is nice to meet you. Fyia has told me much about you.'

'Sounds ominous.'

'Tell me,' said Fyia, 'why did you leave the mountain?'

'It is a long story, but in essence, because the Children of the Lake attacked us.'

'And they did that, because you released those,' said Storm, nodding to the dragons.

Fyia frowned as she tried to keep up. 'I don't follow.'

But before any of them could reply, Sensis vaulted the railings and strode to Fyia's side. 'Your Majesty,' she said with a bow. They hugged, Fyia's grin so wide it hurt her face. This day was better than any she'd had in ... she didn't know how long. Not only was her brother back at her side, but her High Commander, her inventor, and they'd brought two powerful, magical beings. The Gods—all of them—must be smiling down upon her, but when she and Sensis pulled apart, another man was in her eyeline, and Fyia's stomach sank.

'Your Majesty,' said Lord Sollow Antice, bowing low.

They feasted on fresh fish caught by Gabriel as they floated slowly through the air, heading north, for the territory of the Black Hoods. Rouel strummed his lute in the background, and Fyia could have believed they were years in the past, if it hadn't been for Cal by her side, and the dragon pressing against her mind.

Fyia and Cal told the others all they had learned. About the first people to inhabit the kingdoms, how the fire-touched had created dragons and thawed the land, and how those without the fire-touch had used their magic to create new creatures.

They told them of Asesh. How she had hated the fire-touched, and had brought them to their knees. How she had lied, so Fyia and Cal would restart the magma ducts and free the trapped dragons, and how they were heading north, because that was their best hope of training the ancient beasts.

'And this mineral,' said Antice. 'Dragonsprite? It can be used to tame the dragons?'

Cinis scowled. 'You cannot *tame* a dragon. But you can use Dragonsprite to build a relationship. To show them you will reward them for their help, and to exert control, in the rare cases where that is required.'

'But I already have a relationship with my dragon,' said Antice. 'She understands what I want, and she wants to do my bidding.'

It had been a shock to discover Antice was fire-touched, although Fyia couldn't decide if it was more or less of a shock than the covert glances he and Sensis kept firing at each other. Last Fyia had checked, Sensis hated his guts …

Cinis scoffed. 'You have known your dragon for a blink of an eye. She is pleased to have found one such as you, but do not mistake her eagerness to bond as anything other than that. She may understand your wants, and she may choose to obey them, but she could just as easily disregard your wishes, especially if they run counter to her own. She could eat the one you love, or tear up your crops, or enter a fight you wish her not to.'

Antice cast another glance at Sensis, and Fyia stifled a smile. 'So we use Dragonsprite?' said Antice. 'They desire that enough to bend to our will, regardless of their own desires?'

Cinis screwed his face into a ball. 'That isn't how I would describe it,' he said. 'And your dragon may not appreciate that sentiment, either.'

Tense silence gripped them for a moment, then Cinis sucked in a long breath. 'Come,' he said, 'I will show you.'

They all trooped up on deck, to the railing beside where the dragons flew.

'Ask your dragons to fly higher,' Cinis said to Fyia and Antice.

Antice spoke out loud to his dragon, his cheeks flushing a little as all eyes turned to him, while Fyia commanded her dragon silently. Both beasts turned their heads to look at the humans, then lifted a little higher in the sky.

'Good,' said Cinis. 'Now, ask them to fly down under the airships, then up over the top, and return to their current positions.'

Fyia tried, but this time, her dragon just looked at her as though he didn't understand. Antice's dragon dropped beneath the airship, and a punch of jealousy hit Fyia's stomach. But Antice's dragon didn't return, much to Fyia's relief.

'You see?' said Cinis. 'They are stubborn, willful creatures, not unlike petulant children. Your wishes mean little to them. The Dragonsprite gives them reason to obey, but you must use it sparingly, only as a last resort, for if they come to expect it every time you give a command, the whole system will crumble.'

'Because of the Dragonsprite in the clocks?' said Fyia.

'Yes,' said Cinis. 'They must be motivated to go to the clocks, but also, it is a drug to them. Too much, and they will fall into a frenzy, caring only for Dragonsprite.'

'The same happens with the Children of the Lake,' said Storm, 'when they consume too much magic.'

'You should warn your dragons not to follow the magma ducts to the Fae'ch mountain,' said Cinis. 'For if they use that clock, they may not return.'

The thought of losing her dragon so soon after finding him made Fyia shudder. She sent a message to her dragon, imagining the clock under the mountain, showing her dragon that image, then throwing every unpleasant emotion she could through their new bond. She wasn't sure he understood entirely, but she would repeat the message many times, and hopefully, it would stick.

They settled back into their seats in the dining room, and Fyia stroked her wolves, glad of their heat after the frigid air outside. She watched the others as they settled, Essa and Veau dancing around one another, never touching, but always close. Antice and Sensis were still pretending there was nothing between them, but they, too, sat side by side, and Fyia was almost certain their legs were pressed together under the table. Not to mention Rouel, whose eyes had barely left Edu since the moment he'd jumped aboard.

'Messages from your eagles,' said a guard. 'Two of them, although they dropped and fled, on account of the dragons.'

Fyia didn't blame them. She wasn't sure how appealing a giant eagle was to a dragon, but if she were them, she wouldn't hang around to find out either.

Cal slid his hand to Fyia's leg under the table as she opened the scrolls, the first from Starfall, and the second from the Temple of the Sea Serpent.

'A dragon came out of the clock in Selise,' said Fyia, reading the scroll from Starfall. 'It killed several of my subjects before snatching a ball from the clock and flying away. All open dissent across the Five Kingdoms has ceased, and Lady Lyr, of the Starlight Kingdom, has specifically asked Starfall to congratulate me on the return of the dragons.'

Most of those around the table laughed, knowing as they did of Lady Lyr's loud objections to anything magical. How quickly her tune had changed.

'Lady Lyr has also welcomed the magic-folk fleeing the Fae'ch Mountain. A large group recently entered the Starlight Kingdom, and she plans to integrate them into society.'

It was unbelievable, and yet hardly a surprise at all. This was why Fyia hated politics.

'The Kingdom of Moon would also like to congratulate you,' said Antice, holding up his glass in salute. 'We are thrilled to see the dragons returned.'

'So long as you're not here with plans to stage a coup, Lord Antice, I thank you. Although, it seems not every kingdom writes with the same sentiment,' she said, scanning the scroll from the Temple of the Sea Serpent. 'The recently appointed High Priestess Elowyn sends grave news. The hole where their dragon clock once stood is spewing magma. Fire has consumed much of the village. Many have died, and there is no sign of it slowing.'

'I tried to find a way to fix it,' said Essa. 'That's why I went to the Fae'ch, seeking help. I asked Isa if we could use the taps outside the mountain to shut off the flow around the system, but she implied we could not, then threw me out.'

'Can you help?' Fyia asked Gabriel and Storm.

All eyes turned to the couple, and Storm shrugged. 'We did not construct the system. We are not that old.'

'Nor did we help maintain it,' said Gabriel. 'But there are long-lives who could help, if we can find them.'

'If they escaped,' said Storm, darkly.

Fyia wasn't sure what to make of the couple. They had helped her brother, and from what she could glean, had suffered greatly at Isa's hands, but that didn't mean she could trust them. 'And in return?'

'Nothing, aside from what you have already promised,' said Storm. 'We want to return to the land we called home before the Five Kingdoms outlawed magic.'

'The Kingdom of Sea Serpents,' said Gabriel. 'We lived by the water, and would be content to do so again, without fear of persecution.'

'Then we gladly accept your help,' said Fyia. 'And the sooner we can repair those clocks that need it, the more lives we will save.'

Sensis, Edu, and Fyia were the only three left in the dining room, the others having gone to bed two turns before, and Sensis had finally run out of ways to deflect the questions about Antice.

'So ...' said Fyia, turning expectant eyes on her.

'Bedtime, I think,' said Sensis, and although she didn't want to leave her friends, who she'd missed dearly, a new pull tugged at her, one that led to the cabin of her own ship.

'Did you ask him to warm your bed?' said Fyia.

Sensis scowled.

'I wouldn't blame you,' Fyia continued. 'It's cold up here.'

'Maybe Rouel is warming Edu's bed,' said Sensis, in an ill-advised attempt to throw her Queen off the scent.

Edu, who was unusually sullen, put down his beer and leaned forward. *Warrior's balls*; she should have left him out of it.

'Nothing inappropriate has ever happened between Rouel and I,' said Edu, 'but I'm not sure you can say the same about yourself and a certain former prince?'

Fyia laughed, delighted her comrade had joined the sortie, and Sensis felt her cheeks flush.

'Redheads turn the most delightful color when they're embarrassed,' Fyia said to Edu.

'And she wouldn't get embarrassed without reason,' said Edu.

'Urgh ... you two are impossible,' said Sensis, downing her drink. 'He's ... not the person I thought he was.'

'You trust him?' said Fyia, turning suddenly serious.

'Yes,' said Sensis, surprised at how easily the word came to her lips. 'He had to hide who he is, the same as we did.'

'Do you think he'll challenge me?' said Fyia. She didn't seem worried about the prospect, only curious.

'If he disagrees with your plans, it's possible, but I think you and he are more aligned than you'd expect.'

Fyia didn't ask the next question—where Sensis' loyalty lay—but it rang in her ears as she returned to her airship, where Antice waited.

They'd spent every night together since they'd kissed, although they'd done little more than kiss since. It was nice, in a way, to be forced to take it slow. She'd never done that before ... had never been in one place long enough, or found anyone she wanted to get to know.

Antice was still awake when she entered the cabin, staring out of the window at his dragon. 'No matter how hard I try, I can't get her to hear my thoughts as Fyia does,' he said the moment the door clicked shut.

'Fyia has a Cruaxee,' said Sensis. 'She communicates with her wolves and eagles the same way.'

'I guess,' said Antice, reluctantly. 'I wish I could communicate with my dragon without words.'

'Why?'

'Because then I'd always have the element of surprise.'

'If you're riding her, no one will be able to hear your words.'

Antice paled.

'Fyia will be on her dragon the second she gets a chance,' said Sensis.

'With no thought spared for the impact on her people if she dies.'

'You wouldn't have a dragon if Fyia wasn't as she is,' said Sensis, hotly.

Antice took a deep, tired breath. 'I know. Maybe I'm just jealous; part of me wants to be that way, but …'

'It's not your nature,' said Sensis, sitting on the bed and pulling off her boots. 'It would be a disaster if we were all like Fyia. She is no more or less valuable because of her willingness to take risks. Everyone has their own part to play.'

'That's easy to say, as High Commander of the Armies of the Five Kingdoms,' said Antice. 'I haven't yet found my role.'

'You are Warden of the Kingdom of Moon,' said Sensis, with a scowl. 'You have a seat at the Small Council's table. You have wealth, and connections, and grew up a prince.'

Antice joined her on the bed. 'I don't mean it that way. I know I have more than most ever dream of.'

'Then what?' she said, sternly. 'What do you want?'

'I want to fill my time with something I love,' he said, 'but I don't yet know what that is. Not like you ...'

'Then explore,' said Sensis, 'and stop complaining. Or step aside and give your position to someone who will use it wisely, someone who has had to fight for everything they own, who would appreciate the opportunities at your feet.'

'Sensis ... I ...' He tried to take her hand, but she stood and moved away.

He had no idea what she'd been through to become High Commander of Fyia's armies. How she'd fought tooth and nail, even as a child, just to learn the skills she needed. How her family had shunned and belittled her. How the whole Gods-damned Kingdom of Moon had laughed at her, made lewd jokes, and called her mad.

'Sleep in your own cabin tonight,' she said, her back still turned.

Fabric rustled as Antice got to his feet. 'Sensis ...'

'It's been a long day, and I've learned to rest when I can when Fyia's around; you never quite know what she'll do next.'

'I ... I'm ... did I touch some nerve?'

Sensis saw red. Had he *touched some nerve*? He didn't even realize how that question belittled her. Did he really expect her to sympathize because his life wasn't perfect, when many in his kingdom could barely put food on their family's table?

'I'm sorry if my life seemed easier than yours, but it has never been easy ...'

Sensis whirled towards him. 'The poor little *prince*?' she spat. 'And yet it was never bad enough for you to *do* anything. How have you fought for change?

'You could have found purpose in any number of pursuits, but when did you try? What have you done in your whole life that is of any note at all? That benefits anyone but yourself, or the high society of Moon?'

'That's not fair.'

'Leave,' said Sensis, then turned away once more.

'We should talk about this. I don't understand ...'

'I asked nicely. Do not make me ask again.'

Antice let out an exasperated growl, and his dragon screeched. 'Fine, I'm going, but I don't even begin to understand what just happened. If you could find it within yourself to explain—at your earliest convenience—I would be much obliged.'

Fyia awoke early the following morning, slipping out of the cabin before Cal awoke, and heading up on deck. Her wolves followed her to the bow, where she looked for her dragon, calling to him with her mind. She was tempted to ride him, but it was too dangerous, even for her. To fall from this height would mean death, and there were no eagles around to save her; they were all too afraid of the dragons.

'Good morning, Your Majesty,' said a voice from the next-door airship, her words faint, the wind whipping them away.

'Good morning, Essa,' said Fyia. Her friend's formal address was both appropriate and irritating. When Sensis or Edu used her title, they did it out of respect, but underneath the formality was a bond of friendship that had withstood the test of time. It had once been like that with Essa, until she and Veau had lied to her. Sure, they'd been trying to help, but still ...

'We should build a new system,' said Essa, neglecting small talk in her usual way.

'A new system?'

'To replace the magma ducts. There has to be a better way; a safer way.'

'Maybe,' said Fyia, pondering the idea—the enormity, or maybe audacity of it, 'although we have several other hurdles to jump first.'

'It suddenly makes sense though …'

Fyia waited patiently for her to continue, well acquainted with Essa's seemingly erratic ways.

'Towns in illogical places that once were prosperous, but have fallen to ruin, because they no longer have a use. But they are important to the ducts. We should look into that … seek to understand. They are placed at joins in the system. I think they have taps …'

'Essa, I can't say I'm following,' said Fyia, but Antice distracted them as he jumped the railing onto Essa's ship.

'Good morning, Your Majesty,' said Antice, bowing low.

'Lord Antice,' said Fyia, with a brief nod.

'Are you going to ride your dragon?' he asked, as though the question had been burning a hole in his throat.

Fyia gave him an incredulous look at his abrupt tone. 'I should think so, as long as he seems amenable to the idea.'

'Have you asked him yet?'

'Asked him?'

'If he's amenable?'

'How would I do that?'

Antice frowned. 'Mind to mind … how you communicate with your Cruaxee.'

Fyia paused, thinking through her reply, because it occurred to her that Antice could be mining for information. 'It is not that simple,' she said. 'That is not how a Cruaxee bond works, and my connection with my dragon is even less straightforward.'

'How so?'

'Why do you care?'

Antice ran a hand through his short, curly hair, looking suddenly sheepish. It was shocking; the Antice Fyia knew never looked anything but poised and polished.

'Because right now we're the only two people in the known world with dragons,' said Antice.

'Assuming the other dragons haven't found ...'

'Yes, of course, but we're the only two *here*, and I thought ... well, I thought maybe we could work together; compare notes.'

Fyia watched him for several beats, then averted her gaze, noticing that at some point Essa had slipped away. Fyia couldn't take Antice's offer at face value. She'd snatched his birthright when she'd killed his father, the former King of Moon, and all intelligence suggested Antice, and his late uncle, Lord Venir, had plotted against Fyia and supported the rebel cause.

But Sensis trusted him, and Sensis trusted no one. Was she blinded by her feelings for him? He was tall and handsome, and represented the pinnacle of everything Sensis had known as a child, so Fyia couldn't discount the possibility. But Sensis had learned many hard lessons in her life, and she would have been suspicious of Antice, too. He'd done something to win her trust, which was the only reason Fyia didn't dismiss his request outright.

'I will think on it, certainly,' said Fyia.

Antice hesitated for a tick, looking as though he might say more, but then he gave a curt nod. 'Of course, Your Majesty. I will await your decision.'

His deferential response was a surprise, and there was no sarcasm, nor hint of contempt. Maybe he'd hidden those feelings deep down, so they festered inside him, but if so, he was an accomplished actor, and despite herself, Fyia found she wanted to believe he was sincere.

Chapter Eleven

Queen Scorpia sat in the bow of her ship, under a canopy designed to keep the worst of the sun at bay. She'd never been this far north, and she wished the structure's sides were solid, for the air was icy, cold seeping into her bones.

'More tea,' she barked, pulling her cloak more firmly around her.

She could retreat inside, of course, but she disliked the damn rocking, and could not abide being sick in front of her crew. Not to mention, she felt something in the air ... some shift afoot, and she scanned every inch of land that had finally come into view.

'We'll dock by lunchtime,' said the captain, coming to stand beside her chair.

'Good,' said Scorpia, relieved it was almost over ... she needed a flying ship, like Queen Fyia.

They would alight in a small fishing village with a deep-water dock, close to where the Fae'ch Mountains met the sea. Neither Scorpia, nor any of her crew had been here before, so they knew not what awaited.

'It's still not too late to change course, my Queen,' said the captain.

'Where is it you think I should go?' she said, cocking an eyebrow, a move she'd perfected over her long life.

'Home, Your Majesty,' the captain mumbled. 'Leave the northerners to their foolish wars. Something's not right ... I can feel it.'

His words finally caught Scorpia's interest. 'Explain.'

The captain shook his head. 'It's hard to put into words, but ... a presence tracks us. Like something doesn't want us to reach land. It comes close, and then scurries away, as though waiting ... or building confidence.'

'Or maybe there is no danger, and it scurries away because it is scared.'

'It's not,' he said firmly. 'I can't say how I know, but I do. In my bones.'

'We are committed already,' said Scorpia, with a wave of her hand. She would not abandon her birthright, especially not now she was so close. 'What will be will be, and we will stay the course.' She pointed to the small cluster of houses perched above the sea.

The captain bowed his head. 'I thought you'd say that, but for the sake of all aboard, I had to try.'

'What do you mean by that?' she snapped. Few dared to criticize her so openly, and his tone was laced with hopelessness, or ... despair.

The captain closed his eyes. 'It comes,' he said. 'You cannot feel it?'

'Feel what?' said Scorpia, clutching the arms of her chair. She strained her senses, willing them to detect the threat, but other than the general strangeness in the air, she found nothing.

'It is too fast. Much too fast. We will not make it.'

Scorpia's heart thudded wildly. 'What comes?' she demanded. 'Tell me!'

The captain looked out to sea. 'That,' he said.

Alba and Leo flew in silence, Alba fuming she had to be so close to him at a moment like this. Leo had decided they should return to Queen Fyia, rather than seek their own people, and Alba wanted to beat her fists against his damned delectable chest in rage.

They'd returned to the Fae'ch Mountains, intending to report all they'd learned to their leader, but had found the place deserted, the portcullis firmly closed, and a message carved into the stone saying: *To enter is to die.*

Alba wanted to find her uncle, Pips, to ensure he had made it out alive. The uncertainty gnawed at her. 'Don't you care about your parents, or your brother?' Alba said with a huff, as though she hadn't used the same argument ten times already.

Leo tipped his head to meet her eyes as his magnificent wings took another powerful stroke. 'They either made it out, or they did not. Nothing we can do will change that. But our mission has not altered; we are still tasked with gathering intelligence on the Queen.'

Why did he have to be so level-headed? So loyal to their leader, even outside the mountain, where they were free to disobey her at will? And so Gods-damned attractive? It made it very hard to hate him.

'What if Isa's dead?' said Alba, immediately wishing she hadn't.

Leo's features turned dark. 'My mother is nothing if not a fighter,' he said, then looked away, towards the sea.

They'd skirted around the mountains before heading back to the Temple of the Warrior, so they could scan for their people a little—Leo's only concession. But now they'd hit the sea, and caught sight of not one Fae'ch.

'Queen Fyia might not be there any longer,' said Alba. 'It took us days to fly back to the mountain. She could be anywhere by now.'

Leo didn't answer. They'd been over this countless times already, and Leo never budged. Of course, she *could* get him to set her down, so they could go their separate ways, but that wasn't what Alba wanted, and he would probably refuse to leave her, which would be painful for them both.

Alba returned to scanning the land for any sign of their kind, but the sea kept drawing her gaze. The water called to her—she was a water rider, after all—and a ship bobbed a few leagues out, heading to shore.

She wondered who they were, their mission, and if they knew the whole world might be going to shit at this very moment. The ship flew a flag that looked important, and Alba longed to get closer, to find out who it was.

Then whatever impulse pulled her gaze towards the boat shifted into something darker, something familiar and yet not. It reminded her of the monsters that hid in the depths of the lake under the mountain, but more sinister, its intention more powerfully honed.

'Leo …' she said. His arms tensed at her tone. 'Can you feel that?'

'Feel what?' he said, meeting her eyes briefly before scanning for danger.

'In the water … something big, something …' But before she could put the feeling into words, an enormous monster lifted out of the sea, its head that of a snake, its fangs bared, and with tentacles flicking out behind it as it dove beneath the water once more.

'Is that a kraken?' said Alba.

'*By the Goddess*,' Leo breathed.

'It's going for the ship. We have to help them.'

'That is not our mission,' said Leo, although his words were hesitant.

'What if the people it carries are important?' she said. 'And even if they're not, are you really content to stand by and watch them die?'

'But what can we do?' he said. 'I could carry perhaps one other, but that's all.'

Leo altered his course, heading for the ship, and Alba paled. He was right. What could they do? 'One person is better than none,' she said, her mind frantically seeking a better solution. 'Fly faster, or it will be too late.'

Leo shook his head, but he flapped his wings harder, Alba finally grateful for the long hours of flying their assignment had forced them to endure. Leo's muscles had filled out after a lifetime stuck under the mountain. He'd found tricks to help conserve energy, and could fly almost a full day without a break, if he really had to.

So Alba didn't doubt Leo could carry at least one other, but that wasn't enough. The ship's entire crew would die if they couldn't think of *something*.

They got closer and closer, and the kraken raised its head twice more. Each time, Alba could make out more detail, and each time, the beast became more terrifying. It was almost upon the ship now, and Leo's flaps became wild, sweat beading on his brow as he strained for every last ounce of power.

But it made no difference, for they would be too late. They were still leagues away when the kraken lifted itself from the water, then slammed two of its enormous tentacles onto the deck.

The ship listed dangerously as the kraken began to pull itself aboard, and Alba caught sight of an old woman in the bow, dressed in bright pinks and greens, and clutching at the rail. The kraken was midship, and it raised its serpentine head, lunging forward to grab a member of the crew.

As the kraken crunched its victim, a tingling sensation filled Alba's arm, shooting to her fingers, and she impulsively reached for the magical tether in her pocket. Her fingers flexed around the plated rockhopper silk, and she pulled it out, then brandished it in front of Leo's face.

'Drop me on the kraken,' she said, waving her hand.

Leo checked his speed. 'You can't be serious,' he said, gripping her more tightly. 'You'll ... die.'

'I won't,' she insisted. 'Look at its head; it's just the same as every other serpent I've ever ridden.'

'None of those had tentacles, and with them, you knew what to expect. What if the kraken ignores your magic?'

'It won't,' she said. 'Pips told me the magic of the water riders works on any creature that dwells beneath.'

'A kraken can live above or below. Maybe it's not the same for them.'

'It will work,' she said. 'I can feel it.' They were above the boat now, and the kraken was crunching crew member after crew member, inching further aboard with each death. 'Now, Leo. It must be in the water.'

'Alba ...'

'I am not asking your permission,' she said, with authority she hadn't known herself capable of. 'Do it now, or all aboard that boat will die.'

Leo closed his eyes for a beat, then flew over the kraken. 'I love you,' he said. He kissed her temple, then dropped her from his arms.

Alba whipped the tether forward as she fell, her feet landing on the kraken's scaled back as the tether hooked over its head. Its mouth was open, so the silk caught on its teeth, and Alba prayed to every god that it would hold.

Alba yanked the tether tight, and the kraken reared back so violently, Alba released the tension, scared it would fall over backwards and land atop her.

The kraken righted itself, and Alba pulled again, although this time more gently. Its tentacles relaxed, and it slid from the ship. Alba risked a glance up at the crew, who stood slack-mouthed, features filled with awe, looking at her as though she were a gift from the Gods.

She couldn't help but grin, but the kraken sensed her distraction and bucked beneath her, thrashing its tentacles to push itself up out of the water, drenching her, the barrage almost knocking her off her feet.

Alba yanked hard on the tether, and the kraken calmed its movements, although it didn't cease them entirely, which meant Alba still didn't have total control. She tugged as hard as she could, the plated silk cutting into her palm, and finally the kraken stilled.

Alba took a moment to consider her next move, because she hadn't had time to form a plan. Should she swim the kraken out to sea? Or force it to circle? Or stay where she was until the ship made it into dock? She pondered her options, and decided to stay put for as long as she could, because that seemed least likely to go wrong.

It would take a while—at least a turn of the clock—but she was reasonably sure she could keep the connection for that long. Not that she'd ever tried, but she was managing it for the moment.

Leo's shadow danced across the water beside her, the sun making the sea glisten with golden light, the sea calm, only a gentle swell bobbing them up and down. Had it not been for the kraken under Alba's feet, she could have enjoyed the moment, beautiful as it was.

The time passed quickly, the sound of water lapping against the kraken soothing and serene, the ship finally approaching the tiny village where it would dock. A swell of pride rose in Alba's chest that they had saved an entire ship full of people when they could have flown by. Curiosity replaced the emotion, and excitement, for surely Leo would want to discover who the ship carried now. But halfway through wondering who the old woman in the bow could have been, the sea became suddenly turbulent, and Alba's magic alerted her to danger of the most extreme kind. 'Leo!' she screamed, panic flooding her.

Leo dove for her, lifting her to safety only moments before the tentacle of a second kraken appeared out of the water. And then three more krakens raised their heads, their eyes locking on Leo and Alba, who hovered out of reach.

'We have to warn the ship,' said Alba.

Leo was already moving, beating his wings hard once more. But he was no match for the krakens, which slid through the water with breathtaking speed, and Leo was tired from his earlier exertion.

Alba willed him to move faster, but she knew it was hopeless; they would never reach the ship in time.

'Can you warn them with your magic?' said Alba. Her own magic applied exclusively to the water, but Leo was fae, and had magic that far exceeded her own. Maybe he could send a message …

'I ... no,' he said, his forehead scrunched in thought. 'I can't think of a way.'

But it didn't matter, for now the ship had seen the threat, the krakens approaching with their heads above the surface, five of them in a chilling line. The crew pointed and screamed, and some even threw themselves overboard before the beasts could reach them, for it was an absolute certainty every soul aboard that ship would die.

But as they grew nearer, Alba spotted the old woman, still in the ship's bow, her face turned not towards the krakens, but upwards, to the sky. Was she praying to the Gods and Goddesses, asking them for help? Or begging for safe passage to the afterlife, hoping to avoid any of the Seven Hells?

Tears welled in Alba's eyes. They could have saved her. Or if not her, one of the crew. She should have made the kraken follow the ship to shore.

A high-pitched whine sounded overhead, and Alba's eyes snapped up to the clouds. It was loud, whatever it was, but few birds of any large size usually ventured out to sea. It called again, and Alba changed her mind; it didn't sound like any bird she'd ever come across. The sound was a screech, then a scream, and then a roar.

And as the roar vibrated through her bones, Alba caught sight of the mighty beast as it dropped through the clouds, hurtling towards the sea with its wings tucked tight to its sides.

'*Goddess*,' said Leo, at the same moment Alba said, '*Warrior's tits.*'

The dragon dive-bombed a kraken, throwing a torrent of fire down upon it before smashing it beneath the surface with its claws. The dragon disappeared a moment, then broke free of the water, launching into the sky with elegant beats of its red and gold wings.

Leo stopped moving, hovering in the air a safe distance from the action.

'Fyia did it,' said Alba, a disbelieving laugh breaking through her lips. 'She returned the dragons!'

'There are too many krakens,' said Leo, his eyes glued to the beasts. 'It can't kill them all in time.'

He was right. The krakens were almost upon the ship, and although they tracked the dragon with wary eyes, they didn't slow. And the dragon seemed to have lost interest in the krakens, instead flying to where the old woman waited.

The dragon set its talons on the bow, and the ship listed dangerously under the weight, but then two krakens climbed aboard, and a terrible creaking filled the air as the ship began to split in two.

The old woman didn't hesitate, moving so quickly, Alba almost missed her scaling the dragon's leg, as though born to do it. As soon as she'd hoisted herself onto the dragon's back, the beast took to the air, moments before a kraken launched itself onto the bow.

The ship splintered, the four remaining krakens tearing it apart, the crew thrown about like rag dolls.

The dragon screamed once again, and attacked the krakens with fire, but even as the krakens shied back, Alba knew it was too late, the ship already half under. The dragon circled, bringing the old woman close enough to see her features, and Alba gasped.

The wind whipped the woman's grey hair back, her clothes—a riot of green and pink—flooded out behind her, and across her face was painted a picture of intense, wondrous, victorious delight.

The airships decoupled as they approached Anvarn. Cal wanted to see his people, to reassure them, and Fyia wanted to check the assistance she'd promised, to help the Black Hoods grow crops in heated glasshouses, had arrived. But as they floated above the town, they found no signs of life. Not a soul, no footprints in the snow, no smoke …

Cal was tense as he stood at the railing beside Fyia, and her wolves whined at her feet. 'Do you think they're hiding?' said Fyia, although it made little sense if they were; the Black Hoods hadn't hidden the first time an airship had landed in Anvarn.

'They're not here,' he said. His eyes swept the ground, seemingly searching for something specific. 'They haven't been here for days. We should continue to the temple.'

Fyia slipped her hand through his arm and squeezed tight. 'There's no sign of a struggle,' she said in a low voice. 'Everything is in its place, and nothing is damaged. If they left, they did so of their own accord.'

'I agree,' said Cal, 'but that doesn't explain why they left.'

'We'll find them.'

Fyia didn't stop him as he pulled away, heading back inside. Fyia's wolves whined again, and she petted them, then told Opie to change course. Part of her was relieved they would reach the Temple of the Dragon sooner. Her dragon had disappeared—Antice's too— and she hoped they weren't hunting the Black Hoods, that that wasn't the reason Cal's people had left Anvarn. The sooner they learned how to control the beasts, the better.

She scanned the horizon, then the ground, switching back and forth, searching for both the dragons and signs of human life. She found neither, until the Temple of the Dragon finally came into sight, and Fyia's breath caught in her throat.

The ground around the temple was thawing, water dripping off the great sheet of ice that blocked the entrance, and an enormous, oval depression had appeared in the ground behind the temple. 'Gods,' said Fyia, trying to take it all in. And then the people came out of the trees, waving up at the sky as they spotted the airships.

'Cal!' Fyia screamed, racing for the door. 'Cal! They're here!' But before she could make it inside, a bone-chilling screech sounded overhead, and Fyia's magic reacted, flinging her to the ground. A deafening crunch split the air, and Fyia threw her hands over her head as splinters of wood exploded around her, the railing, and half of the central cabin, ripped apart by deadly talons.

The rain of wood ceased, and Fyia jumped to her feet, screaming, 'Down!' at Opie. 'Set the airship down!'

Fyia searched for the threat as she scanned for her dragon once more, using her mind as she would when finding her Cruaxee, but it was useless; she got no sense of him at all.

Cal pushed through the wreckage, as did Edu, reaching her as their attacker dropped through the clouds to show itself. It was the first proper look Fyia had got at the dragon, this one red and gold, and … Gods … a woman in robes of green and pink sat atop the beast, her head thrown back in laughter as she plummeted towards them.

'Queen Scorpia!' said Edu, pulling Fyia back below the rigging, where it would be harder for the dragon to snatch Fyia from the ship.

A pang of jealousy hit her, even as she feared for her life. Scorpia was the first to ride a dragon, and it looked glorious.

'Scorpia!' Fyia screamed, as the dragon came close, circling the airship, looking for an opening. 'What are you doing?'

The dragon went round again. 'Riding my dragon!' Scorpia shouted back, laughing as though she'd chewed one too many imp-cap mushrooms.

'Why are you attacking us?'

'It's not me! Ask my dragon!'

'Shit,' said Fyia. 'She doesn't have control.'

The airship was slowly sinking through the sky, but not nearly fast enough, the dragon seeming more and more frustrated with every passing turn. It slowed, then lurched at Fyia with its head, but Fyia moved before it could grab her, sending a silent prayer of thanks to whichever god had given her magic.

The dragon retreated, Scorpia finally addressing it in a soothing voice, putting some effort into convincing it to cease its attack.

'Fyia,' said Cal, from just behind her. The excitement in his voice was strange, given the high chance they were all about to die. 'My scales are hot. I think they're glowing!'

And before he'd even finished the words, a mighty roar split the air, and a ferocious dragon of green and gold punched through the clouds, heading for Scorpia.

Elation bubbled in Fyia's chest, but alongside it was a deeper kind of fear, because although the red dragon was terrifying, it hadn't attacked them in earnest. If it had wanted to, it could have punctured their sails then chased them to the ground, but it hadn't. The green dragon—Cal's dragon, she supposed—had the feel of a sledgehammer. It wasn't playing as it hurtled towards the other. It meant business, and the dragons were close enough for the airships to get caught in the crossfire.

But what could she do? They were descending as fast as they could, and short of jumping overboard—which would mean certain death—she could only watch as the green dragon challenged the red.

Fyia's heart pounded, concerned for all on her airship, but also for Scorpia, who could do little but hold on and pray.

The red dragon was smaller than the green, and more nimble. It was wiry next to the other's brawn, and it ducked, dived, and wove through the air as though delighted to be chased.

They circled close, then raced away, the airships sinking ever further, but the dragons focused only on each other.

And then Fyia felt the connection with her own dragon flare to life in her mind, but her instant relief fled in the face of his visceral anger. He was fire made flesh in every sense, searing heat consuming Fyia's insides, stealing her awareness of anything else around her.

She felt it as her dragon slammed into the red dragon's side with such force, it was sent sprawling through the air, satisfaction tempering his anger at the direct hit. It calmed her dragon enough that his hold on Fyia's emotions released, and she snapped back into herself to find Cal hovering above her, his hands cradling her face, her body stretched across the deck.

'It's coming back!' Opie screamed, and Fyia tilted her head just in time to see talons shred the largest of the balloons filled with hot air that kept them afloat.

The airship lurched downwards, tipping forward, so they were all thrown towards the stern, and suddenly everything around Fyia went mute, and time seemed to slow. She reached inside herself as her long, dark hair flew above her, and dredged up every scrap of power she could find, throwing it at the airship, demanding it slow its descent, commanding the wind to thicken, to provide more resistance.

And then her dragon was at the ship's side, fending off yet another attack from the red dragon, and Cal's helped too, but Fyia couldn't chance a look. Sweat soaked her brow as the power poured out of her, draining her until she worried there would be nothing left, that the ship would plummet anyway.

But they were close now. If her power gave out, the fall wouldn't be so great. Some of them might survive …

They crept down towards the earth, and Fyia almost began to believe they would make it, but her power lessened with every passing tick, draining from her until she had nothing left to give. Until the edges of her vision blurred, then went black. Until that blackness crept in, so only a pinprick of light remained. Until she could hold out no longer, nothing left to give, and finally, the darkness won.

Chapter Twelve

FYIA BECAME AWARE OF THE world all of a sudden, every limb in her body screaming in pain, the only relief the warm presence pressed against her side that smelled like Cal.

'What happened?' she whispered, her throat dry and scratchy.

Cal stirred, then sat bolt upright and called to someone outside. 'She's awake!'

Bodies scurried in, hands, arms, and faces she didn't recognize suddenly everywhere.

'Get off!' she said, but she didn't have the strength to make them do her bidding.

'Hush,' said a matronly woman dressed in white robes. The woman shooed the others away, then went to a sideboard and busied herself crushing and scraping and stirring.

'Where are we?' Fyia asked Cal, who was back on the bed, holding her hand.

'In the Temple of the Dragon. They're healing you … healing your magic.'

'Who is?'

'The Order of the Dragon. You drained yourself to the point of oblivion ... they had to use a dragon scale to save you. Thank the Gods they were here ... that we were here.'

Cal's distress was obvious, and she rested her head against his leg, the only movement she could manage.

'This will make you feel better,' said the healer, presenting Fyia with a vial of soot-colored liquid.

'Looks like it,' said Fyia.

'If you're capable of sarcasm, you must be on the mend,' said the woman, waggling the vial a little until Cal finally took it.

'Fine, but I can't lift my ...' Cal's hand was behind her head in less than a tick, gently angling it so she could drink down the foul-tasting liquid.

'All of it,' said the healer, her tone brooking no argument.

Fyia did as she was told, then almost vomited. 'Water,' she rasped.

'Nothing else for at least two turns,' the healer countered. 'By then, you'll be back to normal, give or take. In the meantime, you must rest.'

Fyia closed her eyes, and had to admit it felt good. She heard the healer's retreating footsteps, and then Cal shuffled down next to her, slipping an arm under her head and pulling her back into his body, turning her a little so he could press his chest against her.

As his body met hers, a sense of safety and comfort and belonging poured through her, and she sighed as he brushed his lips against her temple.

'What happened?' she asked again.

'You passed out when the airship was still two paces in the air. The ship dropped to the ground and was badly damaged. Several of the crew were injured, and one died.'

Fyia inhaled sharply. 'Who?'

'The cook.'

Fyia tried to shake her head, but a bolt of pain stilled her. 'I was so close.'

'You were,' he agreed, stroking her hair, 'but if you hadn't thought to use your magic at all, no one would have survived.'

Fyia knew that, but it didn't help. She'd wanted to save them all. 'What about Scorpia and the red dragon?'

'They landed, and Scorpia demanded to know if you were okay, insisting she had no control.'

'Well, if that's true,' said Fyia, whatever potion the healer had given her working already, 'it makes me feel better about my own lack of control.'

Cal chuckled.

'What about the green dragon?' she said. 'Is she yours?'

'Yes. My fire-touch warmed when she came near, but I haven't left your side since we landed. I am yet to meet her properly.'

Fyia pushed his arm. 'Go, if you want to! I don't need a babysitter.'

Cal tightened his grip, as though worried she would send him away. 'I'm not leaving you. I thought … when you passed out … and then you were thrown across the deck …'

Fyia laced her fingers through his, imagining their roles reversed, shuddering at the thought. 'It could have been so much worse.' A cloak of heavy silence fell over them.

'My cousin is here, along with all of my people,' Cal eventually said into her hair. She could hear the smile in his voice.

'Thank the Gods,' she said, a weight lifting. 'Why did they leave Anvarn?'

'The clock. It started leaking magma into the hot pool below the library. They didn't know how long it would hold, and then a dragon flew across the sky, circling and screaming.'

'They thought they'd be safer here?'

'Yes, and they're building the glasshouses here too, given the thaw has already begun. They want to move here permanently, for Anvarn to become a small trading post once more. They're building houses, and the Order of the Dragon has taken over the temple. This is the royal wing; they're fitting it out for us.'

'Wow,' she said, trying to wrap her head around the speed of all the changes. It had only been a few days since Asesh had tricked them into putting the balls into the mechanism, and yet already the dragons had returned, and their dreams for the north were coming true.

But at what cost?

She tried to dislodge the lump of dread that suddenly landed in her stomach, but it wouldn't budge.

'The engineers you sent from the Kingdom of Moon were shocked to see Antice disembark,' Cal said with a laugh.

Fyia's face split into a grin, although the dread was still there, dug in, refusing to let go. 'I bet they were. I think there's something going on with him and Sensis.'

'You think?' he teased, kissing her neck.

'I've never seen her like that … ever. And she's always hated Antice, ever since they were kids.'

'Not any longer.'

'What do you think he's really up to?'

Cal pulled her more tightly against him. 'I think he wants to learn about his fire-touch, and how to train his dragon. Whether he's here to spy and plot against us too, I couldn't say. But Sensis trusts him …'

'What if he's manipulating her?'

'Hmm,' said Cal, skeptically, then lapsed into silence, stroking her arm. 'Alba and Leo turned up.'

She swiveled her head to look into his eyes, noting the pain had all but gone.

'Alba saved Scorpia,' said Cal, 'by riding a kraken.'

'She ... what?'

'But then four other krakens showed up, along with Scorpia's dragon. The ship was wrecked.'

'Aren't krakens supposed to be solitary? I didn't think they hunted in packs.'

'Cinis and Storm are of the opinion that Scorpia's fire-touch lured them.'

'Why?'

'Because dragons are the only real threat to krakens. If the krakens take out the fire-touched, it hurts their enemy. Apparently, dragons enjoy being bonded ... just like me.' He kissed her shoulder.

Warmth flooded Fyia, even going some way to dissolving the dread in her stomach. She kissed his arm. 'Me too.'

It took several days for Fyia to recover enough to leave the royal wing of the temple. Cal barely left her side, and the others took turns to visit her, until the healers shooed them away.

On the third day, Fyia finally put her foot down and called a meeting, hosting everyone at the large, round, sand-colored stone table in the royal wing, in the chamber adjacent to their bedroom. Forging a stable alliance was at the top of her agenda, and it couldn't wait another moment.

The noise was almost deafening—their group now large—until Sensis banged the hilt of her dagger against the tabletop, demanding silence.

Fyia sent a nod of thanks to Sensis, who returned it with a flippant incline of her own head, and Fyia stifled a smirk. 'Thank you for coming,' she said. 'I am much recovered and eager to get on with the business at hand, creating a strong and beneficial alliance between those represented around this table. The threats …'

'… are many and varied,' said Scorpia. 'You have done much damage, *Queen* Fyia.'

'As has your dragon, Queen Scorpia,' Fyia replied, her tone neutral. So Scorpia questioned Fyia's ability to lead, or maybe she had ambitions of her own …

'I am glad to see gathered here people from all five of the true Kingdoms of Asred,' said Fyia. 'Scorpia, from the Scorpion Lands, many from my Five Kingdoms, members of the Fae'ch, Cinis, from the Great Glacier, and of course, no shortage of Black Hoods. We must work together to rebuild our world, focusing not on what divides us, but on that which unites.'

'Which is?' said Zhura, Cal's cousin.

'The desire to bring prosperity to all,' said Cal, sending the dark-haired woman a stern look.

Zhura raised her eyebrows, but said no more.

'We have many problems,' said Fyia, 'and I am the first to admit some—maybe most—were caused by me. But the dragons have returned to us. The ranks of fire-touched—those who can bond with dragons—are larger than we realized, and we finally have a chance to set right that which is wrong.

'As I see it, we have three key problems: One, we must repair the clocks, so we can stop the magma flowing where it should not, and use the system to keep magic moving around the world. Two, we must learn to control the dragons, so they are not a danger. Three, we must understand the damage to our lands, and do what we can to reassure our people, lest they panic.'

'And after that?' said Scorpia. 'What happens when we have helped you do these things?'

'It is not for me these things must be done,' said Fyia, a warning in her tone, 'but for all of us. For all our people. I do not have the answers to every question; it is up to us to find those together, one problem at a time.'

'But you see yourself as the new Dragon Queen?' said Scorpia. 'Expecting fealty from us lesser royals?'

'No,' said Fyia. 'I have no desire to dictate anything about your lands.'

'Just all the others?' Scorpia continued. 'You're marrying the King of the Black Hoods. The Great Glacier is practically unoccupied, and the Fae'ch have abandoned their mountains. They will become citizens of lands they do not control.'

'You do not speak for the Fae'ch,' snapped Storm, 'nor should you presume to know what we will or will not do. Gabriel and I lived in these lands long before any of you were born; we have seen what happens when humans fight among themselves. If that is what you wish for this alliance, Queen Scorpia, then you are no ally of ours.'

'Now as ever was,' she replied. 'The Fae'ch were always too good for my lands.'

'Do you hold a grudge on behalf of your ancestors?' said Storm. 'You think it was some slight against them? Against you? Against your lands?'

Scorpia made a tsking sound and turned her head away.

'We liked your people and your kingdom just fine,' said Gabriel, cutting across the tension with his smooth, deep voice, 'but your lands did not like us. Few of the Fae'ch could survive so far south. It is hot, your clock is small, dragons rarely visited, and that made us weak.

Some who pulled power from the water, or the earth, could make it work, but most could not.'

Scorpia lifted her head in a jerk of acknowledgement. She clamped her mouth shut, and the eyes of the room returned to Fyia.

'Those of us with the fire-touch should remain here, and learn what we can from Cinis about the dragons. Essa, I am assuming your chief concern is fixing the clocks?'

Essa nodded. 'I was hoping Gabriel and Storm, or Alba and Leo, could help me.'

'The powerful Fae'ch lived deep under the mountain,' said Gabriel. 'We did not know them all, but Isa frequently boasted that she housed those with the skills you seek. I do not know if that is true, or where they might have gone.'

'We can search for Isa,' said Alba, leaning towards Leo and taking his hand.

Leo seemed reluctant, but eventually nodded his agreement. Storm and Gabriel had told Leo of his father's death at the hands of the Children of the Lake. Axus had sat at Isa's right hand for centuries, and it was strange, even to Fyia, who had only met him once, that he was gone.

Leo, always quiet, had grown even more so, and Alba seemed to watch him at all times, reaching for him whenever she could. To make matters worse, no one knew where his mother, Isa, had gone, and his brother, a fae named Regio, was most likely dead, too.

Alba was keen to find her uncle, a man named Pips, so it was no surprise she had volunteered to go.

'Storm and I will search for long-lives with the knowledge you seek,' said Gabriel.

'And I have dozens of sites to visit,' said Essa. 'The two maps we now have depict many clocks and taps. They're mostly in towns that have fallen to ruin, but we must check and reinforce all points of weakness in the system.'

'I will go with you,' said Veau.

The room went still, and Essa's cheeks flushed pink.

'You do not wish to learn how to control dragons, brother?' said Fyia.

'I have no dragon, and Essa cannot go alone.'

'There are others we can send. She will take an airship, a whole crew …'

'Who will be her guard?' said Veau.

Fyia resisted the urge to point out that Veau was hardly an accomplished warrior himself, but that would have been cruel with such an audience, and Essa was embarrassed, clearly wanting the conversation to end

'I will!' said a voice from the back, and a murmur of surprise rippled across the room. Fyia spun to see Rouel step out from the shadows, a guilty look on his face. 'Sorry, Your Majesty. I'm on guard duty.'

Fyia snuck a glance at Edu, who stood behind her chair, as always. He did not look pleased, and Fyia wondered why Rouel would so freely volunteer to leave him. Rouel was, after all, head over heels in love with Edu … was he not?

Rouel continued, 'It is, of course, not my place to …'

'I would be happy for you to guard Essa,' said Fyia. 'You are a member of my personal guard, so she would certainly be in safe hands, but only if that should meet with Essa's approval, and Edu's, of course.'

Essa nodded, then averted her gaze. Veau's jaw locked closed, his teeth clenched. Edu said in a clipped voice, 'I will consider the most suitable guard for this appointment.'

Fyia shared a covert look with Sensis before moving them on. 'Which leaves our third challenge,' she said. 'Assessing the situation in our kingdoms and reassuring our people.'

'I left my people in capable hands,' said Scorpia, 'and they are not an excitable sort. I need do nothing on that front.'

Fyia nodded. The people of the Scorpion Lands had a somewhat fiery reputation, but she refrained from challenging Scorpia so openly.

'It is fortunate for me we are in my lands,' said Cal, something about the way he said the words sending a thrill up Fyia's spine, 'and I am sure Zhura would tell us if action were required.'

'I took the required action in your absence, cousin,' said Zhura, a teasing smile on her lips.

Cal chuckled. 'Which is why I like to have you around … why I forced your royal title upon you.'

Zhura rolled her eyes.

'There are few hardy enough to live on the Great Glacier,' said Cinis, 'although that will change with the thawing. For now, an eagle to the members of the Order of the Dragon there—the miners—will suffice. They will be delighted to hear the dragons have returned, if word has not reached them already.'

'Of course,' said Fyia. 'Write a message, and I will send an eagle.'

'The Fae'ch can look after themselves,' said Storm, 'assuming the people of your Five Kingdoms play nice.'

'Fae'ch have also come to our lands,' said Zhura. 'We have welcomed them with open arms.'

'As you should,' said Storm, 'for we have much to offer.'

'Which leaves only my kingdoms,' said Fyia.

'And the Kraken Empire,' said Veau.

He was right, of course. The Kraken people did not have the same magic, but the changes wrought on the world would affect them too. Fyia wondered again if their parents were still at the Kraken Court, and if they already knew about the dragons. Would they try to return now? Try to weasel their way back into her—or Veau's—favor? Or would they fear Fyia would set her dragon upon them?

'I will send an eagle to the Empress, and another to Adigos,' said Fyia, hoping Adigos was representing her kingdoms well.

'And I will go to Selise,' said Sensis. 'Starfall will need help, both with managing the people, and the Small Council.'

Fyia was glad Sensis had volunteered. She was the only one Fyia could trust with the task, and it showed their thoughts were still aligned, regardless of the little time they'd spent together of late.

'I cannot think of a better person,' said Fyia, smiling warmly. 'What else?'

'I sent eagles to all the towns with dragon clocks shown on the maps,' said Essa. 'Some returned with messages, and all of those report the banging and creaking inside the clocks has stopped, and that the balls of Dragonsprite have stopped appearing.'

'That is good,' said Cinis. 'The dragons will not go back until there is more, which will only happen when the magic in an area diminishes, and the clock strikes thirteen. If there are other dragons, they will now most likely come here, where there has always been a plentiful supply of Dragonsprite.'

'That's good?' asked Fyia, because his words did not sound positive.

'On the one hand,' said Cinis, with a nod. 'But on the other, now the Dragonsprite is gone, they will remember they are hungry for more.'

'Shit,' said Fyia. 'They'll start eating people?'

Cinis shrugged. 'And sheep, and elephants, and whales, and krakens. There are many better meals than people, but that won't always stop them; they'll run rampant until brought to heel. Luckily, the Circus has almost completely thawed; training can start tomorrow.'

Sensis shut the door to the hut Antice had claimed on the edge of the tree line. It had been hidden before the ice melted, and now the whole area was a slushy mess, no choice but to trudge through pools of water and greying snow.

Apparently, the water would find its way to the aqueduct, and eventually end up in the sea, but in the meantime, Sensis was tired of wet boots. She pulled them off as she entered the surprisingly dry and cozy space. Antice had a fire going in the small hearth, over which sat a rabbit on a spit, and he'd somehow dried the floor and found animal skins, which he'd arranged in a tempting pile.

The hut had little else of note; one window at the front, another at the back, a few shelves and cupboards dotted about. Most of the other huts had been squashed under the weight of the snow, little remaining but debris as they reappeared, but this one had survived with barely a mark.

'It's made of alterwood,' said Antice, seeming to read her mind. 'The hut's walls have grown roots into the ground, and it draws strength from the earth to sustain itself.'

Sensis looked at her feet. 'The hut?' she said, disbelieving.

Antice laughed. 'Sort of.'

'But they killed the tree when they cut it down and turned it into planks,' said Sensis.

'Not entirely.'

'It has no leaves! Trees can't survive without leaves.'

'It will have them somewhere. Roots travel far, especially those of alterwoods, and they connect to one another. This hut may even be linked to the trees on your estate.'

'I'm glad you're finally calling it mine,' said Sensis, sighing as she lowered herself onto the furs. She lay down, stretching out her back, making an appreciative noise as her muscles relaxed. She was tempted to close her eyes—she'd be asleep in less than two ticks—but she resisted. First thing in the morning, she would leave for Selise, and only the Gods knew when she would see Antice again.

'Wait,' she said, raising herself onto her arms. 'So you could spy on the Guild of Magic in Moon, or on my estate, or on anywhere else that has an alterwood tree?'

Antice half-smiled. 'I was wondering how long it would take you to catch onto that.'

Sensis flicked a piece of grit at him. 'Could you?' she pressed.

He took the rabbit off the fire and put it on a metal tray. 'In theory, one could, but in reality, it's not so easy. I've been practicing my whole life, and can finally make out some words, and … well … feelings through the roots, but it's imperfect, and it depends how far they go. The further the distance, the more difficult it is to follow. At some point, there are just too many voices. To identify and focus on one out of the multitude is … difficult.'

'But not impossible?'

Antice cut the rabbit, splitting the roasted meat across two plates, which were already filled with green leaves. Where he had found those, Sensis couldn't begin to imagine.

'In theory,' he agreed. 'Storm or Gabriel might know more. They might even know Fae'ch who could help.'

'Or maybe we're being spied on by the Fae'ch right now,' said Sensis.

Antice halted his movements as he considered that. 'You're right. We should tell everyone to be careful what they say around the alterwoods.'

Antice pulled a jar full of a viscous brown substance from a leather bag, and Sensis eyed it dubiously as he spooned a little onto each of their plates.

'What is that?'

'Delicious,' he said, handing over her food.

Sensis gratefully accepted, her mouth watering at the prospect of the crispy fat and fresh greens. Antice handed her a fork along with a hunk of bread, and she gingerly tasted the brown sauce. An explosion of sweet yet sharp and mildly peppery flavors skittered across her tongue, and her eyes went wide.

Antice chuckled. 'Good?'

'Amazing,' she said, slathering it over a piece of rabbit, then wrapping it in a leaf. 'Who made it?'

'The Order of the Dragon keeps many secrets, and this recipe is one of their best. My uncle, Venir, was a horticulturist, as were his ancestors before him. Venir created this sauce many times, but the exact recipe is a closely guarded secret of the Order. I've never tasted the real thing until today, and it exceeded my every expectation; Venir never got close.'

'You like cooking?' she said, then popped another morsel into her mouth.

Antice looked down at his hands as though embarrassed. 'I love foraging, and my mother's family made a name for themselves through their obsession with growing things, but no one ever let me cook the things I foraged.

'They said it was "not for the likes of me", and if anyone ever found me near the kitchens, they would shoo me away. Even on hunting trips, we took cooks, and you know my military career ended before it began.'

'Cooking is women's work,' said Sensis. 'They rammed that down my throat, too.'

'Aside from the Head Chefs in most of our houses,' said Antice. 'They were all men. I tried to befriend them, but it was more than their jobs were worth to teach me.'

A loaded silence descended as they ate, an echo of their previous fight bouncing back and forth across the room. They had spent little time alone together since.

'What you said before,' Antice said eventually, taking Sensis' empty plate and putting it with his by the fire, 'about me pursuing what I wanted. You were right … I never really tried. But it didn't seem important. I did things I shouldn't have: aided Venir, supported the rebels, disagreed with Fyia's changes. But I didn't have allies.'

He ran a hand through his hair as he positioned himself next to her on the furs, wrapping his arms loosely around his bent legs. 'Fyia has you, and Edu, and her aunt, and … everyone else. I never found my people.'

'You might have, if you'd looked.'

'Sensis …'

'I don't want to fight,' she said, irritated by his tone. 'I'm just being honest. If you don't want truth from me, then we have no future. That kind of relationship—second guessing and dancing around in fear of offending you—is not one I can tolerate.'

'I do want the truth,' he said, then trailed off, watching the glowing coals in the fire. 'It's just ... new. Very few people dare to be so brutally honest with the former Crown Prince of Moon.'

'It has never been that way at Fyia's court,' she said. 'Fyia seeks the opinions of those who disagree with her, then listens when they speak. And if this is all a game. If you're plotting to overthrow her ...'

'I'm not!'

His eyes found hers, and Sensis was relieved to see truth shining in them. 'I believe you, but I need you to know, if I ever have to choose between the two of you, I will choose her. I swore my life to Fyia because I believe in her, and all she stands for.'

Antice inhaled deeply, mulling over her words.

'If that is a problem for you, we should ...'

'It's not a problem,' he said, cutting her off. 'But it is a problem if you don't trust me. I expect the others to look at me with suspicion in their eyes—I have earned that, I know—but I can't bear it from you.'

'You think you have done enough to earn my trust?' she said, her tone turning playful. She didn't want to spend their last night together fighting. She did trust him, and she would vouch for him, for as long as she believed his intentions to be pure. She would stand beside him, and she would even let the world know they were together, much as the thought made her curl up inside.

Antice moved to sit on his knees before her, brushing the hair back off her face, a smile on his lips. 'Do I think I've done enough?' he repeated, his usual cocky self returning.

Sensis' insides clenched, and she raised a challenging eyebrow. 'That's what I asked ...'

He leaned forward, invading her space, crowding her, and Sensis looked up at him with sultry eyes, the sweet, malty smell of him mingling with the woodsmoke from the fire, both travelling deep into her lungs. Their lips crashed together, and every erogenous part of Sensis tingled, longing for attention.

He pushed her flat onto the furs and straddled her, settling his weight on her legs as he deepened the kiss. Sensis' eyes rolled back in her head, and then he shifted his body, lying flat atop her.

'I saw the healers,' said Sensis, when his lips moved to her ear.

Antice stilled, then lifted himself to look down at her, his gaze flicking from one eye to the other. 'And?'

'They told me Fyia's doing well; she's almost back to normal.'

Antice rolled his hips, and Sensis laughed and gasped at the same time.

'And they performed the spell to prevent pregnancy,' she said, then bit her lip.

'Speak plainly, Sensis,' said Antice, suddenly serious. 'Do you want to …'

'Do you?'

'Yes,' he said, without hesitation. 'But the decision is yours. If you do not …'

Sensis silenced him with a finger against his lips. 'I'm hardly a virgin.'

He kissed her finger, then removed it, entwining it with his. 'But do you want to?' he said quietly.

'Yes,' she said, her body screaming to cut the talk and get to the part where they took their clothes off.

'It will be a relief,' he said, rolling his hips again. Sensis almost combusted. 'To have sex in the light … to let another touch me.' Given the location of his dragon scales, he'd rarely let anyone see him naked, or touch his skin.

Sensis reached for his breeches, watching him as she tugged at the fastening. She slipped her hand inside and stroked his length, and he inhaled sharply, his eyes falling closed, a slight crease on his brow.

'Take them off,' she said.

He kissed her, then obeyed, and she pushed him onto his back, tracing the slight ridges of his abdomen, his muscles defined, but not impressive, different to most of the men she'd bedded.

She traced his hips, then kissed her way down the ridge of muscle leading to his straining erection. She ignored that, focusing instead on the tiny, gleaming scales of gold, kissing each in turn.

She looked up to find his eyes black, pupils blown so wide he looked imp drunk. 'Don't stop,' he whispered, his voice tight.

She took him in her hand and stroked, and he groaned as she squeezed him, lifting his hips, encouraging her to move faster. Sensis bent forward, her hair cascading between them, and took him into her mouth. Antice swore loudly, and she laughed around him. He groaned again, fisting a hand in her hair.

'*Goddess*,' he breathed. '*Warrior*. Fuck ... Sensis ... stop.' He pulled her up, breathing hard, and then his lips were on hers, the kiss deep and rhythmic. Antice undressed her as they devoured one another, making short work of her clothes, and then somehow, Sensis was beneath him, and he pressed between her thighs.

She spread her legs wider as he shifted his hips, and then he was where she wanted him most, nudging against her entrance. Their desire had wound tight after endless days of restraint, and Sensis urged him forward, impatient for more. Antice didn't need further encouragement. He pushed inside her, burying himself in a single thrust, and Sensis tipped her head back, a moan escaping her lips.

Her inner walls pulsed at the delicious stretch, and then he pulled out, and she pulsed at the loss of him.

He thrust forward again, and she grasped his shoulders and wrapped her legs around him, determined to keep him inside.

'You think you're in charge, even in here?' he teased, as he stopped moving.

She bucked her hips, but he refused to move, and she let out a frustrated huff.

'Because you're not,' he said, then nipped her neck, not quite hard enough to hurt.

'No?' she said, rocking just enough to feel friction.

'No,' he said, rolling them to the side, his arms around her, locking them together.

He kissed her, overwhelming her senses with his lips and hands and legs, their bodies tightly entwined. He cupped her breast, then her backside, and then Sensis rolled them upright, so she straddled him, her feet on the floor behind his back.

'You're a control freak,' he said as he pinched her nipple.

'And you like it,' she whispered, holding his neck as she lifted herself up and down his shaft.

'Fuck,' he grunted, then sucked on her nipple so hard her legs went to jelly. She wrapped them around him and rocked as he kneaded, nipped, and licked her, Sensis holding onto him as though she were at sea, he her only chance of survival.

'Yes,' she breathed into his neck, 'don't stop. Antice …' She bucked, and release hit her like a storm surge, her legs a vice around him as wave after wave rolled through. He went up on his knees, pumping his hips wildly, then threw them down onto the furs, thrusting twice more, then groaning as his own release hit.

As the shocks subsided, Antice kissed her, tender and deep, languid pleasure seeping through her blood, every nerve relaxed, and every problem chased away.

Antice stirred the following morning to find Sensis asleep in his arms. Her hair was tangled, her limbs strewn out at all angles, but her back was still pressed to his chest, and his heart gave a hard squeeze.

He didn't want her to go ... hadn't wanted to be apart from her since her airship had landed on his uncle's estate ... on *her* estate. Lady Altergate. The title was all wrong for her; High Commander suited her much better. Ladies were constrained, inhibited things, and by that measure, Sensis was anything but. Or maybe plenty of ladies were like Sensis underneath, and he'd just never noticed.

But he'd never found one quite like Sensis. At least, none of the prospects his parents had put in front of him. The thought left a sour taste in his mouth; he couldn't imagine being with anyone but her ... ever wanting anyone but her.

Sensis inhaled, her chest rising, and Antice dropped a kiss on her shoulder. She rolled over, and he tried to focus on her drowsy eyes and not her naked breasts, but her nipples were alluring peaks.

She smiled up at him, and he kissed her, but she pushed him away before it could go any further, hopeful as his body already was. 'I want to stay,' said Sensis, now wide awake and searching for her clothes, 'but I have to go. The sun's already rising; they'll be wondering where I am.'

'I wish I could come.'

'No, you don't,' she said with a teasing smile. 'You want to learn about your dragon.'

'Fine. Then I wish I could come with you and stay here at the same time.'

'Me too,' she said. 'Not least because politics is more your game than mine.'

'I doubt Starfall will leave much politicking to you,' he laughed. She swatted him. 'But she'll need your armies, and I can be of no help there.'

'Which is why you will stay, and I will go.'

'And the absence will make our hearts grow fonder?' he said, with an overly sweet smile.

'Please, I don't want to throw up so early in the day; I haven't even had breakfast.'

Antice laughed as he leaned back and watched her dress. She stood and threw her cloak around her, and then he caught her hand, stilling her, the mood turning serious.

'I'll miss you,' he said, playing with her fingers.

She watched him for several long moments, and a bolt of fear shot through Antice that she would not return the sentiment. She stepped over him and squatted until she sat atop his legs, took his face in her hands, and looked deep into his soul. 'I'll miss you, too,' she said, then kissed him. 'And if you so much as look at any other woman while I'm gone, I'll chop off your balls.'

Antice chuckled, and she kissed him again. 'Fly safe,' he said.

'I will. And you, don't fall off that dragon.'

Sensis' airship was disappearing over the horizon when they gathered at the Circus, Fyia excited and apprehensive about finally learning what her fire-touch would allow her to do.

The Circus was a great, oval space, designed with the express purpose of training dragons. The four dragons had gathered also, each perched on one of the stone plinths that stood at regular intervals around the perimeter wall. And in the middle of the wall's long side, resting on the ground, was a large clock face, but without the symbols that usually adorned the dragon clocks.

The dragons seemed curious, watching their four bonded humans, along with Cinis and Veau. They cocked their heads to one side and pulsed their wings, or twitched their ears like curious horses.

'The Temple of the Dragon does not have a conventional clock,' said Cinis, beginning the lesson without preamble. 'It is not connected to the main magma ducts across the known world, but has a separate system that mimics the larger, which is used for training dragons.

'But before we get onto that, you must first learn the basics. I was never an expert in dragon husbandry, but I will share what I know … what I remember.'

As Cinis collected himself, Fyia cast a look up at her silver dragon, and reached out with her mind. She gave him a mental stroke, and he purred and fluffed up his wings.

'You must spend time with them to understand their personalities and needs,' said Cinis. 'You must build trust and respect, but above all, boundaries. There can be no doubt who is in charge; who is leading whom.

'Each of you must develop your own commands and ways of communicating, but remember this, even if you forget everything else I tell you: do not allow your dragon the upper hand. Dragons are magic made flesh, bound to this world by the scale of a fire-touched. They were created to serve, to assist, but the magic does not always want to obey. It strains against the scale locking it in place, whimsical and playful, and your dragons must place your commands above the impulses of the magic, or chaos will reign.'

To Fyia, there seemed nothing whimsical about the dragons or the magic. But then, what did she know?

'You must ride them to establish the right dynamic.'

'But what if we lose control when we're in the air?' said Antice.

'I doubt very much you'll have any control at all to start,' said Cinis, 'but the Circus was made for training dragons. Should the situation become dangerous, I will release a ball of Dragonsprite into the airlock behind the clockface. The dragons will hear it, and return.'

'And fight for it with us on their backs?' said Antice, his voice thin.

A series of jibes popped into Fyia's mind, but she kept them locked up. It was no surprise the dragons scared him; like her, he was no warrior.

'It's unlikely they'll truly fight here,' said Cinis, 'and I will keep the clock face closed until they settle down. Your dragons are old, and they will know what to do, just as they will know how to navigate the magma ducts.'

Fyia glanced at Veau from the corner of her eye. He was doing his best to look happy, but she knew he wished for a dragon. If their roles had been reversed, Fyia would be imploding from jealousy and disappointment.

'Call your dragons,' said Cinis.

Veau moved back to the stone wall, leaning against it nonchalantly. He sank down onto the now dry ground and rested his arms on his knees.

Fyia wished there was something she could do—to find him a dragon, and to sort out whatever was going on between him and Essa. Essa seemed to be keeping her distance, but Veau's eyes followed her wherever she went. Fyia knew Essa still cared for her brother, but they were both so private, she couldn't just come out and ask for details.

The others had already summoned their dragons, so Fyia hastily called hers. He hopped off his platform, gliding to the floor in an elegant movement.

Scorpia was atop her red dragon in a moment, while the others struggled to scale the legs of their own beasts. Scorpia had spent years climbing onto her pet elephant, but that didn't make Fyia feel any better about her own clumsy ascent. Her dragon stamped his feet, seemingly unimpressed too.

We will practice, she silently told him as she settled into place, but before waiting for more, he launched into the sky, racing the red dragon into the air. Fyia's silver dragon was bigger and heavier, so the red dragon took the lead, but Silver's wings were wider, and after a few flaps, they overtook, Red screeching angrily.

Scorpia shouted, 'No!' at her own dragon, and Fyia chanced a look back to find Red preparing to bite Silver's ankles. For a moment, Fyia thought Red would ignore Scorpia, but then he turned away with a light shake of his head.

Edu reported Scorpia had been spending every waking moment with her dragon, and sleeping next to him too, in a cave not far from the temple. They already had a strong bond, and Fyia resolved to spend more time with her own dragon, because she wasn't so certain Silver would have listened had their roles been reversed.

Fyia clung on for dear life, exhilarated but also scared. This was not like riding an eagle, the wing beats more powerful, Silver's movements so much faster as to not even bear a resemblance, his body able to make snake-like jinks an eagle could never hope to replicate.

She told Silver to turn back towards the Circle, so she could see how the others fared without having to look over her shoulder. Silver obliged, although Fyia almost slid off the side at the speed of his spin, and she thoroughly chastised him. She was sure he was laughing as he straightened up. 'I hope you know how to catch me if you take your tricks too far,' she said, her voice tight.

Cal was up in the air on his green dragon, and despite its ferocity in the fight with Red only a few days before, she was taking care of her human, circling low and at a steady speed.

Cal looked up, found Fyia, and urged his dragon up towards her.

Fyia told Silver to wait for him, so they hovered in midair, and Silver's movements finally became predictable, the up and down almost gentle. Fyia relaxed, starting to really enjoy herself, although she shouldn't have, because as soon as Cal came close, Silver lurched to the side, then dove under his dragon.

'Silver!' Fyia shouted, once again fearing for her life.

Silver righted himself and hovered beside Cal's dragon, and Fyia was surprised to find a grin on Cal's lips. 'Silver?' he said.

'Nice to see my near-death doesn't cause you concern,' she said dryly.

'You looked fine to me. Maybe not entirely in control, but not in any real danger.'

'Don't let Silver hear you say that, or he might step things up a notch, and then I'm done for.'

'Seriously? Silver?'

'He's silver!' Fyia said with a shrug. 'And Scorpia's been calling hers Red.'

'Well, I am not calling mine *Green*,' said Cal.

Fyia laughed. 'Doesn't have quite the same ring to it.'

A scream sounded from below, and they both turned their eyes downward. Antice lay sprawled on his dragon's wing. The dragon coasted steadily back to the Circus, then rolled him off, so he landed in a heap on the ground.

See, Fyia said to Silver through their bond, *that could happen to me!*

Silver shook beneath her, and she clung to his neck. 'Now you're just being mean.'

Cal chuckled, but the sound turned into a cry as his dragon spun under him and dove for the ground. Fyia would have gloated, but Silver did the same, as did Red, and suddenly they were all hurtling towards the Circus together.

'The ultimate test of a dragon rider,' said Cinis, his voice somehow in Fyia's ear, 'is whether your dragon will listen to your commands when it can smell Dragonsprite. If your bond is strong enough to puncture the feeding frenzy, then you truly have control.'

Fyia tried. She screamed through the bond, and hammered on Silver's scales, and even begged, but nothing worked. Finally, when they were so close to the ground she was sure they would smash into the hard earth, she sent a bolt of panicky magic through her fingers.

Silver bucked and pulled up, rearing back so hard, Fyia's brain smashed against the inside of her skull, blackening her vision, and disorienting her so much that she slipped and fell. Fyia landed hard on her side, the breath whooshing from her lungs, her limbs in awkward positions beneath her. To add insult to injury, Silver took to the sky, his wing smacking her as he lifted off.

Fyia vaguely noticed Scorpia's and Cal's dragons facing off, snarling at one another, and Antice's purple dragon standing to one side, both the dragon and Antice looking like cats that got the cream.

'Stand down!' Cinis screamed, although Fyia couldn't see which of them he addressed. Maybe he was shouting at them both.

'Scorpia, Cal's dragon is not posturing. You must stand down!'

'I'm trying!' Scorpia shouted back, but it wasn't doing any good.

Then suddenly, Antice's dragon was lumbering between them, Antice's features screwed up in nervous concentration. Or was it simply fear? He maneuvered carefully, staying closer to Red than to Cal's dragon, bumping Scorpia's irate creature backwards, and breaking the eye contact between the two deadly beasts.

Scorpia slipped from Red's back, then the dragon took to the air with a snarl, sending a plume of fire into the sky before him. He flew through it, then disappeared into a cloud.

Fyia let her head fall back, then gingerly tested her limbs, one after another, making sure they still worked, that nothing was broken. Veau came to her side. 'Smooth,' he said, mocking her in his brotherly way.

'I thought so.'

He reached out his hand to help her up. 'Or should I call the healers?' he asked, suddenly unsure.

Fyia grasped his hand and pulled herself to her feet, wincing at the general pain. She would no doubt find bruises on every part of her body.

Cal's dragon was now snarling at Antice's, and Antice was coaxing his dragon away, talking to her in a soothing, placating tone.

Cal was sheet white, holding on as though not sure what to do, perhaps worried that if he tried to dismount, his dragon would go for him.

'What's his dragon doing?' Fyia asked Cinis, as they joined him at the side of the Circus.

'She's being territorial,' said Cinis. 'Antice's dragon got to the opening in the duct first, and snatched the Dragonsprite. Red arrived next, but Cal's dragon pulled him back, and is defending the opening.'

'Why?' said Veau. 'If the Dragonsprite's gone, what's … wait … what's that noise?'

Fyia and Cinis shared a confused look. 'Noise?' said Fyia.

'It's like … squawking. It's coming from …' Veau moved around, stopping every few paces to listen, following sounds only he could hear.

Cal's dragon turned, now ignoring Antice, instead watching Veau. She snorted and stomped, then bared her teeth.

'It's inside,' said Veau, pointing to the still-open clock face that allowed entry into the ducts behind.

He moved forward, as though to investigate further, but Cal's dragon swiped her tail, blocking Veau's path. She flicked the barb-covered end menacingly back and forth near Veau's face.

'There must be another dragon inside,' said Veau, his eyes lighting up despite the danger.

'Her mate?' said Fyia.

Cinis stepped to one side, revealing a recess in the wall covered in levers and dials. He fiddled for a moment, and the clock snapped shut. He pulled a lever, then spun a cog, then waited.

'Hear anything?' Cinis asked Veau.

'Um …' Veau frowned. They stood in silence for several excruciating moments. 'Nothing,' he said eventually, some of the light leaving his eyes.

Cinis pulled another lever. 'How about now?'

Fyia held her breath as they waited. She so desperately wanted Veau to have a dragon, too.

'There!' said Veau, at the same moment Cal's dragon let out a deafening, terrifying roar. And then, an eruption of squawking and scratching and tapping sounded through the closed metal.

The green dragon roared again, as Cinis played with the cogs and levers once more, and then the door slid aside, revealing not one, not two, but three, tiny, overexcited baby dragons.

Cal's dragon rushed forward, although she didn't seem menacing any longer, just irritated in the way of a long-suffering mother.

She tried to shoo the babies back into the ducts, but they refused to heed her, ducking under her head, then her outstretched wings, then scattering in three different directions. Fyia couldn't help but chuckle as steam poured out of the adult's nose. She roared at the babies, who were attempting—and failing—to take off, then gave chase.

As she rushed one, another—the smallest of the three—made a beeline for Veau, hopping onto his shoulder, causing him to stumble under its weight. The dragon shrieked apologetically, then jumped down and nuzzled his hand, just as a second—the largest—knocked the first out of the way, bundling it across the hard ground and licking Veau's hand.

Veau gasped and ran after it, but it was already back on its feet, hissing and spitting at its sibling.

'Enough,' said Veau, in a commanding voice Fyia had rarely heard from her brother. 'Play nicely.'

His words got the green dragon's attention—Cal still atop her, not daring to dismount—and she rushed at Veau.

The babies scurried behind him, and he stood his ground, although he shook with fear, and his forehead contained a glistening sheen of sweat. The green dragon roared in Veau's face, but before she'd finished, all three babies sprang at their mother, jumping up and pushing at her with their clawed feet, then repeating the movement again and again. The smallest of the babies jumped so high, she landed on the green dragon's face, then scurried up her neck to sit in Cal's lap.

Cal scooped the baby into his arms, then threw his leg over his dragon's back and slid down her scales. He hopped to the ground, then hastily put the baby down, not wanting to test his bond with its mother, and sending the clear signal he was on her side.

The baby scurried back to Veau, joining its siblings in rubbing themselves against Veau's legs. Veau crouched and stroked them, petting them behind the ears as though they were dogs. Cal's dragon retreated, then took to the air with a huff.

'Don't think I didn't notice your dragon dumped you on the ground, Daughter,' Cinis said to Fyia. 'What did you do?'

Fyia struggled to tear her eyes from the babies. Veau had not one, but three dragons, judging by the way they were fawning over him. Veau's face came alive every time one of them did something mischievous, or butted a sibling, or, in fact, whenever they did anything at all.

'I used magic to try and make him listen to me,' said Fyia. 'He didn't like it.'

Cinis gasped, as though she'd crossed some terrible line. 'What possessed you?'

'I thought it might work,' said Fyia, with a defensive shrug. 'How was I supposed to know it was wrong?'

Her words tempered his indignation. 'I suppose you have a point. I keep forgetting how little you know.'

Fyia raised her eyebrows but didn't speak, because if she had, she would have said something petulant.

Antice dismounted, and all five of the fire-touched stood in a loose circle, ready for their debrief, although the babies kept stealing their attention.

'Scorpia, Cal,' said Cinis, 'you made a good attempt at control, but the deepest of bonds will take time. Antice,' he said, turning to face him, 'despite a shaky start, your control when separating the other two dragons was impressive. Your dragon is beginning to trust you.'

'Thank you,' said Antice, and a prickle of jealousy seeped into Fyia's gut. She knew it was stupid, and childish, but she couldn't shake it, not that she tried all that hard. She'd been sure she would have a steadfast bond with her dragon, w, but so far, that hadn't come to pass.

'Same time tomorrow,' said Cinis. 'In the meantime, spend as much time with your dragons as you can.'

'How do we get them back?' said Cal, searching the sky in vain for any sign of his.

Cinis gave an exasperated shake of his head. 'You wait.'

Chapter Thirteen

By lunchtime, the others were all with their dragons, Fyia's the only one still missing. Cal had hesitated before going to his, but Fyia sent him away. There was no use in punishing Cal for her actions, and Cinis had made it clear there was no substitute for time in developing deep bonds, to build the trust and familiarity required for a dragon to obey without question.

Fyia wished she was with her dragon too, as she wandered the halls of the temple, keeping to the shadows so she could watch the work of the Dragon Order. She and Cal hadn't been back to the large cache of dragon scales at the bottom of the temple. It would cause conflict with the Order if they did, and there was no reason to risk the fragile balance of their young community, although a part of her wanted to see the magnificent sight again.

She headed outside, pulling her cloak more firmly around her as she stepped into the chilly breeze. Everything was soggy from the ice melt, the ground a disgusting mess.

Antice's dragon perched at the top of the long flight of steps out of the temple, breathing fire onto the remains of the ice sheet that had, until recently, covered the entrance almost entirely. The Order had requested the fire-touched set their dragons to the task of melting it, worried the ice would come down in a vast block, atop whoever stood beneath.

Soon, the temple's colossal doors would swing shut, although Fyia wondered if they would still hang as they should. She didn't dare to think what would happen if they fell ...

She couldn't wait to experience the inside of the temple with the doors closed, the space big enough to accommodate ten fully grown dragons. Her hair stood on end just imagining what a dragon's roar would sound like, bouncing off the polished walls.

Fyia's guards were drilling in the slush, each of them looking miserable as Edu drove them hard. With Sensis gone, Edu was the only one here Fyia could confide in, aside from Cal. She even doubted her own brother, after he'd lied to her about the metal balls, and it would take time to rebuild what they'd lost.

But Edu had been in a strange mood these past few days. In fact, ever since he'd caught up to them at the Temple of the Warrior, and Fyia had neglected him, too distracted to press him on it.

'Edu!' called Fyia, picking her way around the worst of the puddles.

'My Queen,' said Edu, bowing as she approached. Her guards stopped mid-movement, turning to bow also.

She inclined her head. 'Carry on,' she said, then faced her dear friend.

'What?' he said, in a quiet-yet-snappish voice only Fyia could hear.

'That,' she said, her face splitting into a grin.

'I don't want to talk about it.'

'Yes, you do; you just don't know it yet,' she said conspiratorially, linking her arm through his and pulling him away from the training ground, heading for the trees.

'Fyia, you may have nothing to do with your time, but I am busy. I do not have time to …'

'Oh, hush,' she said. 'Don't make me play the Queen card, and don't think I haven't noticed how hard you're working. You've been drilling my guards, and the young Black Hoods, from dawn 'til dusk. It's like you're avoiding something …'

'I am sharing combat techniques with our allies,' he said sharply, as they stepped into the shelter of the trees.

'Which is more important than the needs of your Queen?'

'You have Cal.'

She swatted him, then pulled him to a halt. 'Stop it.'

Edu shook his head, wisps of his long white hair falling around his face.

'I'm worried about you.'

'You have more important things to worry about.'

'Edu,' she said, weaving until she found his eyes, making him look at her. 'Tell me what's wrong.'

He made a frustrated noise in the back of his throat. 'Is that an order?'

Fyia punched him on the arm, and her wolves, feeling her anger, appeared through the trees.

'What do you want me to say, Fyia?'

'Is it Rouel?'

Edu laughed cruelly, and Fyia paused, looking up at him, feeling as though she'd missed something.

'You indulge him,' said Edu. 'You all do, and he takes advantage every time. You have done nothing but make my job harder.'

'I like him. I almost consider him a friend.'

'You shouldn't. He is not your friend. He's your guard. One who puts finding fodder for songs above all else. I should have dismissed him years ago.'

'And yet, you didn't …'

'No.'

'Because you love him?'

Edu rounded on her with such ferocity, Fyia's wolves snarled. 'If you think so little of the Captain of your Body Guard, I will tender my immediate resignation.'

'Edu! What in the name of the Seven Fucking Hells is going on?'

Edu balled his fists and screamed.

Fyia kicked off her boots, shivering when her feet landed on the wet, frigid ground.

'What are you doing?' said Edu, his features saying he regretted his outburst already. That was entirely in character, even if the rest of his behavior was not.

'Going for a run,' she said, the restorative power of the earth already seeping through her soles. She needed this too, she realized. 'And you're coming with me.'

He looked for a moment as though he might object, but then took off through the trees. A shot of adrenaline entered Fyia's blood as she raced after him, laughing as she wound up to a full sprint, her wolves yelping with glee as they ran at her side.

They weaved this way and that through the trees, which grew closer together the further they ran, scaring rabbits and startling birds. By the time Fyia's lungs burned and her legs ached, the trees were so thick they could only manage a slow jog. They moved in silence, forced to concentrate lest they run into a tree or trip over a root.

They eventually emerged from the trees with little warning, stopping suddenly on account of the steep descent to a small river below. The water moved fast, bolstered by the ice melt, and the sound of it tumbling over rock was further sustenance to Fyia's weary soul.

They climbed down and sat on the rocks, neither noticing the cold, still warm from the exercise, and the wolves that curled up beside them.

'I kept Rouel around because he's a fine guard,' said Edu. 'He's wily and quick thinking. The same instincts that help him sniff out songs are useful for sniffing out trouble. He's often three steps ahead of the other guards, and when his skills are used to keep you safe, I'm glad of them.

'But something's shifted … something I can't put my finger on, and it makes me question his priorities.'

'You don't think he should accompany Essa?'

'It is not that I don't want him to go. I would be happy for Essa to have Rouel as her guard, if I was convinced the only reason he wanted to go is to protect her.'

'You think he would put his songs above Essa?'

'I hope not, but protecting Essa is not the same as guarding you. You are his Queen.'

'And Rouel gets to be with you when guarding me …' said Fyia, shamelessly.

'Fyia, I do not have feelings for Rouel, and I am certain he has grown out of whatever feelings you believed him to have for me.'

'But I thought …'

'You enjoyed the notion of our forbidden love, and I didn't correct you, because it kept you and Sensis occupied.'

Fyia scowled. 'Why will no one tell me what's going on in their personal lives? You and Rouel, Sensis and Antice, Essa and Veau … and don't get me started on Alba and Leo. They're obviously obsessed with one another, but I don't understand it. The only ones that make any sense are Storm and Gabriel, and they had Isa stuck in the middle of their love for hundreds of years.'

'You're short of gossip?' said Edu, scornfully.

'I am short of truth,' she snapped. 'How can I trust any of you when you keep the basic details of your lives from me?'

'We are not entitled to privacy?'

'What if Sensis chooses Antice over me?'

Edu nodded once, but said nothing, and Fyia let the water soothe her as she waited.

'Sensis would choose you over any other. Always. I understand her relationship with Antice not at all, but even if they pledge to spend their lives with one another, have babies, and bicker into their latter decades, if you call, Sensis will answer.'

'I thought the same of Veau,' she said, her voice quiet.

'And you were right.'

'He lied to me,' she snarled. 'He and Essa both.'

'And I don't condone it, but they did so out of a misguided notion of love.'

'And what if Sensis does the same? What if you do?'

'What's making you feel this way?' said Edu, scratching her wolf behind the ear.

'Everything is changing, and nothing is like I thought it would be. My dragon has abandoned me already—because of my own stupidity—and I have no trust in Scorpia or Antice. Their motives are unclear.

'Storm and Gabriel say they want to help, but the Fae'ch have politics so old, who knows what truly drives them? You have been sullen of late, and Cal ...' She trailed off. 'Cal is back among his own people, and he has his dragon.'

'Cal loves you.'

'And so do you, but you're hiding something.' She bunched her fists. 'Nothing is as it should be ...'

'The great Fyia Orlightus is finally feeling unsettled by the changes she fought to bring about?' said Edu, teasing her.

'Don't change the subject.'

'I'm not.'

'Then don't mock me.'

'If I mocked you, I would also be mocking myself,' he said, his shoulders finally relaxing.

She swiveled her head to look at him. 'You feel the same?'

He tossed a stick into the water, then followed its swift movement downstream with his eyes. 'Ever since you left me and headed north with Cal. You didn't even leave a note ...'

Fyia's mouth dropped open as his words punched a hole in her heart. He was right, of course. She had left him, because Starfall and the Spider needed him more than she. But she hadn't told him that, and she'd been so wrapped up in the moment—in Cal—she'd barely considered Edu's feelings.

He was so stoic, able to bear the brunt of almost anything—him and Sensis both—that it was easy to forget they had feelings. That they could be hurt as easily as any other. They might not wear their hearts on their sleeves, but they still beat the same way ... could be crushed the same way.

'Edu,' she said, putting a hand on his arm, 'I'm so sorry.'

He refused to meet her eyes and the tension returned to his shoulders, his lips pursed. Even this made him uncomfortable.

'You're right to be angry ... to be hurt ... to feel like everything is running too fast in all the wrong directions,' said Fyia. 'Gods know, I feel like that. But for as long as you want to be here, I will always need you by my side. I left you behind because I thought the others needed you more, but I was wrong. You were right to follow me, and I'm sorry for everything I put you through.'

'Everything?' Edu joked, cocking an eyebrow.

He always used humor as a defense. Fyia understood the impulse, and she wouldn't push him. She'd take the olive branch for what it was, and be glad their friendship was on the road to recovery.

Fyia scooted closer, wrapping both of her arms around his much bigger one. 'You're right, *everything* would take too long to atone for,' she said, resting her head against his rock-solid arm.

Edu snorted.

'Do you think Sensis feels the same way?' she said, wishing she'd spent more time with her before she'd headed south.

'Sensis has always had a different kind of relationship with you,' said Edu. 'She leads your armies. I ensure you don't get killed. I'm sure she would like to spend more time with you, as she did during the war, but she has more to occupy her mind. I have only you.'

'I'd hoped you had Rouel too ...' He tensed, and she held on tighter. 'I only mean, you are my dearest friend, and I want you to be happy.'

'I am happy.'

Fyia believed him, but she still wanted him to have more.

They sat in silence for many turns of the hand, the simple pleasures of the river, the open blue sky, and her easy companionship with Edu restoring Fyia's inner balance.

'We should go,' she said eventually, worried she might fall asleep if they stayed much longer. But Edu's eyes had locked onto something in the sky.

'Isn't that your dragon?' he said, pointing to a streak of silver scales hurtling across the blue.

'Yes,' said Fyia. A ball of worry sank into her stomach that Edu had spotted Silver first. Did that mean Silver was concealing himself from Fyia in some way?

'He's heading for the temple. Maybe he's looking for you?'

'Maybe,' said Fyia, although she wasn't convinced.

Fyia and Edu pushed themselves hard as they ran, sweat trickling down Fyia's spine by the time they arrived at the temple. They broke through the tree line, and Fyia lifted her arms triumphantly at having crossed first, but her heart leapt into her throat as she took in the scene before them.

Several devouts of the Dragon Order surrounded Scorpia's red dragon, Scorpia atop him, her features fearsome as the Order inched the angry dragon away from Cal. Cal lay on the ground, his arm outstretched towards his own, green dragon, who was baring his fangs at Red. Fyia tried to go to Cal, but Edu grabbed her around the waist and hauled her back.

She didn't fight, because he had a point. She was Queen of the Five Kingdoms, and putting herself in harm's way was not in the interests of anyone but herself, even though her every instinct strained to go to Cal.

But what could she do? She'd most likely end up with an injury, maybe even from her own dragon, who'd just landed behind Red, and was snarling at the smaller dragon.

Fyia was glad her dragon was backing up Cal, but she could find no clues to tell her what had happened.

Cal got to his feet, and mimicked the actions of the devouts, his arms pointed at his own dragon, his hands waving up and down, his mouth moving, although Fyia couldn't hear his words.

Red eventually quietened, and Scorpia dismounted, running her hands over her dragon's neck before he took to the sky. Scorpia stalked inside the temple as Cal's and Fyia's dragons hopped up to perch on nearby pillars.

'What was that about?' said Fyia, rushing forward when Edu finally released her. 'Are you hurt?'

'Only bruised,' said Cal, testing out his limbs, 'and in need of a hot bath.'

'What happened?'

'Scorpia's dragon attacked. She was screaming at Red to stop, but he refused to listen. My dragon dove for the ground and dumped me before squaring up to them.'

'But why would Red attack?' said Edu.

'Because he's got an anger problem?' said Fyia.

'I …' Cal hesitated.

'What?' said Fyia.

Cal made sure no one else was in earshot before saying, 'Do you trust Scorpia? I don't want to sow seeds of doubt in our alliance, but I'm not sure she was truly calling her dragon off. She has the best control of any of us, and yet she says she could do nothing. Maybe the first time it happened, but again?'

'Or her dragon's unstable …' said Fyia. 'The dragons have been stuck together in Hell for hundreds of years.'

'And who knows what history lies between them?' agreed Cal. 'But still …'

'I'll assign a guard to watch her more closely,' said Edu. 'Just in case.'

Fyia considered telling him not to. It was one thing to loosely monitor everyone's activities, but quite another to spy. It would be a breach of trust against one of their closest allies, and if she discovered them, Scorpia would have reason enough to abandon the alliance. But Cal wouldn't have said anything—especially in front of Edu—if he didn't believe Scorpia to be hiding something.

Fyia nodded. 'And I'll speak with her. There's been so little time since we arrived here … maybe all she needs is some care.'

Edu returned to drilling his guards, and Fyia intended to find Scorpia, but as she and Cal headed for the temple's entrance, her dragon hopped down in front of her, blocking her path.

'Hey,' she said, unable to hide her surprise.

'I'm going to the baths,' said Cal. 'Take your time.'

She barely heard him, focusing instead on the enormous face of her dragon that was now inches from her own. 'I'm sorry,' she said aloud, and into her dragon's mind. 'I didn't know not to use magic … I barely know *how* to use it. I just wanted you to listen to me, and I was trying everything I thought might work.'

He head-butted her with such force, she fell backwards, and a shot of fear hurtled through her as he snarled over her, baring his mesmerizing, razor-sharp teeth.

Fyia tipped her head back and forced her body to relax. He was playing with her, showing her he could do as he pleased, that he was bigger and more powerful, and could crush her in an instant.

'I'm sorry,' she said again. 'Truly.'

Her wolves whined from where they stood by the trees, and Fyia threw a mental barrage towards them, ordering them to stay back. *I want us to be partners*, she said to her dragon. *A team. I want people to see our bond and know nothing could ever come between us. I know I haven't made the best start, but I want to try, and I hope you do too.*

Silver stopped snarling, and Fyia reached out her hand, until it was an inch from Silver's scaled face, waiting for him to close the final distance between them.

For what must have been a thousand of her racing heartbeats, Silver didn't so much as twitch, and Fyia worried her arm muscles would give out. She focused so hard on willing her arms not to shake that she almost didn't realize when Silver snorted out a breath that warmed her fingers, then pressed his chin against her palm.

Fyia scratched him there, and like a cat, greedy for attention, Silver tilted his head, his ears twitching comically as she scratched harder. When her arm was shaking from the workout, she dropped it to her side, and he shook his entire body and ruffled his wings. He reminded Fyia so strongly of a horse, she was concerned he would try to roll and scratch his back, but instead, he leapt into the sky, then landed in the lake just downhill of the temple.

It was mostly slushy water atop a still frozen base, and the sight of Silver rolling, scratching, and pawing, then launching showers of slush with his wings, made everyone stop and stare. Children giggled and tried to get closer, but their parents pulled them back, and Fyia laughed along with them, feeling like she might finally be making progress with her dragon.

Fyia didn't want to face Scorpia just yet, not wanting anything to burst the bubble of joy in her chest, so instead, she headed in search of Cal.

The temple held numerous bath houses heated by the magma ducts, some public, and others private, or used for special ceremonies.

The royal baths were a series of pools and chambers, each a different temperature, some frigid, some bubbling, and others with falls of water crashing down from the roof. Some contained only sweet-smelling steam, and one had a pit of hot coals in its center.

Candles flickered throughout the space, sending light dancing across the mosaics of flowers and trees and soaring dragons.

Fyia tossed aside the boots she'd retrieved from the trees, then stripped off her sweat-soaked clothing. By the time she found Cal, in a heated, bubbling pool, not a shred of cloth remained, and his eyes—black in the orange light—stuck to her like glue.

'You should have seen Silver,' she said, elation still coursing through her veins. 'He rolled in the lake!'

Cal laughed as she stepped into the deep, deliciously hot pool of bubbles, her freezing feet stinging at the sudden heat. Whoever had built this temple was a marvel, the pools here more extensive and luxurious than any she'd encountered across the known world, their only rival perhaps those at the Temple of the Night Goddess, where Starfall called home.

She wondered briefly how Starfall fared in Selise, and a pang of guilt hit her hard in the chest. Practically speaking, Fyia couldn't leave the north; she needed to learn how to control her dragon. But that did nothing to help with the hardships her kingdoms were facing.

The most recent message—some days ago now—said the protests against her rule had stopped, and after the initial shocks, things had quietened down. Not before many had lost their lives to spewing magma and hungry dragons, however.

Fyia hoped the wardens of each of her kingdoms would finally work with Starfall to keep her people safe. And Sensis would soon be there, which Starfall would surely be glad of. But guilt slipped like rushing sand through Fyia's torso, landing heavily in her gut, and piling in a heap.

Cal pulled her down onto his lap and wrapped his arms around her waist. 'They're so full of character,' he said. 'The babies so naughty, Red so angry ... but I think I have the knack for placating them. You saw how the Order calmed Red earlier, and I tried it on my dragon. I could feel the effect I was having. It makes me wonder if my mother had that skill ... if she passed it to me.'

'That's amazing,' said Fyia, but his words reminded her how far behind the others she was, and she faltered.

He pressed his lips to her back. 'You'll get there with Silver.'

'I hope so,' she said, 'although I'm not sure the same can be said for my relationship with Scorpia.'

Cal moved her so she sat between his legs, kneading the knots in her back. She squeezed his thighs appreciatively.

'I must speak with her,' said Fyia. 'We need a strong alliance between the fire-touched, and she's a loose cannon.'

'But I can't work out why?' said Cal.

It was a question Fyia had asked herself at least a hundred times. 'Maybe she doesn't like me?'

'Or she's just a grumpy old woman, stuck in her ways, and doesn't like playing second fiddle to anyone.'

Fyia pulled forward and turned her head to look at him. 'She's not playing second fiddle,' she said hotly. 'She's Queen of her lands, as we are King and Queen of our own.' Not that Fyia was fulfilling her queenly duties …

Cal raised his eyebrows, and she turned back so he could resume his kneading, his thumb sliding back and forth over a particularly large knot.

'She's the only one who doesn't seem to realize working together is in everyone's interests,' said Fyia. 'Even Antice is playing nicely …'

'He's been helping with the glasshouses,' said Cal, sliding his hands to her neck.

She closed her eyes and focused on the feel of his fingers and the sounds of bubbling water. 'And foraging, and cooking in the kitchens, and doing whatever he does for hours on end in his hut, and making great strides with his dragon.'

'Don't be jealous,' said Cal, pushing into a spot that made her leap into the air.

'Ow …' She couldn't help her jealousy, or frustration, or uncertainty. Everything was running away from her, paths being trodden by others, leading off in every direction, and Fyia didn't know where she should tread, or if her path would lead where she wanted to go.

Which is where, exactly? Fyia's path had been so clear for so long, and now …

She stood abruptly, and moved to the other side of the pool, bracing her hands against the side. Angst screwed tight in her chest, and she didn't know how to make it unwind.

Cal was back with his people, in his home. It was obvious what he wanted, that he was happy here, but what did she want?

She shut down the unwelcome thoughts. She had to deal with Scorpia, and the clocks, and then consider what came next. Whether they would live in the north, or in her kingdoms, or some combination of the two, was not a problem for this moment. But the anguish caused by her many worries spread out under her skin, sitting there like a coating, and no matter how hard she scrubbed, she couldn't wash it away.

Chapter Fourteen

WHEN FYIA AND CAL LEFT the shelter of the royal baths, they found outfits laid out for them—fancy ones. They shared confused looks, but donned the clothes, Fyia slipping into a dress of shimmering silver, earrings made of tiny, golden dragon scales that cascaded from her lobes, and a flowing, hooded cloak of black and silver. Cal wore the traditional black of the Black Hoods, but with green embroidery on his long doublet, and miniature dragon scales sewn into the cuffs and collar.

Someone—presumably a member of the Order of the Dragon—had left the clothes, along with a note politely requesting their presence in the Hall of the Dragon. They'd wondered if it was a joke, and certainly weren't expecting the lavish celebration already in full swing.

They shared baffled glances, then gratefully accepted the warm, heavily spiced wine offered by a server. Cal slipped his hand into Fyia's. 'You are breathtaking,' he whispered in her ear. He kissed her lips, but Fyia pulled away.

'I must speak with Scorpia,' she said, spotting the old woman leaning against a nearby pillar. She surveyed the spectacle of dancing and drinking and ... oh, Gods ... Veau stood in the middle of the room, sending sparks of magic up into the air, each of his three baby dragons chasing them, to the delight of the crowd. He really had learned to control his power. Something Fyia had yet to accomplish ...

Fyia tore her eyes away, focusing instead on Scorpia, who wore an exquisite red dress with intricate, golden embellishments painstakingly sewn across every inch, including rows of tiny dragon scales. She also had scales pinned into her hair, and a cuff of them along each ear.

'Queen Scorpia,' said Fyia, bowing her head as she approached her fellow queen.

'Queen Fyia,' said Scorpia, barely bothering to incline her own.

'How do you find the frozen north?' said Fyia, her tone light, friendly, and respectful.

'Cold,' said Scorpia, 'bland, and boring.'

'I am sorry to hear that,' said Fyia. 'At least bonding with your dragon is going well? You seem to have a strong connection already.'

'What of it?' said Scorpia, rounding on Fyia with intense eyes.

'I'm jealous, I suppose,' said Fyia, with a self-deprecating smile, forcing her voice to retain its warm edge.

Scorpia cocked an eyebrow. 'It was stupid to use magic on your dragon.'

'So I have discovered.'

They watched as a group of children leapt back and forth along the sunken aqueduct that ran through the middle of the temple's floor. They chased Veau's dragons, who kept diving below the surface, then squirting the children with water, causing them to squeal with glee.

'May I be frank?' said Fyia, tearing her eyes from the children, and turning so her body angled fully towards the Queen.

'It would be refreshing,' said Scorpia.

'You seem unhappy here. When I met you in the south, in your own lands, you seemed to me relaxed, at ease, interested in what we would find, and excited about my quest for the eggs.' Scorpia had also withheld much, including her knowledge of the magma ducts, and the fact she was fire-touched, but Fyia refrained from mentioning that now.

'Since you arrived here,' Fyia continued, 'I have seen nothing of that woman. If we have offended you, or …'

'You took the royal suite,' said Scorpia, cutting off Fyia's words.

Fyia clamped her mouth shut, forcing herself to think before saying something she might regret. 'You would like the royal suite?'

Scorpia sniffed. 'I would not be opposed to the idea. I am, after all, *royal*.'

'Then I will speak with Cal. It was not my people, but his who prepared it for us, and I am sure we can find an arrangement that suits us all.'

'You think yourselves the Dragon King and Queen,' said Scorpia, her tone hostile as she repeated the accusation she'd made before.

'No,' said Fyia. 'We do not consider ourselves above you, or Veau, or Antice. We are equals, each with our own fire-touch, dragons, and responsibilities.'

'Lord Sollow Antice is your equal? And your brother? When you return to your lands, will you no longer rule over them as Queen?'

'We are equally fire-touched,' said Fyia, 'but the dynamic between myself and my subjects is my business. My lands and people are still my own, just as your lands and people belong to you.'

'And if we disagree?' said Scorpia. 'If I must make choices you dislike—as will surely be the consequence of all this—it will be four against one. Meaning whose word is final?'

Fyia took a long breath, forcing calm into her heating blood. 'I do not have all the answers,' she said, 'but I hope it will not come to that. I hope we will discuss our wants and needs and devise solutions that work for the world. I have no desire to emulate the ways of the kings that came before. Just as I have no desire to control the bloodlines of the fire-touched. More of us will emerge, and I will be glad when they do.'

'Until they find a bigger dragon and take your throne,' said Scorpia, with a cruel smile. 'Let us see how *glad* you are then.'

'Fyia!' called a voice from behind her, and she turned to see Cal's cousin, Princess Zhura, moving towards her, dragging Cal in her wake.

By the time Fyia turned back to Scorpia, she was gone, and hot frustration kindled in Fyia's blood. If anything, she'd made things with the old battle-axe worse. But she didn't have time to dwell, because Zhura deposited Cal by her side, and then turned and raised her hand, waving to Aaron—Cal and Zhura's closest friend. Aaron slammed a wooden staff against the floor, and the sound echoed around the temple, silence rippling out behind it.

Cal leaned down towards her, his features a strange mix of trepidation and excitement. 'I knew nothing of this until this moment, but there's no use in fighting it … it would cause great offense to my people.'

What in the name of all the Gods? He squeezed her hand, presumably because she looked like a rabbit caught in lamp-light, and then a rich, female voice of a devout floated across the temple. The devout stood by the dragon thrones, dressed head to foot in white, her face hidden behind her robes.

'All hail Atlas Calemir Talos, King of the Black Hoods, and his chosen consort, Fyia Orlightus, Queen of the Five Kingdoms of the East.'

'All hail!' the crowd chanted. Then the people moved apart, opening a channel between where Cal and Fyia stood, and the aqueduct.

Fyia tried to smile, although, given Cal's words as he leaned in once more, she wasn't convinced she'd pulled it off, and the beginnings of panic flared inside her, mixing with the angst still coating her skin to make a toxic, flammable combination. 'All will be well,' he murmured, 'just follow my lead.'

Cal took Fyia's hand, gently tugging her until she moved with him towards the aqueduct. He squared his shoulders, pride swelling in his chest as his people bowed, respect shining in their eyes. He looked down at Fyia, who'd recovered from her initial shock, and now was every inch the imperious Queen, her hair half swept up in elegant twists on either side of her face, her shoulders back, head high.

He wished he could warn her about what would come next, but what could he say? Certainly nothing that would fully explain, and with only a few words, he might make it worse. So as they reached the aqueduct, he simply whispered, 'To the thrones, my love,' then released her and leapt to the far side.

He set off towards the dais, trusting Fyia would follow, that she would understand they were embroiled in something ancient, and far beyond their control. The crowd pressed back so Fyia and Cal could pass with ease, and soon they'd reached the wide, shallow steps leading to the dragon thrones.

As Cal looked up at the stone dragon, its head hovering between the two thrones, he thought of the last time he and Fyia had ascended these steps together, when he'd felt almost guilty for doing so. They had been alone in the temple then, only the Gods watching. It was different today, with most of his people crowded into the vast space, the ice melting, prosperity returning to his lands with every drip.

The channel of water between them thinned as they climbed, and as they came closer together, Cal offered Fyia his arm. She laid her hand gently atop his and sent him a warm look, although Cal didn't miss the apprehensive edge.

I'm sorry, he tried to tell her, but her eyes had already turned away, the crowd now completely silent, not a sound to be heard aside from the click of their feet against the old stone.

They reached the top, then turned to face their people, and two devouts of the Dragon Order appeared, one from each side, each carrying a golden ring of dragon scales across their palms.

Cal inhaled sharply as the crowns came closer, crowns that had not been used for hundreds of years. There could be no dispute now over Cal's right to sit this throne, not with his dragon outside, and the ice thawing. Soon their people would be a power in the world once more, no longer cowering in the north, foraging for scraps, and forced to trade dragon scales—their heritage—to survive.

The devouts stood before Fyia and Cal, then held the crowns aloft above their heads. Fyia turned to look at him, and as Cal met her gaze, a prickle of concern tingled against his mind, because underneath her smile was something darker, savage and untamed.

The devouts started speaking as one, pulling Cal and Fyia's attention forward once more. 'I crown you, King and Queen of these ancient, sacred lands, before the Dragon God, the people of the north, and your dragons—magic itself made flesh. As we serve you, you shall serve your people and the Gods, lest the magic, the Gods, or your dragons, strike you down.'

They lowered the crowns, offering no opportunity for Fyia or Cal to refuse their titles, as was the tradition. The people decided who would rule, and if those rulers shied from the task, they must face the embarrassment of abdication and exile.

Guilt ripped through Cal as the weight of his crown settled. He should have warned Fyia, should have known his people might do this, but he had never dreamed it would happen so soon—if ever. They'd only been here a handful of days. Everything was still a mess, they knew not how to fix the magma ducts, and they were still developing their bonds with their dragons.

Cal and Fyia hadn't spoken about where they might live, or whether Fyia wanted the responsibilities the devouts had just placed upon her head.

'All hail the King and Queen of the Black Hoods,' said the devouts.

'All hail the King and Queen of the Five Kingdoms of the East!' someone shouted from the crowd.

'All hail the Dragon King and Queen!' shouted another, and the temple erupted, taking up the chant.

'Wait!' Fyia shouted, lifting her arms. 'Wait! We are not the Dragon King and Queen! We have never made that claim, and it is not a title I seek, nor want. Lord Antice, Queen Scorpia, and my brother—Prince Veau Orlightus—please join us. Together we command the dragons.'

The crowd looked on in disbelief, buoyant in one moment, unsure the next. The story was simpler if Cal and Fyia were the only ones to rule, but Fyia was right. The last thing they wanted was a rift between the fire-touched that could tear their dreams to shreds.

Antice and Veau stepped up, standing beside them on the dais, but Scorpia was nowhere to be seen.

The crowd looked for her, a murmur travelling through them as they questioned where she could be. And then a loud, terrifying screech sounded from the entrance, and their heads turned as one. Gasps and screams went up as a plume of fire lit the air above their heads, and then Red, Scorpia atop him, punched into the temple, landed on the steps that led to the dais, and roared in Fyia's face.

Cal moved without thinking, in front of Fyia in a heartbeat, and holding out his hands to the dragon. He had seen the devouts calm Red earlier that day, and Cal channeled the same calm thoughts now, moving his arms as they had.

'Out of my way, *King*,' Scorpia shouted from above them. 'My fight is not with you.'

'If your fight is with my Queen, then you are mistaken,' said Cal, losing the beginnings of the grip he held over Red. 'A fight with Fyia is a fight with me.'

Smoke billowed from Red's nose, and Cal had to step back to avoid being burnt.

'She has you so tightly wrapped around her finger already?'

'No one lays a hand on my wife,' Cal growled, then redoubled his efforts to calm the beast.

'We do not wish to fight you,' said Fyia, stepping to the side so she could meet Scorpia's gaze. 'Stay and celebrate with us, as our equal. Let us create a powerful alliance that benefits us all.'

'You know not of what you speak, *child*,' said Scorpia, although her eyes kept darting to Cal, worry marring her otherwise fearsome features.

'Then leave now, and we will not fight you,' said Fyia, 'for it is a battle you cannot win. Three fully grown dragons await outside that door ...'

'And we will placate your dragon while they rip him apart,' said Cal, with more confidence than he felt.

For a moment, Cal thought she would make the stupid choice, but then she whirled and flew back through the enormous opening. Cal's and Fyia's dragons took to the sky behind her, running her out of the north.

Cal turned to make sure Fyia was alright, and found her cocking an irritated eyebrow at him.

'What was that?' she said, folding her arms across her chest.

'I placated Red! Like the devouts!' he said, feeling a rush as the realization settled in.

'No, not that,' said Fyia. 'You called me your *wife*.'

'Oh,' said Cal, Fyia's words a brick wall before his racing thoughts. 'Yes, I did.'

Gods, she was magnificent when she gave him that look. It made him want to throw her over his shoulder, carry her back to their room, and refuse to come out for days.

'What the fuck?'

'It's tradition here for the people to choose their leaders ... to surprise them in this way.'

'King and Queen both?' said Fyia.

Cal nodded.

'But what if ... what if they chose a king and queen who hated one another?'

'That's never happened, as far as I know. My people are not stupid; they know their leaders must see eye to eye, and anyway, the practice has been dead and buried for centuries.'

'Well, not any longer, *husband*.'

She edged her words with an anger that sent a chill down his spine, but he couldn't stop his feet from moving closer, his heart squeezing in his chest. 'Say that word again,' he murmured, inhaling her scent of wild roses deep into his lungs.

Fyia's eyes told him she was not playing, and Veau coughed awkwardly, piercing the moment. 'Um ... everyone's watching. And do I need to congratulate you? On your coronation and ... wedding day?'

'We're not actually married ...' said Cal, stepping back.

'So if I wanted to marry another?' said Fyia, sharpening her knives.

A bolt of irrational jealousy cut through him, and his heart leapt in his chest. 'We might not be married, but we're as good as, at least in the eyes of the Black Hoods. Once crowned, it is impossible for kings and queens to marry another.'

'They just take lovers instead?'

Cal glimpsed the feral thing behind her eyes once more.

'Fyia!' said Veau, chastising her like only a brother could. Cal would ordinarily be glad of the ally, but not with Fyia like this.

He had to get her out of here. She didn't like being blindsided, was already feeling unmoored, and she had genuinely wanted a strong alliance with Scorpia. Things were spiraling out of her control, and she needed to let it out, rage at the world, find a release. Veau was only making it worse.

'I think you should leave,' Cal said to Veau. 'And we should get some air,' he said to Fyia, desperate to take her somewhere quiet where they could talk, where he could explain, where she could explode in private.

'You get some air, if that's what you need. I need a drink.'

A makeshift bar stood at the back of the temple, and all eyes were glued to Fyia as she descended the stairs alone and made a beeline for it. The crowd parted for her, bowing as she passed, but Fyia paid them no heed.

When she reached the table, she waved aside the tankard of beer the barman offered—that stuff was disgusting—opting instead for a bottle of the potent spirit they distilled from liquid tapped from the elusive Byar tree.

It was fragrant and rich and extremely potent, and Fyia poured herself a liberal measure.

She turned to face the people and threw her arms wide. 'Come!' she cried. 'Drink with me! This is a celebration, is it not?'

Those who had been skulking at the back perked up at her words, needing little encouragement before selecting drinks of their own.

Fyia downed a second measure. 'Music!' she shouted, and Rouel, lute in hand, appeared by her side, as though primed and waiting for this very moment.

He played, and she laughed, accepting another measure from the bartender. Soon the whole place was dancing and singing and drinking, buoyed by relief, for they had not been eaten by a dragon, and would still have a party this night.

Fyia didn't spare a look towards Cal, her sort-of husband. They had planned to wed, of course, but not like this. Not because of some long-dead northern custom, where Fyia and Cal had no say in their own destiny. Maybe if she'd known it was a possibility …

Suddenly, the crowd was too much, and she pushed her way through them, heading for the exit. She found Cinis near the doors, hiding in an alcove, only realizing he was there because her magic alerted her to his presence.

'This way,' he said.

She followed him through a hole at the back of the alcove. The bricks slid closed behind them, shutting out the noise, removing one of the many layers of Fyia's discomfort.

Cinis led her up a narrow, spiral stone staircase, and they popped out onto a balcony at the top. Spy holes on either side allowed them to see both outside the temple and the party below.

'How did you know this was here?' said Fyia. She peered through a hole and found Cal in the crowd, talking with Zhura and Aaron, his body tense, a frown on his brow.

'My brand of magic is helpful in such things,' said Cinis, 'and you looked as though you could do with time away from the crowds.'

Fyia nodded, although it was hard to make sense of anything, her head already swimming from the liquor, which made the frustrated rage inside her even worse.

'Why did you have sex with my mother?' she said, lashing out at the only punchbag available.

Cinis didn't even blink.

Fyia leaned back against the wall. 'Did she tell you her plan? Were you in on it? Apparently, she was quite open with the Fae'ch when she asked them for a sire.'

'It was not the same with me,' said Cinis, 'and the story is simple. She came to the Great Glacier and told me she was an explorer. She was … magnetic, a quality you inherited from her, I think. She was very forward in her advances, and I thought it harmless.'

'Did you know? That she had got with child?' said Fyia, almost disappointed the story was so plain.

'No,' said Cinis, 'at least, not then. I pieced it together later, and then when I saw you … well, it's obvious, is it not?'

Fyia studied his features. Features so much like hers.

'You inherited your mother's ambition too, it would seem.'

Fyia half laughed. 'Some see it that way, but really, I'm just angry at the world. I don't want to rule, not really … never have. I didn't covet Veau's position as heir when we were children, and I never longed for the throne, or a crown. When my parents tried to marry me off to the Emperor, I ran away, and I met others to whom the Five Kingdoms had not been kind.'

'And you decided you would be the one to change it.'

Fyia couldn't work out if he was mocking her, or if the edge she detected was respect, so she paused a moment, studying him.

'Well, here's the thing, Cinis, I had nothing to lose. My life was worth not a thing, aside from as currency, to further my parents' own aims. And if not me—a princess, with a full belly, connections, and sturdy boots on my feet—then who?'

'I don't mean to goad you,' said Cinis.

'Most do.'

'It is truly surprising, what you have done, that is all.'

'Why?'

'I was beginning to think the day would never come when dragons graced the skies once more.'

'Then Asesh saw to it that they did.'

Cinis raised his eyebrows. 'She was never trustworthy, that one.'

'Why should we trust you any more than her?' She shouldn't have said it, especially not in that accusatory tone, but everything was so unsatisfactory. How could this man be her father? How could she not have known? And what were his motives?

Cinis made a disgusted noise. 'I am nothing like that witch. By all means, be wary, as is wise, but never compare me to her. I swore an oath to protect the dragons. Since that time, I have lived thousands of years, and still I have not shirked, nor deviated, nor followed opportunities for personal gain.

'Do you not think I could have done what Asesh did? Befriend kings? Seduce queens? Steer the course of politics and bloodlines, pretending to be a God? But I did not. And in all that time, I lapsed in my duties only once, when your mother sought me out. She knew her ancestors had the fire-touch, but she was greedy, and wanted her children to have more. She wanted them to have magic, and neither her line, nor the King of Starlight's, had any of significance.

'She played a dangerous game, for I am part fae. There was a chance you would inherit too much fae blood, that it would have been obvious you were not the child of the King. Had that happened, they would have killed you both for her treachery. Not to mention, with too much fae blood, the fire-touch will not manifest.'

'You are Fae'ch, then?' said Fyia. 'I am Fae'ch?' Her new identity fit her not at all.

Cinis scoffed. 'What are the Fae'ch in this age? A sorry collection of outcast beings with little magic. I am not a part of that band of unhappy imposters. I am of the old magic, of the kind that flows through the alterwoods and the seas and the ancient algae of the deepest crevices. The kind that was here before. I am not as old as Asesh, but almost. I am descended from the first Fae'ch—when that word meant something—when we helped humans without the touch of fire to hold their own.'

'You came from a breeding experiment?' said Fyia.

'I am part of the ninth generation,' said Cinis. 'By then, people had almost forgotten where we came from. We freely interbred with humans, whose magic was no weaker than our own in those days. It was only when human magic weakened more than our own that the problems started. When they began to fear us.'

'Where do you think Asesh has gone?' The woman had proven herself a worrying threat, and Fyia wondered when she would strike her next blow.

Cinis shrugged. 'She comes and goes as she pleases. She has lived longer than any other alive, and in that time, I am sure she has travelled every inch of the known world, and perhaps further besides. She could be in this very building, concealed in plain sight … it is unfortunate she escaped.'

Fyia wondered why Asesh had wanted to restart the system. Because she knew the fallen clocks would bring death and destruction? Or was there some deeper purpose to her scheming?

'And what of your magic?' said Fyia. 'Given my mother claims to have no magic of her own, it makes sense for mine to be like yours.'

'Everyone has some talent,' said Cinis, 'and now, when the dragons fly over the world, disbursing the magic, more will be able to use theirs.'

'But what of *my* magic?' said Fyia. 'I've pushed it so deep for so long, and now its strength grows, and I'm … What if I hurt someone?' *Like Veau used to.*

'You must find a teacher, but I am not the best candidate. Despite being your father, my earth magic is a poor match for your fiery nature.'

'Earth magic?'

'I have an affinity with the earth, and growing things, and finding veins of minerals in the ground, and passages hidden to most.'

'I like to run barefoot in the woods,' said Fyia, half to herself. 'I find it restorative … like the earth is feeding me.'

Cinis nodded. 'I find the same.'

'But how do you control it?'

'I don't,' said Cinis, harshly. 'What is it with you and *controlling* everything? Have you not learned by now that control is only an illusion? You seek to exert control over your dragon, and your people, and your magic!'

Fyia scowled. 'You said yourself, I need to control my dragon …'

'Yes, but not with sheer force of will, or fire and fury, with *control*.'

Fyia shrugged. 'I don't understand.'

'If you want to control your magic, you must control yourself. You must be calm, and centered, and slow, like the growth of an alterwood tree. You must understand yourself, your intentions and desires, what you want the magic to help you accomplish. Only then will the magic be able to assist.'

'I do understand myself,' said Fyia, not caring that her voice had become shrill. 'I know what I want.'

'You wanted to unite the Five Kingdoms, so you could return the dragons,' said Cinis. 'You wanted to become a legend, even when you discovered the legends were mostly lies.'

'I wanted to right the wrongs of the kings.'

'Wanted?'

'I still want that.'

'Then why are you here, and not in the Five Kingdoms?'

'Because I need dragons to make my people believe in me.'

'You have dragons, and the rebellions in your lands have ceased. So why are you still here?'

Fyia threw up her hands. 'How can I take my dragon to the Five Kingdoms when I have no control?'

'Then leave him here. If all you want is to right the wrongs of ...'

'We must fix the magma ducts first ... the clocks.'

'So it is not righting wrongs that is truly what you want? At this moment, you care most about fixing the magma ducts?'

Fyia growled and turned her head away, anger kindling in her chest anew. 'It is not so simple. I want many things.'

'Simplicity of thought is a challenge in itself. One of the greatest challenges we know.'

Fyia furrowed her brow, but allowed herself to consider his question. What did she want most in this moment? He was right, it wasn't to go to her own kingdoms and fix the many problems rife across them. She felt guilt for leaving Starfall and the Spider to bear the burden, and she knew it was unfair on them, but she had no desire to return. The realization lifted some weight off her soul, and elation filled her liquor-fueled mind.

But then what? What did she want from this mess she'd caused? Cal. She knew with certainty she wanted him, and for her bond with her dragon to be cast from the strongest steel. She wanted her friends around her, and to be free in a way she'd never been before.

'You are finally thinking,' said Cinis, in a patronizing tone that made Fyia want to punch him so much, she lost her train of thought.

'I was getting somewhere,' she snapped, rage bubbling to the surface at the loss.

Cinis chuckled, which only heightened Fyia's fury. 'Even now, you want to *force* your will upon yourself. You want the answer *now*, after only moments of seeking truth.'

'I was getting somewhere,' she repeated, through gritted teeth.

'It will take time. Give yourself permission to explore and …'

Fyia didn't hear whatever irritation flowed next from his mouth. She descended the spiral staircase, her blood so hot it was a wonder she didn't set herself on fire. Why did people always want to change her? Action was *how* she thought, who she was … an innate part of her. Yet few could truly embrace her because of it. She pushed through the stone door, then stepped out, heading for the night air, ignoring the curious looks as she passed.

She didn't think before reaching out with her mind, searching for some part of her Cruaxee who might understand the ball of pent-up fury in her chest. A beast that would spar with her, or run with her, or perform a dangerous dive with Fyia on its back.

No wolf or eagle answered her call as she ran into the woods. Apparently her current state scared even them, but as she searched in vain for her dragon, an unexpected presence pressed against her mind. A roar filled her ears, and then an enormous bear stepped out of the trees. Fyia's face split into a broad, sadistic grin. *Perfect.*

Zhura had been talking for endless spins of the hand about all the marvelous things the return of the dragons meant for the north. About the glasshouses, the things they could grow, the animals they could farm, and how wonderful it was they would no longer have to trade dragon scales just to stay alive.

Much as Cal agreed, and shared her joy, Fyia preoccupied at least half of his brain. Where had she gone, and what was she doing? None of this could be easy for her. The dragons, the worry over fixing the clocks, her new father, Scorpia, and being crowned Queen of the Black Hoods. Ordinarily, Fyia did an impeccable job of holding it together, at least in public, which was why her behavior tonight worried him.

'Antice said something about the alterwoods helping to regulate something or other ... I don't understand it yet,' said Zhura, 'but he's more knowledgeable than the experts Fyia sent. And ...'

A bolt of emotion hit Cal through his Cruaxee bond, shutting out everything around him as he tried to make sense of it. He hadn't seen his bear in some time, and the one time he'd tried to reach out to her, she'd shut him out, batting him away with a furious swipe of her paw.

She was like that—angry—a lot of the time, and Cal had learned through hard-won experience, it was better to give her space to cool off than try and force her to see him. She was angry he'd left her without saying goodbye, but now she was here … close … but it was strange. Cal couldn't decipher her emotions. It had never been like this …

And then Cal's senses heightened, and he could hear and smell everything both inside the temple and out, and that could mean only one thing. Fyia had connected with his bear, and his bear was angry, and so was his Queen …

Cal spun without conscious thought and ran for the stairs out of the temple. His feet had never moved so fast, his people scampering out of his way.

He knew there would be those who followed, curious and concerned, but he couldn't think about that, not when Fyia was in danger. His bear was the most fearsome creature he'd ever known, more dangerous even than his dragon, for she was stubborn and unpredictable and cruel. Cal reached out to her as he ran, the bond showing him Fyia through his bear's eyes, the look on Fyia's face wild as she toyed with death.

Would his bear go that far? One swipe of her colossal paw was all it would take. And his bear was frustrated, just like Fyia. Alone, each was set to explode. Together, Cal didn't dare think …

He surfaced into the night air, pumping his arms as he sprinted into the woods, Fyia's wolves snarling and yapping, guiding him through the trees. But moments before Cal reached them, their snarls became whines, and Cal's blood ran cold.

He burst into the clearing to find his bear hovering over Fyia's body, which was sprawled on the floor. 'No!' he commanded, throwing all his will through the Cruaxee bond. 'Do not hurt her!'

He ran for them as Fyia rolled over, her features a picture of vengeance.

'Fyia! No!'

If Fyia heard him, she showed no sign. She reached out her hand, and a moment later, his bear reared back with an almighty roar. She went up on her hind legs, writhing and baring her teeth, and Fyia dropped her hand, watching with terrible fascination.

Cal threw himself on top of Fyia, covering her with his body, and screamed at his bear, ordering her to stand down. But she didn't take orders from anyone, even him, and as both her paws, and all her weight, came thundering out of the sky towards them, he could do nothing but turn his head away, and breathe, 'I love you,' into Fyia's hair.

Chapter Fifteen

THE GROUND SHOOK AROUND them, and fear like she'd never known coursed through every part of Fyia's being. She'd gone too far; had goaded Cal's bear into wanting to kill her, and now they would both die. 'I'm sorry,' she whispered, clutching onto Cal as tightly as her shaking arms could manage. 'I just needed to feel … something … something extreme. I didn't mean …'

A different roar rent the air, drowning out Fyia's words, and her head snapped up in surprise. Cal's bear turned, facing the new threat—Fyia's dragon—who hadn't thought twice about flattening numerous trees to come to her aid.

Fyia pushed Cal off, then jumped to her feet, euphoria coursing through her every vein. She was not dead, Cal was not dead, and her dragon cared enough to come to her rescue. Cal's bear issued a low growl, then slunk off into the woods, for even she wasn't stubborn enough to face down a dragon.

Fyia ran to Silver and climbed onto his back, following her instincts, something in her saying this was an important moment for their bond. She'd barely settled her weight before Silver took to the sky, the cold rush of air through Fyia's flimsy dress barely registering.

She didn't care where they went, or for how long they flew, Fyia curious to see where Silver would take them. She looked back to find shimmers of blue light cascading through the sky behind them—magic, she realized, or some echo of it—and with each flap of Silver's wings, more of her anguish fell away.

Fyia sat in the crook of her dragon's wing, watching the sunrise in the valley below. They'd flown east, and had spent the night in a cave high in the Fae'ch mountains, Silver's inner fire keeping them warm.

Something about the encounter with Cal's bear had brought them closer together, but Fyia couldn't work out why. It was almost as though Silver wanted Fyia to need him, that he had enjoyed coming to her rescue. Whatever it was, Fyia was glad of it, just as she was glad for this time away from the world.

Her mind turned to her conversation with Cinis the night before, where he'd all but accused her of not knowing what she wanted. Although the idea had not landed well, her head was now clear, alcohol gone, and she could concede his words were true.

Her journey had started as a rebellion against her parents, and then against the world she knew, because it wasn't only she who'd experienced injustices. And if the world was not a place where they—Edu, Sensis, Essa, Veau—could happily exist, then she'd known it must be the same for others, that change was needed, and the only way to truly change the world was with dragons.

Now she had the dragons, and the changes were underway. So, what next? What did she want? She'd never seen herself as a ruler atop a throne, nor as the cornerstone of any political structure, and the idea that the rest of her life would be dominated by audiences with squabbling courtiers made her want to hurl herself from the nearest mountain peak.

A figure landed on the ledge in front of her, flying in from above without so much as a whisper of warning, and Fyia started, although her dragon did not. 'You can fly?' Fyia said to Storm, the short, blond Fae'ch who'd helped her brother.

'I can fly,' Storm confirmed.

'But you have no wings …'

'Solid observation skills you have there,' Storm said, her words dripping with sarcasm.

Fyia watched Storm for a moment, and Storm returned the appraisal, neither looking away. 'Why are you here?' Fyia said eventually. 'Did you follow me?'

'No,' she said, stepping into the cave and sitting at Fyia's side. 'I have been patrolling for signs of the Children of the Lake, for there are many secret ways out of the mountain. I stopped to speak with you, because I know how you feel.'

'About?'

'Everything. You are trapped in a cage of your own making. You feel beholden to others—which you are—because of the decisions you have taken, and you are lost and frustrated and want to run away from it all.'

'I do?'

Storm gave her a coy smile. 'I'm not sure if you realize, but you currently sit in a cave in lands that do not belong to you, far away from your people. But running away only makes things worse. I should know …'

'Oh?' said Fyia. She knew Storm and Gabriel had allowed Isa to lead under the mountain, because neither they, nor most of the powerful Fae'ch, had wanted the job. She also knew that Isa was in love with Gabriel, had forced him to do things he did not want to do, and that Storm had been stuck between the two. 'But you've been under the mountain for hundreds of years …'

'I ran through a portal.'

'A portal?'

'A hole in the fabric of our world leading to a … middle ground, called the House of Portals.'

'The House of Portals?' said Fyia, feeling foolish for repeating everything Storm said.

'It matters not,' said Storm. 'The point is, I ran *away*. I did not run *to*. If one runs anywhere, one should always run *to*, and only after properly dealing with the things one is running *from*. Otherwise, the things one is running *from* will eventually catch up. One can only run for so long, you see, before one needs a rest.'

Fyia just about caught the gist. 'But what if I don't know what I want to run towards?'

'You know,' said Storm. 'But you are not ready to admit it to yourself.'

Fyia scowled, and Storm laughed.

'That wasn't an insult. Remember you have the power to do anything you want in this world. You have earned that right, and you are not beholden to a set of rules, just because others insist they exist. You must make your own rules. Just as you changed the rules of war when you stole the Five Kingdoms, so you can change the rules of peace, and make them whatever you desire, as you have already begun to do in your own lands.'

It seemed harder, somehow, changing the rules of peace. Like the stakes were so much higher. The old kings had called her a cheat, and had spat upon her methods. She'd used trickery, and deception, and magic, and a bow instead of a sword, and she hadn't thought twice, because she would never have won if she'd lined up against them on a battlefield.

'Oh, don't think so hard,' said Storm. 'Take yourself out of the moment. Let it all fall away.'

'How?' said Fyia, her chest screwing up in the way it always did when she didn't understand something. Let what fall away? How could she take herself out of the Gods-damned moment? What did that even mean?

Storm nodded slowly, as though she finally understood. 'Close your eyes,' she said.

Fyia rolled her eyes, but then did as she was told.

'Now, clear your mind.'

Fyia tried. She really did. But an endless string of thoughts peppered her consciousness. Dragons, Cal, Veau, Cinis, Selise, broken clocks, her wolves, Cal's bear, Scorpia, her errant magic …

'Picture only blackness,' said Storm. 'Say to yourself, *blackness, blackness, blackness*. Force your mind to think actively of blackness, and if another thought slips in, redouble your efforts.'

Fyia did as Storm said, looking at the black behind her eyes, saying the word in her head, and she noticed a sensation in the middle of her forehead, a pressure, or a tension.

Her dragon shifted behind her, and the sensation passed, an image of the shimmering blue sky from the evening before sliding into her mind.

'Redouble your efforts,' Storm repeated. 'Only blackness and breathing. Breathe deep into your soul, clear out the stale air lingering in your lungs, allow your chest to rise and fall of its own accord, and then think *blackness* once more.'

Fyia did, and it was easier the second time, the tension in her forehead moving to sit behind her eyes, her eyeballs feeling as though they were rolling back in their sockets. The sensation moved higher, and then spread wide to her temples, then the center of her hairline, and then all at once, her brain relaxed, like it had stepped up to another level, everything below falling away.

Now she felt the pressure in the middle of her scalp, and then it circled in front of her ears and across her nose, as though the skin there pulled tight. And then it was back behind her eyes, and this time, when they rolled back, the sensation sank lower, as though dropping through her brain to the bones at the base of her skull. And then the last of the tension seeped outward, as though her brain had released its hold, and her face went slack, and her hands went lifeless in her lap.

But her eyes still pulsed, lower, then higher, and she had to make an effort to catch onto the higher feeling and hold it, pushing it out to the sides and forcing it to settle. Her brain flicked back and forth between true black, and black with a strange swirl of orange across the surface.

'Open your eyes,' said Storm, and Fyia obeyed, a feeling of calm fatigue washing over her.

'Keep breathing,' said Storm, 'and keep that focus.' Storm threw a bolt of magic at Fyia, and without thinking, she whipped her hand into the air and stopped it dead, then blew the magic away, so it dissolved in the air.

'Excellent,' said Storm. 'You are strong, with much earth ... much grounding.'

Fyia smiled, while her dragon huffed out a breath and ruffled his wings. Storm sent another bolt of magic, and her dragon screeched, because this time, Fyia was too slow to prevent the blow. It threw her backwards, her head smacking against her dragon's leg.

'A good start,' said Storm, 'but much practice is required. Repeat the exercise several times a day and you will improve quickly.'

Fyia wanted to ask, *And then what? I find the answers to all my woes?* But Storm said, 'Now, tell me, do you know what in the Seven Hells is going on between your brother and that damnable girl, Essa?'

Fyia laughed loudly. 'They're impossible.'

'We plan to leave today; Alba and Leo to look for Isa, Gabriel and I to search for experts, and Essa to find the taps. But Veau and Essa have both been moping for days.'

'Believe me when I say I don't get it any more than you do. Why won't they just let themselves be happy?'

Storm shook her head. 'I don't know, but I damn well intend to find out.'

Veau hung back in the shadows, his dragons around his feet, watching as Essa loaded her airship with box after box of whatever it was she was taking with her.

Essa had insisted on separate bedrooms, despite Veau's best efforts to convince her they could share a bed as friends, and as a result, he'd hardly seen her. She'd been holed up with Storm, Gabriel, Alba, and Leo, discussing plans to fix the clocks, and he'd been with his dragons.

Veau wondered just how bad it was in the Five Kingdoms. Had magma eaten up half the streets, or were his sister's subjects merely living with the threat hanging over their heads? Either way, he understood the need to fix the system. Until it was repaired, there was no reliable way to distribute the magic fairly. And once it was, every part of the world would prosper, with abundant crops, ample fish stocks, and plentiful magic for all who needed it.

People who'd thought themselves magicless would find themselves capable of all manner of simple feats. Washing and cooking and repairs done in half the time, not to mention, some would be capable of more impressive deeds, like redirecting rivers, concocting potions, and summoning rain. Veau wasn't sure he would truly believe it until he saw it, but it was a pleasant daydream.

'Are you just going to stand there and watch her?' said Gabriel, batting Veau with a wing.

'She'll skin me alive if I make a scene.'

'Then don't make a scene.'

Veau exhaled loudly. 'It's not that simple. She's … complicated.'

'You think Storm is straightforward?'

Veau laughed, the sound catching Essa's attention as she headed to her make-shift workshop in a nearby hut.

'If you hesitate, you will regret it,' said Gabriel, then he flew to the airship to help load.

Veau took a deep breath and followed Essa, not allowing his brain to think, to reason the pros and cons, mainly because he wasn't convinced the pros would win.

Essa was heading back out with a box by the time Veau reached the hut. 'Hi, Veau,' she said, then made to step past him.

Veau lifted the box from her hands. 'Let me help,' he said, and she nodded, then turned back inside to get another. Veau followed her and placed his box on the floor. Essa turned at the sound, looking first at the box, and then at Veau.

'I thought you wanted to help,' she said, her tone businesslike, her mind in work mode.

'I do, but I also want to say goodbye,' he said. 'Here, where it's only us, with no prying eyes.'

She nodded once, then turned back to the task of selecting her next box. 'Goodbye,' she said.

'Essa ...'

'What do you want, Veau? A fanfare? A declaration of love? A kiss?'

'Yes,' he said. 'I would like all the above, aside from the fanfare; I could live without that.'

Essa picked up a box and moved to his side. 'I love you, Veau,' she said quietly, then kissed him on the cheek.

Veau blocked her path, and she looked away, her eyes scanning the slushy ground beyond the door as though checking for observers. He slid a hand to her cheek, forcing her eyes up to his. 'I love you, too,' he said, and then stilled, waiting for her to pull away.

She didn't, and the longer she looked up into his eyes, the tauter the air pulled between them, Veau's head spinning, for he barely dared to breathe. Her eyes flicked to his lips, and she swayed minutely towards him. It was all the encouragement he needed, and he tugged her gently towards him, then lowered his lips to hers.

The occupants of the Dragon Temple fell into a steady rhythm, the days passing slowly, filled with endless work.

Glasshouses went up, seeds were sown, slush was cleared, huts were built, and Fyia, Cal, Veau, and Antice bonded with their dragons.

Cinis showed them how to get their dragons into and out of the magma ducts, and how to encourage them to swim through the magma. The older dragons were happy to oblige, eager for the Dragonsprite reward, but Veau's babies were suspicious, and mischievous, and downright defiant. Even Cal's dragon—their mother—had given up on them. Instead of helping train them, she'd taken to stealing their rewards. She'd succeeded the first time, resulting in much angry chatter from the babies, and they'd learned to be more careful after that.

Fyia spent most of her free time trying to master herself, as Storm had instructed. She could feel nuances in her magic, and sense magic in the world around them, and she was calmer, more level, able to keep at bay the rush that so often threatened to consume her.

Cal was pulled by the needs of his people, who demanded audiences and decisions, and wanted to take him on tours of the new glasshouses. Fyia rarely joined him, happy for the time to focus on her magic and prioritize her dragon.

'I wish you would come with me,' he said, as they watched Veau coax the most stubborn of the three babies into the magma duct. The other two were becoming almost reliable, but Fyia was losing hope the third would ever cooperate.

'Why?'

He took her hand. 'Do you really need to ask?'

'Because you want your people to get to know me?' It was selfish of her not to accompany him, but she'd never enjoyed shaking hands and kissing babies while people fawned over her for no good reason.

'And because it would make the whole thing more bearable if you were by my side.'

Fyia laughed. 'I suppose it would strengthen my cause for making you accompany me when we return to the Five Kingdoms. Just think … at least five times the demands on our time.'

Cal stiffened beside her, and she turned to look him in the eye, wondering if they would finally discuss the topic they'd been dancing around for days.

He searched her eyes, and she half-smiled, daring him to do it. Neither of them had wanted to ruin the time they had alone, but they would have to address it eventually.

'What are we going to do?' he said, and Fyia's shoulders relaxed, happy to finally deal with the thorn in their sides.

'We can't live in six kingdoms at once,' she said. 'I had the same problem when it was only my five, which is why I chose Selise as my capital.'

'Because it was central?'

'Yes, but even that is not perfect. Far from it. Selise is too far from the principal cities in each kingdom to be any real deterrent to dissent. The high families will do as they please, I will not even learn about half of it, and the rest I will learn about too late. The Spider's network is excellent, but it was never meant for a task so broad as running five kingdoms.'

'Could we find better wardens?'

'I would like to, but they would have to be respected by the high houses to be effective, or the high houses will simply cut them out.'

'No simple task,' said Cal.

'Perhaps impossible.'

They wrapped themselves in silence, distracted as Veau finally coaxed his errant dragon into the mouth of the magma duct. He threw the Dragonsprite into the airlock, and Cinis tried to close the door, but the dragon was too quick, grabbing his prize and leaping free with time to spare. The dragon screeched, as though laughing at their failure.

'So what do we do?' said Cal. 'Live our lives endlessly touring six kingdoms? Trying to stay abreast of all the goings on?'

'That is not what I want.'

'Nor me,' said Cal.

'But if I let the high houses regain control, my kingdoms will return to life as it was before. Women will have no rights, no education, and corruption will run rampant.'

'Then we must find wardens we can trust; that is the only option.'

'And where will we live?' said Fyia, her words sucking the air from the space between them.

Cal lifted their joined hands and kissed the back of hers. 'I want to be wherever you are; I will sacrifice much for that.'

Fyia believed him, but that alone didn't solve a single problem. An eagle swooped out of the trees, landing by their feet, a piece of parchment attached to its leg. The eagles had taken to flying low, to avoid the dragons, and Fyia stroked a reassuring finger across its head, then crouched to retrieve the missive.

She unrolled the parchment, her eyes scanning back and forth, her blood running colder with every passing word.

'What is it?' said Cal, already on his feet.

'It's from Sensis. They need me. We must fly south.'

Cal tailed Fyia as she made for the temple. Edu had already gone to find Opie, to alert him to prepare Fyia's newly repaired airship, and Cal felt like everything was running ahead of him, just out of reach.

'Fyia!' he said, pulling her to a stop below the dragon thrones they were yet to sit upon.

She rounded on him, and he dropped his hand from her arm. 'I have to go, Cal. Now. I've neglected my people for too long, and because of us, my lands are burning and flooding all at once.'

'You'll go to Selise?'

'Where else?' she said, her tone causing hurt to skitter down his spine.

'I can't come with you,' he said. He immediately wished he'd softened the blow, but he couldn't think amid the turmoil.

Fyia's face fell, and Cal's chest cratered, the air rushing from his lungs.

'I want to come,' he said. 'The idea of you leaving without me makes me sick, but I can't abandon my people again.'

Fyia closed her eyes for a moment, and when she opened them again, all warmth was gone, replaced by an icy wall of resignation. 'Of course,' she said, 'your people need you, as mine need me.'

'I *want* to come,' said Cal, taking her hand.

Fyia nodded. 'And I wanted to make the world better … more prosperous, but instead, I've made it worse. And I am here with you, restoring the north, while all five of my kingdoms go to ruin.'

'Fyia …' She was lashing out, choosing words she knew would hurt, but he had already left his own people once.

'I have to go,' she said, but Cal held her tight.

'You can't make a clock without breaking an egg,' he said, the old saying surfacing from the recesses of his mind.

'Eggs don't exist.'

'But the sentiment remains. Nothing worth having is ever easy.'

'People are dying, Cal. *My* people.'

'And if we hadn't done this ... if we hadn't returned the dragons and warmed the lands, then eventually all would have perished. You heard Cinis. When our ancestors came to these lands, there was nothing but ice. No life.'

She avoided his eyes, shaking her head.

'Fyia, we did what was needed.'

'I have to go. I'm taking Antice and Veau, and I'll send word to Essa.'

Cal stepped into her space and hooked a finger under her jaw, forcing her eyes up to his. 'We did what was needed,' he repeated, his heart breaking at the uncertainty in her eyes. 'If we hadn't done this, we all would have died.'

'But not today,' said Fyia. 'Maybe not for a hundred years ...'

'Stop it,' said Cal, a flood of irritation filling him. 'This is not you. You think I don't feel responsibility? You think I don't feel the loss? But what's done is done; we can't go back. And would you change it, even if you could? Because I wouldn't.'

Fyia lowered her eyes, and Cal pulled her into his chest, wrapping her tightly in his arms.

'We did what we had to,' said Cal, kissing her hair.

'I know,' said Fyia, her voice softer than before. She looked up at him as she slid her hands inside his cloak, grabbing handfuls of his shirt. 'I'm going to miss having your voice of reason in my ear.'

He pressed his forehead to hers, then kissed her, the kiss deep and all consuming, like they were trying to absorb one another's souls.

Fyia pulled away. 'I have much to do.'

Cal nodded, somehow ignoring his body's screaming demands to go with her, to not let her out of his sight. He watched her go, and it was like she was tearing a strip of his being with each parting step. She had to go, and he had to stay, and only the Gods knew how they would each run their own kingdoms, and be together. But there would be time for that later, after they'd helped their people through the many disasters he and Fyia had brought down upon them all.

Chapter Sixteen

'WE'VE RUN OUT OF EAGLES said Starfall, banging her fist against the table in the council chamber. 'So you take one of those eagles Fyia gave you, and you tell my niece to get her backside down here immediately.'

Sensis' eyes flicked from Starfall to the Spider—who was slumped in a chair—and back again. Both women looked beat, frayed in a way she'd never seen before.

'Of course,' said Sensis, 'but could you tell me why?'

'Tell you why?' said Starfall. 'So you really don't know? No whisper of the carnage running rife across the Five Kingdoms has made it to your ears? Or Fyia's? Or anyone's north of the mountains?'

Sensis shook her head. 'We've been fighting battles of our own,' she said, although it sounded as though training dragons and relocating the Black Hoods was not a patch on what the Five Kingdoms had endured.

'Where to start?' said Starfall, lowering herself into a seat.

'We've lost control of the Small Council,' said the Spider.

'What?' said Sensis. 'Then who is running the Five Kingdoms?' Had they really lost everything they'd worked so hard to win? And so soon after victory?

'The new High Priestess of the Sea Serpent—Elowyn—has assumed control of that kingdom,' said the Spider. 'The magma from the fallen clock destroyed half of the town below their temple, and continues to flow. And now they report the sea level is rising. Lady Nara Orchus—Fyia's Warden—could not reassure the people, so they turned to the temple instead.'

'Shit,' said Sensis, dumping her leather satchel on the floor and joining them at the table.

'Oh, High Commander,' said Starfall, 'we're only just getting started.'

Sensis steeled herself as she waited for them to continue.

'Lady Letta and her mother Lady Otterly of the Kingdom of Moon have assumed control of Medris, and are working their way out from there. They have removed the University's Chancellor, and are using the University as their base.'

'What of the military academy?' said Sensis. She'd trained the soldiers stationed there, and couldn't believe they would defect so easily.

'Good question,' said the Spider. 'We await the answer by courier. We ran out of eagles days ago, and now messages must travel by horseback.'

'I have eagles,' said Sensis.

'I doubt you have enough,' said Starfall.

'Lady Lyr Patrice is welcoming the Fae'ch into the Kingdom of Starlight with open arms,' said the Spider.

'After all the fuss she made about magic,' said Starfall, making a disgusted sound in the back of her throat. 'She's up to something.'

'The Kingdom of Plenty is stable for now,' said the Spider.

'Because the army is still stationed in Selise, and because so many here saw the green dragon with their own eyes,' said Starfall.

'And the Warden of Plenty—Lord Fredrik—doesn't have the backbone for open rebellion,' added the Spider.

'It will take time for news of the dragons to spread,' said Sensis. 'For sightings to become common. They're all being trained in the north, so I suppose they haven't been around much for people to see.'

'Whose idea was that?' said Starfall.

'The fire-touched needed to become acquainted with their dragons,' said Sensis, 'and Fyia wanted to form a strong alliance between them all.'

'More have the touch?' said Starfall.

'Lord Antice for one,' said Sensis, her heart lurching at the mention of his name, 'and Queen Scorpia. They're both with Fyia in the north.'

'Then maybe Scorpia's lost control of her people too,' said the Spider. 'Otherwise, why are they fleeing north?'

'They're doing what?' said Sensis.

Starfall rubbed her face with her hands, a movement so unlike her, Sensis did a double take. 'Shortly before your arrival,' said Starfall, 'we received word that many from the Scorpion Lands are fleeing north, into the Kingdom of Sky.'

'Why?' said Sensis.

'We've run out of eagles,' said the Spider, 'so we will know in a few days, when the riders return, but we have no Warden in the Sky Kingdom …'

Sensis sat back, processing all they'd told her: two kingdoms in open rebellion—Sea Serpent and Moon. Two kingdoms whose loyalties were unknown—Sky and Starlight—and only one, Plenty, still fully under their control.

Magma in Sea Serpent, rising sea levels, unknown motives across the board, and now a possible invasion from the south. Starfall was right, Fyia had to return immediately, or they would lose everything they'd worked for years to obtain.

Fyia had no choice but to leave Cal in the north. His people needed him, just as the Five Kingdoms needed her, but it had felt brutal when she'd waved him goodbye. She had Veau, Edu, and Antice at her side, the adult dragons keeping pace beside the airship, but the words in Sensis' message ate at her insides.

Her kingdoms—the newest of which she'd held for barely a turn of the moon—were slipping through her fingers, and the strangest thing of all was that she wasn't sure she cared. She certainly didn't want things to return to how they had been before, where women had no rights, and corruption ran rife, but neither did she want to live her life travelling from kingdom to kingdom to ensure things remained fair.

Antice had been especially keen to accompany Fyia south, and his eager energy rubbed off on Fyia as they stood at the railing together, floating above the Kingdom of Plenty, heading for Selise.

'At least one of us is excited to return,' said Fyia.

Antice turned a broad, uncharacteristic smile upon her. 'You're leaving Cal,' he said, 'and I'm …'

'Chasing after the one you love?' Fyia finished for him, cocking an eyebrow.

Antice chuckled. 'Your words, not mine.'

'Break her heart, and I'll throw you in a dungeon so deep, not even your dragon will find you,' said Fyia, although he was so lovesick, she didn't believe he had it in him. Such a change from the scheming, brooding man she'd thought she understood.

'You're more likely to do that than I,' Antice shot back, and Fyia recoiled at his words.

Fyia would never …

'Oh, don't look so self-righteous,' said Antice. 'I only mean that her devotion to you tops anything and everything else in her life. Sensis has been quite clear on the matter.'

Now it was Fyia's turn to smile, the news welcome. She'd never really doubted Sensis, but they'd spent so little time together of late, and love had caused vast swathes of terrible choices and broken friendships throughout the epochs.

'Don't look so smug,' said Antice, 'although I suppose it's a welcome change from your sullen brooding.'

'Sullen brooding?' said Fyia, wondering if she should remind the upstart she was still his Queen.

'Sullen brooding,' Antice agreed, with an expression that said: *I am merely the messenger, don't blame me.*

Fyia rolled her eyes. 'What were you doing in the hut when I came to get you?'

Antice turned back to watch the soaring dragons. 'Listening through the alterwoods.'

Antice had previously told Fyia's court that the alterwoods had ears, but Fyia had been too preoccupied to quiz him for details.

'And?' said Fyia.

'And what?'

'What did you hear?'

Something like frustration replaced the smile on Antice's lips. 'I am still learning,' he said, 'and the voices are not clear, but something of the rebellion in Moon came through. At least, I think that's what it was, but it's so far away, the voices were broken ... I've heard nothing of any real use.'

Fyia nodded. There was so much in the world they didn't understand ... that had been lost when the kings outlawed magic. And now Lady Lyr Patrice of the Kingdom of Starlight was welcoming the magical into Fyia's own home kingdom, no doubt with plans to court the most powerful, to win them to her side and wield them like a weapon.

But that was not Fyia's most pressing problem. As they'd crossed the snow-capped Fae'ch mountains into the Kingdom of Starlight, they'd followed the course of many tiny streams, more plentiful and lively than usual, running down from the high ground.

They'd become formidable torrents, thrashing over rock, and hurling branches and other debris down their descents towards the sea. It was exhilarating to watch—proof that the north truly would be prosperous once more—but now, in the flatter lands of the Kingdom of Plenty, the water had collected with such abundance, the rivers had burst their banks, the flow fast and ferocious as it plowed through villages, towns, and farms. The water was an unstoppable force, taking houses and livestock, and people, as it rampaged through these usually peaceful lands.

But it was worse still, because when they caught sight of the sea, the water level there too was higher than it ever had been, the cliffs halfway covered, the villages that hugged the shores in chaos, people rushing to leave.

There had been floods before, and it made sense, with the rapid ice melt in the north, but the further south they travelled, the worse it became, with more water and fewer signs of hope.

By the time Selise came into view, Fyia's blood stood still in her veins, for the streets were gone, submerged, small wooden boats the only form of transport. Sensis had said nothing of this in her message. Could all this really have happened over the course of just a few days?

Every soul aboard the airship looked down in horror as they floated above the terrible destruction. Rescue crews pulled lifeless bodies from the water, a torrent of white steam rose from the middle of the city, and scared faces peered out from the upper windows of half-submerged buildings.

A flurry of activity was underway on the plaza in front of the council building, one of the few dry areas, raised as it was on the city's high ground. The army was coordinating boats, and handing out food and blankets, the scene desperate.

Three women exited the council building and looked up at the airship, and Fyia's insides roiled with mixed emotions. She couldn't wait to see the women she relied upon, but was also apprehensive, because surely they—and everyone—would lay the blame for this devastation squarely on Fyia's shoulders. As well they should, for if she had not returned the dragons, none of it would have happened.

But if she hadn't returned the dragons, could she have held the Five Kingdoms together? And how long would it have been before the Black Hoods had been forced to leave the north? How long until the freeze had travelled further south, and it had forced her own people to migrate?

The soldiers tried to form up in ranks to mark their Queen's arrival, their eyes frequently flicking to the flying beasts circling above, but Sensis promptly sent them back to work, and Fyia was glad she did.

Opie set the airship down with practiced precision, and Fyia barely waited for the gangplank to slot into place before rushing to the ground.

'When did this happen?' said Fyia, not bothering with a greeting. She fell in beside Starfall, who led them inside.

'Two days ago,' said Starfall. 'A huge torrent wiped through the capital. We sent out scouts on airships to try and ascertain the broader damage, but they haven't yet returned.'

'The Kingdoms of Plenty and Starlight have flooded too,' said Fyia, her mind supplying images of the scenes they'd witnessed on their journey.

'And we know the Kingdom of Sea Serpent is also,' said Sensis.

'No word yet from Moon or Sky,' said the Spider, as they passed under the dragon clock.

'We are glad you have *finally* returned,' said Starfall. Fyia forgave her sharp tone; it seemed she deserved it.

'What is the smoke in the middle of the city?' said Veau, who had ordered his dragons to remain on the airship.

Starfall stopped in her tracks, turning to look at the plume of white. 'That is all that remains of our Queen's new palace,' said Starfall.

'There was a collapse,' said Fyia, recalling a report from some time before. 'They found magma below.'

'Magma that does not like to be covered with water, apparently,' said Starfall.

'The magma ducts must run that way,' said Sensis.

'A poor decision to put the palace there, then,' said Fyia, her shoulders slumping.

Starfall led them to a small chamber just inside the building's entrance; their war room.

'How bad is it?' said Fyia. She pushed the strands of hair that had whipped free from her low bun back behind her ears, then squared her shoulders. They would get through this.

'Worse than it looks,' said Starfall. 'Most of our food washed away, we are yet to get a sense for how many have perished—although we already know it is a great many—and the water has become contaminated with sewage.

'The army is working around the clock to rescue those still alive, treat the injured, and distribute what food we have, but there is only so much we can do in the face of all this water.'

'And we don't think it will subside,' said Sensis.

'You don't?'

'The ice melt from the north has to go somewhere,' said Sensis.

'Into the sea?' said Fyia.

'And the rising sea will flood inland, up the river valleys,' said Sensis.

'Many more will lose everything they've ever worked for,' said Starfall.

'People will have no choice but to leave their homes,' said Sensis.

'And go where?' said Fyia.

'Wherever they can survive.'

'But the existing occupants of those areas will not like it,' said Starfall. 'We will see disputes over territory, and food, and …'

'We could send them south?' said Antice. 'The Kingdom of Sky is only sparsely populated.'

'It seems Queen Scorpia has had the same thought,' said the Spider. 'For not only do we face open rebellion in our own lands from Sea Serpent and Moon, but Queen Scorpia's people have pushed up into the Sky Kingdom from the south.'

'Why?' said Fyia. 'Why would they leave their homes?'

'Because the world is getting hotter,' said Starfall, 'which means the Scorpion Lands—already unbearably hot in most parts—are beginning to burn.'

'We must take Medris back,' said Starfall, 'or give it up forever.'

They'd been going round and round for hours, discussing the rebellion in Moon, but had yet to come to any meaningful conclusions.

'They won't give it back without a fight,' said Antice. 'I know them, and Lady Otterly has been looking for an opportunity to seize control for as long as my father has been dead.'

'And Medris is a fortress at the top of a mountain,' said Sensis.

Fyia knew that only too well. It had taken them months of sieging and skirmishes before she'd eventually put an arrow through the King's heart from the back of an eagle. Then they'd called her a cheat for using her Cruaxee and had accused her of being a coward. The people of Moon had never quite moved past it.

'City walls mean little to dragons,' said Fyia.

'You would burn the city to the ground?' said Antice, with a start.

'No,' said Fyia, with a coy smile, 'but it would be fitting for the Moon Kingdom's prodigal son to return home on one.'

'You want me to fly into Medris on the back of my dragon?' said Antice. 'And then what? Assuming they don't put an arrow in my back the second they can.'

'They won't risk angering your dragon,' said Fyia. 'The threat of attack will be a powerful deterrent, and Sensis can fly in with you as your personal guard.'

'To do what?' said Sensis, her features frosty at Fyia's suggestive tone.

'And take back the military academy. The commanders there should be loyal to you, should they not?'

'The commanders there have done little to oppose the rebels,' said Sensis. 'They could be just as likely to lock me up as listen to me.'

'Not with the threat of the dragon,' said Fyia.

Sensis sat back, considering Fyia's proposal. 'I suppose it's not the most reckless plan we've ever had.'

Fyia beamed at her friend, feeling alive in a way she hadn't in months. This was how it had been during the war, Sensis and Fyia concocting mad plans that they somehow managed to execute.

'And they will listen to Antice,' said Fyia, 'for he is a man, and Letta and her mother are mere women.'

'So you're happy to use the old rules when they suit you?' said Antice, his arms crossed, although he seemed to be coming around.

'I will use the shortcomings of my enemies against them whenever practical, yes,' said Fyia.

'And what then?' said Antice. 'After we reclaim Medris in your name. What next?'

Fyia's heart thundered in her chest. She had worked so hard for so long to claim the Five Kingdoms as her own, so what she was about to do seemed ludicrous. 'Then you rule, as King of Moon,' said Fyia, and the air whooshed from the room in a rush.

Starfall made a choked sound, Sensis inhaled sharply, and Veau laughed. The Spider and Edu threw meaningful looks to one another, and Antice's mouth dropped open.

'But you must rule within certain parameters, and agree to my armies being stationed in your lands,' said Fyia. 'As I see it, our choices are perpetual war, for which I, and I am sure my people, have little appetite, or we can make changes that work for us all.'

'You would hand the Kingdom of Moon straight back to the very family you overturned?' said Starfall, waving her hand in disgust.

'Lord Antice is not his father,' said Fyia.

'You think the people of Moon will remember that when you put him on the throne?' said Starfall.

'What other choice do we have?' said Fyia. 'We have been circling for hours, and still we have no hint of another resolution. Not to mention, I cannot be in five kingdoms at once—six, including the Kingdom of the Black Hoods—so I can either cling to power, to the detriment of my people, or I can be pragmatic.'

The words felt perfectly right to Fyia, and she breathed an inward sigh of relief.

'Pragmatic,' parroted Starfall. 'I'd call it stupidity.'

'I never set out to be a ruler,' said Fyia. 'I set out to change things … to return the dragons. And now we must change the way we run my kingdoms, for it cannot go on like this.'

'And what if Lord Antice reverses all the changes you've made?' said Starfall.

'I won't,' said Antice.

'Of course you'd say that here,' said Starfall. 'You'd say whatever you must to take back your kingdom. Why should we believe a word from your mouth?'

Antice smiled at Sensis, who sat beside him, her features a careful mask. 'Because I happen to like your changes. To outlaw magic would be to outlaw myself, and Sensis would kick my arse if I ever suggested women were lesser creatures.'

'And if the two of you have a lovers' quarrel?' said Starfall, her back ramrod straight.

'We won't,' said Antice, 'but I will happily agree to whatever terms you set out. You may not believe me, and who would blame you, for you have only ever seen my public mask, but the way things were before you overthrew my father ... they did not work well for me, either.'

After that, the remaining problems seemed simple. They would send contingents of soldiers to the areas most affected by the floods, who would help move people to higher ground, build new houses, and salvage what food they could from whatever stores they could find. It would be a tough winter, but if they rationed what they had, they would make it through.

'And what of Queen Scorpia's invasion?' said Starfall. 'What assistance will you send to the Kingdom of Sky?'

'I will fly south and treat with her myself,' said Fyia.

'Without an army?' said Sensis. 'The risk is too great.'

'Edu and my brother will be with me, and I have my dragon.'

'As she will have hers,' said Starfall.

A guard rushed through the door, and Fyia was glad for the reprieve, because she would treat with Scorpia, regardless of what any in the room might say.

'Your Majesty,' said the guard, bowing low. 'You must come quickly ... the dragons!'

By the time Fyia and the others had boarded the airship and flown to the other side of the city, the dragons had almost finished the job of fixing the hole billowing steam into the air. Opie refused to get too close, fearing damage from the heat still thundering skyward, but they could see the scene clearly enough.

Silver sat atop the magma, like a swan on water, his wings outstretched across the open void, forming a perfect arch. The flood water still flowed into the hole at the edges, streaming across her dragon's wings, while Veau's babies—who'd ignored his order to remain on the airship—flew back and forth to the parts of the surrounding area not under water, sifting through the debris, and carefully selecting rocks, which they then hauled atop Silver's wings. Antice's purple dragon rearranged the rocks, so they lined up just so, occasionally breathing fire upon them, then bashing them against the ground to change their shape first.

'They know how to fix the magma ducts,' Fyia breathed.

'Maybe they know how to fix the clocks too,' said Veau. His eyes were glued to his dragons, who were being bossed around by Antice's. 'We should send word to Essa.'

Fyia nodded, unable to tear her eyes away either. When the hole was fully covered, the middle stones the last to be placed, Antice's dragon breathed fire over the whole structure. She first boiled away the water, then fused the stones together, and when she'd finished, water rushed back over, and their work disappeared from view.

'How will Silver get out?' said Veau.

Fyia's heart gave a worried thud.

'The clock,' said Antice.

Fyia turned her gaze to the clockface. 'How do we open it?'

'Cinis said the clocks would strike automatically, when the magic in an area waned,' said Veau, 'but …'

As they watched, a third hand appeared on the clock face, and Fyia held her breath as it progressed past the first three numbers, then as it passed the halfway mark, until it stopped, pointing to a symbol Fyia couldn't make out, between the numbers nine and ten.

The deep, booming bell of the clock tolled across the city, and Fyia waited, expecting it to sound again, but instead, the clock's face spun open, revealing a huge black hole. Silver appeared, to gasps and cries. He used his wings to lever himself out, grabbed the ball of Dragonsprite that had dropped onto a runner, then hurtled into the sky.

Chapter Seventeen

SENSIS HELD TIGHT AROUND Antice's waist as his dragon took to the air. Not much scared her, but she wasn't ashamed to admit that she was terrified of the dragon's jerky movements, and the thought of falling leagues through the air to her death. But Veau had taken Sensis' airship to look for Essa, and Fyia had needed hers to fly south in search of Queen Scorpia.

Antice rested his gloved fingers over hers, stroking her through the leather. 'My dragon will look after us,' he said, turning his head so she could hear over the wind. 'I was scared at the start, remember? But I trust her with my life.'

Sensis believed him on a practical level, but that did nothing to ease the fear gripping her limbs.

'What's our plan?' said Sensis, forcing her mind onto something other than the danger. They'd had little time to prepare, and the journey on dragonback wouldn't take long.

'We'll land on top of the university,' said Antice. 'I'll make an announcement from there, telling the people that with Fyia's blessing, I am now King of the

Kingdom of Moon. While I'm doing that, you can slip away to the military barracks and take back control.'

Sensis laughed. 'You plan to stand atop the university and simply announce you're in charge?'

Antice nodded. 'Yes,' he said cockily. 'Never underestimate the power of confidence. And my people love me ... or at least, the idea of me.'

Sensis rolled her eyes, because it was probably true. 'And if the military side with Lady Otterly? What then?'

'Then you get arrested and thrown in a cell, and I leave you to rot forever more.'

Sensis pinched him, and he exhaled a childlike laugh.

'If Lady Otterly has the army, then you'll be in a cell beside me,' she said, but Sensis couldn't believe the commanders she'd left in charge would turncoat so easily. They had been loyal to her—and to Fyia—since the beginning of their campaign. They believed in Fyia's vision for a fairer world, and most importantly, they were not power hungry. Sensis hoped they were okay, that they hadn't been slaughtered by ambitious soldiers further down the ranks ...

But that was the problem; they had no intelligence. They were going in totally blind, and that made Sensis nervous. It was reckless ... downright stupid, but they also had little choice.

'The people will support me,' said Antice, 'and most of the resistance will, too. I'm sorry to say, but for as long as the kings were in power, only the word of men held weight. Not much has changed in the short time Fyia has been Queen.'

Sensis didn't like it, but she knew he was right, and at least in this case, it would work in their favor.

'And they'll be awed by my dragon. That will buy us some time.'

Sensis nodded into his back, pressing herself more firmly against him, getting used to the motion. She'd missed Antice more than she'd thought possible, and something taut inside her had unfurled when he'd landed in Selise. The idea of being parted from him again was ... she pushed the thought aside, instead planning the route she would take from the university to the military academy when they landed. It was one she knew well, but she went over it again and again, visualizing every step.

'I want you to stay,' said Antice, pulling Sensis back from her thoughts. It took her a moment to interpret his words, which were half lost to the wind.

'In Medris?' said Sensis.

'With me.'

Sensation cascaded through her, and her mind went fuzzy, so she couldn't think. 'I can't abandon Fyia,' she blurted, but the words were a defense, a way to buy time.

'You wouldn't be. In fact, you'd be doing her a favor, keeping me in line.' Sensis squeezed him, her chest constricting at the smile in his words. 'And your work as a conqueror is done. Your job now is to maintain Fyia's armies, and you can do that from the military academy in Moon. And your estate is here ...'

The cloud cover cleared, and Medris came into view. 'One thing at a time,' said Sensis, although she buried her nose in his neck, digging through the fabric until her skin rubbed against his. She kissed him, and he dropped a hand to her leg, squeezing it against his.

'Think about it,' he said, 'but I love you, and I want you by my side, and to be at yours when you need me.' He released her, the people below staring and pointing, drawing their focus.

Sensis' heart gave a loud thud in her chest, but she didn't have time to dwell, because as they flew over the city wall, the people of Medris raced this way and that, pointing and screaming and shielding their children from the threat above.

'Well, I guess our entrance will be memorable,' said Antice.

Sensis gripped him hard, the changes in speed and direction sending new bolts of fear into her blood. It was only when they landed, and Sensis leapt from the dragon's back, that the rushing stopped in her ears.

'Good luck!' Antice shouted.

She sprinted for the military academy, surrounded by shouts of fearful wonder as Antice's voice projected out across the city from above.

Antice informed his people that dragons had returned, that a new order had begun, and that he was now their King, by order of Queen Fyia Orlightus.

Sensis came to a grinding halt, because outside the gates into the military academy stood four armed guards. The gates had been bracketed shut, and new bolts dug into the ground, fixing them in place.

So that's how they'd controlled the military; they'd locked them in. The sight made Sensis' chest swell with hope. A stamp of boots suddenly sounded from behind the gates, then shouts as the men and women inside spotted Antice standing atop the university. Sensis recognized several of the voices as those of her commanders.

The guards at the gate looked nervously to one another, obviously unsure what to do in the face of Antice's proclamation he was now their King. They were not professional soldiers, and one of them left his post, heading closer to Antice and his dragon.

The others hesitated for only a moment before racing after the first, one shouting, 'Come back!' the others yelling, 'Wait up!'

Sensis hid until they were out of sight, then ran on light feet to the gate, swiftly removing the bars and pulling up the bolts. She swung the gates inward, and surprise registered on the faces of the commanders who milled on the other side.

'High Commander,' said one, saluting.

Only the most senior ranking officers stood before her.

'They separated us from the rest of the academy,' said another, seeming to read her mind.

'Go to the other gates,' said Sensis, pointing to officers she trusted, 'and take them back. I am assuming command of the academy. Our mission is to secure Medris, then find and detain Lady Otterly and her daughter.'

The soldiers scrambled to obey, but as she turned back to look at Antice, she saw one of her tasks was already complete, for Lady Otterly and her daughter had taken up positions on the roof, one standing on either side of Antice's dragon, as though he'd asked them to be there all along.

Sensis loosed the breath she'd been holding. Their compliance changed the game from perilous to political, meaning no blood need be shed that day.

Fyia entered Scorpia's war tent flanked by Edu and her wolves. She had come in peace, but if Scorpia sensed an ounce of weakness, Fyia would fail in her mission, and she might not even make it out alive.

'Queen Scorpia,' said Fyia, with an incline of her head—respectful, but not deferential.

'Queen Fyia,' said Scorpia, not bothering to stand from her throne.

'How nice of you to visit,' said Fyia. 'You appear so very comfortable in my lands.'

Scorpia's lips pulled into a feral smile. 'Quite comfortable, thank you. So comfortable in fact, I doubt I'll ever leave.'

'Well, that is good news.'

She let the words settle, and watched as Scorpia tried to hide her shock.

'I am glad you think so,' said Scorpia.

'Why would I not?'

Scorpia cocked an eyebrow, but her lips remained shut.

'I have a proposition for you,' said Fyia, walking the perimeter of the lavish tent. Scorpia did have a penchant for luxury …

'Yes?' said the old woman, impatiently.

'I find myself in need of strong, reliable leaders to run my kingdoms in my stead. Five kingdoms are too many for one person, and yet those with the skills required are scarce.'

Scorpia's lips curled in disbelief. 'You expect me to believe you will willingly hand the administration of this kingdom to me?'

'There will be conditions.'

'Even so, what about the people here? They will not be pleased …'

'The Sky Kingdom is only sparsely populated, and I'm sure you'll placate them, skilled as you are. Especially when they know you rule with my blessing.'

'Rule?' said Scorpia, going still.

'You will retain your title, along with full ownership of the Scorpion Lands.'

'Whatever is left of them …' said Scorpia, bitterly.

'I should imagine the Temple of the Whore will survive,' said Fyia. The temple had a clock and was built on the highest point of the island.

'And perhaps my capital,' said Scorpia.

'And you have a dragon, so no need to brave the krakens when travelling back and forth.'

'I want an airship,' said Scorpia, leaning forward.

Fyia nodded. 'Done. But you must leave in place the legal changes I have made, and I will keep control of all armies across the Five Kingdoms. All military training will be completed at the academy in Moon, led by Sensis, and you will retain only a small private guard for your own protection.'

'And if we disagree?' said Scorpia. 'What then?'

'I will maintain regular meetings with the rulers of each of my kingdoms.'

Scorpia flinched. 'You're giving them all away?'

'I am not *giving* them away,' said Fyia. 'I am supplying them with strong, present leaders to help them prosper. I have no desire to manage every tiny detail, and will only involve myself in issues of great consequence.'

'It is an intriguing proposition,' said Scorpia, playing with one of the many bracelets adorning her wrists, 'but ...'

A ruckus outside interrupted Scorpia's words, and a blur of movement rushed into the tent. Edu was in front of Fyia in a heartbeat, but then he fell, slumping to the ground, his legs buckling beneath him. Fyia tried desperately to understand what had happened, her eyes flicking first to Edu's stunned form, and then to a short woman with wild hair and mis-matched eyes: Asesh.

'You,' snarled Fyia, her voice full of loathing. She wanted to look down, to see if Edu was okay, but she couldn't afford to take her eyes from Asesh for even a heartbeat.

'Who else?' said Asesh, tilting her head to one side. 'So kind of you to return the dragons, so I am reunited with mine.'

'*Your* dragon?' said Fyia. Only the fire-touched had dragons ... didn't they?

'My late consort's ... mine by extension,' said Asesh. 'The Dragon King loved me so deeply, he would have lain down his life had I asked him to. Nice of Queen Scorpia to look after Red until I could return.'

Fyia tried to read between the lines. Was Scorpia working with Asesh? And if so, why? Fyia didn't dare chance a look at Scorpia, but she was willing to bet the old woman wasn't happy her dragon had been snatched away, especially by one such as Asesh. So maybe Scorpia was Fyia's ally in this moment.

'And where will you go?' said Fyia. 'Now you have him?'

'Go?' Asesh laughed. 'Go? I will not *go* anywhere. These are *my* kingdoms. The Dragon King bequeathed them to me, but they tricked the dragons ... tricked me ... took all that was mine and locked it away.' Asesh stepped forward. 'But I have been waiting. I have been biding my time and watching for the signs, and now ...'

Fyia acted almost without thinking, pouring all her strength into a single thought: kill.

Not one part of her objected, or hesitated, or faltered, and as she flung her hand towards Asesh, a flood of power left her. Asesh responded a tick too late to prevent the blow entirely, but she hadn't survived so long without tricks of her own. She rolled her body, deflecting most of the magic.

But Fyia sent a second bolt straight after the first, and this one hit Asesh square in the chest. Asesh's shoulders and head flew back, but she balled her fists, and suddenly, a visible stream of magic arched between her and Fyia, Fyia unable to shake the connection from her hand.

Fyia might have panicked, if Edu hadn't at that moment cried out, because he'd tried—and failed—to get to his feet. The noise galvanized her, and she pushed magic through the connection between them, sending with it all the anger and hatred she felt for the woman.

But it had no noticeable effect on Asesh. If anything, she seemed to gain in strength as Fyia emptied herself of magic. A smile formed on Asesh's lips, and Fyia realized too late it was a trap. Asesh had grabbed hold of Fyia's magic and was stealing it, draining her dry ... and then what would happen? Would Asesh take Fyia's life force? Was this how her life would end?

'No!' said Fyia, trying desperately to pull her magic back. But nothing worked, and her vision blurred. Horror crept through her, melding with her exhaustion as Asesh sucked everything she had.

Fyia vaguely noticed a figure behind Asesh. Scorpia? She was small and seemingly fragile, but she moved with determination and carried a metal rod in her hand. It must be a hallucination, Fyia thought, as the blackness stole her sight, her well sucked dry. Of all the people Fyia could count on to rescue her, the Queen of the Scorpion Lands was not one.

Veau had memorized Essa's route. He'd coerced her into telling him every tiny detail, not taking no for an answer. Then he'd written it down, just in case. He checked the parchment for the hundredth time, once again wondering if he'd made the right decision, because although he knew her planned route, he knew not how long she would spend in each place, nor if her plans had changed after they'd said goodbye. All he could do was hope luck was on his side.

They floated over his home kingdom—the Kingdom of Starlight—heading for a village that had been all but abandoned for decades. Maybe it was nostalgia that pulled Veau there, because his family had holidayed close to the village every summer, high over an enormous lake.

Essa had accompanied Fyia and Veau on their final holiday, before Veau had abdicated and gone to the Fae'ch. Before Fyia had refused to marry the Emperor. It all seemed a lifetime ago now.

The sun was setting by the time they spotted Essa's airship by the lake, and Veau's heart leapt into his throat. What if she was unhappy to see him?

It was all so confusing between them. Essa had always kept her cards close to her chest—one of the things he loved about her—but she'd taken it to another dimension. He knew she was worried about the clocks, and thought she'd failed by not fixing them, but it wasn't her fault. If anyone was to blame, it was his sister …

Veau hopped overboard the second they touched down. He threw aside the flaps of the communal tents, but not a soul remained in camp. Was that unusual? Should he be worried? But coals still glowed in the fire, and nothing seemed out of place, so he followed the path around the lake, his disobedient dragons on his tail.

They chattered and squawked at one another, happy to have a new place to explore, that the confines of the airship were behind them. Veau zoned them out, listening instead for any sounds ahead.

They rounded a corner, and Rouel appeared from the undergrowth, Veau so surprised, he jumped a foot in the air. 'Fuck! Rouel!' he said, trying to get his heart back under control.

'Sorry,' said Rouel, with an impish grin. 'Couldn't resist.'

'Where is everyone?'

'This way, I'll show you. Essa found a tap, and then an *ancient* Fae'ch appeared. He's as obsessed with the taps as Essa. He seems trustworthy, and Essa's been quizzing him for … oh, I don't know … two days? The man looks as though he could conk out at any moment, and he speaks sooooo slowly, but Essa's like a pig in shit.'

Rouel led Veau to a cave they'd never discovered when they were kids. Inside, Essa and a tall, old man with greying hair sat by a copper pipe, which ran vertically up the wall, and then bent at ninety degrees, forming a handle. Essa and the man were completely absorbed, discussing what would happen if they should twist the handle.

'If you turn it all the way, it will turn off the magma,' said the old man, in a ponderous voice. 'But the longer the tap is turned, the more pressure will build. It is not advisable to shut off the flow for long; the taps are primarily to regulate the magma, not stop it.'

'But each clock has a tap?'

The man nodded.

'And to repair the broken clocks, we can use the taps to shut off the magma, make the repairs, and then turn them back on?'

'So long as you have someone who knows *how* to make the repairs.'

'It takes magic?'

'Always,' he confirmed. 'Different types for different repairs. And to make a new clock, you must break an egg.'

Essa went still at his words. 'What does that mean?'

Everyone knew the saying, but as to the exact meaning ...

'The word *egg* was once common parlance for anything used to make something else. The balls needed to restart the system of magma ducts, the compound needed to create Dragonsprite, and the scales of the fire-touched needed to create dragons ... or a dragon clock.' As he finished, he turned to look at Veau.

Essa inhaled sharply, finally noticing him.

'How many scales?' said Veau.

'Just one,' said the man.

'How?' said Essa. 'How do you remove them?'

The man gave her a quizzical look. '*I* don't.' His eyes moved back to Veau. '*He* does, or one like him.'

The hairs on Veau's skin stood on end at the thought of removing one of his scales. His nerves contracted, pulling tight. 'With a knife?' he said. 'I cut it off?'

'You peal it off,' said the man, 'and then a witch breaks it in half, and places one piece on each side of the new clock.'

Veau shuddered. 'With my bare hands?'

'I suppose you could use an implement of some kind. I've never seen it done firsthand; too grizzly for my tastes.' The man's eyes found Veau's dragons. 'It is good you have some little ones. They're the best for securing clocks. They can get into all the hard-to-reach places.'

Essa frowned.

'The dragons repaired the hole in Selise,' said Veau, 'without anyone asking. They just ... knew what to do.'

Essa nodded slowly. 'So the dragons could help repair the clocks? Or fix a new one in place?'

'Assuming you can find someone capable of making a clock in the first place,' said the man, 'and infusing it with magic.'

'But you can help with the taps?' Essa asked. 'So we can shut off the magma for long enough?'

'I can,' he said.

Storm spotted them before Gabriel, a group of Fae'ch sitting around a campfire in front of a cave. They'd flown the length of the Fae'ch mountains, looking for their kind. Then they'd met with Lady Lyr Patrice, the Warden of the Starlight Kingdom, who had welcomed them, and told them where to find their people. But the places she'd pointed them—the towns and cities of Starlight—had not held the old, powerful Fae'ch they sought.

So they'd flown further, all the way to the eastern mountains, to Lake Sulu. Night had settled, so they could not see the water that lapped at the shore below, but the fire was a beacon, and Storm could feel the magic of those who sat round it, so they cautiously approached.

They landed by the water, keeping their distance, and Storm conjured a ball of flame in her hands to announce their presence. 'We come in peace,' she called.

The group watched as Storm and Gabriel approached, although Storm couldn't yet make out their faces, still in shadow. But as they neared, a fae woman stood, her wings the color of amethyst, and Storm froze, as did Gabriel beside her.

'Isa,' said Storm, then threw the ball of light, so it hovered above the group of Fae'ch, illuminating them all.

Leo and Alba sat on the far side of the fire, beside Pips, Alba's uncle, and Regio, Leo's brother. 'Regio!'

said Storm, almost without thinking. 'It is good to see you.' She'd come to like the arrogant fae, but had feared the Children of the Lake had killed him.

'Likewise,' said Regio, with his usual smooth smile.

'How did you get out?' said Storm.

But before Regio could answer, Isa said, 'Why are you here?' Her eyes were locked on Gabriel, whose face was a blank mask.

Storm wanted to punch Isa—her own half-sister—but that would not help their cause. And out here, free from his oath to obey, Gabriel could fight his own battles … if that was what he chose to do.

'We seek a witch to help us create a dragon clock,' said Gabriel. His eyes flicked to Leo and Alba, whose task had been to find Isa, to ask if she knew where the old Fae'ch had gone.

'We only got here earlier today,' Alba blurted guiltily. 'We were just about to ask …' Leo took her hand, silencing her.

'Help *you?*' said Isa.

'Help the world,' said Gabriel.

Isa tisked.

'The old Fae'ch are here also,' said Regio.

'Stop,' hissed Isa. 'Do not help them.'

Regio ignored her. 'They're in caves all around the lake. We like it here … the peace …'

Isa disappeared, materializing half a tick later before Regio, throwing him backward onto the ground, her hands around his neck.

Storm moved without thinking, hauling Isa off Regio and hurling her towards the cave's edge. Isa disappeared before hitting the rock, and when she reappeared, she held a knife to Gabriel's throat.

Storm saw red, her eyes going wide, her blood going still, and she reached out with all the power that had been bestowed upon her, and used it to take hold of Isa's arms. Storm held tight with her magic, so when Isa tried to disappear once more, she couldn't.

Storm wrenched her sister's arms wide, and pushed her back from Gabriel, so she stood, in the shape of a star, at the edge of the firelight.

'Gabriel,' Isa whispered, all she could manage as she strained against Storm's superior power.

Gabriel moved to stand behind Storm and slipped a hand into her hair. He pulled her head sideways and dropped a kiss on her lips. 'Do as you please,' he said, then kissed Storm once more. 'I am intrigued to see what you devise.'

'No,' said Isa. 'My love …'

Storm grabbed Isa's tongue with her magic, then pulled, and Isa's face froze in abject horror. Gabriel wrapped his arms around Storm, pressing her back to his chest, the feel of him against her a reminder of everything they'd endured at the hands of this woman. How she'd raped Gabriel, and forced him to lie with Veau's mother. How she'd ruled the mountain as though it were her personal playground. How she'd advanced the fae, thinking them superior, and all but stamped out the water riders—and who knew what other forms of magic. How she'd hated Storm since they were children, because their father had loved Storm's mother more than Isa's.

Isa cared not for anyone but herself. She would see the whole world burn rather than help Queen Fyia, and she still had the audacity to call Gabriel—Storm's own soulmate—her *love*. Storm slapped Isa with her magic, and Isa's head snapped to the side, but Storm held her tongue tight, and the action ripped it clean out of her mouth. Storm let it drop to the sandy ground.

'No!' screamed Leo, flying to his feet, Alba just behind him. 'Don't!' But he didn't dare get too close, nor use his magic.

Isa didn't even bother to look at Leo, the only one willing to speak out in her favor. Her eyes were still fixed on Gabriel, so Storm wrapped her magic around Isa's throat and squeezed.

Isa made a terrible choking noise, and Leo violently shook his head. 'Please,' he begged, 'don't kill her. She's …' But he seemed to hesitate, like he couldn't physically say the words.

'She's his mother,' said Alba, in an unusually quiet voice. 'She bound him, so he could never tell anyone, and she tortured him too.'

'Alba, no,' said Leo, taking a step towards her.

Alba looked up into Leo's eyes, but didn't stop. 'Leo's powerful,' she said, 'and Isa used his blood to strengthen her own magic. He has scars all over his back.'

'Alba, please …'

Regio was on his feet now. 'She did what?' Blood magic was not common among the magical. It was dangerous, and manipulative, and resulted in lethal medleys of power that could send one mad.

Leo grabbed Alba, lifted her into his arms, and took to the sky. Storm was glad he'd found the water rider; he would need much help to heal the wounds his mother had inflicted.

Isa was too busy sobbing for her own loss to care about her son, blood leaking from her mouth, tears streaming down her face. And then Storm felt a shift in Gabriel, as though he'd had enough, ready to be done with this woman for good. He drew his dagger, made of iron laced with magic from the forges of old, then threw, and the blade flew true, piercing Isa's heart.

Isa's body slumped to the ground, and Storm pulled the dagger free, then set Isa on fire with a single flick of her hand. Gabriel watched her burn, his face still devoid of emotion.

'I will perform the right,' said Regio. He stood over Isa's flaming body, flecks of blue already flying up, her magic escaping back into the ether. Regio would see to it all her magic escaped, and what he did with the ash that remained, Storm didn't much care.

'Come,' said Pips, with a deep sigh. 'I will take you to those who can build a clock.'

'The old magics told you of their powers?' said Storm. They were usually private, keeping their secrets to themselves.

Pips chuckled. 'I'm a trader, and I trade knowledge, along with all the rest. The old magics like me, and like to keep me sweet, for few others remain who can get them what they need.'

A weight sat over Fyia's airship as they flew northwest, towards the Kingdom of Sea Serpents. Essa and Veau had sent word to meet there, and seeing as Sensis and Antice had control of the Kingdom of Moon, and Selise was now almost entirely under water, it wasn't like Fyia had anywhere else to be.

Aside from in the north, with Cal …

After Asesh had drained Fyia of her power, Fyia had been out cold for days, but her first thought when she'd woken was of Cal, and her mind regularly pulled her back to him, her chest going tight each time.

Asesh was dead, killed by Queen Scorpia, who hadn't hesitated when both Fyia and Edu went down. Scorpia had personally hauled Asesh's body from her tent, then instructed her dragon to incinerate it. Then she'd packed up camp and headed straight for the castle where Fyia had stabbed King Perdes in the back.

She'd wasted no time before declaring herself Queen of the Sky Kingdom, and had held audiences with all the high families before Fyia had even come around.

'They were surprisingly amiable,' Scorpia had said, when she'd outlined her immediate plans for the kingdom. 'Of course, many I knew already through trade, but if anything, they seemed glad of the clarity.'

'The Kingdom of Sky has never been ambitious,' said Fyia, 'at least until Lord Eratus Venir got his claws into their late King.'

'Yes, well,' said Scorpia, 'both are dead.'

Scorpia stayed behind in Sky, more interested in running her new kingdom than fixing the clocks, a spring in her step Fyia hadn't seen before.

Fyia was glad to be rid of her, still not trusting the woman entirely, but she would be a great asset to the Sky Kingdom.

Edu had descended into a pit of despair, and tears welled in Fyia's eyes just thinking about it. Edu had protected her, without a thought for his own well-being, and it had cost him dearly, for his legs would no longer support his weight. All feeling on one side was gone entirely, the other barely functioning, so he could no longer walk, even with a stick.

He'd barely said a word, refusing to meet Fyia's eyes as guards carried him onto the airship, communicating only when he needed something. He remained in his cabin, staring out of the window whenever Fyia sat with him, flinching when she put her hand on his arm.

They reached the Temple of the Sea Serpent as the sun was setting, and Fyia's mouth dropped open, but it wasn't the cloud of steam and smoke that shocked her. They'd seen flooding everywhere, but here …

The Temple of the Sea Serpent now sat alone on an island, the houses in the hollow below entirely submerged. The platform at the back of the temple, which had once stood acres above the water, was now only a few feet up, magma pouring from it into the sea. Fyia gaped, mesmerized by the terrible sight.

They landed on the mainland—now a league from the temple—next to a settlement that hummed with life. Voices burst through every window, the streets full, the tavern raucous, and above it all, Veau's dragons hovered.

Hope finally bloomed in Fyia's chest. The message from Veau and Essa had sounded promising, and she spotted many magical creatures here too.

'We've found a way,' Veau said excitedly, as Fyia strode into the hall that appeared to be their headquarters.

'To fix the clock?'

'I must give up a scale,' he continued, 'but Storm and Gabriel are here. They found an old Fae'ch who knows how to infuse a clock with magic. And Essa found another who taught us about the taps. And the dragons will help attach the clock to the existing duct, just like they helped fix the hole in Selise.'

Fyia tried to keep up with his excited words, her mind slow, still recovering from Asesh's attack. 'But a scale is needed?' said Fyia, the idea of her own fire-touch being pried from her back making her nauseous.

'I don't relish the thought,' said Veau, 'and I am sure it will be painful. But you have only one scale, and none of the others are here. I have many …'

Fyia couldn't argue. She needed her scale, for she could not call herself fire-touched without it, and might even lose her dragon, she supposed.

'We're doing it tonight,' said Veau. 'You arrived just in time.'

'We're doing it now,' said a voice from behind them. 'Your Majesty.' Essa dropped into a bow, then stood. 'We should get going.'

'The clock is mostly built,' said Veau. 'It awaits my scale at the temple.'

'And it would be helpful to have your dragon with us,' Essa said to Fyia.

'Of course,' said Fyia, although she felt like a spare part in a whirlwind, 'but before we go, I have something to run by you both.'

Fyia flew to the temple on Silver, while Gabriel and Storm carried Veau and Essa. Gabriel was sullen, and it made Fyia wonder if removing a scale was dangerous for Veau. He'd said the risks were small. Was he lying?

In fact, now Fyia paid more attention, they all seemed somber. Was that strange? Or were they just focused on the task at hand, knowing how important it was?

She put the thought from her mind and wondered instead what Cal was doing at that moment. Was he riding his dragon? Drinking with his cousin? Out in the woods with his bear? Or was he mulling some problem, or holding audiences with his people? Such was the lot of a ruling monarch.

The High Priestess, Elowyn, greeted them in brisk fashion. She gave only the hint of a bow to Fyia before directing everyone to their stations. Fyia was glad they were in decisive hands.

The new clock was already halfway along the tunnel to the platform, and a team of Fae'ch stood by, waiting for their cues.

'I guess it's now or never,' said Veau, trying to sound upbeat, but fooling no one.

Fyia hugged her brother, as did Storm, then Gabriel, and then Essa. Essa was not one for public displays of affection, and although Veau was visibly fortified by her touch, it only made Fyia more nervous.

Essa tried to move back, but Veau caught her hand, and she stilled, remaining by his side when he dropped her hand. He wanted her close by, and whatever was going on between them, she would do that for him.

'Turn the taps,' said Elowyn.

It would take a few turns of the hand for the magma to stop flowing entirely, and in that time, Veau would rip a scale from his face. The witch Gabriel and Storm had found would then divide it in two, and place the pieces in the waiting clock Essa had made under the witch's direction.

A messenger ran to the old Fae'ch by the tap, and Veau closed his eyes, preparing himself.

Fyia wanted to look away as Veau raised his hand to his face, finding the upper most scale and tracing the edge with his fingers. Essa handed him a wicked-looking metal tool with flat hooks on one end, and he held it up to the scale, checked the position in the mirror Gabriel held, then dug it under the edge.

Veau cried out, and Fyia squirmed. She wrapped her arms tightly across her stomach and forced an encouraging look onto her face.

'That's it,' said Essa. 'Now yank it free.'

Gods. *Yank it free?* Fyia wanted to hurl as a trickle of blood dripped down Veau's face. And then he closed his eyes once more, and did what he had to do.

The place became a flurry of activity. Essa snatched the scale from Veau's shaky hand, then disappeared down the corridor to the clock. Gabriel cast aside the mirror and caught Veau as his legs gave out, while Veau's dragons skittered after Essa, at Veau's worryingly weak command.

Fyia's dragon already waited by the platform, ready to do his part. All that was left was for Fyia to sink to the ground beside her brother and wrap him in her arms.

Chapter Eighteen

Days later, Fyia cast her eyes over the large group before her. 'Thank you for coming,' she said, bone weary, but also hopeful. They were nearly at the finish line, only one hurdle left to jump.

They'd installed the new clock in the Temple of the Sea Serpent, and then flown to all the other clocks in need of repair. It had worked. Everything felt different already; more in balance, less on edge, no plumes of steam to be seen.

Hopefully now her kingdoms could adjust, rebuild, and create a new kind of normal, even if the homes of many would forever be under water.

'It has been a difficult period for us all,' said Fyia, 'and I thank you for your hard work in repairing what was broken.'

Faces from all corners of her kingdoms looked back—leaders, all of them—and Fyia would give them the positions they deserved.

'As you know, I have established a new structure of leadership across the Five Kingdoms. My aunt, Lady Starfall Orlightus, has borne the brunt of managing these lands while I have been ... otherwise engaged, but it would be unfair to expect that of her indefinitely.'

Starfall cocked an eyebrow. 'You can say that again.'

Veau and Essa chuckled, but the High Priestess did not.

'So I am pleased to announce that new rulers will lead the Five Kingdoms, by proxy, from this day forth. King Atlas Calemir Talos and I will reside in the lands of the Black Hoods, and all rulers will convene twice annually to discuss important matters of state.

'All have agreed to uphold the legal changes I have already made, and will act in accordance with the spirit of those changes going forwards. None shall raise an army, and Lady Sensis Deimos will remain High Commander of the Armies of the Five Kingdoms. Responsibility for all military training and engagement will fall to her.'

Silence rippled out across the open expanse inside the Temple of the Sea Serpent. The moment was momentous, so it deserved a little pomp, and a ball of emotion welled in Fyia's chest. She tamped it down as her eyes landed on Veau, his face still bandaged after his ordeal. They'd all been through so much ... but now they would heal.

'Kneel, Lady Starfall Orlightus, High Priestess Elowyn, and Lord Veau Orlightus.' She drew the ceremonial sword at her hip, and used it to touch each of the kneeling rulers on both shoulders.

'Arise, Starfall Orlightus, Queen of the Kingdom of Plenty, Elowyn, High Priestess of the Sea Serpent, and Queen of the Kingdom of Sea Serpents, and Veau Orlightus, King of the Kingdom of Starlight.' Fyia's voice hitched as she said her brother's title, for it had always been his, and yet she'd never thought she would see this day.

They rose as one, bowed to Fyia, and waved at the cheering crowd. Veau took Essa's hand as he returned to his place at her side, and to Fyia's surprise, she didn't pull away. Maybe Essa would become Queen of Starlight one day after all …

Fyia bid the new rulers goodbye, and flew north on dragonback. Edu and her wolves would follow on her airship, but she couldn't bear to spend another moment cooped up with Edu, and the journey was quicker by wing.

She hated herself for her frustration with him, given everything he'd faced—everything he'd done for her—but what could Fyia do? Essa had made him a wheeled chair, so at least he could move around by himself, although it wouldn't fare well on the airship, or the soft, slushy land in the north, nor on the steps of the Dragon Temple …

Asesh had taken Edu's legs, and by extension, his role as Fyia's bodyguard—his purpose. It would be a hard road for Edu, and right now, he had no interest in forging a new path. He needed time to process, and maybe he just needed to wallow for a while.

Edu would have a place by Fyia's side for as long as they both breathed air, but such a large part of his identity was wrapped up in his terrifying skills as a warrior. He needed to feel valuable, and Fyia didn't know how to show him she still needed him. But she would find a way.

The closer Fyia flew to the Temple of the Dragon, the bigger the knot of excitement in her stomach became. She'd been imagining her reunion with Cal for almost as long as she'd been away from him, and she prayed they could slip away quickly and avoid their duties for a while.

She flew over Anvarn, where the buildings, which had once been half-submerged in snow, were now fully visible. Someone had built a set of steps to the upstairs tavern window they had once used as a door, and Fyia chuckled as she took it in. She imagined there must be those who refused to use the fully functioning door below, because *the window had worked perfectly well all this time*. She could practically hear their voices in her ears.

As Silver headed even further north, Fyia's heart leapt, and a laugh escaped her lips, because a mighty winged beast had risen from the trees a few leagues in front, and atop it, sat Cal.

'Go, Silver,' she said, without thinking. Silver shot forward with such speed, Fyia had to grab hold, scared she would slip from his back.

Cal's dragon hurtled towards them, and soon Fyia could see his billowing black cloak, his dark, wavy hair, and then, just before each of their dragons lunged sideways to avoid a collision, his deep green eyes.

'You gave away your kingdoms?' said Cal, kissing Fyia's neck, his naked body flush against hers in their enormous bed.

Cal had snuck them in through a secret tunnel that led right into the royal wing, and not a soul had seen them. They'd wiled away hours already, enjoying their reunion, and had instructed the dragons to lie low, so no one would realize Fyia had returned.

'I didn't give them away,' said Fyia, stroking his hair. 'I delegated.'

Cal rolled over her, settling between her thighs, and Fyia hummed with contentment.

'You *delegated* …'

'So I could live in the north with my terrifying Black Hood husband … and run barefoot through the woods.'

Cal looked down into her eyes. 'That's truly what you want? Because …'

Fyia put a finger on his lips. 'My motivation was never to rule an empire. It was to change the ways of the old kings, and to bring back the dragons. I think it's safe to say I've done both those things …'

'Then you don't want to rule the north?'

'The north is not an empire,' said Fyia. 'I think I can manage a single kingdom, especially when my husband is such a wise and talented man, capable of … what was it again? Oh, yes. Capable of looking after those he loves.'

Cal pushed inside her, and Fyia moaned at the delicious fullness. 'Lucky for you I love you, then,' he said.

'Mmmmm,' said Fyia. 'Lucky me.'

He flicked her nipple, and Fyia arched as much as she was able, Cal's hips pinning her down.

'So you can do all the hard work,' she managed, barely able to focus, 'while I frolic like an imp among the …' She moaned as he rolled her breast in his hand.

'Do go on,' said Cal, plumping up her flesh then flicking her nipple with his tongue.

'Among the trees,' she moaned.

Cal pumped his hips, and Fyia grabbed his neck, both because she needed something to hold on to, and to urge his mouth to do more.

'Among the trees,' he said, between licks and sucks. 'Where my bear will hunt you down?'

Fyia bucked as he nipped her. 'Cal,' she moaned.

He chuckled, then started up a slow, steady rhythm, moving his hands to either side of her face, holding her in place as he locked his eyes with hers.

He kissed her, and Fyia surrendered to the big, heavy body pressing her down. She gave herself over to the sensations he sent cascading through her, pulsing with him, arching her back as he rubbed against her core.

Moans escaped her as he moved, ratcheting with every passing stroke. She bit her lip, tipped her head back, and grabbed handfuls of his hair.

'I'm going to come, Fyia,' Cal growled in her ear. His words, and the gravel of his voice, sent a shock of excitement straight to her core. Her climax hit hard, and nothing aside from exquisite release registered for a thousand of her fluttering heartbeats.

When she came down, Cal was reaching for something on the table by their bed. He rolled them, tucking her into his side, her head on his chest, and then he dangled a small metal object in front of Fyia's eyes. A ring. A simple band that gleamed gold and pink and greenish blue all at once.

Her heart raced as she held out her hand, and he slipped it onto her finger.

'I love you, Queen Fyia Orlightus Talos.'

Fyia sat, pulling him up with her, and straddled him, wrapping her arms and legs around him, so not a single sliver of air kept them apart. 'And I love you, King Atlas Calemir Talos Orlightus.'

'Cinis helped me make it,' he said, 'from what I took from the mine.'

Fyia smiled into his hair, and they stayed there like that for several spins of the hand, their chests rising and falling together, each inhaling the other deep into their lungs.

'He's gone back to the Great Glacier,' said Cal, 'to oversee Dragonsprite production. The Order of the Dragon will keep the clocks stocked around the world. They're delighted their purpose has been restored.'

It made sense, for what were any of them without a purpose? 'Starfall plans to run the Kingdom of Plenty from the Temple of the Night Goddess,' said Fyia, pulling back a little so she could see his face.

'I can't see Lord Fredrik Feake liking that very much,' laughed Cal.

'He's too busy preparing to wed Lady Nara Orchus,' said Fyia, smiling broadly, 'so I'm not sure he cares at present.'

'What of the Spider?' said Cal, his hands resting on her hips.

'She will come and go as she pleases. She's suspicious of Lady Lyr, and thinks she might cause trouble for my brother. She'll keep an eye on her, and also on the Kingdom of Sea Serpents. The High Priestess doesn't seem to like me very much ...'

'And what of Edu?'

Fyia sighed deeply. 'I thought of sending him to Sensis, so he could teach at the military academy, but I don't think that's what he would choose, and first he needs to recover. I hope the healers here might be able to help ...'

She rested her head on his shoulder, relishing his scent, wishing she could press herself closer still, that she could climb inside his skin and live there for all eternity. He tugged gently on her hair, pulling her head back, and kissed her, as though he too needed more, as though nothing would ever be enough.

She had never felt contentment until Cal, at least not of the true, bone-deep peace variety. Even with the worries about the new leaders of her kingdoms, and Edu, and whether the Black Hoods would fully accept her as their Queen, as she rested in Cal's arms, his fingers drawing lines along her spine, the world fell away, as though nothing but the two of them existed.

'I still can't believe Scorpia saved my life.'

'From what I hear, she's already turned the Kingdom of Sky into a trading powerhouse, and she's set up a competition to find her heir!'

'She's what?'

'She's not getting any younger …'

'She's supposed to agree things like that with me!'

'Maybe she plans to present the winner for your approval,' he said, in a mildly mocking tone.

She pinched him, and he kissed her, then lifted her off his lap. 'Get dressed,' he said.

Fyia didn't argue, sliding her hand in his as he led her to the Hall of the Dragon, where the dragon thrones stood.

The hall was empty, lit only by flame torches, and Cal threw her a mischievous smile. 'Race you to the top,' he said, then tried to drop her hand. Fyia clung on, and pulled him backwards, then released him and ran.

Fyia sprinted, but Cal easily caught her, and she squealed as he grabbed her around the waist and pulled her to a stop. He kissed her cheek, then took off again, taking the steps two at a time and reaching the top with a victorious raise of his arm.

Fyia stepped up beside him, then said, 'I win, for this is my throne. You are on the wrong side.' Her face split into a smile at Cal's expression.

'No, I won. The race was to the top, not to one's own, particular throne.'

Fyia giggled, and Cal kissed her. 'I love that sound.'

When he pulled back, Cal moved to stand before his own throne. A snarling roar sounded from the entrance, and the hairs on Fyia's arms stood on end as the sound bounced off the walls. A second roar joined the first, and a gasp flew from Fyia's lips as a tingling sensation covered her skin.

Their dragons flew into the temple, and Fyia bit her lip, tears of joy pricking at her eyes. She cast a look at Cal, and found an expression of wonder on his face that surely mirrored hers.

How long had Fyia envisioned a moment like this? The old kings dead, the north thawed, the Five Kingdoms led by those whose motivations matched her own, dragons, and Cal … the kind of match she'd never dared dream of.

As they lowered themselves onto the dragon thrones—the only throne that had ever felt like home—Fyia wondered what other dreams might come true. What they could do for the north, and their people, and each other. But for now, she was content to savor that which they'd exchanged devotion, and blood, and lives for. She looked once more to Cal, who took her hand, and as their skin met, their dragons roared.

I hope you enjoyed *Dragons of Asred*. If you did, I would really appreciate a rating or review wherever you buy books, on TikTok (especially here), or on any other social media.

Just a rating, a few words, or a line or two would be absolute perfection, and will help others find my stories. Thank you for your support.

Want more from the *Shadow and Ash* world? Then check out Storm and Gabriel's story in *House of Storms and Secrets* here:

https://books2read.com/stormsandsecrets

Or join my newsletter to read Alba and Leo's story, *The Water Rider and the High-Born Fae*, for free:

https://hrmoore.com/blog/sign-up-kosa/

READ NEXT: *Nation of the Sun*. Here's the blurb:

Their demon lives spun around each other, their souls, like magnets, pulled back together in every lifetime.

Amari has a perfect life. She's a successful food critic, and is marrying a high-flying human rights lawyer. But the day before her wedding, a stranger, Caspar, tries to solicit her help. She sends him away, but can't shake the feeling that she knows him.

When Amari's new husband has to leave the country before their honeymoon, Amari tells Caspar she'll help him. But Amari and Caspar are attacked by an assassin, forcing them into hiding at the London headquarters of the Pagan Nation. Here, she discovers she's an ancient and powerful demon, someone who reincarnates, and that Caspar is her soulmate.

As she's drawn into Caspar's world of standing stones and feuding nations, Amari can't deny the deep connection that pulses between them. But she can't remember her past, she has a husband, and finds herself torn between two irreconcilable lives. And not only that, but the Pagans have secrets they refuse to reveal: Why did Amari avoid Caspar for a hundred years? And what happened between Amari and the leader of a rival nation in the past? To determine if she can trust Caspar, if she should help him, she must wake her demon soul, and bring back her memories. For one thing is certain: when that happens, the tables will turn.

Nation of the Sun is perfect for anyone who loved A Discovery of Witches, and those who fantasize about stone circles containing magic.

Nation of the Sun is book one in the complete Ancient Souls *series. It's available in ebook, and paperback through all major retailers, and as an audiobook from Amazon and Apple.*

CONNECT WITH HR MOORE

Check out HR Moore's website, where you can also sign up to her newsletter:
http://www.hrmoore.com/

Find HR Moore on Instagram and TikTok: @HR_Moore

Follow HR Moore on BookBub:
https://www.bookbub.com/authors/hr-moore

See what the world of *Shadow and Ash* looks like on Pinterest:
https://www.pinterest.com/authorhrmoore/kingdoms-of-shadow-and-ash/

Like the HR Moore page on Facebook:
https://www.facebook.com/authorhrmoore

TITLES BY HR MOORE

The Relic Trilogy:
Queen of Empire
Temple of Sand
Court of Crystal

In the Gleaming Light

The Ancient Souls Series:
Nation of the Sun
Nation of Sword
Nation of the Stars

Shadow and Ash:
Kingdoms of Shadow and Ash
Dragons of Asred

Stories set in the Shadow and Ash world:
The Water Rider and the High Born Fae
House of Storms and Secrets

http://www.hrmoore.com

Printed in Great Britain
by Amazon